I0776592

THE HAUNTING BETWEEN US

PAUL MICHAEL WINTERS

MAELSTROM PRESS

A Maelstrom Press publication
maelstrompress.com

THE HAUNTING BETWEEN US

Ebook ISBN: 978-1-965-64300-6
Paperback ISBN: 979-8-218-41040-7
Hardcover ISBN: 978-1-965643-01-3

Cover Illustration by Marcela Bolívar
Cover Design by Valerie Gomez

First edition 2025

CONTENT WARNING:
This book contains sexual language and content that is fade-to-black, which may only be suitable for mature readers. Depictions of mild violence, homophobia, bullying, past death of a parent, discussions of past violence, mourning, social anxiety, and past trauma.

THE HAUNTING BETWEEN US

PAUL MICHAEL WINTERS

MAELSTROM PRESS

A Maelstrom Press publication
maelstrompress.com

THE HAUNTING BETWEEN US

Ebook ISBN: 978-1-965-64300-6
Paperback ISBN: 979-8-218-41040-7
Hardcover ISBN: 978-1-965643-01-3

Cover Illustration by Marcela Bolívar
Cover Design by Valerie Gomez

First edition 2025

CONTENT WARNING:
This book contains sexual language and content that is fade-to-black, which may only be suitable for mature readers. Depictions of mild violence, homophobia, bullying, past death of a parent, discussions of past violence, mourning, social anxiety, and past trauma.

To every queer kid feeling alone, left out, or misunderstood, you deserve happiness as much as everyone else. Let no one tell you differently.

1

CRIMSON HOUSE: CAMERON

That hideous house will eat me alive. It almost did once.

Every town has a house like this—abandoned with an overgrown lawn and peeling paint. It howls, creaks, and makes strange sounds at night. When people walk past, they pick up their pace and don't dare peek back. In my town, that house is 16 Sycamore Lane.

I live at 15 Sycamore Lane, right across the street.

Lucky frickin' me.

As I hike through the forest on my way home from school, the crooked roofline of Victorian turrets and dormers appears through the trees, forming a jagged silhouette against the gray sky. The scar on my calf aches whenever I'm near that damn house, a frequent reminder of when it took a chunk out of my leg—the worst moment of my life.

And here the house is, tormenting me again after another terrible moment. Another link in the chain of bad things:

Boy problems.

Well...more like lack-of-boy problems.

I spent all of summer break dreaming of asking Noah on a date, and now, just a week into junior year, it's already over. I finally worked up the courage to talk to him but could barely string two words together, and I almost threw up. His reply still bangs around in my mind: *Sorry, Cameron, my boyfriend in Canada might get jealous.* Seriously? Canada? He couldn't even come up with a decent excuse? Of course he'd never go for a guy like me—awkward, pudgy Cameron. Everybody's friend, but only ever a friend. Why did I think I had a shot? I'll never ask a guy out again.

Maybe that's why I'm at the edge of the forest, hesitating, wondering if the fifteen minutes I'd save cutting through the yard of Crimson House—Port Townsend's notorious haunted murder mansion—is worth the risk. I swear that house has it out for me. It feeds off bad energy, and today, I might have enough for it to swallow me whole.

Come closer, Cameron. You were so tasty at age twelve. I bet at sixteen you're a real treat. All your doubts and fears are delicious, and they've only multiplied. Let me finish the job I started.

I shut my eyes and shove out the negative thoughts.

I won't let that house get to me, boy problems or not.

So, I grit my teeth and take a determined step onto the lawn. The moment I do, the temperature drops, and a shiver runs through me. I rub my hands up and down my arms to warm up. Years' worth of decaying leaves squish under my feet, letting off the moldering smell of rot. Crows circle in the sky above. Broken shingles hang from the steeply pitched gables like loose teeth, and darkened windows glare down at me. The house feels alive—breathing, with a heartbeat of its own.

Eyes fixed on the overgrown grass, I cut through the sprawling backyard of this demon seed of a house. My family's little bungalow shines like a beacon right across the street, but something in the corner of my eye makes me look. Thick velvet drapes have covered the large bay window on the side of Crimson House for as long as I can remember. I swear they just moved.

Ignore it, Cameron. Keep walking. Don't let the house trick you.

Another flash of movement, and an irresistible pull sinks its claws in, luring me toward the window. When I'm just feet away, a buzz in my hand makes me jump, launching my phone into a pile of leaves. I dig it out, wipe it on my jeans, and look up, stunned. The drapes in the bay window, which were most certainly closed a few moments ago, are now wide open. The sunlight fights to penetrate the murky glass. Beyond the haze, something walks across the room. Scratch that—it slinks. Something slinks across the room.

I'm twelve again, held captive in the darkened hallway as something circles me and a crow tries to peck my eyes out. From the shadowed corners, a voice whispers: *You left me. Now I have you.* But it must be just the wind buffeting the walls. My stomach churns at the memory, and ice runs through my veins.

Every instinct begs me to walk away, but the lure of the house is irresistible, and I inch closer, craning my neck to peer inside. Through the window, half obscured by shadows, an old woman with long gray hair and a flowing white dress turns her head in my direction as a crooked yellow smile spreads across her wrinkled face.

I blink, and she's gone.

I'm frozen. Did I imagine that? A trick of the light, maybe? It can't be her. It's not possible.

The White Lady of Sycamore Lane is a legend in the area—an old woman who lived in Crimson House and snatched up unsuspecting kids. Now her ghost wanders the lonely halls in an endless search for her next victim.

A tale told by parents to keep their children away from the derelict old house.

Or so I thought.

The piercing shriek of a crow breaks my paralysis; it's perched on the gutter above the window, aggressively flapping its wings. First shadow women, now crows. I'm so done. With chills running down my back, I race across the street and don't stop until I slam my own front door behind me, eyes wide, chest heaving. That *goddamn* house.

Another buzz in my hand. Oh, right. I pause for a moment, waiting for my heart rate to slow, then take a deep breath and bury myself in the comfort of my cell phone.

Abby: Sorry about Noah [sad face emoji]

Abby: You doing okay?

I thumb a reply.

Cameron: Ugh! Noah

I almost forgot about him, thanks to that damn house.
Well, not really.

Abby: Know what'll cheer you up?

Cameron: A trip to Hawaii

Abby: Movie night!!!!

My mood brightens the slightest bit. I had hoped to hold Noah's hand at the Uptown Theater tonight—and a bit more, if I got lucky—but there's nothing like bingeing Netflix shows with my best friend.

Cameron: That would be awesome

Abby: Yay! On my way!!!!

Abby loves her exclamation points, and a smile breaks across my face. But then I'm struck by all the parallels between now and four years ago: rejected by a boy, a shadowy figure in Crimson House, and even a stupid crow. What does that damn house have against me? It's all too much. When things stack up like this, it's easier to ignore everything. That's basically what I do with anything guy- or ghost-related.

I run to my bedroom, rip off my jeans and T-shirt, and slip into a sweatshirt and an old pair of sweats, taking care to avoid my mirror. The last thing I need is a reminder of why Noah rejected me. I'm determined to forget my problems and lose myself in cheesy movies.

I make my bed and shove all my dirty clothes into the closet.

Perfect. Room cleaned.

The doorbell rings, so I race down the stairs and open the door to see Abby with a smile on her face and a longboard at her side.

She puts out a fist, and I bump it.

"Ready for movies?" she says, the stud in her nose glinting in the afternoon light.

"So ready. And no talking about you-know-who."

She mimes zipping her lips.

Abby's dressed in black corduroy overalls over a pale green sweatshirt. Longboarding is her primary mode of transport, so she likes comfortable clothes. Her white socks have little cheeseburgers embroidered on them, and I puff out a laugh.

"What's so funny?" She snaps her head toward me, pushing her long black hair out of her eyes.

"I was admiring your socks."

She beams. "You like them? I got them on Etsy." She twists her foot around to give me a better look.

"They're making me hungry."

She smacks me on the shoulder. "You're a riot. Let's go watch movies."

As we head up the stairs, Dad calls from his office, "Is that you, Cam? How was school?"

"Hey, Dad. School was fine. Abby's here to watch movies."

"Okay. Make sure you leave the door open while you two are up there."

A jolt of adrenaline courses through my veins. "You know that's not necessary, right, Dad?"

"C'mon, bud, just do it for me. Okay?"

"Fine. Whatever." I shake my head, and Abby rolls her eyes.

I told Dad I liked guys when I was twelve, but he still doesn't get it. I guess it won't really sink in until I have a boyfriend. He keeps clinging to the hope that Abby—my best friend for more than half my life—is secretly my girlfriend. As in, the kissing kind.

Um, no.

Abby and I sprawl on my bed, drinking AriZona lemon teas and scrolling through Netflix on my laptop, searching for something we haven't seen yet. It's pretty bleak. She scrolls into the horror section, and I flinch. Typically, I'd be excited about horror, but I'm not in the mood after today's encounter with Crimson House. I can't tell her about my freak-out earlier. I already feel like a wimp, and I don't want to add to the mounting pile of evidence. Plus, she can get overly enthusiastic about ghost-related things.

"How about something lighter? Like a comedy?" My voice cracks.

She stares at me, her forehead crinkled, her dark brown eyes questioning. "You love horror."

"I'm just not feeling it today."

My eyes dart to the window and the ominous house beyond for only a moment. But nothing escapes the eagle eye of Abby Nguyen. She'd give Holmes a run for his money.

She narrows her eyes. "Why did you just look out the window?"

"No reason," I say, my voice jumping three octaves.

"You were looking at Crimson House, weren't you?"

I've already lost this battle, so I say nothing. Best not to dig myself in deeper. But I have an awful poker face, and guilt radiates from me. Never take me to Vegas.

"Did something happen with Crimson House that you're not telling me?" Abby asks.

Crap. She knows my moods better than I do. Why did I think I could hide this from her?

"Maybe?" I squeak.

She sits up on the bed, arms crossed, laser-focused on me. "Spill it."

"It's nothing, really." I lower my head, avoiding her piercing gaze. "I saw the drapes move."

"They moved? Like, by themselves?"

"I don't know. It all happened so fast. It was the ones in the side bay window. They were closed when I passed. I glanced down for a sec—when you texted, actually—and when I looked up again, they were open. Like I said, it's nothing."

"Nothing?" She nearly spills her tea. "That's the opposite of nothing!"

"Okay. I guess it's not nothing." I slump my shoulders, defeated. This will be the main topic of conversation for the rest of the night. Movie night is slipping through my fingers. At least talking about the house will distract me from thinking about you-know-who, but ghost-hunting isn't the kind of get-over-the-guy therapy I wanted tonight.

"Did you see anything else?" she asks.

I wince. "I might have seen something moving in the house. An old woman, maybe?"

"An old woman *moving*?" Abby glares at me like I punched a kitten. "You saw the White Lady of Sycamore Lane? What else are you not telling me?"

"That's it. I promise. I might have imagined all of it."

She ignores me. "This calls for a paranormal investigation."

She jumps up from the bed, heads to my closet, and pulls out a massive box filled with the ghost-hunting equipment she keeps at my house since I live across the street from paranormal central. Abby has binged every ghost-hunting reality show ever made. She knows all the terms—EVP, apparition, residual haunting—and she uses them properly. Like in full sentences.

She even went on a ghost hunt at Manresa Castle, the haunted hotel in town, hosted by two ghost-hunting celebrities, including the cute gay one with a cleft in his chin. I wasn't jealous at all. Well, not about the ghost-hunting part, anyway.

"Abby," I whine. "I thought we were watching movies."

"That's before I knew we had poltergeist activity," she says with a totally straight face. Because she's serious.

"It's probably just a trespasser."

She scowls. "Cameron. You and I both know that house has been locked up tight as a drum ever since…that night."

That night. During a game of Truth or Dare at my twelfth birthday sleepover, Abby dared me to sneak into Crimson House, go to the attic, and post a selfie on Instagram. With the boy I secretly had a crush on staring right at me, I couldn't say no and look like a wimp.

I don't want to go into all the gory details—and yes, it was gory—but there were dark, twisty passageways, a crow roosting on the third floor that tried to peck my eyes out, and a shadow that circled me, whispering words. My foot crashed through a rotten floorboard, holding me captive, with splintered wood digging into my flesh and blood pouring out of the gash in my calf.

A full twenty minutes passed before paramedics sawed through the wood to get my leg out. There was blood everywhere. I got fifteen stitches and a tetanus shot. My parents were furious and grounded me for a week. To sum it up, the house *bit me*.

"Earth to Cameron." Abby waves her hand in front of my unfocused eyes. "You there?"

"Yeah, sorry." I grin sheepishly. "Spaced for a sec."

"Well, snap out of it and help me with this gear."

She hands me a digital voice recorder and an EMF meter, then takes the ghost box and configures her phone into *creator mode*, as she calls it. She puts it on a selfie stick and attaches a ring light and an external mic with a fuzzy bit to prevent wind noise. She got all this stuff on eBay from a ghost hunter who was unloading it for cheap—something about having to make rent.

Once we're outside my house, Abby pauses. "Okay, we need a setup shot. It's four o'clock. The light is perfect."

I roll my eyes, but she ignores it.

With our backs to Crimson House, she starts recording on her phone and then holds up her selfie stick.

"Recording in three, two, one," she says, all businesslike. "Welcome, everybody, to *Teen Spirits*, where we're about to delve into the latest in a long line of paranormal incidents here at Sixteen Sycamore—dang it! There's a car in the shot!"

We spin around to look at the blue SUV that has crossed into the frame. Our mouths gape as it pulls into the driveway of Crimson House.

"They must be turning around." She shakes her head in disbelief.

"I dunno. Looks like they're parking."

We both watch as a man gets out of the car. He has short brown hair and dark olive skin, and he's wearing faded jeans and a flannel shirt. He stretches like he's been on a long drive, then stares at the house, assessing it. With a press of the key fob, the SUV's lift gate opens, revealing a trunk filled to the top with luggage and boxes.

Abby looks at me, deflated. "Well, there's our poltergeist. Guess somebody was finally crazy enough to buy that house."

Relief floods me. That old lady must have been a relative or a real estate agent, not a ghost. My life can go back to normal now. "I told you it was nothing."

She glares at me as we turn around and head back into my house.

The man from across the street calls into his car. "Hey, Hugo. Put down your phone and help your old man unload all this stuff. Then you can go pick your bedroom."

"Okay, Pa," a deep but youthful voice replies.

The passenger door opens, and out steps a guy about my age. *Hugo.* He has medium olive skin, and his face is smooth and rugged at the same time—undeniably masculine yet beautiful, with a strong jawline, wavy brown hair, and a straight nose. He has this intensity to him, which only adds to his mystique. My stomach somersaults as I stare at the guy before me.

Guess I figured out how to take care of my boy problem: Replace it with an even bigger boy problem. He's like Noah times ten.

Hugo and his dad walk up to the house, pointing and talking. Then Hugo turns and glances my way. His eyes pierce me for only a moment before I can't take it. I turn away fast, a wave of self-consciousness washing over me. I wrap my arms around my stomach and shrink down, trying to be small and invisible. *Hey, Tubby, your stomach is poking out of your shirt. You're so fat.* Those memories torment me—I was bullied for being the "fat kid" through all of middle school. Since then, I've shot up four inches and stayed the same weight, but this spare tire will never go away. Abby's told me a million times that I'm cute, and it's starting to sink in. Maybe. Kinda. I'm working on it, anyway.

I force myself to look back at Hugo, but he has already moved on to something else, talking with his dad. Opportunity lost. Typical Cameron.

Abby has a knowing smile and shuts my gaping mouth with her index finger. "Uh-oh," she says with a laugh. "I think I can predict your next crush."

"Shut up," I say in a hushed voice. "You don't know me." I smack her on the shoulder.

"Um, yeah, I do. No one knows you better."

She's right, of course. She does know me. This is my dream guy. And he's moving into the house of my nightmares.

2
New Arrivals: Hugo

We had all the time in the world. Until we didn't. Now I measure time in the few months it takes for Pa and me to flip a house. We're constantly moving from town to town, switching schools, and running from the pain that Pa can't escape—that I can't escape. I miss Ma so much.

Houses fly by outside the SUV window. Any of them could be our next home. Well, not a home, exactly. Our next project. Our next burden. It might be okay, or it might be a wreck. Unpredictable, like my entire life.

The SUV slows, and Pa pulls up to the ugliest house I've ever seen, turning into a driveway choked with weeds.

"*That's* the place?" I ask.

"That's it," Pa says.

"Needs a lot of work, don't you think?" I try to hide my disbelief.

He shrugs. "We've fixed up worse."

"Really? Worse than this?"

"What about that place in Sacramento?"

That was like the Four Seasons compared to this dump. I keep the words to myself, but I guess my expression speaks volumes.

Pa shakes his head. "C'mon, Hugo. It's not as bad as it looks."

These days we never stay in the same place for more than six months, but something tells me we'll be here longer this time. Everything from the roof to the siding needs replacing. This house is old and decrepit, but it's more than that. It's *strange*. Dormers jut out at odd angles, and rooflines pitch too steeply. Vines have swallowed the front of the house, extending up to a third-story turret right in the middle. Red streaks drip down the siding, making the whole place look like a murder scene. This place *feels* wrong—we should probably just tear it down and start from scratch.

Pa opens the car door, gets out, and stretches. My phone buzzes in my pocket—a text from my sister, Carla, who escaped all this madness by running off to college.

Carla: At the new house yet?

Hugo: Yeah and imo pa has lost it

Carla: That bad?

Hugo: Worse

Carla: Sorry mano [grimace emoji]

Hugo: I'll live. I think

Carla: Any cute neighbor boys at least?

Hugo: [eye roll emoji] We literally just pulled up

From outside the car, Pa calls me to help him.

Hugo: Gtg ttyl

Carla: [heart emoji]

Carla is lucky. She got out. But I'm still here, alone with Pa and all these damn projects and this never-ending cycle of working and moving.

I peer up at the house through the windshield. Just looking at it sends a shiver through me, making me squirm in my seat. Maybe it'll be better up close. I hop out of the car and walk up to it.

Nope. Still sucks. Worse, maybe.

Pa comes up next to me and firmly pats my back. "See, mijo? It's not that bad."

"Why is the house bleeding?"

Pa squints at the walls. "Water must have gotten under the siding. Gotta be from rusty nails." He waves me forward. "C'mon. Let's go check out the inside."

"Watch your step." I point to a spot on the porch where the floorboards are rotten.

"Easy fix." He avoids the bad spot and heads to the front door. "It has good bones. You'll see."

While Pa fusses with the lock, I check out the yard and the surrounding houses. At least the rest of the neighborhood isn't run down like some of our previous places. Little bungalows with well-kept lawns surround us. Looks like a scene from a sitcom about a family in the suburbs. Our house is the worst on the block, hands down. The neighbors will be glad we're fixing this place up.

Speaking of neighbors, a guy and a girl around my age are across the street, looking this way. *Gaping* this way might be a better description. The girl has long black hair and golden skin, and she's holding this elaborate selfie stick setup. Probably a TikTok influencer wannabe. The guy has a mop of brown hair and a pale freckled face. He's holding these strange-looking electronic devices, standing there with his mouth hanging open, looking ridiculous. As soon as I glance his way, he looks away fast. Great. I have weirdos for neighbors.

I turn around and follow Pa into the house.

The moment I pass through the front door, the temperature drops. I'm hit by a gust of frigid air carrying the scent of must. Goose bumps form on my arms, and a full-body chill makes me shake. I wrap my arms around myself, but it does little to fight the cold spreading through me.

The foyer is large, lined with oak paneling cracked from neglect and covered in a thick layer of dust and cobwebs. A long staircase with warped steps and broken spindles leads to a second-story landing. Wooden archways open onto the living and dining rooms on either side of the foyer. Every window is foggy, each one topped with creepy stained glass that casts spiderweb patterns onto the walls. Looks like nobody's lived here for decades.

Pa smiles and nudges me with his elbow. "Pretty nice, huh?"

It's the opposite of nice.

"Who'd you bribe to get an occupancy permit?" I say.

His smile melts away. "Try to see past the dirt. When we fix it up, we'll be rich. This place is a gold mine."

I'd rather live in a home than a gold mine, I almost say, but I think better of it. Pa's got enough to deal with without me mouthing off at everything. "Okay, show me around."

Pa beams and starts the tour. Despite my unease, I have to admit the house has potential. This is the largest one we've ever renovated, with spacious rooms.

"I know it's run down," I say, "but how did we afford this house?"

Pa's eyes shift away from me. "Let me worry about the finances, okay?"

It's not like Pa to hide things from me. In fact, sometimes he overshares about money, which is part of why I worry so much. There's something he's not saying, and that unsettles me almost as much as this eerie old house.

Pa and I head back to the foyer and climb the rickety stairs. The landing opens onto a long hallway lined with doors, and then the stairway turns and continues upward. This place is absolutely massive.

"What's up there?" I tip my head toward the next flight of stairs. Shadows shroud the third-floor landing.

"Just a few odd-shaped hallways and spare rooms," Pa says. "And the attic."

"Let's check it out."

"Okay, but be careful," Pa warns. "Some floorboards need fixing."

On the third floor, the ceilings are lower, angled from the pitch of the roof. The hallway snakes around in a way that seems unnecessary.

Pa points to a gap in the floorboards. "Watch out for that. It'll be the first thing we fix."

I walk over to check it out. A two-foot section of the floor is missing, sheared off like a saw cut through it. I peer through it and see only darkness, so I turn on my phone's flashlight. Spread across the subflooring is a deep red-brown stain. I cry out and fumble with my phone as it nearly slips from my fingers. "Holy shit!"

"Language, mijo!" Pa says, then heads over and peers in. "What *is* that?"

"Pretty sure it's dried blood."

Pa's face pales. He can get superstitious about things like this. But he shrugs it off. "Nah. It's from rusty pipes. Look, there's a pipe running through right there."

Rust again, huh? That'll be his excuse for everything. But the last thing I need is him freaking out, so I shrug it off too. "Yeah, you must be right."

We head back to the second floor. Pa points to a door at one end of the hallway. "That room's mine. You can pick any other one you want."

I choose the bedroom farthest from Pa's because...reasons. It also has the best natural light. My easel and painting supplies will fit perfectly in the corner between the two large windows with views of the massive front and side yards filled with towering oak trees. It might be fun to paint one of those.

As I turn to leave, a flash of motion in the side yard catches my eye. An empty tire swing hanging from an old oak is rocking back and forth. A chill runs through me as I imagine the ghost of a child kicking their legs back and forth. I shake my head and laugh. Just the wind. This house is already getting to me.

Once Pa and I unload the car, we set up our air mattresses and sleeping bags. The rest of our stuff will come next week. We order Chinese take-out and sit in the kitchen in folding camp chairs, eating General Tso's chicken and broccoli beef right out of the cartons with chopsticks.

"Food's not bad," Pa says.

The food *isn't* bad, but the move has put me in a foul mood. This place will be a ton of work to fix up, and I already miss the friends I had to leave behind. "Meh. Could be spicier."

He ignores my comment. "So, Hugo. About school."

I groan.

"I just found out this school district starts earlier than our last one," Pa says. "They started last week."

Typical. Perpetually being the new kid is hard enough, but now I'm behind in school and will get stuck with lame classes. This crappy move just got crappier. I clench my jaw, but my anger spills out. "Goddammit, Pa!"

"Hey, what did I say about language?" Pa's face darkens. "It couldn't be helped. I only got the keys yesterday. This was the earliest we could move."

It *could* have been helped. He could have found out about the school district and gotten me registered. We could have driven here earlier and stayed in a cheap motel. He could have thought ahead, but he didn't. He isn't great at the parenting stuff that requires attention to detail, especially details that impact only me.

"Ma would have figured it out," I snap. Regret hits my gut as soon as the words escape my lips.

Pa's face craters from anger to sadness. "I'm sorry about school."

My throat gets thick, and I stare at my feet. Any time Ma comes up, the hurt is still so raw, even after all these years. "I'll figure out the school stuff. It's okay."

"Hey, mijo, come here." Pa opens his arms for a hug, and I step into them. I clamp my eyes shut and fight the waves of grief trying to flow out. Then Pa puts his hand on my shoulder, holds me at arm's length, and looks at me with glossy eyes. "You know what?"

"What?"

"This house will take us a bit longer than usual. We might be here for the entire school year. And if we can fix this place up real nice, we'll make enough money to afford another place in this area. I can't promise anything, but maybe you can go to the same school next year. How 'bout that?"

Having my junior and senior years at the same school would be a dream. I'd feel like a normal kid. Not that I know what normal feels like. "That sounds nice," I whisper.

Pa pats me on the back. "This place will be good for us."

Maybe it will be. Despite being weird and run down, it could be nice if we fix it up right. Maybe it does have good bones.

As I head back to my room, my spirits lift at the prospect of having the same friends for more than six months. I could have a steady boyfriend and finally work up the nerve to come out to Pa. Ma knew I liked boys. I was thirteen when I told her, and she said she'd always known and that she was proud of me for being true to myself. That meant everything. We planned to tell Pa together, but I kept chickening out. She said it was okay and I could do it when I was ready. We had all the time in the world. Until we didn't. Ma died in a car crash the very next month, and my entire world shattered.

Once she was gone, telling Pa was the last thing on my mind. We had way bigger problems to worry about. And since we moved around a lot, it was easy to avoid the topic. I've always just been the new kid, a perpetual loner, but now it's possible things will change for the better.

I can't help but smile as I head to my new bedroom.

And that's when I see it.

From the second-floor landing, I peer into the bathroom shrouded in darkness. Beyond the door, I swear I see something—a *figure*. I draw in a sharp gasp as coldness descends on me. I'm frozen to the spot.

Looming in the bathroom is a shadow that looks like a woman with long flowing hair. It's the right size and shape to be a person, but it's still as a statue. With shaking hands, I turn on my phone flashlight and shine it at the figure. And just like that, it's gone.

I let out a single short laugh. I'm freaking myself out in this spooky old house. It was nothing—a trick of the shadows. I turn off my flashlight, and the dark shape returns. That proves it. I laugh at myself again for being such a wimp, jumping at shadows in the night.

And that's when the shadow moves.

"Who's there?" I shout.

"What's that, Hugo?" Pa yells from downstairs.

I turn away for only a second. "Pa, come here!" But when I turn back, the shadow is gone. *Vanished*. I race into the bathroom and switch on the light.

The room is empty.

3
Cookies: Cameron

After movie night, I sit in bed for a long while, tapping away on my laptop, working on my short story and peering over at Crimson House. I'm so used to it being dark that seeing lights on inside is surreal. A second-story window shines a soft amber hue. I bet that's Hugo's room. I wonder what he's doing right now.

I'd be lying if I didn't admit he's taking up a chunk of my mental space. The more I try to concentrate on my story, the more my mind drifts to the guy with the wavy dark hair and the serious demeanor. *Hugo.* Even his name is cool.

I fear for him a little. Everything about that house is wicked, and I don't like the idea of anybody living in it, so I send good thoughts in his direction. Not that I believe doing that will help. It just makes me feel better.

I sit awake, staring at the house but not focusing on anything in particular. At some point, the light on the second floor goes out. Without that constant reminder, I'm able to take my mind off Hugo and fall into sleep filled with dreams of harsh rejections, spooky old women, and cute new guys.

The next day, I roll out of bed, do my morning routine. A glance at my phone shows that Abby is already at it. I guess she's working overtime trying to hang out with me after the Noah incident.

Abby: I need your help

Cameron: What's up

Abby: I'm at Manresa Castle

Cameron: [eye roll emoji] Ghost hunt?

Abby: Maybe

Cameron: Yes or no

Abby: I felt cheated after yesterday

Cameron: So that's a yes

Abby: I need you!!!!

Cameron: You know I hate ghost hunts

Abby: But you're the best at asking the ghosts questions

Cameron: Because I'm a good bullshitter

Abby: Also more ghost stuff happens when you're around. I NEED YOU!!!!

Lucky me. Human ghost magnet.

Abby never gives up, so I may as well bow to her unrelenting will. But it's okay. Honestly, I enjoy hanging out with her. Making her happy makes me happy. Plus, I can cut through the yard of Crimson House, and maybe I'll bump into Hugo or catch a glimpse of him through a window.

Cameron: Be there in 15

Abby: YAAAAAYYYYYYY!!!!!!!

On my way to the kitchen for sustenance, I pass my older brother, Jack, who's headed for the front door. He's dressed in his red-and-white soccer kit, our high school colors. He's the sporty one who takes after Dad, which is fine with me cause it takes the pressure off. He and Dad can blab for hours about sports. But I do enjoy watching Jack play soccer and often go to his matches.

"Off to slay the soccer beasts?" I ask with a smirk.

Jack shakes his head. "That's not an expression."

"I've never been good at sports banter."

"Clearly." Jack laughs. "So. I saw people moving into Crimson House."

"Me too. Wild, huh?" My cheeks heat as Hugo flashes through my mind.

"Yeah, wild," Jack says. "I saw them unpacking their car—a man and his son."

"Hugo!" I blurt. God, play it cool, Cameron.

"Huh?" Jack gives me a questioning look.

Heat spreads from my cheeks to my entire face.

"The son's name is Hugo," I clarify. "I overheard them."

Jack has this wry smile. "A new friend for you?"

"Maybe."

"Or a *boyfriend*." Jack's smile goes wide.

"Oh my god. I'm not having this conversation with my straight older brother."

"What can I say? He's about your age and good-looking." Jack laughs, but it's a kind laugh. He has good intentions, even if he is an idiot.

"Have you been consulting with Abby?" I ask.

"Nope. I know a good-looking guy when I see one."

"I'm done." I wave him off and veer toward the kitchen.

"Later, dweeb," he says with a laugh as he heads out the front door.

"Bye, freak," I shoot back.

Mom and Dad are at the breakfast table, sipping coffee and staring at their phones, reading the news, liking posts on Facebook, and commenting on their latest scores on whatever word game they've been playing. Boring parent stuff.

Dad's wearing a light blue polo and khaki shorts—ready for a day on the golf course, no doubt. His sunglasses rest on his short brown hair, which is speckled with gray.

He glances up from his phone. "Morning, Cam. So glad you've joined the land of the living. I was about to send out a search party."

Just as funny as the other five hundred mornings when he's said the same thing. Dad desperately needs new dad jokes.

"Hey, sweetie," Mom says without looking up from her phone. She got in late from her shift at the hospital last night, and judging by her scrubs, she's likely headed back soon. Being one of the top heart surgeons in the region is demanding work, so we don't see her a lot. "How was your movie night with Abby?"

"It was fun," I say as I grab an Eggo waffle from the freezer.

Dad glances up from his phone. "Are you finally going to work up the nerve to ask Abby to homecoming?"

I sigh. Loudly. "I don't know. Maybe we'll go as friends?"

Dad shakes his head, lips pursed, then stares back down at his phone.

Dad always does this. His never-ending passive-aggressiveness wears on me. After several frustrating years of correcting him, I started letting things slide cause it's easier than sounding like a broken record. But each time I do, I feel sick to my stomach. I swear, having to deal with this takes years off my life. The thing is, Dad and I used to be friends, and I miss those days. Now it's like he doesn't know what to do with me.

I head for the door, munching on my Eggo. "I'm hanging out with Abby."

"Okay, have fun, Cameron," Mom says, still half distracted. "Just be home by six o'clock for dinner."

"I will. Love you."

Mom nods while fussing with her phone, and Dad doesn't even look up from his breakfast. Now that he's dropped his heteronormative bomb on me, he can't even be bothered to say goodbye.

Let's see if this'll get their attention. "A man and his son moved into the old house across the street. The son's about my age, and he's really cute."

That does it.

Mom and Dad look up at me as if waking from a dream, but their expressions couldn't be more different. A smile spreads across Mom's face, while Dad tries and fails to look neutral as his jaw clenches and his eyebrows twitch.

"Cute, huh?" Mom's smile widens. "Did you introduce yourself?"

"Not yet. He looked busy unpacking." I stare dreamily into the distance for dramatic effect.

"Well." Dad clears his throat. "Glad somebody's finally moving in. Hopefully they'll fix that place up. It's a real eyesore." He looks back at his phone. A typical dad deflection.

Between Mom's busy schedule and Dad's low-grade lack of acceptance, sometimes it's like I'm on my own in this house. I mean, my parents do love me, and at least Jack's cool. I guess things could be a lot worse, but that doesn't mean I don't want them to be better.

That's enough parent torture for one morning, so I turn to go, Eggo in hand. "I'm outta here. See you later!" I say, then shut the door behind me before they can respond.

Freedom.

The whole day is ahead of me. I love Saturday, the best day of them all. I get to sleep in and stay up late. No other day compares. So full of potential.

Fueled by enthusiasm, I run across the street toward Crimson House, and for once, I'm excited to walk by it. That's something I've never been able to say before. This house is a scourge, but today a run-in with Hugo is possible.

Even with all this positive energy, a chill rolls through my extremities the moment I step onto the lawn. The house glares at me with coldness and malice. I peer up at it, searching for signs of life inside, but everything is still. I've stepped into a void. No birds chirp. No insects buzz. An unnatural calm descends on everything.

I step up my pace and race past the horrible house, but as I enter the backyard, the creak of a door cuts through the silence. My whole body shivers.

Part of me doesn't want to know what caused the noise, but it might be Hugo. This might be my chance to meet him, so I turn toward the house, preparing myself for the worst. The back porch door is open, only darkness behind it.

"Hello?" My voice cracks as I break the absolute quiet.

An elderly woman emerges from the shadows. I'm pretty sure she's the one I saw yesterday, with her flowing gray hair and old white dress. Deep wrinkles cover her face, and her mouth is frozen in a crooked smile. She's looking in my direction, but her unfocused eyes stare past me.

If I hadn't seen Hugo and his dad move in yesterday, I'd be a blubbering mess right now. She's exactly how I imagined the White Lady of

Sycamore Lane, but she must be Hugo's grandma. Plus, she's too solid to be a ghost.

"Hi. My name is Cameron." I wave. "You must have just moved in."

The woman doesn't react, just continues to stare. She must be hard of hearing. I clear my throat to repeat myself, but then she finally speaks.

"I made some cookies. Would you like some?" Her voice is hollow, like an old tape recording. Her smile widens, exposing jagged yellowed teeth.

"Oh—um—no, thank you." I stumble over the words. "I have to be going."

"They're fresh out of the oven." She beckons me toward the doorway as she drifts into the darkness beyond. "Come, Cameron."

I shudder as my name escapes those lips. A breeze picks up, howling as it blows across the porch, carrying the scent of cookies. I swear the wind whispers my name. *Cameron.* A trick of my overactive imagination, no doubt.

I suddenly regret telling the woman my name, like it was an invitation or an unwritten contract between us. Bile rises in my throat, my stomach threatening to reject my few bites of Eggo. Something about this is wrong. Very wrong.

"I—um." I don't even try to finish before I turn around and run.

The moment I step off the property and into the forest, a weight lifts off me. Even in the shade of the trees, it's about ten degrees warmer. The sudden temperature change sends chills running down my back.

I'm a good ten feet into the forest before I dare look back at that godforsaken house. The back door is closed, and no one is around. Like it never happened.

4
THE BASEMENT: HUGO

The stately oak tree outside my bedroom window calms me as it sways in the late summer breeze. I pull in a deep breath. I love the firmness of the wooden brush handle, the scent of the paint, the bristles' light swishes as they spread color over the canvas, and the way my mind can escape. I've been escaping a lot over the last few years.

After seeing the moving shadow in the bathroom last night, I needed the stability only my art can provide. I couldn't believe my eyes—I floated above my body, disconnected, like I was watching someone else. I must have imagined it. It *can't* have been real. Shadows don't move on their own.

After I yelled out, Pa ran upstairs to find out what was wrong. I couldn't tell him the truth, not if I couldn't believe it myself. Instead, I told him a rat ran by, and now he's called the exterminators. A total waste of money, but I had no choice.

See, Pa is—well, he's superstitious. He believes in spirits, ghosts, bad omens, all of it, and the last thing I need is him freaking out, especially since this house could be my key to a normal life. He's clearly dumped his life savings into this place, and leaving now would ruin us. I'll keep my mouth shut and hope the shadow is something my mind made up.

The tree is half roughed out on my canvas when a sharp tap-tapping gets my attention. Out the window, a black crow sits on the rain gutter, pecking away at the glass like it's trying to break through. I race over to shoo it. It flaps its wings and caws, then flies away, but something else catches my attention through the window—a kid is cutting across our yard down below.

It's the guy who stared at me from across the road yesterday. The dork with his hands full of electronics, looking dumb. But today there's something different about him. He's more focused, walking with long, confident strides as the sun filters through his wavy brown hair. He's got a medium build, and his shorts show off muscular legs. No one would mistake him for a twink, but that's good in my book. He's strong in a natural way, not like he spends hours at the gym. Perfect, really.

I shake my head and laugh. I shouldn't pine after every guy I see. Still, as he cuts through our yard, my eyes can't help but follow. I wonder where he's going.

He passes into the backyard, disappearing from sight. I run to the back bedroom and spot him again, heading toward the woods beyond our property.

Then he stops in his tracks like somebody yelled *freeze*. It's almost comical. After a moment, he turns toward the back of the house. He says something, though I can't make it out—must be talking to Pa. I hope Pa's not giving this poor kid shit for cutting through our yard. He can be a dick sometimes.

The kid runs off like he's scared for his life.

"Crap, Pa! You need to chill!" I shout, though I doubt he can hear me from downstairs.

I race down the steps and head to the kitchen, but the room is empty. Out the back window, I see the kid all the way to the edge of our property, looking back.

"Pa!" I yell. "What the heck did you say to that kid?"

No answer.

"Pa?"

No sign of him anywhere on the main floor, but the door to the basement is ajar. The staircase descends into darkness.

"Pa?" I call down the steps, but I get no response, so I switch on the light and head down.

I'm no wimp. I lost my fear of basements years ago, but this basement is Creepy with a capital *C*. Thick cobwebs cover everything, and there's a pervasive smell of mold. Ceiling high windows with years of caked-on dirt let in only the smallest amount of sickly yellow light, casting everything in a dull, eerie glow. Cracks in the concrete floor form irregular patterns and spread in every direction. Old moldy boxes are piled high in the corner, collapsing under their own weight.

Cutting through the stagnant air, a cold breeze dances at my feet—not uncommon for a drafty old house like this. I delve deeper into the basement, searching for the source, curiosity piqued. An ancient boiler about the size of a VW Beetle emits a low rumble, burning fuel deep within its bowels, the occasional flicker of golden light escaping at the seams.

I follow the breeze past the boiler to a part of the wall that looks different from everything else around it. A section of plaster about three feet wide blends into the concrete walls on either side, smoothed out but a shade lighter. At the bottom, the plaster has cracked away, exposing a narrow hole. A cool gust of air tickles my fingers, whistling against the hole's jagged edge.

Well, that solves the mystery of the draft, but now an even bigger mystery takes its place. What the heck is behind there?

From the hole comes a faint scratching and chittering, barely noticeable over the gusts of air pushing through. I lean closer, trying to identify the noises. There must actually be rodents in the walls. This is karma getting back at me for lying to Pa about seeing a rat.

But as I listen, the noises change, taking on a familiar cadence. I swear it's the faint sound of laughter. Or it could be sobs. Okay, now it's somebody sobbing for sure. What the heck?

I back away from the hole in a flash. Icy-cold fingers grip my shoulder from behind, and I jump out of my skin. "Holy shit!"

I spin around, expecting the figure—the shadow that moved. Instead, it's only Pa, laughing.

"Jesus Christ, Hugo." He's almost falling over, clutching his stomach in fits of laughter. "You should see the look on your face."

I glare at him. "Thanks, Pa. You want to give your sixteen-year-old son a heart attack?"

"Maybe?" Pa chokes out. "If I had recorded that, it would have gone viral on TikTok. We'd be rich."

"That's not how TikTok works, Pa."

"Whatever." After his laughter subsides, he asks, "So, what's up?"

"Did you just come down here? Did you talk to that kid in our yard?"

Pa scrunches his brow. "I've been down here for an hour checking out the electrical panel. That whole thing has to go. Why? What kid?"

A chill goes down my back. The unexplainable things in this house are piling up. "It's nothing. Some kid cutting through our backyard. I think he lives across the street. I thought he talked to you."

"Nope, wasn't me. But if you see him, tell him not to cut through. Don't want our yard to turn into a freeway."

I roll my eyes. "Don't be a jerk, Pa. I doubt there are hundreds of kids cutting through."

"Fine, whatever," Pa says. "But I reserve the right to change my mind. Anyway, back to work."

Pa walks off, leaving me alone in the dark corner, and I shiver again. Why is this basement turning me into a scared little kid? I grew out of these fears years ago. *Toughen up, Hugo.*

I lean down to touch the hole again. The breeze has stopped, and the air is stagnant. The noises have fallen silent, and the basement is as quiet as a tomb.

5

MANRESA CASTLE: CAMERON

In a seaside Victorian village chock-full of spooky places, near the top of the spooky list is Manresa Castle—Port Townsend's famous haunted hotel. I mean, it's no Crimson House, but the creep factor is still pretty solid. Still, you wouldn't know from looking at the outside. Everything is pristine: pale stucco walls, European arches, pointed turrets, and a steep slate roof. It wouldn't look out of place nestled among the German Alps.

I race up the short flight of steps and enter the lobby. I've been here a thousand times, so the front desk staff don't even give me a second glance. Abby's dad knows the owners, who give her the run of the place.

Wall-to-wall antique furniture fills the foyer, the dark wood, wingback chairs, and Persian rugs creating a spooky atmosphere. I'm still freaked out by the old woman on the porch of Crimson House, so this isn't an aesthetic I'm excited about at the moment.

I take out my phone.

Cameron: In the lobby

Abby: We're in the turret

Cameron: We?

> **Abby:** Chloe's here

> **Cameron:** I thought you didn't want her on ghost hunts

> **Abby:** I love Chloe

> **Cameron:** Doesn't she "interfere with the evidence-based approach"

> **Abby:** I can't explain how she knows stuff, and that bugs me. But she's almost never wrong

> **Cameron:** True

> **Abby:** And lots of YouTube ghost hunters have psychics

There it is. Abby will do anything for her YouTube channel.

> **Cameron:** Fair enough. I'll be right up

I pocket my phone and head for the stairs. On my way, I pass a familiar face—Mr. Peterson, head librarian of Port Townsend Library, sits in a chair by the fireplace, tapping on his phone. Who knew librarians ever left the library?

I've spent countless hours working on my story at the library, so Mr. Peterson knows me well. He glances up over his reading glasses as I walk past. "Hello, Cameron."

"Hey, Mr. P."

"Everything okay?" He tilts his head. "You seem unsettled."

"I'm fine. Just tired," I lie. I guess that old lady really got to me if people can read it on my face.

Mr. Peterson nods.

"What brings you to Manresa Castle?" I ask.

"I'm leading a ghost tour," he says, smiling. "Part of my responsibilities as a member of the historical society."

"That's a coincidence. I'm here to help Abby with a ghost hunt."

Mr. Peterson laughs. "That sounds like the Abby Nguyen I know. I subscribe to her YouTube channel."

"I didn't know you were into ghost stuff."

"I am," he says. "I've enjoyed it since I was about your age."

Apparently everybody in this town is ghost crazy except me. Living across from Crimson House is more than enough. God, that stupid house. My shoulders tense at the thought of it. But if Mr. Peterson is such an expert on ghosts, he might know something about the house. I should drop it, but my curiosity gets the best of me.

"Hey, Mr. P, you remember that abandoned house across from mine? Sixteen Sycamore Lane?"

"Yes," he says with a slight twitch of his eye. "It's hard to forget. Didn't you have an incident there a few years back? I seem to recall stitches."

"Yeah, that was me." I don't elaborate on it since it's not one of my prouder moments. "Have you heard anything about the lady who lived there?"

Mr. Peterson nods. "Emily Thornburn. Yes, we have a thorough history of her life and the house. Next time you're at the library, I'll show you what we've got."

The way he rattled that off so fast makes me think he must know a lot about her. A strange mix of curious excitement and fear swirls through me. Everything about that house is a contradiction.

"Thanks. I'd like that." I wave goodbye as I walk away. "Gotta run. Abby's waiting."

"Cameron, can I give you a bit of advice?" Mr. Peterson says. Something in his tone makes me stop in my tracks.

"Sure."

"I wouldn't get mixed up with that house." Mr. Peterson's eyes bore into me. "It's dangerous. But you already know that, right?" He glances down at the scar on my leg.

"Yeah. Thanks. I'll keep that in mind," I say as I start up the steps. That was ominous, and more than a little odd. Then again, Mr. Peterson is odd in general.

I race up three flights of stairs and enter the hotel's unfinished attic. Exposed beams and rafters crisscross the space overhead, and the underside of the roof is plain to see. Despite it being clear and sunny outside, the wood creaks and howls, buffeted by the wind from Port Townsend Bay. It's no wonder people think spirits haunt this place.

I wind my way past storage boxes, broken furniture, and chests filled with long-forgotten items leaking the scent of mothballs until I reach the main turret of Manresa Castle. The cone extends upward, coming to a point about thirty feet above. Wooden chairs with purple velvet cushions form a circle, and a noose hangs from a rafter—a nod to the monk who is rumored to have taken his life here and now supposedly haunts the hotel. I chuckle to myself. All just stage dressing for the ghost tours.

Abby stands in the middle of the turret, speaking into her digital voice recorder, hoping to catch ghosts talking back while a video camera on a tripod captures the scene. Even though I'm not crazy about ghost hunts, watching Abby do what she's passionate about always makes me smile. She never does anything halfway.

Standing near her is our friend Chloe, her bright red pixie cut and pale, freckled skin standing out in the dim room.

Since Abby's recording, I keep quiet and hide in the shadows. I'm tempted to scare the crap out of her and Chloe, but I'm way too nice for that. Maybe.

"If you're in here, give us a sign," Abby says, looking upward toward the rafters. "Did you take your life because you broke your vow of celibacy? You knocked once. Can you do it again?"

Silence follows, other than the occasional gust of wind making the entire turret groan as the wood flexes and bends, filling me with cozy, spooky vibes. I'm a bit of a romantic and would love to be snuggled up here during a windstorm. With Hugo. Yep, one-track mind.

Abby peeks over at Chloe, who's standing still, eyes closed, hands out to her sides. "Anything?" Abby asks.

Chloe's eyes open. "No. Nothing at all."

"Really? Not even a peep?" Abby scrunches her lips. "Isn't there some way to, like, switch it on or something?"

"I told you. It doesn't work like that. I'm not like one of your EMF meters. I don't have that kind of control over it. I either feel things or I don't."

"Well, that's not very helpful for my YouTube channel." Abby sighs.

"I haven't even decided if I want to *be* on your YouTube channel," Chloe replies. "You know I don't like people knowing about my ability."

"I doubt we'll have much usable footage anyway," Abby says as she scrolls through the video. "An entire hour, and all we got was one soft knock. And for all we know, that was the housekeepers."

This pretty much sums up why I don't like ghost-hunting. The vast majority of the time, nothing happens and I'm bored out of my skull. On rare occasions, something scary happens, but that's not fun either, since it dredges up old memories of Crimson House.

I step into the room and speak a touch louder than necessary. "I heard the suicidal monk rumor was made up by a bartender to get better tips."

Abby and Chloe jump in surprise, but then Abby smiles.

"Cameron! You made it!" She runs over and gives me a hug. "You're just in time. Nothing's been happening. We need your ghost energy." Abby laughs to let me know she's mostly kidding. Mostly.

"Hey, Cameron," Chloe says, walking over. She has a big smile, but the closer she gets to us, the more her smile fades until it becomes a frown.

"Hey, Chloe," I say. "Everything okay?"

Chloe backs up a step, wobbles on her feet, and sits down hard on one of the velvet chairs lining the room. Abby and I lunge forward to steady her.

"Chloe, what's wrong?" Abby says, panicked.

"Um, it's nothing," Chloe says. "I just got lightheaded."

"Take it easy for a minute and take slow breaths," Abby says, rubbing Chloe's back. "Breathe deep through your nose. The same thing used to happen to me when I was a kid. Low blood pressure."

"Is there anything we can get for you?" I ask Chloe.

"Some water would be nice," Chloe says. "Abby, can you go get me some?"

"Sure." Abby stands up from her crouch. "I'll be right back. Cameron, you stay here and make sure she's okay."

"Will do."

Abby heads for the door. The moment she's gone, Chloe turns to me. "Hey, Cameron, is everything okay?"

I laugh. "Aren't I the one who's supposed to be asking you that?"

Chloe doesn't laugh back. "Has anything happened to you today? Anything unusual?"

Why do people keep asking me that? Is there something written on my face? Did somebody tape a sign to my back saying spooked by a creepy old lady?

"It's nothing," I say. "Just, some new people moved into Crimson House."

"Crimson House? Huh." Her emerald-green eyes gaze into mine, searching for something.

I love Chloe so much, but when she says vague and ominous stuff like this, it freaks me out. She has these abilities—I don't know a better way to describe it. She dreams about things she shouldn't know or things in the future, and she's scarily accurate. She also gets these feelings in certain places or with certain people. Prickly soft, she calls it, but she doesn't like flaunting any of it.

When she directs her attention at me, it's a special kind of uncomfortable.

"Chloe, is there anything I should be worried about?"

Something shifts in her face. "No. It's okay. I'm feeling better now. I think Abby was right. It must be low blood pressure."

"You sure?"

"Yep." Chloe forces a smile. "It's nothing."

But her smile doesn't reach her eyes.

6

FIRST DAY: HUGO

My phone screams at me to wake up. I fight the urge to throw it across the room.

"I hate you, phone." The phone glares back, taunting me with its display, which shows five forty-five a.m. Getting up early to register for school is never fun. I drag myself out of bed and get ready for the first day of class.

Port Townsend High School must be more than a hundred years old, made from red bricks faded from age. My eyelids are heavy as I make my way through its halls. I've seen so many high schools in the last few years that they all blend together. Drab institutional colors, ugly speckled tiles, and dark green lockers greet me as I head to the school office. It's early, so only the occasional teacher and a handful of kids are milling about.

The school office has a half wall of windows with a crisscross of wire mesh, similar to the guard station of a prison. The door has the words PRINCIPAL'S OFFICE stenciled in fading letters. Inside, two students sit in chairs, waiting. They're older guys with buzzed haircuts and scowls on their faces. Thick. Tough. *Bullies.* Their eyes follow me as I walk into the room.

Behind the front desk sits a middle-aged woman with pale skin and a tight bun. She glares at me through her cat-eye glasses, a sour expression plastered on her face. A nameplate on her desk reads MRS. APPLEBER-RY.

"Can I help you?" she asks with an edge to her voice, as if doing her job is a huge inconvenience.

"Yes—uh—Mrs. Appleberry. I'm Hugo Cruz. I'm new here. I'm supposed to register."

Her face turns even more sour. "Registration is over."

"Yeah, I guess my dad missed it," I say. "He called the office last week and arranged things."

She sighs and starts typing on her computer. A moment later, she sighs again and hands me a clipboard. "I need you to fill this out. Then head over there and handle your class registration." She points to a computer in the back corner.

I fill out the form, hand it back to her, and head to the computer.

"Hilarious," she says. "I need your actual address."

I turn around and grab the form, confused. Maybe I wrote something wrong? I move so often that it wouldn't be the first time I've made a mistake, but I scan the document, and everything is correct. "This *is* my actual address."

"Sixteen Sycamore Lane?" She stares at me over her ridiculous glasses. The guys in the office look up.

"Yes?" I say. "Is that a problem?"

"Only cause it's a piece of shit," a guy with buzzed red hair and a face like a pig says with a sneer.

"And haunted," the guy with blond hair says. "You ever notice how it looks like it's bleeding? It's called Crimson House."

Haunted?

"I don't know what to say." I shrug. "That's where I live."

"Good luck with that," the red-haired guy snaps, and both guys laugh.

"Have you seen the White Lady yet?" the blond guy says with a wicked smile.

"White Lady? What do you mean?" The shadow in the bathroom flashes through my mind.

A heavyset man with a balding head comes out of an inner office with MR. ANGUS—VICE PRINCIPAL stenciled on the door. "Bryce. Jimmy. My office," he says in a sharp tone, and gestures for them to join him.

Both jerks follow him, snickering at me as they go.

"See ya later, Spooky," the redhead says as he passes me, leering.

"Nice one, Bryce," the blond guy says, and they bump fists, heading into the office.

Bryce. Asshole. Noted.

So, people think our new house is haunted? It *looks* haunted, and all the red running down the siding doesn't help. Normally, I'd dismiss it as a bunch of dumb rumors, but that damn shadow moved.

"You done?" Mrs. Appleberry points to the clipboard in my hand.

"Yeah." I shake off the thought and hand the clipboard back to her.

"I'd stay away from those two. Trouble." She starts typing.

"Yeah, I got that impression. What did they mean about the White Lady?"

"Well, I really shouldn't say," she says, then starts rattling off facts. "People say the White Lady is Emily Thornburn. Her father kept her locked up in that house her whole life. She was either the sweetest thing you ever saw or she was a nightmare, throwing tantrums and biting people."

"Wow, I had no idea," I say, heading to the computer.

Before I can escape, Mrs. Appleberry continues. "Kids went missing while she lived there, but no one ever proved she was involved. The house has been empty since she died. A family moved in but left within weeks."

"Um. Wow. That's a lot."

"You didn't hear it from me." Mrs. Appleberry looks down and clatters away at her keyboard.

"What happened to the people who lived there?"

Mrs. Appleberry's phone rings. She answers it with all the enthusiasm of a sloth. "Port Townsend High School principal's office. Mrs. Appleberry speaking. How can I help you?" she drones.

Nothing more from her, I guess. And that's probably for the best. I might never finish registering for my classes if she starts talking again.

As expected, my classes are terrible. I sign up for all the basics, like history, trig, literature, and chemistry, but the good electives are all full: advanced painting, computer illustration, graphic design. The only thing even close is theater tech. Maybe they'll need some backdrops painted?

When I finish, Mrs. Appleberry is still chattering on the phone. She waves me over and hands me a sheet of paper. Printed on it is everything I need for the day, including my schedule, locker assignment, and combo. She waves me off without a second glance.

All day I wander the unfamiliar halls, trying to find my classes, and always end up arriving a minute or two past the bell. Each teacher seems annoyed that I'm starting a week late. Soon I have a pile of homework assignments I'm already behind on.

The kids aren't any better. At first they just look at me curiously because I'm the new kid. But by the second period, word of my address has spread throughout the student body, and over and over I hear the words *16 Sycamore Lane, the White Lady,* and *Spooky.* Thanks, Bryce and Jimmy—two hours into school, and I've already got a nickname. But it's better than *Jose Cuervo* or some racist shit like that. Small wins.

I show up to my fourth-period trig class one minute late, and as usual, the only seats left are in the front. Only one period left until lunch, and I need a break. The teacher, Mr. Whitmore, is about a hundred years old and is utterly confused when I show up. He says it'll be a couple of days before he can sort out my assignments from last week. Great. I hate math, I'm already behind, and it'll only get worse with each passing day.

As he writes out some nasty linear equation on the screeching chalkboard, the kids behind me are out of control, laughing, yelling, and throwing wads of paper at the trash can by the teacher's desk. Mr. Whitmore ignores it all, lost in his math. This man has zero control over his class. I sink into my desk as the chaos unfolds around me.

"Hey, Spooky." It's the voice from the office this morning. Bryce. I ignore him.

"You seen the White Lady yet?" Bryce taunts.

I spin around and glare at him. A smirk appears on his ugly face.

"At least you know she's not your grandma," he says with a nasty laugh. "She is the *White* Lady, after all."

A few guys around him laugh and high-five. Half of the class *oooohhhs*. My blood boils. I've had enough of his shit.

"Fuck off!" I shout and flip him off as my words echo around the room.

The entire class goes deathly quiet.

"Mr. Cruz," Mr. Whitmore's icy voice calls out. "We don't allow that kind of talk here."

Oh, great. *Now* he pays attention to his class.

"But you're okay with racist talk? That's bullshit," I shoot back before I think better of it.

"Office, Mr. Cruz. Now!" Mr. Whitmore points to the door.

Sent to the office on the first day. That's a record, even for me.

As I enter the office, Mrs. Appleberry shoots me a look like she's not surprised to see me. I'm already living up to people's low expectations. Mr. Angus gives me a day of detention, which he'll let me do next week at lunch, and says he won't call Pa. Small wins.

By lunchtime, I've had it. I grab my tray of awful-looking cafeteria food, ignoring all the stares and whispers, then find an empty table in the back corner of the lunchroom. With no one to talk to, I eat the nasty excuse for pizza on my plate and bury my head in my phone to block out everything.

I'm scrolling through Instagram when two kids walk up to me and stop. I can't take much more of this day. I glance up to see the brown-haired guy who cut through my yard and the girl with the selfie stick. The guy has this ridiculous grin, dorky but also kinda cute, I have to admit. Adorkable.

He stands there, saying nothing. The girl glares and elbows him in the ribs.

"Ouch!" he cries, rubbing his side.

"Go on," she says through gritted teeth.

"*Okay*, jeez."

I hold back a laugh. This kid is nervous enough already without me making it worse.

He forces his gaze my way. "Hey, um—Hugo, right?"

"I guess my reputation precedes me." I smile.

"Sorry." The guy's cheeks turn a pale shade of pink. "We...uh...we were on the sidewalk across from you when you pulled up to your house Friday. I overheard your dad say your name. Didn't mean to eavesdrop."

The girl whispers to him, "Tell him *your* name."

"Oh! I'm Cameron." He waves.

"And I'm Abby," the girl adds.

I smile again and nod.

"Mind if we join you?" Abby asks.

"Well, I was kinda saving these seats for all my friends." I let out a sad laugh. "But go ahead."

Cameron and Abby set down their lunch trays and settle in on the other side of the table.

"I live right across the street from you," Cameron blurts. "My bedroom window looks right into yours."

I raise an eyebrow, and Abby gives Cameron a look that says, *That's a creepy thing to say.*

Cameron's eyes go wide. "Oh—no—I didn't mean it like that! I don't have binoculars or anything."

"*Not* better." Abby laughs.

I can't help but laugh too.

Cameron goes beet red. "I'm sorry. I—I'll just shut up now."

"That's probably for the best," I say between laughs.

Cameron and Abby seem chill, and we talk about our classes. Overall, I'm relieved to have people to talk to who aren't asking about my haunted house, calling me Spooky, or talking about the White Lady.

But just as I'm getting comfortable, Cameron yanks the rug out from under me.

"Hey, I met your grandma," he says.

I freeze. "Say what?"

"The old lady with the long hair and white dress? Your grandma, right?" He asks it with a straight face like he's not trying to tease me, but I don't appreciate it. This ghost bullshit is pissing me off, and this hits a nerve after all of Bryce's bullying.

"That's not fucking funny!"

"Hey!" Cameron says, eyes wide. "What's wrong?"

"You gonna call me Spooky next?" I shoot back.

"What?" Cameron has this confused and innocent expression. Quite the actor. "Why would I do that?"

He's trying to backtrack, but it's only making me more pissed. I've had it.

"Whatever. I'm outta here." I stand up to leave. "Oh, and my dad says don't cut through our yard."

I thought Cameron and Abby were different, but I guess everybody in this town is a dick. I turn around and don't look back.

7
THEATER TECH: CAMERON

Abby and I sit in stunned silence as Hugo storms off. He shoves the cafeteria door hard on his way out, and several people look up. But he's gone.

I turn to Abby. "What did I say?"

Abby shrugs. "Dude's got anger issues."

"I feel terrible. Should I go after him?"

"I don't think that's a good idea. He seemed pretty pissed off."

From across the cafeteria, our friends Taylor and Matty appear. The two of them are hard to miss. Taylor's bright tie-dye shirt is about three sizes too big, and Matty's hair is platinum blond at its roots, but the rest is a rainbow flag left over from when he dyed it during pride month.

"What was that about?" Taylor asks as they sit down next to us. They might have on the slightest bit of eyeliner to make their pale blue eyes stand out from their creamy complexion.

"I have no idea," I say. "His name's Hugo. He moved in across the street from me. Something I said pissed him off, apparently."

Recognition dawns on Taylor's face. "Ohhhh. *That* was him."

"What do you mean?"

"He was in my trig class last period," Taylor says. "I thought I recognized him. He's cute."

"Um..." My face heats.

"Wait, you're crushing on him, aren't you?" Matty says, smiling.

I say nothing and try to disappear into my chair. Matty will tease me for the rest of the school year if I let on that I like Hugo.

"He totally is," Abby blurts with a wide grin.

Thanks, Abby.

Matty reaches across the table, pinches my cheek, and smiles. "You're so cute when you blush."

My face explodes with heat. Matty is one of the cutest guys in the eleventh grade, and his letterman jacket makes him even cuter. I swear he flirts with me just to see me squirm. He's not queer, but I get the impression that he wishes he was—he calls himself a proud ally. But who knows? Maybe he fits somewhere on the rainbow.

"It hardly matters now that I scared him off." I throw my hands in the air. "And I have no idea what I did."

"Well, in trig, Bryce Hunter made a racist joke about the *White* Lady not being his grandma, and Hugo told him to eff off." Taylor laughs as they pull their long, curly hair back into a ponytail. "Bryce had it coming. He's such an asshole. But Hugo got sent to the office."

Realization slaps me in the face. "Oh crap! I asked Hugo about his grandma. That's why he freaked out."

"His grandma?" Matty asks. "Why'd you ask him that?"

"Because I saw her. Saturday morning, when I was cutting through Hugo's yard."

Abby slaps the lunch table. "Wait! You saw the White Lady again?"

"No. It was, like, a real lady," I say. "She invited me in for cookies and everything."

"That's the exact thing the White Lady would do to lure kids inside!" Abby shrieks.

"I'm telling you, she was real. Solid. Not ghostlike at all." I'm blabbering, trying to convince myself more than anybody else. Seeing that old woman freaked me out so much. Even thinking about it again make me feel off-kilter.

"Well, either way, dude, you pissed Hugo off," Matty says.

"Yeah. I guess I owe him an explanation." I sigh, shoulders slumping. "He must have thought I was teasing him. This sucks."

"You owe me an explanation too." Abby shoots me a withering gaze. "How come you keep holding back stuff about Crimson House?"

"Cause there's nothing to tell. It was an actual lady."

Abby's glare says she doesn't buy it. And to be honest, I don't buy it myself. Something's going on in that house, and I can't explain it. And poor Hugo's living in it.

"Well, now you *have* to talk to him again," Abby says. "We need to figure out what's going on in that house. I need some more footage for my YouTube channel."

I roll my eyes.

The rest of the day goes by with no further excitement, other than Abby badgering me to apologize to Hugo. I also don't want him to be mad at me, but for different reasons. Reasons involving me wanting to kiss him. But there's no sign of Hugo. We don't have any of the same classes, and I never bump into him in the halls. It's totally possible he's avoiding me on purpose. This blows. How did I make such a bad first impression? Typical Cameron, scaring off every cute guy I bump into. I'm cursed.

The last period of the day finally comes, and it's my favorite class: theater tech. A whole fifty-one minutes of doing nothing but building props, talking to my friends, and goofing off with theater folks. My people. We're all misfits, but we all fit together.

The classroom butts right up to the backstage area of the theater, next to all the rigging, lighting equipment, and the flats we'll paint for scenery. Abby's got orchestra this period, so she's not in class. Also, she told me I create enough drama in her life, so she doesn't need to take an entire class about it. I didn't think that was particularly funny.

But the rest of our friend group is here. Taylor and Matty sit across from me. Next to them are Chloe and her girlfriend, Maya.

Maya's one of the prettiest girls in the school, but she doesn't make a big deal about it, which makes her even prettier. She has this luscious, curly black hair cascading over her shoulders, complementing her warm brown skin. Her complexion is flawless. She's wearing a loose-fitting red floral cami dress. *Stunning.* Despite her sweet exterior, Maya is fierce and takes zero crap from anyone. Once a guy made a lewd comment to her and Chloe in the hall. After she was done with him, his voice was about three octaves higher.

"What show do you think we'll do this year?" Matty asks the group as he adjusts his bow tie with little Darth Vaders on it. "I hope it's something by Andrew Lloyd Webber."

Matty knows all the words to tons of Broadway shows, plus he plays football. It's like a theater geek, a jock, and a queer boy had a three-way and somehow had a baby. He's all over the place. But he's awesome.

Maya groans. "I hope it's by anyone *but* that overhyped cheeseball. He's like the turducken of composers."

"Turducken?" Matty asks.

"Yeah. He overstuffs all his musicals, trying to please everybody while satisfying nobody."

Matty puts his hand to his chest and shrieks, "Sacrilege!"

"Maya's entitled to her opinion," Taylor cuts in. "I agree with her somewhat, but *Phantom* is a classic."

"See?" Matty squeals. "Classic."

"One word," Maya says. *"Cats."*

Mr. Spencer, the drama teacher, walks into the room right as the bell rings—a pudgy middle-aged man with a round face and a friendly smile. His frumpy clothes, wool socks, and Birkenstocks scream comfort. He's one of those "cool teachers" who's friends with all the students but somehow still keeps his class under control. He has some kind of special teacher magic and is my favorite instructor by far.

"All right, class, quiet down," Mr. Spencer says as he walks to the front of the room. "I have an announcement to make."

The class goes from loud chatter to total silence in two seconds flat. When Mr. Spencer talks, people listen. Matty sits up with rapt attention like the secrets of the universe are about to be revealed.

"For this year's musical—" Mr. Spencer waits a beat for dramatic effect. He's nothing if not dramatic. He is a drama teacher, after all. Matty is about to explode.

"—we're going to perform *Oliver*!" Mr. Spencer calls out.

The class erupts in cheers. Matty's face craters and his hands slump at his sides.

"Consider myself re-lieved," Maya sings to the tune of that song from *Oliver*. Matty stares daggers at her, and the rest of us laugh.

The classroom door opens, and someone walks in. I can't believe my eyes.

It's Hugo.

My stomach does gymnastics.

The whole classroom gets quiet as everyone stares at the new kid. The tips of Hugo's ears go pink.

"Ah, you must be Hugo Cruz," Mr. Spencer says. "Welcome to the class."

"Sorry I'm late," Hugo says in a husky voice, then clears his throat. I melt into my chair.

"Make yourself comfortable." Mr. Spencer gestures to the class. "Take any open seat."

Hugo glances around the room, and we make eye contact. He holds it for a second, frowns, then averts his gaze and walks over to an empty chair on the opposite side of the classroom. My heart crushes like an aluminum can somebody stepped on.

Mr. Spencer addresses Hugo. "We were discussing this year's musical, which will be *Oliver*." Then he turns to the rest of the class. "There'll be lots of sets and props, so we'll have our work cut out for us. But it will be fun!"

The class begins to murmur again. Matty peeks over toward Hugo. "Well, isn't he a hottie?"

"Are you sure you're not queer?" Maya says, and Chloe laughs. Taylor shoots me a sad look.

Chloe glances at Hugo, her brow crinkled. She peeks back at me, then at Hugo again.

"What?" I ask her.

"Nothing," she says. "He just looks familiar."

Perfect. More vague, ominous stuff from Chloe.

For the rest of the class, I keep shooting glances over at Hugo, but he never looks back. He's keeping to himself.

The bell rings, and I wait for the rest of the students to empty into the hallway before I walk toward Hugo's table. I'm determined to apologize for what happened at lunch, but the closer I get, the more my hands shake, and my chest clenches like there's a vise grip around it.

A few feet away, the shaking gets worse. Emergency abort! I veer to the right at the very moment Hugo gets up, staring at his phone. Only my last-second lurch keeps us from smacking into each other. That must have looked supercool. *Great job, Cameron.* He looks up, and his neutral expression turns to one of annoyance.

We're standing face-to-face, staring at each other—it's too late to escape. I clear my throat. "Uh—hey, Hugo."

He rolls his eyes, even more annoyed. "What is it?"

"I'm sorry about what I said at lunch. I didn't mean to piss you off. I wasn't teasing you."

"Whatever." He turns and heads for the door.

"But I saw an old lady. She asked if I wanted cookies. I thought it was your grandma."

Hugo spins around, fists clenched. "Look, it's been a shitty day, okay? Enough with the White Lady crap," he snaps, then storms off before I can say another word.

For the second time today, I'm stunned as I watch Hugo walk away. It's clear he wants nothing to do with me. I guess I'll take the hint.

Theater tech is the last class of the day, so I head to the sports fields next to the woods I hike through to get home, my mind reeling from Hugo's latest rebuff. He said I'm not allowed to cut through his yard anymore, but I've been doing it my whole life. The hike through the forest is my after-school therapy, and the idea of losing that makes me even more distraught.

What's his problem, anyway? I don't get it. I was only trying to be friendly. Then again, why am I surprised? He's out of my league. Besides, I'm sure he likes girls, like every other guy I'm half interested in. In a couple of weeks, he'll be hanging out with all the jocks and dating a cheerleader.

As I cut across the football field, the scent of freshly cut grass wafts past me on the breeze, and loose green blades cover my new tennis shoes. I shake them off as I head past the sidelines and the bleachers, then walk along the tree line. Near the far corner of the football field, a trail cuts into a dense forest of evergreens, maples, and oaks.

The moment I'm in the woods, the stress of the day lifts off my shoulders. The only sounds are the crunch of pine needles under my feet and the occasional call of a bird. A light breeze blows through the boughs, making them sway and carrying the sharp scent of pine sap. I draw in a deep breath and take in the forest as my problems fall to the ground like dead leaves.

A sharp tug on my backpack rips it away, the straps burning against my shoulders. A shove to my back sends me sprawling to the ground. I throw my hands out just in time to keep from smashing my face on the jagged trail, but rocks and branches dig into my palms, drawing blood.

My heart rate spikes, and my mind goes into overdrive, scared as shit but ready to do what I need to do to protect myself, even if it means getting my ass kicked.

"Hey, Tubby," a voice spits out. "You come back here to suck dicks? I hear this is where all the fags like to do it."

I'm far too familiar with that distinctly hateful tone. I've heard it all too often over the last few years. Things don't get much worse than this. With my backpack in his hands and a menacing smile plastered across his ugly face, Bryce Hunter glares down at me.

8

DAY BY DAY: HUGO

I race out of theater tech, heading for my locker, wanting to get the hell away from school as fast as possible. My jaw clenches so hard that a headache pounds at my temples. The farther I go, the more I regret what I did. The expression on Cameron's face as I stormed off is stuck in my mind. He was shocked and obviously hurt by how I treated him.

I know what this is. I learned the term from my counselor after Ma died: misplaced anger. And I do it a lot. It's been such a bad day, but that isn't an excuse to take it out on Cameron. Guilt drags me down like an anchor.

I turn around and head back toward the classroom hoping to catch Cameron, but not sure what I'll do or say when I get there. The whole way, I'm deep in my head, trying to figure out how to undo what I did. But when I arrive, the door is locked. Through the window, I see Cameron cutting across the sports fields in the distance, so I head in that direction and pick up my pace. Soon he turns down a path into the trees.

Moving fast from the other direction is one of the last people I want to see. I can't believe my bad luck. Bryce Hunter heads toward the same trail like an apex predator hunting his prey.

Shit.

I break into a jog and follow the two of them down the path. Someplace nearby, I hear Bryce shout, "You come back here to suck dicks? I hear this is where all the fags like to do it."

Cameron's reply echoes through the forest. "Give me my backpack, asshole!"

My pulse skyrockets, and my jog turns into a run. On the path ahead, filtered through the trees, I see Bryce shove Cameron, making him stumble. "What did you call me, you little faggot?"

But Cameron gets up and shoves Bryce back, yelling, "I called you an asshole!" His voice quivers, and his legs shake beneath him. Still, I'm impressed that he's not letting this jerk walk all over him.

Bryce grabs Cameron by the front of his shirt and shouts into his face, droplets of spit flying from his mouth. "You are so dead!"

I close the distance between us and shout, "Hey, get your fucking hands off him!"

Bryce spins around, shakes his head, and lets out a wicked laugh. "Well, if it isn't Spooky. I didn't know you and Tubby were boyfriends."

"Just give him his backpack." I clench my fists, ready for the worst. People like Bryce only understand one kind of communication.

"Come get it." Bryce holds the backpack out, taunting me. "You need a good ass-kicking."

There's zero chance he's giving the bag to me. As I reach for it, Bryce snatches it back and shoves me hard. I plant my feet and head straight for him, my heart pounding against my rib cage like it's going to explode.

Bryce predictably swings his fist as I approach, and I duck beneath his arm, sending him off balance and flailing forward. I crouch and spring, punching upward and hitting Bryce in the jaw with an uppercut. A sharp snap comes from his teeth as his mouth smacks shut, and his head jerks back. He tumbles to the ground, stunned, clutching his jaw. I stand over him, breathing hard, fists still clenched.

"You're gonna regret that," Bryce cries as he cowers, but the bite is gone from his bark. He almost sounds scared.

"Oh yeah. I'm shaking in my boots." I lurch toward him, and Bryce scurries back. He jumps up and starts running away.

"Just wait!" Bryce yells as he runs.

"I'll be waiting!"

"Holy crap," Cameron says, eyes wide as Bryce hightails it down the trail. "Where'd you learn to hit like that?"

I grab Cameron's backpack, which is lying on the ground, and hand it to him. "Here."

"Thank you," he says, taking it from me. "For everything."

I rub my fist, aching from the impact of Bryce's jaw. "Didn't plan on making enemies on my first day of school. But Bryce is an asshole."

Cameron lets out a short laugh. "He really is."

"He shouldn't have said those things about you." I shake my head.

"Well, I didn't like his word choices, but he wasn't lying. I do like guys."

That hits me right in the chest, way harder than anything Bryce did. I can't catch my breath. Cameron likes guys, and he came right out and said it. I want to reply, but the words stick in my throat. This shy and awkward guy is braver than me when it comes to being true to himself. I want to tell him I like guys too, but the only word that comes out is "Oh."

The silence continues, getting thicker by the second. I need to say something, but I can't sort the words out in my mind. Cameron's Adam's apple bobs as he wraps his arms around his stomach, drawing into himself, getting smaller by the second. An overwhelming need to escape this awkwardness hits me like a punch. I have to leave before things get worse.

"I...uh...I should go," I say. "Pa is picking me up at school."

Cameron nods, his smile forced. "Yeah, I should go too. Before Bryce comes back with backup." He pauses for a moment, an uncomfortable energy in the air. Then he puffs out a breath, turns, and heads down the path without another word.

I run the other way as fast as my feet will carry me, pissed at myself and pissed at life. On my first day of school, I've already made an enemy of the school bully and alienated someone who could have been a friend. Every time we move, I have to come out to a new set of people. I'm terrible at it, and it makes me sick to my stomach. Why am I so bad at life sometimes?

I stop and turn back. Maybe I can catch him, apologize properly, and come out to him. But Cameron is down the path and out of sight.

***

"How was your first day?" Pa asks on the ride home.

"Okay." I stare straight ahead. I don't want to talk about anything. Half of the reason school sucked was because of Pa's lack of organization. I don't want to go into the other half.

"Just okay?" Pa takes his eyes off the road, looking my way.

"Yep."

"Anything you want to talk about?"

"Not particularly." I focus on the horizon.

"Make any friends?"

"I said I don't want to talk about it," I snap. Pa takes the hint and shuts up, but my mind immediately goes back to Cameron and how much I messed up, making my stomach ache.

Neither of us speaks the rest of the ride back, and it's not a comfortable silence. It's thick with unsaid things. He seems to be on the verge of saying something, then stops. Suits me. Bullying, homophobia, and racist bullshit are parts of high school, and I don't want him overreacting to things I can handle myself. He's got enough to worry about with the house and our finances.

We pull up at home, and Pa finally speaks. "I won't be able to drive you to school every day. It's not too far, so you can walk."

"Fine." I jump out of the car and head to the house. I guess that's what he was trying to say the entire ride home. Thanks for the heart-to-heart, Pa.

When I step inside, a chill hits me like a sheet of ice. I swear I'm suddenly heavier, like somebody slipped a five-pound weight into my pocket—subtle but distinct. The house is stifling.

The way kids called this place Crimson House and said it was haunted by the White Lady bangs around in my mind. It's just a stupid house. I'm not like Pa. I don't believe in all that superstitious bullshit. My therapist would say, *The shadow you saw is a manifestation of all your anger and anxiety. The mind can do terrible things under stress.* Yep. Checks out. I'm delusional.

Pa follows me into the house. He obviously has words on the tip of his tongue, but the last thing I want to do is to talk with him. I race up the stairs to my bedroom, shutting the door. My half-finished painting of our oak tree sits on the easel beside the window. It looks like crap. How did I ever convince myself that I'm an artist? I fall onto my bed and bury my face under a pillow. Maybe if I stay this way forever, the world will forget about me, and I won't have to keep pretending to be a normal kid.

The exhaustion from the day sinks into me, and my eyes fall shut.

I'm walking through our house, but it's changed. The walls are darker and covered with mold. Plaster falls off the ceilings, and the floorboards bend and bow. I take every step with care to avoid tripping over the uneven surface of the wood.

A smell hits my nose—it's not unpleasant. Something baking. *Cookies.* I head to the kitchen to find the source, but the closer I get, the more the scent changes. First it smells like *burnt* cookies, but it keeps evolving. Now it's the acrid scent of something charred in a fire, and then it turns sticky sweet and rotten.

I keep searching, but I make a wrong turn. I *was* heading straight to the kitchen but have somehow ended up in the library. Bookcases line every wall, filled with leather-bound books cracked from age and covered with dust and spiderwebs. The smell changes into an overwhelming scent of musty books and mold, making me cough. All at once, the books fall off the shelves, kicking up dust so thick that my hands disappear just inches from my face.

The shadow appears, and my blood turns to ice. I'm paralyzed as it moves through the cloud of dust, becoming more distinct as it gets closer. Only feet away, the form of an old woman with long flowing hair and a white dress comes into focus through the haze, heading right for me, arms outstretched.

I gasp.

Dust chokes my throat and burns my eyes, so I hold my breath, clamp my eyes shut, and turn to run, but I trip over my feet. I should hit the ground right away, but I keep falling as darkness envelops me, plunging through a vast expanse of nothing.

I scream myself awake, sitting up with a start.

I'm back in my bedroom, safe on my bed, clutching my pillow, fighting to catch my breath, with beads of sweat dripping down my forehead. A goddamn nightmare. Was I dreaming the first night when the shadow appeared? Maybe the line between dreams and reality is fading.

Like confirmation, the scent wafts in again. *Cookies.* I must still be dreaming, so I pinch my arm. Ouch. Nope, I'm awake. The smell must have worked its way into my dream, but cookies aren't typical for our household. Pa isn't the baking type.

As I head to the kitchen, the parallel between my nightmare and reality casts a surreal fog over my perceptions, but this world is solid, and the house hasn't changed. However, the cookie smell is real, and it gets stronger the closer I get to the kitchen.

The kitchen is empty. No Pa. No cookies. My stomach grumbles.

"Pa?" I call out. "Where are the cookies?"

Pa yells from the other room, "What's that, Hugo?"

"Who made the cookies?" I shout back. "Did you eat them all?"

Pa walks in. "What's this about cookies?"

"Exactly. Where are they?"

"Where are *what*?"

"Cookies! You can't smell them?"

Pa sniffs a few times. "All I smell is dust. Are you having a stroke?" He laughs.

"You really want me to die an untimely death, don't you?" I laugh back. "Better record it for TikTok."

"Oh, good idea." He pretends to take a video with his phone. I roll my eyes.

I draw in a deep breath. Nothing. I guess I've gone nose blind to the cookies.

Cameron's words echo in my head. *I saw an old lady. She asked if I wanted cookies.* That's an odd coincidence.

What am I doing, looking for patterns that aren't there? *Chill, Hugo. Stop making shit up and freaking yourself out.*

***

"Hey, Spooky, how's your grandma?" some dick in my history class says on Tuesday morning. I don't even know him, but he thinks he's entitled to pick on me. I bite my tongue. He's trying to piss me off, and I can't afford to get sent to the principal's office again. Best to ignore him.

After trig, Bryce comes up to me in the hallway, all puffed up and leering. He pokes his finger into my chest. "Don't think I forgot about what happened yesterday, Spooky. Payback's coming."

A crowd of kids forms around us.

"I'll knock you on your ass anytime you want, Bryce," I shoot back. The crowd *ooohs*.

Bryce shoves me, sending me tumbling into a locker. A hot jolt of adrenaline hits me as I steady myself, ready to defend against his attack. He comes at me, fist clenched, just as Mr. Angus runs up and puts his arms between us. "No fighting!"

A kid in the crowd yells, "Bryce started it! Hugo didn't do anything."

"Bryce. Office. Now," Mr. Angus says in a punching staccato rhythm, pointing down the hallway.

"Yes, Mr. *Anus*," Bryce shouts, shoving through the crowd.

"You're just making this worse for yourself," Mr. Angus calls back. Bryce flips him off while strutting away.

Mr. Angus sighs. "Hugo Cruz. Trouble seems to follow you around, doesn't it?"

"I'm not looking for any."

"And yet you seem to have caught Bryce Hunter's attention. Is there anything you need to talk to me about?"

"No." I avoid his stare. "I'm good."

Mr. Angus nods. "Okay." He hands me a card from his pocket. "This has my contact info on it. If you need anything, I'm just an email away."

I nod, take the card, and head off, feeling the eyes of Mr. Angus and a hundred kids follow me down the hallway. Sometimes I want to disappear.

The week drags on slowly. By Thursday, I can't wait for the weekend. Theater tech is my one respite during the school day. I told Mr. Spencer that I wanted to paint the backdrops for *Oliver*. He was delighted to have somebody who was excited about that, so now my last period is painting old London. It's the best hour of my day, as I lose myself in my artwork.

Cameron seems to have lost interest in me. He hasn't tried to sit with me at lunch and ignores me during tech, our only shared class. I glance his way from time to time, but he's busy with his friends. I want to clear the air between us, but each time I try, I freeze up. It's easier to ignore it and keep to myself. That's what I'm used to, anyway.

On Friday, I'm working on my backdrop, painting roofs and smoke-stacks on top of the sunset I painted yesterday.

"That looks amazing," a voice says behind me.

I turn around and recognize Taylor, one of Cameron's friends. Taylor is friendly to everybody and has a welcoming smile. I answer, "Thanks. Yeah, I'm pretty happy with it."

"Where'd you learn to paint like that?"

"I dunno." I shrug. "Just picked it up. Lots of YouTube."

Taylor laughs. "YouTube is the best. That's how I learned guitar."

"Nice. I suck at anything related to music. I'll stick to painting."

"Definitely keep it up." Taylor smiles. "You're awesome at it."

The bell rings, and the room erupts in activity as kids put away their projects and race for the door.

"Have a nice weekend," I say as I gather my painting supplies.

"Hey," Taylor says. "Some friends and I are going to this burger joint. You interested?"

Cameron is putting away props on the other side of the room. A single lock of his wavy brown hair falls into his face, and he brushes it away, which sends an unexpected pang through my chest. His eyes flash over at me for a second, but then he turns away fast.

This would be the perfect opportunity to talk to Cameron, but my mind plays back all the times I've made friends at my previous schools, only to lose them a few months later. It's depressing. We always say we'll stay in touch, but we never do. Long-distance friendships don't work, and the occasional like on Instagram doesn't count. It's even worse with boyfriends. The longest I've dated a guy is two weeks. Everyone ends up leaving me in the end, so why bother with any of it? I'm better off on my own.

"Thanks for the offer," I say to Taylor. "But I promised my dad I would help with unpacking." That's not a total lie. We still have some unpacking to do, but I doubt Pa will want to do it on a Friday night.

Taylor nods. "Okay. Well, if you change your mind, you're always welcome."

"Thanks."

As I clean up my painting supplies, Cameron and Taylor head for the door, talking. Cameron's eyes are downcast, like a lost puppy. There's a lump in my throat, and I swallow hard.

A buzz from my phone.

> Pa: Hey Hugo, this is Pa.

Pa's severe lack of texting skills always makes me laugh.

> Hugo: I know it's you. You don't have to say that in texts. What's up

The three dots on my phone pulse for over a minute as Pa writes an entire novel.

> Pa: I had to go to Portland to fix broken siding on the last house we worked on. I thought I'd be done today, but it's worse than I thought. I'll be gone all weekend until Sunday evening. There's frozen pizza in the fridge. My credit card is on my desk if you need anything. Will you be okay by yourself?

Typical Pa—running off to do jobs and leaving me alone. I'm used to it.

> Hugo: I'm good

> Pa: Okay. Thanks for understanding. I love you. Call or text if you need anything. Have a good weekend.

> Hugo: You too. Later

Alone for the entire weekend. Well, now I feel like even more of a dick for blowing off Taylor and Cameron. Maybe I should reconsider, but when I look up, the room is empty. They've already gone. Guess I'm destined for a lonely Friday night.

That's when it hits me: This is the first time I'll be alone in that damn house. I always go with Pa when he runs to the store or picks up takeout. Now I don't know if that's a coincidence or if I've been trying to avoid being alone.

I make a beeline for the door, sick to my stomach.

9

Salty's Burger Saloon: Cameron

"That's all he said?" I ask Taylor as we leave the high school grounds, heading down the hill toward our favorite burger joint. "He has to unpack?"

"Yep, that's it."

"Nothing about me?"

"Nope," Taylor says, with the sympathetic eyes they are famous for. Taylor has a heart like a puppy's.

"Am I a magnet for bad excuses?" I ask. "He might as well have said he has to wash his hair."

Taylor shrugs. "If it makes you feel any better, it seemed like he wanted to say yes."

"Doesn't help much."

I sigh as we weave our way through various neighborhoods, passing Victorian houses, white steepled churches, and old shingled bungalows on our way to Water Street, the main drag running right along Port Townsend Bay.

We're at the top of the staircase heading to the heart of downtown when longboard wheels on pavement roar up from behind us. Abby rounds a curve so fast that I cringe, but she's never crashed in all the years I've known her. She approaches at breakneck speed and, at the last second, spins and digs her heels into the board, stopping feet away from Taylor and me. Taylor flinches, but I hold steady. I've learned to trust Abby's longboarding skills.

Abby smiles, kicking the board into her hand. "Scared you pretty good, didn't I, Taylor?"

"I swear you're going to kill yourself one of these days," Taylor says with a stuttering laugh. "Or kill me."

"Cam knows better, don't you?" Abby puts out a fist.

"Damn straight," I say, bumping it. "Abby's better at longboarding than most people are at walking."

"You two were separated at birth, right?" Taylor says.

"Obviously," Abby says as we wrap our arms around each other, squishing our faces together while I hold up my phone to take a selfie. Her golden complexion is extra rich against my pale, freckled skin.

"Say cheese," I say, taking the photo, and then I post it to Insta with a "besties" sticker.

"No Hugo, I see," Abby says with a crooked frown.

"Nope," I say. "I even had Taylor invite him. Taylor is like loner kryptonite."

"No one can resist my charms." Taylor laughs. "But somehow, Hugo did."

"He'll break eventually," Abby says. "You'll see."

I shrug. "I dunno. I should probably give up after the way he reacted when I came out to him in the woods. I have to learn to stop crushing on straight guys."

Abby bumps her shoulder into mine with sad eyes and a small frown. "Sorry, Cam."

"I'll get over it."

But inside, I'm a jumble of emotions. Hugo's been here for only a week, and it's been a roller coaster. First he was nice, then he stormed off. He rescued me from Bryce, then freaked out when I came out to him. I even sent him a peace offering in the form of Taylor, but he "has to unpack." It's emotional whiplash, and I'm ready to get off the ride.

From the top of the bluff, we climb down the long flight of stairs, lined by deep green lawns and trees on both sides. At the base of the steps is a bronze statue of Galatea, the Greek sea nymph, surrounded by cherubs spraying water out of horns in arcs that splash into a basin.

Our destination is a few blocks away through downtown Port Townsend. Old two-story brick buildings with intricate facades line the street, echoes of the bustling port town this was a hundred years ago, but used bookstores, art galleries, and eclectic restaurants filled with tourists have replaced the bait shops and fish markets. We pass them on our way to Salty's Burger Saloon. It turns into a bar at night, but they allow kids before nine p.m., and our friend group makes the most of it.

"Hang on a sec," Taylor says, peering through a shop window. "Isn't that Chloe?"

"Yeah, it is," Abby says. "That's her aunt Margaret's shop."

"Really?" Taylor's eyes go wide. "I didn't know Chloe's aunt owned The Spirit's Edge."

"Let's go say hi," I say.

Inside, we're hit with the aromas of lavender and sandalwood. Dimly lit shelves cover every square inch, stuffed with gemstones, charms, candles, and essential oils. Farther into the shop, the merchandise gets decidedly more mystical: tarot cards, planchettes, bundles of sage, and old leather-bound journals covered with strange symbols.

Chloe is at the counter, talking to a woman with long red hair and a green turtleneck who looks very much like Chloe plus about twenty-five years. She has the same pale complexion, deep tan freckles, and emerald-green eyes.

As we approach, Chloe's eyes widen.

"Oh—um—hi, everybody," she stammers.

"Hey, Chloe," Abby says. "You coming to Salty's with us?"

"Yeah. Maya's there already. I—uh—I needed to talk to my aunt first." Chloe trails off and glances downward.

A moment of uncomfortable silence descends, which Abby squishes like a bug. "Aren't you going to introduce us?"

"Oh, yeah," Chloe blurts. "Sorry. This is Aunt Margaret. Aunt Margaret, these are my friends Taylor, Abby, and—um—and this is Cameron."

As soon as Chloe says my name, Margaret's eyes light up. She stares at me intently for a moment. What the heck is this about? Just as I'm growing uncomfortable, her face relaxes, and she smiles.

"Nice to meet all of you," she says in a friendly voice that's the tiniest bit gravelly.

We all say hello.

"I love your shop," Taylor says. "This is where I buy my scented candles. I didn't realize you had Wiccan stuff back here."

Margaret laughs. "Yes. This is what I call the heart of my shop. My real passion. I love the candles in the front, but they mostly help pay the bills."

"Well, we should get going," Chloe says, cutting in. "Thanks, Aunt Margaret."

"Anytime, Chloe," Margaret says with a smile. "Remember what I said."

Chloe nods and shoos us out. "C'mon, let's go."

As we walk down the street toward Salty's, I whisper to Abby, "Do you think Chloe's acting strange around me?"

"Chloe always acts a little strange," Abby says.

Taylor holds open the old wooden door, and we file into the lobby of Salty's. It takes a moment to adjust to the dimness of the old tavern. A long wooden bar runs the entire length of the room, lined with old leather swivel stools. A few regulars dressed in fishing gear are cozied up to the bar with icy beer mugs in their hands.

Archie, the bartender, waves at us as we enter. "Hey, kids!" A white apron spans his ample belly, and he dabs sweat from his bald head. "Your friends are in the back."

"Thanks, Archie," I reply with a wave as we head past the bar and into the back room.

A myriad of faded posters and nautical decorations, nets, and old wooden buoys cover the walls. Sunlight streams through a bank of windows on the far side of the room that provide a view of the dark waters of Port Townsend Bay. An eclectic mix of antique wooden tables and chairs sit in random spots with no discernible pattern. Old vinyl booths line the room, big enough for large groups of people. This room feels like home to me. So comforting.

Maya and Matty are chatting in a booth with smiles on their faces. As we approach, they say hi.

"How's it going?" I ask, sliding in next to Matty.

Maya's smile turns into a frown. "No Hugo, huh? I thought having Taylor ask would do the trick for sure."

"Nope," I say. The constant reminders are depleting my energy. "And maybe let's drop the Hugo talk, okay? It's getting depressing. I need to accept that he isn't interested in hanging out."

Maya's frown deepens as she stares at her girlfriend. Chloe glances down and avoids my gaze. Okay, something's definitely going on.

"What?" I glance between them.

Chloe says nothing.

Maya can't take it any longer and blurts, "Chloe had a dream."

"*Maya!*" Chloe chides. "I told you not to say anything."

"But he should know," Maya says, gesturing to me.

"What's up, Chloe?" I ask. "You can tell me."

I knew it. Chloe's been sending me strange vibes all week. A feeling is one thing, but now she's having dreams about me? That's a whole new ballgame, and to be honest, it kind of freaks me out. Chloe's dreams are not to be ignored.

A few months ago, she dreamed that lightning struck the old church on 4th Ave. and it burned down. A week later, it happened. Last year, a seven-year-old boy went missing, and Chloe was sure he was stuck in the old abandoned military bunkers in Fort Worden on the edge of town. She left an anonymous note at the police station. They found the boy with a broken leg at the bottom of a metal ladder. One rung embedded in the concrete had broken free, and he'd fallen twenty feet. He was bleeding and banged up. They were lucky to have found him so fast. She might have saved his life.

Chloe stays silent, and Maya whispers something in her ear. Chloe nods slowly but remains quiet.

"Go ahead," Maya says.

Chloe sighs. "It was a dream about you and Hugo. But it was a fuzzy dream."

"Fuzzy?" I ask.

"Yeah. Sometimes my dreams are vivid—those tend to be things that have already happened, and they're pretty accurate. Fuzzy dreams are usually things in the future. They aren't precise. More like feelings. Things that *could* happen."

"You had a fuzzy dream about Hugo and me?"

"Yes." Chloe pauses, choosing her words carefully. "About you, Hugo, and"—she takes a deep breath—"the house."

"The house?" I stare at her, mouth agape. "You mean Hugo's house? Crimson House?"

She nods. "I saw the two of you standing in a dark room. I know it was Hugo's house. Don't ask me how."

"What were we doing?"

"It was fuzzy. I don't like talking about fuzzy dreams."

"Chloe, please." I hate to push her, but this is important.

"You two were doing something. Hugging, maybe? Or crying?"

"Hugging *or* crying?"

"See? I'm not sure. It was too fuzzy." She sighs. "I felt that you two and the house were connected somehow."

"Connected? What does that mean?"

"That's just it," Chloe says. "I don't know. It's fuzzy. That's why I didn't want to say anything."

Our waitress walks up, a twentysomething woman in jeans and a plaid shirt. Her mousy brown hair is in a ponytail, and she has a no-nonsense appearance.

"Hey, kids. Ready to order?" she asks. The expressions on our faces give her pause. "Am I interrupting something? Should I come back?"

"No, it's okay," Chloe says. "I'll have a Diet Coke, please."

I guess that's all Chloe is going to tell me for now, but I'll do some more digging later. She can't drop heavy stuff like that and expect me not to ask questions.

Everybody gets sodas, and we order a large plate of nachos for the table. Matty orders a cheeseburger too. He's been able to eat whatever he wants for as long as I've known him, and somehow he keeps his athletic build without putting on an ounce of fat. It drives me nuts.

When our waitress leaves, I'm dying to shift the attention off of me. "Does anybody else want to talk about *their* love life? Or nonexistent love life, as the case may be?"

"I asked Sophia to homecoming," Matty says with a smile, but his eyes are sad.

"And?" I ask.

"She said she'd get back to me."

A collective groan erupts from the table.

"Sorry, Matty," I say, grimacing.

"It's okay. I'll give her some time. But I have backups."

Matty smiles a genuine smile. He's always cheerful. Nothing gets him down. He's one of the best-looking guys at school, so he'll have no trouble finding a date. But he also has a big personality and comes across as odd if you don't know him. For instance, his favorite show is *Ru Paul's Drag Race*, and he won't shut up about it. And his fashion sense is very…eclectic. His current outfit includes plaid pants, a striped shirt, and a letterman jacket. But those things make him fun and unique, and any girl who doesn't recognize that doesn't deserve him. I might even ask him out myself if he wasn't hopelessly into girls. He likes attention so much that there's a good chance he'd say yes anyway.

"I assume you two are going together," Matty asks Maya and Chloe.

"Well, sure," Maya says. "But a girl still likes to be asked." She gives Chloe a cute little pout, batting her eyelashes.

"Maya, will you go to homecoming with me?" Chloe asks in a singsong voice.

"Does this answer your question?" Maya pecks Chloe on the lips. Chloe answers by giving Maya a big kiss. Like, a passionate one, with tongue and everything.

"Get a room, you two!" Matty laughs.

"And miss out on nachos?" Maya says after separating from Chloe.

"I might ask Liam Cooper," Taylor says unprompted, which is cool. Taylor doesn't talk about their love life much. "He's been flirty with me in trig class. But then again, I might stay home and binge some shows."

"I might join you," Abby adds. "I don't have anybody to ask." Taylor smiles at that.

Matty cuts in. "I thought you liked Jessica Quint, Abby. Or was it her brother Elias?" Matty taps his chin. "Maybe you should ask both of them."

Abby gives him the evil eye. "Behave, Matty."

"What?" Matty puts on his signature faux-surprised look. "You're lucky. You have, like, way more options than the rest of us."

"I haven't been feeling any of those options lately," Abby grumbles.

"You need to hang out with Cameron less," Matty says, pinching my cheek. "His cuteness is intimidating, so everybody's afraid to ask you."

"Matty!" I groan. I swat away his hand as heat spreads across my face.

"Just calling it like I see it," Matty says matter-of-factly. "If Hugo doesn't snatch you up quick, I might ask you out."

"Stop it!" Abby scolds. "Now you're just teasing him."

"Hey, a guy can dream, can't he?" Matty says. "Sometimes I think that if I try hard enough, I might start liking guys. It hasn't happened yet, but I *do* have eyes, Cameron. You're, like, totally hot."

"Okay!" I blurt, my face burning, slapping my hands on the table. "That's enough about me, my hotness, and anything related to Hugo. Next subject, please!"

Matty shrugs. "The football team is going to suck this year."

***

After we've had our fill of nachos and soda and said goodbye to our friends, Abby and I head back to my house, weaving through the quiet town. She rides her longboard, kicking off slowly as I walk alongside her.

"You know," Abby says, "even though Matty can be over the top, he's not wrong. You're a total catch, Cameron."

"Ugh. I feel fat. I need to lay off the nachos." I grab my love handles. They've hounded me my entire life.

"Stop it!" She stops moving, her eyes piercing into me. "You're fine! You're not skinny to the point of being unhealthy like an underwear model, but that's a good thing. Okay?"

"Okay," I groan. It's starting to sink in. But the memories of bullies pushing me around and teasing me haven't disappeared even after all her compliments. When I stare into the mirror, that pudgy twelve-year-old still looks back at me. My self-esteem is a work in progress.

"And Hugo will either like you for who you are or he's not worth your time. End of story."

"I still don't even know if he likes guys," I say.

"You check out his socials?"

"Of course. Couldn't find anything. I don't think he even has accounts."

"Bummer," Abby says. "Guess he's a true loner."

"Also, that was strange what Chloe said about Hugo, me, and the house being connected."

Abby nods, eyebrows scrunched. "Yeah. No idea what that was about. But Chloe's never wrong about anything."

"But what does it mean?"

Abby shrugs.

"Okay. No more talk about Hugo. What about you?" I ask. "You really don't have your eye on anybody?"

"You know me. I don't get crushes."

"Yeah." I nod. "But let's be honest, you've seemed a little distracted lately."

"Have I?" She glances at me for a moment, then looks ahead. "A lot going on at school, I guess."

"It started before school."

Abby's cheeks turn the subtlest shade of pink. "Let's talk about something else, okay?"

"Okay." I don't push it. She'll tell me when she's ready. Like she said, she doesn't get crushes as easily as most kids do. She needs an emotional connection. It's definitely not me she's got her eye on. We've had that talk. Best friends and nothing else.

For the rest of the way home, we debate what movies to watch. It's a welcome distraction, but my mind still drifts back to Chloe's words. I've had enough of Crimson House to last a lifetime, and the idea that it's tied up with Hugo and me somehow is disturbing. She's never wrong.

As we near my home, I glance at the dark, ominous house across the street. It's leering at me. A shadow moves across an upstairs window, and I suppress a shudder. Maybe it's Hugo, maybe it's not, and I'm not sure I want the answer.

10

HIDDEN SECRETS: HUGO

The house is deathly silent save for the creaky floorboards as I wander the shadowed halls. The house feels strange. Not bad, just different. Lonely, but also welcoming in a strange way, almost as if it *likes* that it's only the two of us here.

Ugh! Why am I personifying this house? It's only a pile of wood and bricks. It's only me wandering around with my thoughts. Nothing more.

The hours tick by as I work on my homework at the kitchen table. I'm almost caught up on trig, my worst subject, but I'm two chapters behind in lit. *The Catcher in the Rye* is an interesting book, but it's not a page-turner, and it's not the book I want to read in my current mood.

Frozen pizza for dinner. How exciting. I throw it in the oven and wait for the timer, scrolling through my phone. No new messages from anybody, and I have only myself to blame. I could be hanging out with Cameron, Taylor, and all their friends right now. Instead, I eat a few slices of pizza in utter silence, then wrap the leftovers in foil, toss them in the fridge, and head upstairs.

A light shines on the third-floor landing. Pa must have gone up there and forgotten to turn it off. The third floor creeps me out. Perhaps it's the odd angles of the roof or the twisting hallway. I jump at every squeaky floorboard and glance twice at every shadowed corner.

Something has changed up here. Where there used to be a sawed-out hole, fresh floorboards now make a jigsaw-like pattern. Pa fixed the floor.

Did Pa clean up the blood before he repaired it—or the rust, or whatever it was? I'm almost certain he didn't. That's the kind of detail he would skip. The back of my neck prickles as I imagine the blood sitting under the floorboards forever, but it can't be helped. Now it's part of the house, for better or worse.

I look up from the hole and let out a shout. Every single door along the snaking hallway is open wide. Was it like that when I came up here? It must have been.

I follow the twists and turns, closing each door until I arrive at a single unopened one. I turn the knob, but the door doesn't budge. Beneath the knob is an old-fashioned keyhole. Pa's keychain doesn't have any old keys like that, I'm sure of it. A peek through the hole reveals only darkness.

From behind the door comes a slight scraping sound, similar to the sound coming from the hole in the basement. My imagination goes wild, picturing the moving shadow on the other side. *Stop it, Hugo. Stop!* Fully creeped out, I race back to the safety of the second floor. Why is this house making me such a wimp?

Back in my dark bedroom, I see a glow emanating from a window across the street. With the lights still off, I peer out at it, an invisible observer. Cameron said he could see my house from his bedroom. It might be his room. I squint at the shapes moving through the window across the street. Then I actually see Cameron.

Oh crap.

I'll have to be careful about keeping my drapes closed—or not. The thought makes my cheeks heat up.

He's bobbing his head around and laughing with Abby, who's there as well. An unexpected pang hits me in the chest.

I snap the drapes shut, trying to get that guy out of my mind, then head for my bed with *The Catcher in the Rye* in hand. What an exciting Friday. Maybe I can read a few pages before I nod off.

I don't.

Two pages in, my eyelids are like lead. The next moment, I wake with my face resting on a wrinkled page and a puddle of drool soaking into the paper. A glance at my phone reveals that it's 2:20 a.m. Wow, I guess I was tired.

A missed text shows on my phone from more than two hours ago.

> Carla: Hey mano. Just checking in. How's your Friday

I smile. At least my big sister remembers I'm alive, but I don't want to bug her at this hour. Plus, I don't want her to find out how lame my Friday was.

I hop out of bed to take a leak, glancing through the drapes on the way. Nothing but darkness in Cameron's room. Guess he's asleep, snuggled in bed, wrapped in a blanket. Wonder what he wears? Full-on pj's, or only boxers or tighty-whities? *Or nothing.*

Man, what's going on with me? It's the third time I've thought about Cameron this evening; no matter how I distract myself, my mind drifts right back to him. Heading to the bathroom, I try to think of anything else: schoolwork, Pa's house projects. It doesn't work.

After I pee, I stare at my reflection over the sink. Other than a zit forming on my right cheek and my messy bedhead, I'm happy with the person looking back at me. My family has always been proud of our Mexican heritage—half Mexican, half Irish on Ma's side—and despite the occasional asshole like Bryce Hunter, I like who I am and wouldn't change it even if I could. What does Cameron think of me? Ugh! Fourth time.

The mirror over the sink has three little doors that fold out with a medicine cabinet behind them. Two of the mirrors hinge outward opposite each other, and if I hold them at the right angle, the double reflection gives me an idea of how people truly see me. It's startling—a new perspective on a face I've seen almost every day of my life.

As I angle the mirrored doors, the medicine cabinet shifts forward. I struggle to grab it as it begins to topple toward me. Dammit—add this to the ever-growing list of crap that's falling apart in this house. This place is a dump.

The medicine cabinet housing hangs halfway out of the wall, so I yank it off and set it on the ground next to the sink. I'll have to secure it with stainless steel screws.

But when I straighten back up, I'm met with quite a surprise. Where I expect a solid wall, there's only darkness—a hole leading to who knows where. I peer in and see nothing but blackness. What the heck?

In the hallway, I pace off the distance between the bathroom and the next bedroom door, going heel to toe. Fifteen feet. I do the same thing in the bedroom. Five feet. That's ten feet unaccounted for.

A hidden room.

No sign of an entrance is visible on the hallway wall, but when I inspect the baseboard trim, I find the slightest imperfection marring the wood—a nearly imperceptible line patched over and painted. Impossible to spot unless you know where to look for it. There's a similar line three feet to the right: traces of an old covered-up doorway. Why would someone seal up an entire room?

Back in the bathroom, I peer into the hole, straining my eyes. A void. Inky blackness. An unsettled feeling forms in my gut as I stare into the dark abyss.

I shine my phone flashlight through the hole, moving it from side to side. An ancient, dust-covered bed and a bookcase sit along one wall. Someone boarded up this room without even bothering to clear out the furniture. What would possess someone to do that?

Climbing halfway up on the sink, I lean through the hole, shining my flashlight around the room. The beam of light crosses a shadowy figure, and I let out a shout.

An old woman with flowing gray hair is standing in the corner, facing away from me, casting a shadow against the wall. Her head jerks to the side in a jarring, inhuman movement. Ice flows through my veins.

She turns and stares in my direction with foggy eyes, smiling with crooked yellow teeth. I'm frozen. My body stops taking signals from my brain. I open my mouth to scream, but only a choked gasp comes out.

The woman continues to stare as her lips curve into an even wider smile. Unnaturally wide. Her hands lift as she lurches toward the hole, a harsh and jarring noise escaping from her mouth—a laugh like shards of glass scraping together, making my skin crawl.

That horrible noise snaps me out of my paralysis, and my silent scream becomes a real one—loud and from the depths of my lungs. I race out of the bathroom, hands over my ears, trying to escape that hideous noise.

But now she's at the end of the hallway, right by Pa's bedroom door. How the hell did she get there? A tattered white dress yellowed with age flows down her skeletal form, and her wicked laugh and crooked smile continue.

With my heart pounding against my rib cage, I sprint down the stairs three steps at a time, tripping halfway. I fumble to catch the railing, my fingertips keeping me from tumbling down the rest of the way. Steadied, I continue my rapid descent.

I'm out of the house in a flash, slamming the front door behind me, not stopping until I reach the sidewalk, where I peer back at the house, expecting the woman to chase me. But the door stays shut, and the house looks like it always has—run down, odd, uninviting.

I swear the house settles like it's sighing with relief, glad to be rid of me. *Feeling's fucking mutual.*

As I stand outside, waiting for my heart rate to slow, my head spins, and the chilly night air seeps through my thin cotton T-shirt, making me shiver. No way I'm going back into that house tonight. Screw that.

But what are my options? I could call Pa, but what would I say? "Pa, please come home because I saw an old lady in a hidden room behind our medicine cabinet who teleported into the hallway?" He'd think I was crazy. Heck, *I* think I'm crazy. How can I accept what I witnessed as something that actually happened?

Carla is off the table. My sister is more than a thousand miles away in California. She'd also think I've lost my mind.

What, then? Sleep under a bush?

Cameron's words echo in my head. *I did see an old lady. She asked if I wanted cookies.*

It hits me like a brick wall. Cameron *wasn't* teasing. He truly did see an old lady. The cookie smell is too much of a coincidence not to be related. But all he said was that she offered him cookies on my back porch. He didn't say there was some ghoul in a hidden room in my house. Would he even believe me? Plus, I haven't exactly been friendly to him. He'd be perfectly justified if he turned me away.

With no other options, I head across the street to Cameron's house, eyes fixed on the window where I saw him and Abby laughing. I swipe a pine cone from under a tree, draw back my arm, and aim.

11

Second Chances: Cameron

I'm on stage wearing a top hat and a jacket three sizes too big, tails hanging just above the floor. An old man with ragged clothing and a wispy beard stands next to me, holding several handkerchiefs and pocket watches, singing about reviewing the situation. It's my verse, but I can't remember the lyrics. Oh god—I forgot my pants. I'm in my underwear, and everyone around me is pointing and laughing.

I blink my eyes open, and the relief is instant. Stupid acting nightmares, preying on my stress. This always happens when my mind is cluttered with anxiety and uncertainty, and lately I've got enough of both to fill it several times over.

The bedroom is dark, and all is quiet. I swear a sound woke me, but now there's absolute silence, so I roll over and cover my head with my pillow.

There it is again—a slight rustling outside my window. Perhaps a nocturnal squirrel? Is there such a thing? That's dumb. Maybe an owl? I sit up and stare at the window, waiting, watching, and listening, but nothing happens.

I snuggle back into the warmth of my bed. Must be nothing.

A pine cone hits the window squarely in the center. Okay, that is no squirrel, unless it's an exceptionally strong squirrel with a grudge. Unlikely.

I slip out of bed, and the cold sends a shiver down my back, covering my bare skin in goose bumps. I bundle into my robe and head to the window.

When I peer into the darkness, the front yard is empty, but the light is on in Hugo's bedroom. He must be a night owl.

Another pine cone strikes the window, and I follow its trajectory to the source. Shrouded in gentle moonlight, a dark figure stands by a tree in my side yard with pine cones in hand.

It's Hugo.

A bittersweet mixture of emotions hits me hard in the gut. He was nice for half of lunch on Monday before he stormed off, but the way he reacted to what I said in the woods still sits wrong in the pit of my stomach. Life is too short to deal with people who don't accept me for exactly who I am.

It's not like I haven't reached out. Okay, maybe I had Taylor do my dirty work, but they were also unable to crack through Hugo's prickly exterior. And everybody likes Taylor.

But Chloe's words echo in my head. She thinks the two of us and the house are tied together for some reason, and part of me is excited that he's outside. A cute guy is throwing pine cones at my window. Countless teen movies start like this, followed by people kissing. Warmth spreads across my face.

I crack open the window and call out in a loud whisper, "Hugo? Is that you?"

Hugo steps out of the shadows and approaches, shaking, his arms wrapped around his body. "Hey, Cameron," he says, his voice quivering. "I know this is a lot to ask, but can you come down here? I need to talk."

"It's, like, two in the morning. Can't this wait?"

"No, it can't." He glances back at his house with an expression I know well.

Fear.

Fear of that goddamn house.

He truly does need my help. Chloe's right again. "I'll be right down."

I throw on the jeans and T-shirt sitting on my floor, slip on my sneakers, and then tiptoe down the hallway. Jack's door is closed, and Dad's snoring echoes out to the hallway. Mom's next to him, face slack, dead to the world. I make my way downstairs and slip out the front door.

Hugo stands in the side yard wearing a long frown. He's got that whole brooding teenager look nailed. Annoyance still seethes at the corners of my mind, but those dark puppy dog eyes are hard to resist. In fact, here in the moonlight, he's gorgeous. The pang in my chest is impossible to ignore.

"Hey," Hugo says, staring at the ground.

"Hey," I say back, fighting a smile. He's even cuter when he's bashful. He looks up, and we watch each other until the silence becomes unbearable. "So..."

"So...um...I don't quite know what to say." Hugo kicks at a pine cone. "Sorry for how I acted?"

"That sounds like a question."

"No! I really am sorry," Hugo blurts. "Monday was a shit day. I overreacted at lunch and in the woods after..." He trails off and can't make eye contact.

He's still uncomfortable about my whole coming out thing, so much so that he can't even say it, and it's starting to make *me* uncomfortable. "What's this all about? Why are we outside in the cold at two in the morning?"

"Um. This is going to be hard to believe—"

I finish for him. "You think your house is haunted, and you saw an old lady."

His jaw drops. "How—why—um—you believe me?"

"See this?" I lift my pant leg and show off my scar. "Your house did this to me. I *hate* that place."

Hugo puffs out a quick laugh. "I'm starting to agree with you."

"What happened?" I put my hands in my pockets, fighting the chill.

Hugo shivers. A thin T-shirt and shorts are the only things protecting him from the bitter cold.

Hugo stares at the ground again. "This is asking a lot, but any chance we can talk about it inside? I...um..." He glances back at his house. "I don't think I can go back in there right now."

He wants to go *inside my house.* Emotions swirl through me again. It's hard to believe that this adorable guy who ignored me all week suddenly wants to sneak into my house, but the fear in his eyes is real. I relate to that fear.

"Yeah. Come on in. But be quiet." I wave him inside. It doesn't hurt that sneaking a guy into my house is one of my top five fantasies.

I listen for sounds inside the house. Silence. We tiptoe up the stairs to my bedroom, and I lock the door behind us. Hugo and I are together in my bedroom. Is this happening, or is this another dream?

"Um... it's a little messy. Sorry." I kick my dirty laundry toward the closet. "Have a seat." I point to my desk chair and then sit on the end of my bed.

Hugo sits in the chair and blows out a long breath. "So. On Monday, when you said you saw my grandma, you weren't messing around, were you?"

"No. I really saw her. She offered me cookies and invited me into your house. But I was so creeped out, I just left."

"Was that Saturday morning?"

"Yeah. How did you know?" I ask.

"I was upstairs in my room, and I saw you cutting through the yard. You did seem super creeped out."

"Something felt off," I say. "I take it that wasn't your grandma?"

"Nope." Hugo shakes his head. "Both my abuelitas died years ago. What did she look like?"

"Very old. Long gray hair and a ratty old dress."

"Crooked yellow teeth?" Hugo asks.

"Yeah, exactly!"

Hugo's face goes pale. "I saw her too. Exactly like that." He pauses for a beat, then whispers, "I—um—I found a hidden room behind the medicine cabinet in my bathroom. She was in there."

"Holy shit, really?" I blurt, then cover my mouth and whisper through my fingers. "Is she still in there?"

"You won't believe me. I can barely believe it myself."

"Try me," I say. "You'd be surprised what I'll believe when it comes to that house."

"I ran out of the bathroom, but when I got to the hallway, she was already there. The only entrance to that room is boarded up. There's no way to explain how she got out there before me. That's when I ran out of the house." Hugo's hands are shaking, and he fidgets with them. "I don't know what to do."

"Is your dad home? Has he seen her too?"

"No, he's out of town. I'm by myself. If he knew about any of this, he'd freak out." Hugo's shoulders slump. "We'd move out tomorrow. He'd sell it immediately."

"You shouldn't go back tonight. You shouldn't be alone in that house."

"I don't want to, but I don't have a choice. I don't know anybody in this town. I have nowhere else to go."

I feel for him, but my mind returns to his reaction in the woods. Still, I believe in second chances. Let's see how this goes.

"Look, Hugo. I know firsthand how bad that house is, but here's the deal." I sigh. "In the woods, the way you reacted when I said I liked guys...I don't have space in my life for people who are uncomfortable with who I am."

Hugo's eyes go wide. "Oh. No. I—um—I think you got the wrong idea."

"Did I?" I stare right at him. "I saw the look in your eyes. I've seen it a hundred times, and I know what it means." *Homophobe*, but I don't say it out loud.

"I'm totally fine with you liking guys. It's cool, even. It just threw me off," Hugo says. "You have to understand, my life is complicated. Pa moves us every six months, and I have to make new friends every time. Lots of places we've lived aren't as accepting as here, and when you told me you liked guys...well, I kinda freaked out."

I knew it. Homophobe. "You freaked out because I like guys."

"No!" Hugo blurts, then whispers, "I freaked out because you caught me off guard. *I* wasn't ready to come out to *you* at that instant."

My jaw drops. "Come out?"

"Yeah." Hugo's cheeks go pink, and he shrugs. "What can I say? I like kissing guys too."

My head spins as my whole mental image of Hugo rearranges itself in a matter of seconds. "You're not messing with me, right?"

"I wouldn't kid about something like that." Hugo shakes his head with vulnerable eyes.

I could get lost in those eyes.

As we've been talking, we've leaned in toward each other more and more, and I'm suddenly aware of our proximity. In a fit of self-consciousness, I jerk away. "I—um." I need to defuse this sudden awkwardness, but my mind is blank. Hugo stares at me with a startled expression. Even getting close to him freaks me out. I must seem like such a loser to him. Sure, he likes guys, but it's stupid to think he'd be interested in me.

Hugo stands up. "Sorry. I should go. I'll figure something out."

"No! You can stay here," I blurt. God, play it cool, Cameron. Don't freak him out. I have to show him we can be friends. Now that he's talking to me again, I don't want to push him away.

"Really?" Hugo sits back down. "Are you sure? Will your parents be okay with that?"

"They don't have to know."

He hesitates as if weighing the idea.

I add, "I mean, you don't *have* to stay."

"No. I want to. Thank you." He smiles. "As long as you're sure it's cool. I can sleep on the floor."

"It's totally cool. Abby sleeps over all the time. I have a sleeping bag and a camping pad you can sleep on." I pull them out of my closet and lay them on the ground at the foot of my bed. "Tomorrow I'll text Abby about what you saw. She's super smart and totally into paranormal stuff. She'll know what to do. If you're okay with that."

"Yeah, that sounds great." He looks relieved and smiles again. What a beautiful smile. And he's smiling at me. It's hard to believe.

Hugo settles into the sleeping bag, and I nestle into bed. If anybody had told me a few hours ago that this super-cute guy who blew me off this entire week would soon be sleeping in my bedroom, I'd have laughed at them, and yet here he is.

The room goes silent except for Hugo's soft breathing. It's soothing.

"Thanks, Cameron," Hugo says, breaking the silence. "For letting me stay and for being nice even after I was a dick."

I pause for a moment and think. He is adorable, and that's hard to resist, but it's more than that. Something about our mutual connection to that house makes this feel important. I whisper, "Everybody deserves a second chance."

***

Sharp knocking on my door jerks me out of a deep sleep. Hugo lies on the ground, wrapped in the sleeping bag, and panic hits me. Disorientation clouds my mind for a moment, and then the details of last night come back, but still with a dreamlike quality.

"Cameron, it's nearly ten o'clock," Mom calls from outside my room. "There are pancakes down here, but they're getting cold. Come grab some before I throw them out."

Hugo stirs in his sleeping bag, his hair standing on end and his face squished from his pillow. My breath catches, and my cheeks warm. He's so adorable I can barely stand it.

I put my finger to my mouth and mime a shushing sound. Hugo nods.

"Okay, Mom," I call back, trying hard to sound normal. "I'll be down in a bit."

Mom's footsteps retreat down the hallway. I whisper to Hugo, "We need to sneak you out. I'll see if Abby can come over. Will you be okay by yourself until then?"

"Yeah. I'll be fine." He scratches his head. "In daylight, this whole thing seems kind of silly."

"There's nothing silly about that house."

Hugo nods.

"Let me text Abby now," I say, thumbing a message on my phone.

Cameron: You'll never guess who spent the night

Abby: Umm, you're right. No idea. Matty?

Cameron: Try Hugo

Abby: WTF! [two boys in love emoji]

Cameron: [eye roll emoji] He slept on the floor. He saw the white lady last night and freaked out and asked for my help

Abby: Chloe was right!!!!!!!!!!!

Cameron: Don't mention that

Abby: How come

Cameron: It's embarrassing. Don't want to weird him out

Abby: K, I promise

Cameron: Can you come over in an hour

Abby: Omg yes!!!!

"Abby's in," I say. "She'll be over soon."

"Okay." Hugo gets up. "I'll head home and try to take a shower without getting too freaked out."

"Good luck with that." I laugh, but the image of Hugo in the shower flashes through my mind, instantly sending blood southward.

"Give me your number." Hugo takes out his phone. "Text me before you head over."

Hugo wants my phone number. I struggle to keep my voice calm as I tell him the digits. My phone buzzes.

Hugo: Thanks for everything

Cameron: np

I sneak behind my closet door to change into some clothes. I would die if Hugo saw me undress. Not to mention that taking off my clothes with him in the room is causing some inconvenient side effects below my waist.

Dressed and ready to go, Hugo and I sneak down the stairs. The path to the front door is clear, so I motion for him to head out as I distract my parents in the kitchen. I clear my throat loudly as he opens and shuts the door, and he escapes undetected. Mom and Dad stare at me.

"Morning, Cam. Something caught in your throat?" Mom asks.

Dad doesn't even glance up from his phone. "You need to start those allergy meds again?"

"I'm fine. Just some morning phlegm."

"Mmm," Dad replies, nose in his phone.

As I sit at the table eating my pancakes, my phone buzzes in my pocket. It's a message from Abby that she's on her way. "Oh, Abby's coming over in a bit."

Dad looks up from his phone. "You ask her to homecoming yet? You know that girl is crazy about you, right?"

My jaw drops open, and a tiny jolt of adrenaline swirls through me. "Dad, are you serious?"

"Of course I am. I've seen the way she looks at you."

I shake my head, and my nostrils flare. "We're just best friends."

Dad says nothing, but he has this annoying smirk on his face as he looks back at his phone. This is classic Dad. He can't just say that shit to me and get away with it. I've had it.

Just as I open my mouth, Mom gets up and puts a gentle hand on Dad's shoulder. "James, help me with the dishes, okay?"

Dad gets up, and Mom shoots me a sympathetic smile. I sit at the table for a moment, taking deep breaths, letting my pulse slow. I was this close to having it out with Dad. This mixture of feelings swirls in my gut. It needs to happen, but I'm also glad it didn't. I have other things to concentrate on, and I'm so used to the way he always acts. I shrug it off.

After breakfast, I spend extra time messing with my hair in front of the mirror. Of course it won't cooperate today. This stupid spot in the back sticks up no matter how much hair crap I put in it.

I lift my shirt, grab the blubber around my midsection, and let out a grunt. There's no way Hugo will like me if he ever sees this. Is emergency liposuction a thing?

Abby shows up, and we head to my room. She forces me to tell her about last night in excruciating detail. I explain three times that nothing happened between Hugo and me.

I recount what Hugo saw last night: the White Lady, the hidden room, all of it. Abby is more excited than I've ever seen her. After all, two of the top things on her priority list are finding a ghost and finding me a boyfriend. I'm glad to oblige her on the boyfriend part, but I'm less than excited about the ghost.

We root through the ghost-hunting box and stash several things in a backpack that Abby says are "critical for a successful ghost hunt." I take her word for it.

I text Hugo.

Cameron: Abby's here. Heading over

Hugo: K. I'm outside

Outside. Hmm. I hope nothing more happened.

We arrive at Crimson House to find Hugo on the tire swing hanging from the old oak tree in the side yard. He swings back and forth with his head resting on his hands. As we approach, he hops out.

Compared to this morning, his hair is tame, and he's wearing a new set of clothes: a Hurley T-shirt and tight-fitting jeans. The arms bulging from his T-shirt are extremely distracting, and I can barely look at his butt in those jeans without blushing.

"Hey, Hugo." I wave as we approach. "You remember Abby from lunch on Monday?"

Hugo looks down. "Heh, yeah. Um...sorry I was such a dick."

"We're cool," Abby says with a smile. "Cameron explained everything."

Hugo smiles back. "Cool."

"How come you're out here?" I ask. "Something happen inside?"

"No." Hugo shrugs. "Just needed some air."

I'm not sure if I buy it. The slightest bit of apprehension flashes in his eyes when he looks at the house, and I know that feeling well.

"So, can we go in?" Abby asks with more enthusiasm than Hugo and me combined. "Upstairs bathroom, right?"

"Yep." Hugo gestures toward the front door. "Be my guest."

Abby takes several things out of the backpack. She hands Hugo a digital recorder after pressing the record button. "Hold that and keep it recording." She hands me an EMF meter with a row of green, yellow, and red LED lights across the top. "Let me know if you notice any spikes." She takes out a small square box. "I'll hold the ghost box. This is how ghosts can communicate with us," she explains to Hugo. She turns it on, and faint static emerges from a speaker on the side. "Okay, let's go."

As we approach the house, the occasional word comes out of the ghost box speaker.

...peace...

"How does that work?" Hugo asks, pointing at the ghost box.

"It scans radio frequencies. The theory is that ghosts can manipulate electromagnetic frequencies and tune in to certain words to communicate," Abby says. Hugo nods and says nothing, but his body language says he's more than a bit skeptical.

The closer we get, the more the nervousness in the pit of my stomach builds. Years have passed since I've been in this house, and I swore I'd never go back, yet here I am, trying to be brave for this cute guy. I'm not sure love is blind, but it sure is stupid. I'm not saying I *love* Hugo, but you know what I mean.

...onion...

Hugo walks through the door, followed by Abby, and I'm the last to cross the threshold. A distinct change in energy sweeps over me, like the raw crackling of electricity.

"Whoa," Abby says. "Did you feel that?"

"I thought it was only me," Hugo says. "That happens every time I walk into this house. It's like a weight comes down on me."

"Yeah, exactly. Like a weight." Abby nods, glancing around the foyer as if she can somehow find the source of the weight in the walls.

"But that was more intense than usual," Hugo says.

"It might be because three of us came in at the same time." Abby shrugs. "Anything on the EMF meter, Cameron?"

...ocean...

I open my mouth to speak, but I'm hit by a wave of nausea. I lean over, hands on my legs, taking deep breaths, fighting back the bile rising in my throat. The scar on my leg itches, but I'm 95 percent sure it's my imagination.

The crow. The blood. The shadow. The hopelessness and the dread. They all roll through my mind like a sick waking dream.

Then there's a voice. *You left me. Now I have you.*

Was that in my mind? Or did I actually hear it? My head swims, and darkness floats at the edges of my vision.

Abby's eyebrows scrunch. "Cameron, you okay?"

I hold up my hand and nod as I take deep breaths, fighting the light-headedness and the sour taste in the back of my throat. "Sorry. I'm okay. Just felt sick for a moment. Bad pancakes."

Abby scrutinizes me with narrowed eyes. "Let me know if anything changes."

I nod. "It's passing. I'm good."

"Okay. Let's get this ghost hunt going, then," Abby says.

She walks through the foyer. "Is there anybody here who wants to communicate with us?" she asks, peering upward. "We mean you no harm."

The three of us head up the staircase to the second-story landing. More memories from four years ago flash through my mind, but this time I'm ready and feel more in control.

"Are you the White Lady?" Abby makes a sweeping turn, arms wide. "Can you give us a sign?"

...changes...

"Does that ever say anything that makes sense?" Hugo asks, pointing at the ghost box.

"Sometimes," Abby replies with a huff. "You have to be patient and know how to interpret the words. Where's the bathroom?"

"In there." Hugo nods toward a door at the end of the hallway but doesn't go in. Abby marches straight through the door without hesitation. Reluctantly, I follow, and Hugo brings up the rear. As he described, the medicine cabinet rests up against the toilet, and a hole in the wall leads into darkness.

...lost...

"Are you lost?" Abby asks, looking around.

"Can we turn that off?" I point to the ghost box. "It's giving me the creeps."

"Are you kidding?" Abby gapes. "It's just getting good."

She grabs a massive flashlight from her backpack and flips it on. The beam is so bright it could serve as the beacon for a lighthouse. She stands on tiptoe, shining the beam into the darkness.

"You saw the White Lady in here, right?" Abby asks Hugo.

"Yep." Hugo pauses for a moment. "Then out in the hallway."

Abby peers in. "Well, I can't see anything now. I'm the smallest, so I should go in."

"Whoa!" I cry. "Nobody said anything about anybody going in there!"

"Yeah." Hugo nods. "I don't like the sound of that. Pa would kill me if anything happened."

"What could happen?" Abby protests.

"Lots of things could happen," I say, voice cracking. "You could get your foot caught in a floorboard, for instance."

"Don't be such a worrywart. I'll be fine."

As though the discussion is over, Abby sets down the ghost box and flashlight, then climbs onto the sink and sticks half her body through the hole before Hugo or I can utter another word. She goes in stomach up and grabs the top of the hole, hoisting her feet up and in.

This is what the house does—lulls people into complacency. *It's just a spooky old house, after all. What could go wrong? Let's have an adventure and hunt for ghosts. It'll be fun.* Until it isn't. Until you're bleeding and stuck, being attacked by birds and watching as shadows circle you.

"Abby," I whine, "please be careful!"

Halfway through my sentence, Abby drops to the floor behind the wall.

"The floor is solid," she says. "Hand me the flashlight."

I pass it through to her, and she shines the beam around. It's hard to make out much from this side, but Hugo and I lean over the sink to peer through the hole. Hugo's shoulder brushes against mine, sending a tingle through me.

"Sorry," Hugo says, and pulls his shoulder away.

"It's okay." My voice breaks on the last word, and I clear my throat. We stare at each other for a moment. I gulp.

"There's an entire room back here," Abby says, redirecting our attention. "And it's furnished, and there's a bunch of old gross stuff lying around."

The flashlight beam bounces off the walls and various pieces of furniture, but it's hard to make out much from this side.

"It looks like a little girl's room. There's a wrought iron twin bed and old-fashioned toys and dolls sitting here on a shelf." Abby leans down to inspect something. "But everything is covered in a thick layer of dust and mold. I doubt anybody's been here in forever."

The temperature drops, and goose bumps form on my arms like there are a hundred baby spiders crawling on my skin. "Abby, maybe you should get out of there."

...cookies...

My heart skips a beat, and Hugo and I exchange glances, eyes wide. "Did that box just say cookies?" I ask.

Hugo nods, eyes wide.

"The box just said cookies!" I shout.

"There's a spiral staircase in here." Abby either didn't hear or she's ignoring me. "But it goes right into the ceiling. It's boarded up. This place is intense. You two should see this."

...trespass...

"I think you should come out," Hugo says, his voice firm but shaky toward the end.

"Um." Abby's voice is strange. Distant. "Hey, I feel—" She slurs the last words.

"Come out of there!" I cry, extending my arm toward her. "Grab my hand."

The flashlight falls out of Abby's hand with a loud thud, making shadows dance as it rolls across the room.

Abby falls to the floor.

12
THE PLAN: HUGO

"**A**bby!" Cameron cries, staring into the darkness. He turns to me with desperation in his eyes. "We have to help her."

His care for Abby is palpable—he can barely contain his panic. There's a strange tug in my chest, and I'm not sure what it means.

"I'll give you a boost." I bend down on one knee and cup my hands together.

Cameron grabs my shoulder with a firm grip. The warmth of his hand penetrates the fabric of my shirt. I hoist him up, and in a flash, he's up and through the hole, slipping into the next room.

...friendly...

That damn ghost box. "Yeah, real friendly," I say under my breath. I call to Cameron, "Is she okay?"

"I think so." Cameron's muffled voice comes from the other room. "She's waking up."

"Should we call 911?" The thought of this spiraling out of control makes me sick to my stomach. How was I stupid enough to allow her to go in there by herself? Pa is going to kill me.

"No. It's okay. But come help me."

"Be right there."

Thoughts of the White Lady with her jagged yellow teeth flash through my mind. Fewer than twelve hours ago, she was in this room, chasing after me with that harsh laugh. But Cameron and Abby need me, so I shove those thoughts to the back of my mind as I climb onto the sink, hoist myself through the hole, and drop to the floor.

...alone...

The room is dark and dusty, and the air is stale. Cameron kneels next to Abby, who's lying on the floor. She blinks a few times. With Cameron's help, she sits up. "Easy now, Abby."

She rubs the back of her head. "Ouch. That'll leave a bump." She winces. "What happened? I don't remember anything."

"You fell over suddenly," Cameron says. "You were in the middle of a sentence." He rubs her back in small circles.

"Wow. I used to have fainting spells when I was a kid, but it's been years," Abby says. "Did you see her?"

"Who?" Cameron and I say in unison, shooting worried looks at each other.

"The old lady. She was right there." Abby points to the spiral staircase.

"You saw her!" Cameron shouts.

"Yes. I mean, I think I did." Abby rubs the bump on her head. "Everything's a little fuzzy now. Maybe I imagined it."

I swipe Abby's flashlight off the ground and point it at the spiral staircase in the corner of the room. Ornate black wrought iron, filled with twists, swirls, and filigree, extends right up to the ceiling. But no old lady anywhere.

...secret...

"Well, she's not here now." I shine the flashlight around the rest of the room. "And you didn't mention her before you passed out."

"Maybe I made her up," Abby says, rubbing the back of her head.

"We've both seen her too," Cameron says. "We're not doubting you."

I nod in agreement, continuing to search the room, although to be honest, the last thing I want is to actually find anything. I'd like to board this room up and forget about it.

"Can you stand up, Abby?" Cameron asks.

"I think so." He helps her off the ground. Her feet are steady. "I feel better. I think I'm okay."

"Just take it easy for a bit," Cameron says, watching her like a concerned parent seeing a baby take their first steps.

I scan the room's perimeter with the beam of the flashlight. Jackpot. The door leading to the hallway is right where I expect, but it doesn't budge. Ends of old rusty nails poke out along the door frame. "Found the door, but it's nailed shut."

"Check this out," Cameron says, inspecting the far wall. "I think there's a boarded-up window behind this. It's just a piece of plywood nailed into a window frame."

"Maybe we can pry it off," I say. "Be right back."

I climb out of the hole and run to the dining room, where Pa keeps all our tools. I grab a hammer and a crowbar. Back in the bathroom, I hand them to Cameron through the hole in the wall.

...open...

That damn ghost box is giving me the creeps, so I shut it off, then climb back into the hidden room.

I take the crowbar, and Cameron uses the hammer while Abby holds the flashlight. We work from both sides, prying the plywood away from the wall. The nails groan as they loosen, and sunlight streaks in around the edges as the gap gets bigger. With one last pull, the entire piece of plywood comes loose, and we set it down against the wall. A window caked with years of dirt is now exposed. Vines cover the outside but let in enough dappled sunlight to cast the room in a golden hue, revealing details that I'd guess no living soul has seen in decades.

Shelves line the walls, holding dolls and stuffed animals half-eaten away by mold and decay. A broken wooden playhouse sits in one corner, covered with dust. An old rocking horse sits next to it. Flaking white paint covers the wrought iron bed, and a tattered yellowing quilt rests on a lumpy mattress. Childlike pictures of clowns and horses hang on the walls, their frames cracking and canvases faded.

A standing birdcage rusted with age is in the room's far corner. The skeleton of a long-dead bird rests inside it. Probably the remains of a crow, based on its beak and size.

"This is seriously creepy," Abby says. "Who keeps a crow as a pet? And what would cause somebody to board up an entire room without even clearing it out?"

"No idea," Cameron replies. "But those vines explain why we've never seen this window from the outside."

"I wonder when this room last saw sunlight?" I ask.

"Probably before I was born," Cameron says.

"And where does this staircase lead to?" I ask, peering up at the curved railing ascending into the ceiling.

Cameron grabs the hammer off the ground. "Maybe we should try to break in?"

"Hold up," I say, raising my hands. "I need to think about this before we open up new parts of the house. I haven't even figured out how to explain *this* to Pa." He's going to freak the second he finds out. Part of me wants to board this room back up and forget about everything. But visions of the old lady run through my head. Ignoring it won't make her go away.

"You've met our friend Chloe, right?" Abby asks me. Cameron shoots her a look I can't quite read.

"Uh...she's in theater tech, right? Redhead?"

"That's her," Abby says.

"I haven't met her, but I've seen her in class. Why do you ask?"

"Would you mind if she came over?" Abby smiles, but Cameron looks sick to his stomach.

"I guess that's fine." I shrug. "Why?"

"Chloe is unique. She has dreams and can sense things," Abby says in a mysterious tone.

"You mean she's, like, a psychic or something? I—um—I don't really believe in that stuff." Then again, my beliefs have broadened lately.

"I get it," Abby says. "I'm a woman of science myself, but Chloe is special. She's not like a circus act or one of those dumb people on psychic reality TV shows who asks leading questions. She just has these dreams sometimes. She doesn't even like to talk about them, so it's not like she's doing it for attention or anything. But when she has them, they're pretty spot-on."

"So, did she have a dream...about this house?"

"Yes!" Cameron cuts in with a side-eye toward Abby. "About the *house*."

"What did she dream, exactly?" I ask.

"She didn't say much," Abby says. "Just that she dreamt something would happen between the house and—"

"With the house," Cameron cuts in, and glares at Abby. There's something they aren't telling me.

"Like, what kind of something?" I glance between Cameron and Abby, searching for answers. "That's pretty vague."

"Exactly," says Cameron. "That's why Abby wants her to come here, to see if she can be more specific. Right, Abby?"

"Okay. Sure." Abby sighs. "Let me text her."

"Look, Pa can't know about any of this," I say. This could get out of hand fast, and the more people know, the harder it will be to hide it.

"Chloe is awesome," Cameron says. "She can totally keep a secret."

After a flurry of texts, Abby peeks up from her phone. "Okay, Chloe can be here in twenty minutes, on one condition."

"What's that?" I ask.

"She wants her girlfriend, Maya, to come too."

"Sure, might as well invite everyone." I laugh, more to shake off my nerves than because anything is funny. Involving even more people isn't great, but I'm in over my head and need all the help I can get, so I let it slide. "No, it's fine. I understand."

None of us is excited about hanging out in my house for twenty minutes, so we climb out of the room and wait outside. Abby plays back the voice recording, an intense expression pasted on her face as she rewinds and relistens to various parts.

"What are you doing?" I ask.

"I'm listening for EVPs." She sees the question on my face. "Have you never watched *Ghost Hunters* or anything?"

I shrug. "Not really my thing."

"Electronic voice phenomena. We ask the ghosts questions, and sometimes they answer back, but you can only hear it on digital audio."

"And does that work?" I lift an eyebrow.

"Yes!" she blurts. "Of course it works."

"How many have you recorded?"

"Me?" She looks away. "Well, I haven't personally recorded any. But I've heard plenty on the internet."

The internet. Well, that proves it, I want to say, but I bite my tongue. Instead I say, "Okay. Well, let me know if you find anything."

After waiting in my front yard for a while, listening for EVPs, Chloe and Maya arrive. Maya looks stunning, like she's headed to a fashion show, in a short sage skirt, white top, and denim vest. Chloe's wearing faded jeans and a spaghetti strap top.

They're walking side by side, holding hands. Their wide-open affection makes me smile. Cameron glances my way and smiles too, but then his cheeks turn rosy and he averts his eyes.

"Hey, you two," Abby says, and they both say hi back. "Thanks for coming over."

Chloe peers up at the house. "I hate this place, but it sounded important."

"It is," Abby says. "And we appreciate it."

"We really do," I add.

"It's something I need to do more of, anyway," Chloe says. "I've been working with my aunt. She's like me, and she wants me to do more things like this, work on my active abilities."

"Well, this house will give you plenty of practice," Cameron says, puffing out a short laugh.

Maya wraps her arm around Chloe, her face as tough as nails. "Nothing in there better mess around with my girlfriend, or I'm gonna kick some ghost ass."

"Do ghosts even have asses?" Cameron asks.

"Well, I'll kick them somewhere," Maya says, glancing at her nails.

"No time like the present," Chloe says as she heads for the door. "Let's get this over with."

As Chloe crosses the threshold, she shivers, and Maya pulls her closer.

"So, how does this work?" I ask Chloe. "What do you need to do?"

"Honestly, I don't even know," Chloe says. "I never *do* anything. I just get these feelings. Sometimes it's a taste or a smell, or I feel cold or hot, prickly or soft. And sometimes I dream about things."

"What do you feel now?" Cameron asks.

"Cold," Chloe says. "Very cold."

"We shouldn't ask the ghost questions or anything?" I ask.

"I mean, you can ask questions if you want." Chloe laughs. "But I don't think it'll make a difference to me."

"Honestly, that makes me feel better," I say. "Asking questions to thin air feels silly."

Chloe smiles, but Abby's affronted. "Hey, don't dis the EVPs!"

I put up my hands. "Sorry! No disrespect intended."

Abby glares at me. "I'll get one eventually. Then you'll give me a real apology." She finishes with a smile to show me she's joking, but I get the impression that she's half serious.

Chloe walks slowly down the hallway and into the kitchen, pausing occasionally to glance around as the rest of us follow behind. Cameron scoots closer, and I don't mind one bit. Our shoulders bump. I smile, and he smiles back, this time without looking away or turning beet red. Being around him is having this giddy effect on me, but I don't want to act like a smiling fool, so I focus my attention on Chloe, trying to get Cameron out of my mind.

"It's warmer in here," Chloe says as she circles the kitchen, running her hand along the countertops.

"Do you smell anything?" I ask, thinking of the scent of the cookies and my weird dream.

"No," Chloe says. "Be careful about asking me leading questions. I don't want to be influenced."

"Sorry!"

"You saw the White Lady, right?" Chloe asks me.

"Yeah. I saw her in—"

"Don't tell me where!" Chloe cuts in.

"No influence." I nod.

"No influence," she echoes.

Chloe continues to explore the house, and we follow. In the library, Chloe shivers. "So cold in here."

Everyone trades glances. The library is not cold. In fact, it's on the warm side.

"Did you see her in here?" Chloe asks me.

"I saw her here in a dream," I say. That horrible dream where she appeared through the dust of a thousand old books and then I fell. I fell for a long time. The memory makes me squirm.

"Interesting," Chloe says. "I have some of my more intense feelings in dreams. They can be powerful. Has she ever physically touched you?"

"No. But I've never let her get near enough."

"That's a good sign. Hopefully it means she's not powerful enough to command the physical world," Chloe says. "If she ever touches you or manipulates an object, let me know."

"Will do," I say.

She could get *more* powerful and even touch objects? Or me? A knot forms in the pit of my stomach.

Chloe continues her tour of the house. She returns to the foyer and climbs the steps. At the top, she heads right to Pa's bedroom door and stands in the exact spot where the White Lady stood last night. That's quite a coincidence. I keep my face neutral, trying to not give her any signals that something happened there.

"It's very warm here," Chloe says in a whisper. "And soft. I feel safe here. Did anything happen here?"

"That is exactly where I saw her last night," I say.

Chloe nods like she's not surprised in the least. A slight murmur of amazement comes from everyone else.

Chloe walks along the hallway, her fingers grazing the wall as her feet move forward one delicate step at a time. Near the bathroom door, she pauses, eyes narrowing, body stiffening. "I don't like this place. It's cold, and my skin is prickly." Her face darkens, and she looks sick.

Maya places a hand on her arm. "Are you okay, Chloe?"

Chloe nods. "I think so. The feeling isn't going away, but I'm getting used to it. It came on so strong. Hopefully we don't need to go into that bathroom."

Abby and Cameron shoot worried glances at each other, and I grimace at Chloe.

"That's where we need to go, isn't it?" Chloe says, her face drawn into a frown.

"I'm afraid so," I say.

Chloe breathes in deep and nods. "All right, let's do it, then."

In the bathroom, the air is heavy and oppressive. Her shoulders slump at the sight of the hole in the wall leading into the creepy little girl's room.

"In there, I take it?"

I nod. "We found a hidden room."

"Of course you did." Chloe laughs, shaking her head.

"We are *not* going in there!" Maya blurts, and tugs on Chloe's arm. "No way! Let's go, Chloe."

Chloe takes Maya's hand. "It's okay. I can do it."

Maya frowns. "We've talked about this. You do not need to put yourself through anything you don't want to do. You have nothing to prove."

I cut in. "I agree. I don't want anybody hurt or sick on my account."

"But I think it's important," Chloe says in a steady voice as she glances between Maya and me. "I think we need to do this. I can feel it."

"Goddammit," Maya says under her breath, shaking her head. "She can feel it. Argument over." It's not sarcasm, just resignation and acceptance, like Maya has experience with this.

"Okay," I say, following Maya's lead. "But the second anybody gets sick or passes out, we're done."

"Agreed," Chloe says.

One after another, we climb through the hole until the five of us stand in a circle in the middle of the room. The soft afternoon light streams through the vines covering the window.

"You sense anything?" Maya asks Chloe, studying her face. Maya is clearly so devoted to her girlfriend. I want someone who is protective and will care for me no matter what. I glance at Cameron. Why do I keep doing that?

"It's strange, actually," Chloe says, examining the room. "I feel both warm and cold. Prickly and soft. But they balance each other out so it almost feels like nothing. Does that make any sense?"

"Kinda." I shrug. "Do you think there are two ghosts?"

"No. It doesn't feel like that," Chloe says. "One entity, but with two distinct personalities."

"Like a split personality?" Cameron asks.

"Something like that."

Chloe continues her tour of the room until the spiral staircase catches her eye. "A spiral staircase to nowhere?"

"Someone boarded up the top," I say, pointing to the slats of wood nailed to the ceiling.

Chloe puts her hand on the twisting railing, gripping the wrought iron tight. Her knuckles turn white as her jaw clenches. "This is it. This is the source of the cold."

"That's right where I saw the White Lady," Abby says, eyes wide.

"Do you think we should open the top and see where it leads?" Cameron asks the group.

"That sounds like a horrible idea," Maya says. "It's like the start of a bad horror movie."

"I agree," I say. "I don't want to open it until we know what we're getting into." We've already been pushing the limits of my comfort, and breaking into new parts of the house will send my anxiety into overdrive.

"Do we know what's up there?" Abby asks me. "Do you have the original plans for this house?"

"Nope," I say. "Pa checked. It was built in the late 1800s, and the online records only go back to the 1920s."

"I bet we could check the city archives at the library," Abby says. "My dad found the plans for our house, which is also super old."

"Cool, I know the head librarian, Mr. Peterson," Cameron says. "He told me he had more info on this house. I can go and talk to him."

"Good idea," Abby says. "You and Hugo should do that. It'll go faster if there are two of you."

Cameron and Abby share a look, but it's hard to read. Those two communicate simply by looking at each other. It's intimidating.

Cameron turns to me. "That sound okay, Hugo?"

"Yeah, sounds good," I say. Spending more time with Cameron sounds awesome to me.

But what if this ends like everything else has? All the friends and boyfriends I've left behind flash through my mind. Any connection I make will be severed in a heartbeat if Pa decides we need to leave, especially if he finds out about any of this ghost shit. An undercurrent of worry eats at my gut.

"What are the rest of you going to do?" I ask.

"I've been recording audio this whole time," Abby says. "I'm heading home to use my good headphones, spend some more time listening for EVPs."

"I want to talk to my aunt," Chloe says, "and ask her about the two personalities."

"I'm going with her," Maya says.

We all agree to the plan. We'll split up and meet back at my house in a few hours.

It's different each time I leave the house. This time there's relief combined with the slightest twinge of sadness, an odd mix that doesn't feel quite right. I'm dying to leave this house, but part of me wants to stay, which doesn't make any sense.

Abby, Chloe, and Maya wave goodbye to us and head down the street. I start to follow, but Cameron tugs at my shirt. "This way."

"We don't need to go that way to get to the center of town?" I ask, pointing to where the girls are walking down our dead-end street.

"We can take the shortcut through the forest." Cameron smiles.

"Oh, so *that's* why you're always cutting through my yard," I tease. "I seem to recall telling you to stop."

Cameron puffs out an incredulous laugh. "Do you want to learn the shortcut or not?"

I smile and gesture toward the woods. "Lead on."

Cameron guides us to a small trail heading into the trees at the back of my yard. The path forks several times, twisting through the evergreens, maples, and oaks, but Cameron never pauses. In the short time I've known him, I've seen two distinct sides to him. Sometimes he's shy, reserved, and draws inward, shoulders slumped. Other times, like now, he radiates confidence. The confident Cameron is a joy to watch.

"You really know your way around here, don't you?" I ask, blindly following him through the forest.

"I've been hiking through these woods since I was old enough to walk."

"I can't imagine what it would be like to live in one place your whole life," I say.

"A little repetitive, to be honest. My family has lived in this town forever. My four-times great-grandpa built our house. Your family moves around a lot, huh?"

"Every time Pa and I finish fixing up a house, we move—about every six months. It sucks. I'd take repetitive any day. It'd be so nice to have one place to call home."

"It's okay." Cameron shrugs. "This is a better place to be a queer kid than most small towns, I guess, but I still want to see the world. At least you've been able to experience different places."

"I've experienced some pretty crappy places. Places I haven't felt comfortable being who I am. It's cool how you're out to everybody, and everybody seems to be cool with it."

"For the most part. Not Bryce Hunter." Cameron laughs.

I laugh back. "Bryce Hunter can suck it."

"Maybe he does. Wouldn't be the first closeted bully," Cameron says. "And even though some people say they accept me, I don't always believe it. My dad hopes this 'gay thing' is a phase."

"At least you're out to him." I sigh.

"Oh, your dad doesn't know?" Cameron asks. "How about your mom?"

"My ma knew." A lump forms in my throat.

Cameron glances at me, his face melting into concern. "I'm sorry. We don't have to talk about it."

"No, it's okay. I told her I liked guys when I was thirteen. She was great about it." I take a deep breath. "She died in a car accident a month later. She was driving me to soccer practice. I escaped with a broken leg and a few scrapes."

God, it still hurts so much to talk about it. The memories flash by: Ma in the car, smiling. A noise like an explosion. The car crumpling around me. Everything going black.

I peer up at the leaves blowing in the light breeze, fighting back the grief that's welling up. "Ma died the instant the truck hit the driver's side door."

Cameron stops on the path and looks at me with kind, sad eyes. "I'm so sorry, Hugo."

I'll lose it if I keep looking at him. I turn away fast and start down the path again, keeping my head down. "We got through it."

Emotions pound on my insides, trying to spill out, but I choke them all back. Something I've perfected over the last three years.

We hike in silence for a while, concentrating on the sounds of the forest. It's serene, and it soothes me a bit. When the emotions have ebbed, I continue. "Anyway, yeah, I haven't told Pa. We move around so much that he's hardly noticed I haven't had a girlfriend. And I've only dated guys for, like, a week at a time, so it's hard to even call them boyfriends. Just guys I've kissed."

I peek over at Cameron. He's smiling and fighting a blush.

"What?" I say with a smile.

"Nothing."

"Nothing?"

Cameron laughs. "Just seeing somebody like you talking about kissing guys."

"What about it?"

"It makes me smile, that's all."

"How about you?" I ask. "Any boyfriends?"

He loses the battle with his blush. "Uh, no. No boyfriends."

"Girlfriends?"

"Definitely not!"

"You and Abby seem close. Never been anything more than friends?"

"Me and Abby? Oh my god! You sound like my dad." Cameron laughs. "Abby and I have been best friends since the third grade. But yeah, only friends. I'm pretty exclusively into guys."

"Cool." I nod. "Yeah, me too."

We walk in silence, the only sounds the pine needles crunching under our feet and the occasional chirping bird. But in the dappled light of the forest, Cameron's smiling, and I can't help but smile too.

13

The Library: Cameron

Hugo and I make our way along Lawrence Street, the main drag of Uptown Port Townsend. And by "main drag," I mean a few random shops, a neighborhood pub, the Uptown Theater, and the Port Townsend Library. The tourists rarely make it up this far from Water Street, so everything here caters to locals.

Like everything else in this town, the library is more than a hundred years old, a white painted brick building with architecture from the Victorian era. Despite its age, the building is in pristine condition with trimmed hedges and not a spot of dirt on the walls. We climb the flight of stairs to the front entrance, passing wrought iron globe lights. The words CARNEGIE LIBRARY are etched on the stone facade above the entrance. Hugo opens the door and gestures me in.

"Thanks," I say with a smile.

"My pleasure." Hugo smiles back.

"What a perfect gentleman you are," I say, dripping with sarcasm.

"Get in before this door smacks you in the ass," Hugo says, laughing.

Inside, bookshelves line every wall and form several aisles in the middle of the room. Scattered people sit at old wooden tables, reading books, typing on laptops, or resting their heads in their hands, taking afternoon naps. Oak-trimmed windows line the walls, providing ample natural light for reading. Box beam ceilings and antique lamps complete the classic aesthetic. I'm a bit of a bookworm, and I've spent many an hour here. It's like a second home.

Mr. Peterson sits at the front desk, eyes on his monitor, clicking his mouse. A cardigan sweater covers his button-down shirt, and he's got on khaki chinos and brown loafers. His style screams librarian, and it suits him to a tee. As we approach the desk, he looks up from his computer. "Cameron. Good to see you again."

"Hi, Mr. Peterson. This is my friend Hugo."

"Hey." Hugo waves.

"Hello, Hugo. A pleasure to meet you." Mr. Peterson nods.

"You said you had stuff about 16 Sycamore Lane, right?" I ask.

"Yes," Mr. Peterson says with a sigh. "You really want to know more, huh?"

"Yeah. I'm doing an essay for school. I was hoping you had old plans or some history about the place?"

"We do," he says with a snap to his voice. He gets up from his chair. "Ms. West, can you watch the front desk while I'm gone?"

A squat woman with dark skin and locks looks up from the other side of the desk. "Will do, Mr. Peterson."

"Thank you. Follow me, gentlemen."

Mr. Peterson turns with a flourish and leads us down two flights of stairs, then along a long hallway. In the basement, the only light comes from old yellowed ceiling lamps illuminating drab olive walls. This is my first time in the archives. It's unsettling, a bit like a morgue—the exact opposite of the warm and welcoming upper floors.

We come to a metal door, and Mr. Peterson takes out a massive key ring with no fewer than twenty keys, poking out in jagged spikes like some kind of medieval weapon. He riffles through them until he inexplicably finds a key identical to the ones around it.

"Here we go." He opens the door, and I'm hit with stale air and a waft of musty paper. With a flip of the switch, fluorescent lights flicker several times, then glow steadily, revealing a large room with row after row of metal shelving filled with white banker's boxes, each labeled with care.

Large metal file cabinets with wide, short drawers sit in the middle of the room. Mr. Peterson runs his finger along the drawers of a particular cabinet until he gets to one labeled *So–Sy*.

Fragile documents faded with age fill the drawer. He thumbs through the papers, then stops on an especially yellowed one.

"Okay, here we go," Mr. Peterson says, pulling out a few large sheets. "The original plans for 16 Sycamore Lane, circa 1880. These are fragile, so I'm afraid I can't let them leave this room."

"Can I take a few photos with my phone?" I ask.

"Sure. Just no flash, please."

Hugo helps Mr. Peterson hold up each page of the plans as I take pictures. After we're done, Mr. Peterson delicately places every page back into the drawer while Hugo and I go through the photos.

"Look," I whisper, pointing to the second-story floor plan. "There's the hidden room."

"Let me see that." Hugo leans closer, his shoulder brushing mine, and my stomach tumbles. "Wow. It really is a whole separate room, just boarded up. What about the third story? Where does that spiral staircase lead to?"

I swipe to the next photo, and Hugo gasps. "I know that room! The door is locked, and we don't have a key." He shudders. "I just gave myself the heebie-jeebies."

"It is totally freaky having locked and hidden rooms in your house," I agree. "I wonder what's in there?"

Mr. Peterson finishes putting away the plans and turns to us. "So, how much do you two know about the history of 16 Sycamore Lane?"

I shrug. "Just that Emily Thornburn died in that house and strange stuff happens there." I've heard more about the hauntings and rumors of missing children, but I don't want to repeat things I heard secondhand from friends. And of course I keep our recent experiences to myself.

"I heard she inherited it from her father," Hugo adds.

"That's right." Mr. Peterson has a glint in his eye. "But do you want to know the *full* story? I've spent hours researching that house. Bit of a local history buff, I'm afraid."

"That'd be awesome," I say.

"Follow me." Mr. Peterson waves us deeper into the archive room, passing rows of bookcases lined with endless boxes. He turns down one aisle and finds a box with the word THORNBURN written on the side. With the box in hand, Mr. Peterson guides us to a table with a desk lamp, where we sit. He opens the box filled with papers, photographs, and newspaper clippings.

"Charles Thornburn was a war hero and the sole heir to his father's lumber fortune. By all accounts, he was an upstanding citizen, but the war changed him. He returned with a bizarre fascination with death and became the town's mortician." He shows us a fragile-looking photograph of a man in a military uniform and a pregnant woman in a white dress.

"Mind if I take pictures?" I ask, taking out my phone.

"Be my guest."

I take a picture of the photo and keep my phone out.

"He built 16 Sycamore Lane in 1880 both for the family business and for his wife, Greta. They intended to have a big family."

"Are you telling me that house was a mortuary?" Hugo says, eyebrows raised.

"That was the intent, yes. But it never came to pass," Mr. Peterson says. "Greta went into labor only a week after she moved into the house. The delivery did not go well. She died giving birth, and there was something wrong with the child. That child was Emily Thornburn."

Hugo and I trade glances.

"The White Lady of Sycamore Lane, if I'm up to date on the local folklore." Mr. Peterson looks at us, eyebrows raised.

"That's right," I say. "At least that's what I've heard kids call her."

Mr. Peterson nods. "After that, Charles Thornburn became a recluse. He blamed himself for his wife's death and his daughter's condition. Sometimes Emily was sweet and docile. Other times she was a nightmare. Her tantrums were famous. People could hear her screams all over town."

I give Hugo another glance, and he nods. That must be why Chloe sensed both good and evil in the house: the two opposing sides of Emily's personality.

Mr. Peterson continues, "Mr. Thornburn and Emily never left the house. The only person who ever saw them was Emily's nanny, Agnes Finch. She purchased food and supplies and kept the house running." He pulls out a photo. "This is one of the few photos of Emily and Ms. Finch."

A little girl in a frilly dress sits in a wingback chair with a wide smile. Too wide. Her eyes are vacant. A silver locket shaped like a heart hangs from a chain around her neck. Next to the girl is a pretty young woman in a black dress with a white lace collar, her hair drawn back into a bun. "This was taken shortly before Emily's father died. She was ten years old."

Hugo's face contorts for a moment. He was only thirteen when he lost his mom. He doesn't acknowledge my gaze.

"How did he die?" I ask as I take a picture of the photo. Digging into the death of a parent might upset Hugo, but I'm overwhelmed by curiosity. Plus, it could be an important detail.

"Gunshot wound to the head," Mr. Peterson says in a grim tone. "The local sheriff ruled it a suicide. But neighbors reported a young man around Ms. Finch's age sneaking into the house on a regular basis, though no one ever got a good look at him. People assumed it was her lover. The town erupted into rumors that Mr. Thornburn's gunshot wound was not self-inflicted."

"Did they think the young man did it?" I ask.

"That was the popular theory. People speculated that Mr. Thornburn had taken a liking to Ms. Finch and that he walked in on her and this young man together and it ended in a gunfight. Others think Emily went into one of her famous rages and got her hands on a firearm or that Ms. Finch did it. Emily was the sole heir to her father's fortune, but it went into a trust until she was eighteen, controlled by Ms. Finch."

"What do you think happened?" I ask Mr. Peterson.

"The simplest explanation is usually the right one. Mr. Thornburn was a troubled man." Mr. Peterson's lips press into a tight line.

"What happened to Emily after her father died?" Hugo asks.

"Emily and Ms. Finch lived alone in the house for many years, and no one saw the young man again. People saw Ms. Finch in town from time to time, but it became less frequent as she got older. Eventually, even she stopped leaving the house. All the food and supplies were delivered on a schedule and left on the back porch. People sometimes saw Emily bringing in the supplies, always wearing a white dress. Hence the nickname White Lady."

"What happened to Ms. Finch?" I ask.

"Another mystery. No one knows. She immigrated from Ireland and had no local family. The sheriff checked in on her after people in town hadn't seen her in over a year. Emily told the sheriff that Ms. Finch had left for good a few months prior. No one ever tracked her down. But after the sheriff's visit, things got *really* strange."

Mr. Peterson takes out a stack of yellowed newspaper clippings. "There were many unsolved cases of missing children in Port Townsend in the 1940s and 50s. There was no evidence linking Emily Thornburn to them, but of course the townspeople had their own ideas. There was one day when many of them gathered outside the house to demand answers, but nothing came of it. To this day, those cases remain unsolved."

Mr. Peterson pauses with a distant look in his eyes. We stand in silence for longer than feels comfortable. I clear my throat. He comes back from wherever he was and sighs. There's a distinct change in his demeanor. When we started, he seemed excited to talk about the house, but now he's quiet and withdrawn. "Well, boys, this has been fun, but I should get back to work."

"Thanks, Mr. Peterson," I say. "Mind if we look through the rest of this box?"

He nods absentmindedly, his thoughts obviously elsewhere. "Sure. Just leave it here when you're done." Mr. Peterson waves goodbye and heads back upstairs.

Hugo and I spend a few minutes searching through the remaining contents, finding articles about the missing nanny, Emily's death in 1959, and the unsolved cases of the missing children. There are even some highly speculative articles about the nanny's lover, saying he was a local fisherman who called off the relationship out of guilt after Mr. Thornburn's presumed murder.

Another photo of Emily catches my eye. She's wearing the same white dress as in the first picture, but in this photo, she has a terrible scowl, fists clenched, and eyes shooting daggers.

"She was a real Dr. Jekyll and Mr. Hyde, I guess," I say as I take a picture of the photo.

"I bet that explains why Chloe senses both good and bad in the house. There was something wrong with Emily's mind." Hugo's brow wrinkles, and he frowns. "Kinda sad, really."

"Emily is certainly a tragic figure." I sigh. "Let's get outta here. This place gives me the creeps."

On the way home, we cut through the forest again. The mid-September days are getting shorter, and the air has a touch of chill. Dappled light through the trees casts long shadows on our path.

Hugo's hiking ahead of me, trying to find his way back. I've corrected him only once. Not bad for his second time through the mazelike trails of the forest. He stops at each fork in the path, pauses for a moment, and then chooses without looking back. He exudes confidence, but not in an arrogant way. He's just good at everything he does without making a big deal of it.

"Hey, Hugo," I call. "I'm not sure I properly thanked you for your help with Bryce last Monday."

Hugo sighs. "I hate fighting, but sometimes it's the only choice with people like that. Plus, that asshole had it coming. But I hope I didn't make things worse for you."

"Since I came out years ago, Bryce has never missed an opportunity to make a homophobic remark every time he sees me. But he hasn't made a peep since Monday."

Hugo cracks a smile. "Glad to hear it. Let me know if you have any more problems with him."

I smile back. "Thanks! I will."

My phone buzzes.

Abby: Chloe wants to meet at the house in an hour. She talked to her aunt

Cameron: Cool

Abby: Matty found out and wants in too

Cameron: Of course [eye roll emoji] I'll check with Hugo

Abby: And Taylor

I laugh out loud, and Hugo stares at me.

"How do you feel about inviting half the theater tech class over?" I ask.

Hugo's laugh has a touch of nervousness. "As long as Pa doesn't find out, the more the merrier."

We have time to kill when we get back, so we stand outside the ominous house, staring at the imposing structure. Several uneasy minutes pass without a word between us. The wind blows through the trees, making the leaves flutter. A whistling sound comes from the porch, an eerie chorus.

"I hate that damn house," I say, glaring at its decaying walls. "But I'm also dying to know what's at the top of the spiral staircase."

"Me too," Hugo says. "We'll be okay if we go in together."

I doubt it, but all I say is "Okay." Another dumb thing I'm going to do to impress a cute guy.

We both take a deep breath and head through the front door. The same oppressiveness as before envelops me, but this time it's mixed with a strange undercurrent of excitement.

You left me. Now I have you. Those same words echo in my mind again, but this time I'm 95 percent sure I imagined them.

Hugo heads upstairs, and I follow. We hover near the entrance to the bathroom, neither of us willing to be the first one to go in. A nervous laugh escapes my lips. "Let's do this."

Hugo nods, and we both head in, bumping shoulders, then climb through the hole into the secret room. The afternoon sun shines through the window, extending the shadows and making the room appear even more ominous than it did earlier. We size up the spiral staircase with the hammer and crowbar in hand.

"Well, here goes nothing," Hugo says as he climbs the stairs and wedges the crowbar into a seam between the ceiling and the wood. I squish in next to him and shove the hammer claw into the other side.

"Pry the wood on three," Hugo says. "Ready? One, two, *three!*"

The timbers creak and groan, sending bits of wood shrapnel spraying down, covering us in splinters. On the third try, the nails release, and the wood comes crashing down, clattering onto the spiral staircase and falling to the ground, missing my head by an inch. Above us, the staircase ascends into darkness.

A blast of stale air shoots out of the hole, carrying the smell of something else—the sickeningly sweet scent of decay.

14

A Circle of Friends: Hugo

"Oh, that's awful!" Cameron retches, coughing out the words. "Smells like something died up there."

I hold back a dry heave. "Let's hope we didn't just find the missing nanny."

"The nanny!" Cameron's eyes go wide. "Oh god, I didn't even think about that!"

"Should we keep going?" I ask.

"We've come this far. Let's finish the job."

We ascend the staircase, me in front, cellphone flashlight in hand. My heart pounds harder with every step.

At the top is a room filled with antique furniture, but less childlike than the room below. A window, half obscured by vines, provides dim light, revealing a twin bed in the corner covered with a molding quilt. Next to it is a vanity filled with old combs, brushes, and glass bottles. Cracks radiate from the middle of the mirror, making a fun house effect, a dozen broken images reflecting back at me.

"I think this might actually be the nanny's room," Cameron says, inspecting the furniture.

"Makes sense that her room connected to Emily's room," I add. "But why would he board up the room?"

"Mr. P said Mr. Thornburn was ashamed of Emily. He must have boarded up the entrance to Emily's room, trying to hide her away. That was one messed up guy."

As we continuing to explore, the beam of my flashlight hits the wall across from the bed, revealing hundreds of hash marks scratched into the plaster wall.

"What the heck is this?" I say. The marks are neatly arranged in in rows and columns. The sheer number of them, all painstakingly carved, is startling. This could only be the product of an obsessive mind.

"Wow," Cameron says, inspecting the marks and doing quick math on his fingers. "Each row has twelve sections, and there are about thirty marks in each. Somebody was counting the days in a year."

"Fifteen full rows and a partial row on the bottom." I tap my finger on the hash marks in the last row, counting them. "Fifteen years, three months, and ten days."

"You know who makes hash marks on walls?" Cameron asks, then answers his own question. "A prisoner."

"The nanny went missing," I add. "Do you think maybe Emily held her against her will?"

"I guess the whole family was messed up," Cameron says, but then his nose wrinkles. "Wow, it stinks in here. I really hope we don't find the nanny someplace." He plugs his nose.

I continue to scan the room with my flashlight, then find the source of the smell.

"Well, it's not the dead nanny," I say as I point the beam at a dark corner. "But those rats have seen better days." Piled up in the corner is a nest holding countless dead rats in various states of decay.

"Oh, nasty!" Cameron frowns as he inspects the carnage. "They didn't die too long ago. I wonder what happened here?"

"That's one mystery I think I can solve," I say. "When I first saw the shadow of the old lady, I lied to Pa and said we had rats. He called an exterminator. Looks like it wasn't a lie after all. They must have eaten rat poison and crawled back to their nest."

"Hey, here's the door," Cameron says, heading toward it. "Look! There's a key in the lock!"

"This is the locked door on the third floor. Interesting that it's locked from the *inside*."

Cameron turns the key, and the locking mechanism clicks. He opens the door, walks into the hallway, and then stops, staring at the floor with a strange expression I can't quite read—he almost snarls. He's hovering over the patch job where Pa fixed the sawed-out hole in the floorboards.

"You okay?" I ask, stopping beside him.

"Yeah." Cameron sighs. "Went somewhere else for a moment."

With two sets of thick rubber gloves Pa and I use for demolition work, we throw the dead rats into a black plastic bag. Not how I imagined spending my Saturday, but I'm doing it with Cameron, so I'm not complaining too much. He keeps making rat puns and *Ratatouille* references, cracking me up. Somehow he makes cleaning up decomposing rodents funny.

"When we're done, this place will be squeaky clean," Cameron says with a big silly grin. Okay, so the puns aren't all winners, but I laugh anyway just to see him smile.

With the help of the crowbar, we open the window to try and get rid of the rancid smell of decay. In no time, it has gone from a horrible rat murder room to a slightly less horrible creepy nanny's room. Small wins.

"The good news is, we don't have to climb in and out of the hole in the bathroom anymore," I say with a smile.

"Way to look on the bright side of having two spooky hidden rooms in your house." Cameron laughs.

***

"This place is huge," Matty says, looking around the foyer as Abby and Taylor follow him through the front door. "And spooky. We could throw an awesome Halloween party here."

Matty spins around, like he's already planning where the punch bowl will go. My stomach churns, imagining a hundred drunk teenagers trashing the place. Another item on the long list of things Pa would kill me for.

Cameron cuts in. "Let's start with introductions before we plan any parties. Matty, have you met Hugo?"

"Hey, how's it going, Hugo? I've seen you in theater tech, but nice to meet you for real."

"Same." I nod.

"And you know Taylor, of course," Cameron says.

"Hey again." Taylor waves, and I wave back.

Cameron peeks out the front door. "Where're Chloe and Maya?"

"They're on their way," Abby says. "Chloe said something about having to prepare."

"Prepare?" I ask, hit with visions of a séance and a Ouija board and us holding hands around a table with a bunch of candles, asking spirits to communicate with us. This better not be a mistake.

"Chloe asked her aunt for advice," Abby clarifies.

"Advice about what?"

"I'm not exactly sure. Something about calming the spirits. Chloe wants to talk to you about it before she does anything."

I'm still skeptical about Chloe's abilities, but everybody's impressed with her, and I have no reason to doubt her other than my general lack of belief in spirit stuff. Still, the things that have already happened in the house are hard to deny, so I'm keeping an open mind. "If Chloe can figure out how to help, I'm all for it."

"You find any EVPs?" Cameron asks, glancing at the digital recorder in Abby's hands.

"No." Abby scowls. "At first I thought I heard one, but then I realized it was you squeaking."

"Hey!" Cameron whacks Abby on the shoulder with a playful smile. "I don't squeak."

"You totally squeak," Abby says.

Cameron turns to Taylor and Matty for backup. "I don't squeak, right?"

"Sorry, dude. I've heard you squeak many times," Matty says. "But it's kinda cute."

Matty's right. It's totally cute when Cameron squeaks, and I fight a smile.

"I'm staying out of this," Taylor says, putting their hands up and backing away. Cameron scoffs, cheeks turning a subtle shade of pink. He's so easily flustered in the most adorable way, which makes me want to tease him more just to see him squirm. But I'm not that mean. Well, sometimes I am.

The doorbell rings.

"Saved by the bell," Cameron says, side-eyeing Taylor.

Everyone greets Chloe and Maya. It's quite the group. Looks like Matty is getting his party after all. Good thing Pa is gone until Sunday. If he showed up right now, I'd be so grounded. Probably. Hard to say, actually. I've never had this many friends, so this is unfamiliar territory.

Abby takes charge and ushers us all into the living room. "We need to debrief. Is it okay if we sit in here, Hugo?"

"Be my guest."

The living room is one of the few that Pa and I have furnished. A sofa and love seat are arranged near the TV. We don't have a lot of stuff, but being comfortable while watching our shows is high on the priority list.

Abby stands in front of the TV, waiting with her hands behind her back, looking every bit the leader of this friend group. "Everybody take a seat, please," she says.

Maya sits on the love seat and holds out an arm to Chloe, who snuggles in next to her. They make a cute couple and look so comfortable around each other. It's something I've seen little of, and it gives me a glowing feeling.

Matty takes one end of the sofa, and Taylor flops down beside him. It's clear the two of them are close friends. Cameron sits on the other end of the sofa, leaving enough space for me, but it's a tight fit. If I squeeze in, half my body will press against him.

A tug hooks in my chest, but then the usual inhibitions come crashing down on me—this fear of making connections only to have them ripped away when we inevitably move. Turning off my feelings is much simpler than getting my hopes up and having them stomped on. It never gets easier.

I start toward the kitchen to get a chair to sit on, but Cameron sends a bashful glance my way, and my heart melts. He's watching me, nervous and half expectant.

Screw it.

I shove all the inhibitions to the back of my mind and plop down right next to him, not caring that our legs and arms rub against each other. I even lean into it a bit. The warmth radiating from him sends waves of electricity running through me. He's got the cutest shy smile, and I smile back.

Abby appears pleased as she addresses the group. "Okay, everybody. Let's each give a quick update. On the EVP front: total bust. No unusual sounds on our digital recorder." She paces back and forth, eyes moving from person to person. "Cameron and Hugo, can you give us an update on what you found at the library?"

Cameron tells the group about the plans we found and all the history we learned from Mr. Peterson, including the details of Emily Thornburn's tragic life, her father's possible suicide or murder, the nanny's lover, her disappearance, and all the missing children. Everything he says is factual, but he has this ability to make a story sound exciting, like we're watching a movie. He really has a gift. The news is met with *ooh*s and *aah*s from the entire group. When he mentions Emily's split personality, Chloe listens with particular interest.

"That lines up with the things I was feeling," she says. "The hot and cold, the prickly and soft. I feel both sides of her. It's like she's at war with herself, but in a strange way, the sides balance each other out."

Abby nods. "Chloe, have you sensed the nanny at all?"

"Not that I've been able to detect."

"Speaking of the nanny, Hugo and I opened up the spiral staircase," Cameron says. "Oh, but Hugo, it's your house. You should tell them."

"No, you go ahead," I say as everyone looks at me with anticipation. "You'll tell it better."

Cameron is a *much* better storyteller than I am, filling his account with dramatic flourishes. I smile as he recounts how we opened the staircase, smelled the dead rats, and found the nanny's room, the hash marks on the wall, and the missing key.

"So, you think that Mr. Thornburn boarded up his daughter's room and locked her away?" Taylor asks.

Cameron nods. "That's how it looks. The only way to get in there is through the nanny's room and down the spiral staircase."

"Or through the hole in the bathroom wall," Maya adds. "So glad we don't have to do that anymore. You have any idea how hard it is to climb through in a skirt?"

"And those hash marks make it sound like Emily also held the nanny captive," Abby says.

"That's our best guess," Cameron replies.

"That leaves us with you." Abby's gaze descends on Chloe. "What did you find out from your aunt?"

"I told her everything I felt. She said split personalities are extremely complex and rare. If the spirit is in harmony, it's better to leave it alone.

But if the spirit is manifesting in disruptive ways, then something has thrown it out of balance. Something external has disturbed it." Chloe's gaze bores into Cameron and me. I'm not sure what she's expecting.

"How do we find out what's disturbing it?" I ask.

"Just the fact that you and your father moved in could be part of the disturbance," Chloe says. "But I think there's more to it. Something deeper."

Something deeper? I don't like the sound of that. I'm in deep enough. "How do you know?"

"Well, I don't *know*, exactly." Chloe glances upward and around the room as if searching for something invisible. "I felt it in my dream. None of this is scientific, I'm afraid."

"So, what can we do to calm the spirit?" Taylor asks, appearing fascinated by the whole situation. I suspect they would feel different if they had experienced the White Lady themself.

"Do we need a sacrifice?" Matty asks, laughing.

Chloe cuts in. "You shouldn't even joke about that, Matty."

"Sorry." He stares at his feet. "I'll shut up now."

"But," Chloe continues, "you aren't completely off base. I talked to my aunt about this. She gave me some things to try tonight. If things don't improve, she says she's willing to help. We might have to find out what's binding the spirit here in order to free it. But that can take time. First we need to understand the spirit better."

"We'll have to wait for another time when my dad is away," I say. "He can't get a whiff of any of this or he'll flip out. I'm begging all of you, please keep this stuff a secret. Don't tell my pop. Don't tell your parents. Don't tell anybody at school. If he finds out, I'm screwed."

Everybody nods and promises not to say anything. Trusting them is all I can do at this point, but I'm so far beyond my comfort zone already. My stomach is a viper's nest of nerves.

I turn to Chloe. "What do we need to do?"

We all head to the third floor and enter the nanny's bedroom. Expressions of half-wonder and half-horror spread over everyone's faces. We've entered a time capsule, everything as it was sixty years ago, with the addition of a thick layer of dust and mold. The cleaning Cameron and I did has helped, but the sickening stench of dead rats still lingers.

Taylor takes one look at the hash marks on the wall, bobs their head for a few seconds, and then says with utter certainty, "Five thousand, five hundred and sixty-eight hash marks. Or fifteen years, three months, and ten days."

"Wow!" I say. "How the heck did you do that?"

Taylor shrugs. "I've always been fast at math."

"You should see them play poker," Matty says, smirking. "I can't wait until we turn twenty-one and can go to casinos."

Abby glares at us. "Hey, everybody, keep it down. Chloe's trying to concentrate."

"Sorry!" Matty cringes.

Chloe walks around the room, taking in everything, her face expressionless. She pauses at the vanity, walks by the wall with the hash marks, and then stands motionless by the bed, saying nothing.

After more than a minute of total quiet, Abby speaks. "Do you sense anything?"

Chloe rests her hand on the mattress. "There's something here. Prickly."

"Let's check it out," Abby says.

Chloe steps aside as Abby tries lifting the delicate quilt, but it crumbles in her hands, kicking up a small cloud of dust. Beneath the tattered remains are dingy sheets and a mattress, but nothing else.

"Nothing," Abby says with tight lips, but then her eyes light up. "Hang on a sec."

She runs her hand between the mattress and the box spring, and her eyes go wide as she pulls out a yellowed envelope. "Jackpot."

Scrawled on the outside, barely legible in faded ink, are the words *Dearest Agnes.*

"Love letter?" Cameron asks.

"Let's see," she says, setting the letter down on the bed and taking a picture with her phone. Taking great care, she opens the flap, which makes soft cracking noises like the crunching of dry fall leaves, as if age drained all the moisture out of the paper long ago.

"Careful," Cameron warns, hovering over Abby.

She glares at him.

"Sorry," he says, backing off.

With the hands of a surgeon, Abby extracts an ancient piece of paper from the envelope. Opening the single fold, she reveals a whole page of the same flowing script as on the envelope, but darker and more legible, protected from the elements.

After taking another photo, Abby reads the letter out loud.

April 14, 1890

Agnes,
It is with a heavy heart that I must end our courtship. The
girl's actions are inexcusable, and our inaction makes us
equally accountable. I cannot bear to see her again. It will
only remind me of that horrible night. I will try to find for-
giveness in my heart and make peace with what happened.
I recommend you do too.

Luke

Several drops of liquid, long dried, have smudged and streaked the ink.

"Well, we have a first name for Agnes's lover now," Abby says. "Another piece of the puzzle."

"What did he mean by *the girl's actions*?" Cameron asks.

"The death of Charles Thornburn, I bet," Abby says. "Maybe it wasn't a suicide after all and one of Emily's famous tantrums led to an accident."

"Or perhaps it wasn't an accident," Chloe says, just above a whisper.

The room is quiet as a tomb as the weight of Chloe's words descends on us. The air is oppressive and stifling, and the dappled light through the vine-covered window dims.

"This place gives me the creeps," Matty blurts, shattering the silence.

Abby scowls at Matty, then turns to Chloe. "Do you sense anything else?"

"Nothing more in here."

One by one, we descend the spiral staircase until we're all in Emily's room.

"I know I said the last room was creepy, but that was before I saw this one," Matty says with nervous laughter. "Creepy little girl's room with old moldy toys? No thank you."

"Don't forget the boarded-up door and the hole behind the medicine cabinet," Cameron adds.

Abby rolls her eyes. "Chloe, what can we do to help?"

"I assisted my aunt with calming a spirit a few months ago," Chloe says, reading notes from her phone. "She said spirits feed off the energy of the people around them. So we need to project calm and comfort. Let Emily's spirit know we mean no harm."

"Do we need to burn sage or anything?" Taylor asks.

"Other than making it smell nice, that wouldn't do much." Chloe laughs. "Let's all sit in the middle of the room in a circle."

Chloe sits down, legs crossed, palms resting on her knees. Everyone copies her, forming a circle. Cameron sits down next to me, and there's a little flutter in my insides. I scoffed at the idea of holding hands earlier, but now it doesn't sound so bad.

Like she is reading my mind, Abby asks, "Should we hold hands?"

"If you want," Chloe replies. "What's most important is that we're comfortable."

"Let's do it," Cameron blurts, peeking at me and then turning away fast. I fight back a smile.

Everyone joins hands. I grab Taylor's hand on my left and Cameron's on my right.

"Okay, everyone," Chloe says in a soothing voice. "Close your eyes and clear your mind. Breathe slow and deep." She pauses for a moment, then continues. "Push out unwanted thoughts. Picture a place where you've been happy. Think about what it looks like. Think about the smells. Think about the sounds. Think about how it makes you feel."

I search my mind for such a place, but Cameron's warm grasp captures all my attention. His palm is soft and smooth. His grip is firm enough that I can feel his strength, but not too tight. I squeeze his hand, and he squeezes back. Such a simple gesture, but it fills me with a little glow. Perhaps *this* is my happy place, holding Cameron's hand.

Chloe continues in a deep monotone, "If you've found your place, let your whole mind think of nothing but how you feel there. Let all other thoughts drop away."

I clear my mind and think only of Cameron and me together, holding hands, smiling, being happy in each other's company. The feeling of someone you like liking you back is such a fundamental thing for many people, but it's one that has eluded me for much of my life. Cameron squeezes my hand again like he's telling me he's also feeling it. A warmth I've never felt spreads through my chest. I don't want this moment to end.

A pleasant scent hits my nose. I'm so deep in my happy place that I think it must be my imagination—the unmistakable scent of cookies.

"Do you all smell that?" Matty blurts, shattering my bubble. I blink my eyes open. Everyone's slowly coming out of their happy places, sniffing and glancing around.

"I totally smell cookies," Taylor says, and everybody else chimes in, saying they do too and nodding.

Cameron and I trade knowing looks. We've both smelled this, but having everyone else experience it is validating in a way that's hard to describe. It means I'm not delusional. Either that or we are all delusional and having a group hallucination.

"This is what you two smelled before, right?" Abby says, glancing between Cameron and me.

We both say yes.

"I just totally got goose bumps," Matty says. "You're telling me that's not a real smell?"

"I swear I'm not making cookies," I tell Matty. "And there's nobody else in the house."

"So, what, that's a ghost smell?"

Chloe nods. "Spirits can manifest in many ways. Sometimes you can see them, sometimes they make a sound, and in this case, it's a smell. In other words, yes, it's a spirit manifestation. Or a ghost smell, if you'd prefer, Matty."

"I'm not sure I'd *prefer* anything," Matty says, eyes wide. "This whole thing is freaking me out."

"Something about cookies must be significant to the history of this house," Chloe says.

"Is this a good sign?" Abby asks. "It's a good smell, so does that mean our positive thoughts are working?"

Chloe's expression is complex. "I'm not sure. The goal is to calm the spirit and have the manifestations go away. But that isn't what happened, good smell or not."

The cookie smell morphs from pleasant to acrid in a matter of seconds, and the group collectively groans. The memories of my nightmare in the library rush back.

"Well, that can't be good," Abby says. "Now what?"

Chloe glances at the notes on her phone. "I guess we can try again but be more forceful—"

Crack!

I shout in surprise, and the group lets out a chorus of yells and screams.

"What the heck was that?" Matty screeches.

"Look!" Taylor says, pointing to the floor at the bottom of the spiral staircase.

Abby shines a flashlight at the spot. Hairline cracks spread from the center in a circular pattern, like pie wedges.

"Good eye, Taylor," Abby says.

Taylor smiles, blushing a bit.

My anxiety ratchets up at the sight of the cracks in the floor. "Crap. I hope we aren't ruining the house," I say. I'm still hoping to keep all of this a secret from Pa.

"Hang on a sec," Abby says as she consults her phone. "I was looking at those floor plans you sent over, Cameron. Here, check out the plans for the second floor, first floor, and basement. What do you see?"

Cameron and I crowd around her phone as she swipes between the three photos.

"Holy shit!" I say. "There's a room in the basement that lines up with this one. And what's that space on the first floor?"

"At first, I thought it was the coat closet off the foyer," says Abby. "But the coat closet is on the other side. Right, Hugo?"

"Yep."

Cameron's eyes go wide. "Steps. These cracks look like steps retracted into the floor. It looks like they open."

"Exactly," Abby says as her lips curve into a smile.

"You mean the spiral staircase goes down as well?" I say.

Abby nods. "There must be a switch around somewhere to activate it. Help me search, everybody."

Everyone walks around, scouring the room with their phone flashlights, looking beneath moldy toys, searching the walls for seams, and scanning the baseboards.

"Hey, come check this out," Matty calls, standing next to one of the old brass wall sconces beside the window. "This thing moves."

He pulls the sconce out of the wall until it clicks, then glances between it and the staircase, excited for something to happen.

Nothing happens.

"Hmm," Matty says, hand on his chin, looking deflated. "I was sure that was going to work."

"Let me see that," I say. "I have a hunch."

A quick jiggle reveals the sconce turns on its axis in the wall. It won't go any farther clockwise, so I turn it counterclockwise. As I do, each little wedge of the floor descends at a different rate, creating steps headed down.

"It's working!" Matty screams right into my ear.

I keep spinning the sconce until it clicks and won't go any farther. Stale air wafts up from the now-revealed staircase leading to darkness. We stand in a circle around it, peering into the depths.

"This house is absurd," Abby says, shaking her head as she heads toward the stairs without a moment's hesitation. "Let's go check it out."

I whisper to Cameron, "Is she afraid of anything?"

"Nope," Cameron says, shaking his head. "Literally nothing. Wait! Scorpions. She hates scorpions for some reason."

"Then let's hope there are no scorpions down there."

15

The Crow: Cameron

I follow Hugo, who's on Abby's tail, the rest of our friends right behind us. The staircase descends into a long, narrow channel leading through the first floor. The walls butt up against the railing on all sides. Abby swipes at years of cobwebs as she leads us into the darkness, her phone flashlight providing the slightest illumination. We descend until we hit the concrete floor of the basement.

We've entered a room that reminds me of a dungeon from a fantasy movie. A rough wooden table rests against one wall, various metal tools and clay jars scattered across it. A reinforced iron door with large rivets dominates the far wall, with a simple iron bar for a handle and an old-fashioned keyhole. A makeshift burlap mattress stuffed with rotten straw sits in the corner, and there are iron chains attached to the walls, ending in manacles. Etched into the wall are thousands of hash marks, covering nearly every square inch.

"What the hell am I looking at?" Hugo asks, shaking his head.

"Torture chamber?" Matty says.

"More like a prison cell," Abby says. "Emily had a split personality. This must be where they put her when she was bad."

"Those are like the hash marks we saw in the nanny's room, but there are way more," I say. "Maybe this *was* a prison."

My whole life, this house has radiated sorrow, and this seems to be its epicenter. It's no wonder Emily's soul is so tortured after enduring such a life, being caged like an animal for years. The house reflects her loneliness tenfold.

"Do you sense anything, Chloe?" Abby asks.

"The same things I've sensed before, only more so. Hot and cold. Prickly and soft," Chloe says.

"Eighteen thousand and eighty-seven," Taylor says after examining the hash marks for an absurdly short amount of time. "Or forty-nine years, six months, and eight days."

My jaw drops. Who knew they were so talented at math. "Taylor, you're amazing," I say. Taylor just smiles.

Abby takes notes on her phone. "Okay, some of these numbers are making sense."

"They are?" Hugo and I say in unison, glance at each other, and smile.

"Yep. What if..." Abby pauses, making sure she has everyone's attention. "Now, hear me out. Emily was born in 1880. Her dad died under mysterious circumstances ten years later. After his death, nobody saw the nanny's lover, Luke, again. And the letter explains why."

Cameron cuts in. "You think Emily had something to do with her dad's death and Luke couldn't handle the guilt?"

"Yep," Abby says, nodding. "Agnes was so distraught about losing Luke that she locked Emily up down here. Nobody saw Emily again for the next forty-nine years, until she appeared again in 1939. That lines up with the hash marks."

"Forty-nine years!" I say. "That's horrible. And the fifteen years of hash marks in the nanny's room?"

"Emily must have escaped. Perhaps she locked up the nanny as revenge."

"Kids started going missing in 1939," Hugo says, "right when the nanny disappeared. It must have been Emily."

Hugo's face contorts. Something about this is hitting him hard, and my heart aches. He's no stranger to loss and hard family situations. I put my hand on his back. "You okay?"

Hugo nods, meeting my eyes. "When it's a story, it's one thing. But seeing this room..."

Chloe stares at Hugo and me, her eyes shifting between us. Oh crap. That usually means she's about to drop a bomb.

"Chloe?" I ask, voice cracking. "What's going on?"

Chloe's eyes brighten. "I think I know what went wrong with the spirit calming."

"You do?" Abby asks.

Chloe's eyes bore into me. "Cameron, what was the safe space you imagined right before we smelled the cookies?"

I was thinking about how nice Hugo's hand was in mine, and to be honest, I imagined kissing him. But no way am I going to say that in front of Hugo and everybody. My face burns like the surface of the sun. "Umm..."

Chloe smiles and nods. "That's what I thought. Hugo, what were you thinking?"

"I...uh...I was imagining..." Hugo glances at me, then looks down fast. He wasn't imagining the same thing as me, right? How is that possible?

Chloe's eyes light up like she just solved a puzzle, and Abby smiles, shaking her head.

"I know how to fix it," Chloe says, marching toward the spiral staircase. "Everybody back upstairs—get into a circle."

We follow her instructions. Back in Emily's room, Hugo heads toward me, but Abby intercepts him and guides him to the opposite side of the circle. Well, that sucks.

"Right here, Chloe?" Abby asks.

"Perfect. Let's try it again," Chloe says. "This time, everyone put your hands on your knees and clear your mind. No good thoughts, no bad thoughts, nothing at all."

With my eyes closed, I try to clear my mind, but all these thoughts keep popping up. Who knew thinking of nothing would be so difficult? Holding Hugo's hand. The hidden room we just found. The cookie smell. It's all banging around in my head.

Chloe continues to talk, her deep soothing voice like butter. "Whenever a thought enters your mind, gently push it away. Breathe deep. In through your nose, out through your mouth."

I take a long breath and concentrate on the timbre of her words, fighting to block out everything else. Eventually the individual thoughts drift away like pillowy clouds. Thinking of nothing is oddly freeing. The world melts away with only Chloe's voice to guide me.

We sit in calm silence for a long time, save for the steady drone of Chloe's words. I'm no longer aware of the specific things she's saying. The words are lyrical, like a song in a long-forgotten language. Minutes pass, and nothing changes. Gradually, a weight lifts off my shoulders, and I feel distinctly lighter, like I could almost float off the ground. I had no idea what a heavy burden I was carrying until it was gone. Whatever force was holding me down has left, and I hope it never returns.

"Okay, everybody," Chloe says, her gentle words breaking through my bubble of soothing calmness. "Anchor to the sound of my voice and slowly return. When you're ready, open your eyes."

Bit by bit, I return to the land of consciousness and blink my eyes open. Everyone around me is doing the same, some with calm faces, some smiling.

"Wow, that was something," Taylor whispers.

"Yeah, I've never been so relaxed," Matty adds. "Chloe, you should do that for a living."

"Do you all feel it?" Abby asks. "The oppressiveness I've always felt in this house…it's gone."

A murmur of agreement comes from everybody.

"Chloe, do you think we did it?" I ask. "Did we fix the house?"

Chloe peers around the room, taking deep breaths. "We did something, that's for sure. The personalities are still there, but they feel…" She pauses to find the right word. "Smoother? More in balance. Calm."

"That's amazing!" I smile shyly at Hugo. "Do you feel it too?"

"Yeah!" He smiles back. "This house has never felt so peaceful."

Matty hops up, raising his hands over his head. "It's Saturday night! Let's celebrate!"

***

We all head downstairs with bubbly exuberance. The oppressiveness is gone, and it's strange. Living next to the house for my whole life, this low-grade dread has always churned inside me, and now that it has lifted, the difference is profound. It's like I've had an itch my entire life and I finally got to scratch it.

In the living room, the group chatters, excited by what we've done. I sneak over to Abby and whisper to her, "It seemed like you knew what was going on in there. Why did it work the second time? Why did you separate Hugo and me?"

"You just answered your own question." Abby laughs. "Chloe said you two and the house were connected. Something about your and Hugo's teenage hormones was messing with it."

"Mine *and* Hugo's?"

"Duh. I saw the way he was looking at you."

My heart speeds up. "Really?"

"For such a smart guy, you sure are dumb sometimes," Abby says, laughing. She nudges me toward him. "Go talk to him."

I gulp, swallowing my fear as I approach.

"Hey," I say to Hugo.

"Hey," he says back, smiling, but then his brow knots. He looks around at our group, which—let's be honest—can get a little rambunctious.

"You okay with all this?" I wave my hand vaguely at the group.

"It's fine." Hugo manages a smile. "Just not used to having so many friends."

"We can move to my house if you want."

He shakes his head. "Nah. Pa isn't due back until tomorrow. Might as well take advantage of it."

Hugo puts a couple of frozen pizzas into the oven and sets out a few two-liter bottles of soda. Several of us pile onto the couch and turn on the TV. Everyone agrees scary movies are off the table tonight, so we pick a superhero movie instead.

I take my spot on the couch from earlier today, hoping Hugo will sit next to me again. I'm not disappointed. He stands above me holding two paper plates.

"Pizza?" he asks, holding one out to me.

"Thanks." He got pizza for me. It's the smallest gesture, but it makes me glow. It means he was thinking of me.

He plops down next to me with his plate. We eat and watch the movie with our sides pressed against each other. My eyes are on the TV, but I'm not really watching—all my attention is focused on Hugo. The way his chest moves as he breathes. The way he laughs at the funny parts of the movie, heartfelt and genuine. The way he brushes his hair from his eyes. The way he licks his lips—so kissable. Thinking of anything else is impossible.

After I finish my pizza, Hugo takes my plate and drops it off in the kitchen. I'm not used to getting this kind of attention from a guy. I could get used to it. When he returns, he sets his hand right next to mine. Our pinkies touch, and my pulse speeds up.

Is Abby right? Is it possible he really likes me? My mind races at the thought.

On the next couch, Abby steals glances at us and smiles. Maybe this is for real. I lean into his shoulder. I don't want this moment to end.

But just as I'm getting comfortable, Hugo's arm shifts, and my shirt rides up, showing a slice of my midsection where my pants pinch into my belly. Confidence kryptonite. I pull my hand away and squirm to shift my shirt down before Hugo sees my ugly belly fat. For the rest of the movie, it's all I can think about. My stomach ties up in knots. Did he see it? Was he grossed out? God, I have to get rid of these love handles.

The credits roll, and people shuffle out of their seats.

Matty stands and stretches. "Well, I gotta head home. Curfew. But it's been fun. Thanks for the pizza, Hugo."

"No problem," Hugo says, getting up from his seat.

Despite being sick to my stomach for half the movie, I miss his warmth the moment he's gone.

"Yeah, me too," Taylor adds. "Gotta run home before the parental units freak out. It's almost ten."

Almost ten? Crap. I texted my family earlier that I was having dinner with friends, but I haven't checked in for a while. I try to wake up my phone, and the screen stays dark—dead battery. Double crap.

Everybody gets up, says goodbye, and heads to the door. I'm about to follow the crowd when Hugo puts a hand on my shoulder.

"Hey, Cameron," he says with a gentle smile. "You think you can stay for a bit? I want to reattach the medicine cabinet, and I could use a hand."

"Sure," I say before I think better of it. My dead phone glares at me. I ignore it.

"See ya later, Cam," Abby says, shooting me a barely perceptible wink. Or I might have imagined it.

"Bye, Abby. See you on Monday."

She heads out the door, leaving Hugo and me standing side by side in the foyer. He smiles with welcoming eyes. My face heats as I gaze at his soft lips.

Hugo puffs out a laugh and shakes his head as if he had considered something and thought against it. He grabs my hand and tugs. "C'mon. The sooner we get this done, the better I'll feel."

I half hope he's forgotten about the medicine cabinet and has other ideas, but to my disappointment, he grabs a drill and some screws, and we head upstairs to the bathroom.

He lifts the cabinet, places it back in the hole, and looks my way. "Can you hold this steady?"

"Sure."

I lean over the sink with a hand on each side of the cabinet, keeping it still. To my total shock, he ducks under my outstretched arm and slides in front of me, his back to my front, pressed against me. His body is solid muscle, and his cute butt pushes right into me. I can't take much more of this without something super embarrassing happening. Blood heads south, and I force my brain to think of anything else. I think of my grandma. I think of school. I think of dental work. Anything but his hard body pressed against mine. But I fail miserably.

"Hold it steady," Hugo says.

"I'm trying." I gulp.

Hugo places each screw in the cabinet, and with a few quick whirs of the drill, they sink in tight. In only a few seconds, the cabinet is secure.

"Okay, you can let go," Hugo says.

I pull away, and not a moment too soon. I race to adjust my pants before Hugo turns around. God, I hope he didn't see that.

"Thanks," Hugo says with a gentle smile, apparently unaware of how that moment made me melt into the floor.

"No problem," I say with a squeak. God, I *do* squeak. Why hasn't anyone ever told me I squeak?

We leave the bathroom and head into the hallway outside his bedroom door, pausing a beat as we look at each other. Direct eye contact still makes me wilt like a flower in the hot sun, but I pour every ounce of courage I have into not turning away. A lock of Hugo's wavy dark hair falls in front of his eyes. He brushes it back.

"So," he says.

"So," I echo. I don't want this night to be over. I don't want to leave yet, even though I'm pushing it with my family and my dead phone. I peek into the bedroom to the left, where a bed with wrinkled sheets and a bedspread that's hanging half off catches my eye. "Is that your room?"

"Oh, yeah. Um—" Hugo says, startled. "I don't usually have people over. It's kind of a mess."

"Seems only fair, since you've seen my room," I tease. "You've even slept over."

"That was a special circumstance," Hugo says, but it's clear from his tone that he's joking.

I give him my best sad face, perfected from years of trying to finagle what I want from my parents. It never fails.

"I guess it's okay." He laughs, shaking his head, then heads to his room.

I follow him, victorious. Works every time.

Hugo stands with his hands in his pockets, eyes shifting around his room. The room is lived in but not *too* messy. Mine's been way worse. A queen-size bed with brown sheets and a dark blue comforter sits against the far wall. The jumble of sheets and bedspreads is surprisingly intimate, and I imagine Hugo tangled in it. I imagine myself and Hugo tangled together, which causes the same physical reaction that happened in the bathroom. My eyes dart around the room for something to distract me.

Art supplies cover a large desk in the far corner, tubes of paint, brushes, and half-painted canvases spread across it in an ordered chaos. A canvas sits on an easel in front of the window. On it is a half-painted picture of an oak tree in an Impressionistic style using broad strokes and bright colors. Streaks of light shine through the limbs, bringing the tree to life in a way I've never seen. It's stunning.

"You're a fantastic artist," I say. "The backdrops you're painting in theater tech are great, but this is amazing."

"Thanks." Hugo glances down at his feet. "It's okay. I still have a lot of work to do before it's finished."

Hugo is too modest. He's really talented, and I'm not just saying that because I like him. He's better than any other kid in all the art classes I've taken.

"Honestly, it's incredible," I say. "I've been staring at that tree for most of my life, and I've never seen it so alive."

"How about you?" Hugo says, seeming eager to change the subject. "Got any hobbies?"

"I like to write. Short stories, for the most part. Urban fantasy with gay characters." I laugh.

Hugo's eyes light up. "Cool! I'd love to read some."

"No way! I never let people read my stuff."

"Hey, you saw my paintings," Hugo says. "It's only fair."

"It's not going to happen."

Hugo makes a pouty face. It's adorable, and it forces a smile out of me. I guess he's perfected his own sad face. Most people don't care about my writing, so his interest is a little startling.

"I'll be nice," Hugo says. "Honest."

"Perhaps. But probably not."

"That's better than a no." Hugo's got this ridiculous grin, and a laugh escapes my lips. He joins in. It must be contagious, cause now both of us are laughing at nothing.

After our giggles die down, we both stand there with comfortable smiles. This is the longest I've been able to face him without blushing furiously and averting my eyes. I'm starting to like Hugo. Like, a lot.

The sharp sound of glass shattering nearby cuts through the silence, snapping us back to reality.

"What the heck was that?" I shout.

"Oh crap!" Hugo's eyes widen. "Was that the medicine cabinet falling?"

He races to the bathroom with me on his heels, but the medicine cabinet is intact above the sink, right where we put it.

"Huh," Hugo says with his hands on his hips.

I scan the room. "If it wasn't that, what made that—"

"Shh!" Hugo's index finger is over his mouth. A faint noise comes from beyond the medicine cabinet. We both stand in total silence, straining our ears. There it is again—a rustling and the scraping sound of broken glass.

"In there," Hugo whispers, pointing to the hidden room.

A creeping dread spreads over me as the noises continue. We got a couple hours of calm, and now this damn house is already back to casting its nasty spell on me.

We both head upstairs toward the nanny's room. Hugo moves with care, and I stay behind him, trying hard not to seem too afraid. But in reality, I'm terrified as I revert to my twelve-year-old self—scared, trapped, and alone. We pass by the very spot where the house nearly bit my leg off, and I shudder. My eyes dart around, half expecting to see the shadow that circled me, but the hallway is empty.

Hugo guides us with his phone flashlight. With the sun down, the nanny's room is pitch black. We pause for a moment to listen.

"Down there," Hugo says, pointing to the spiral staircase descending into darkness.

Hugo continues to lead, flashlight in hand, descending each step at a slow and deliberate pace. At the bottom, we're met with a grizzly sight. A crow flaps its wings, tangled in the vines outside the window. But the window has smashed into long, nasty shards, and the crow has ugly red gashes dripping with blood. It flails around, trying to break free, but that only cuts it up more. Rivulets of blood streak down the razor-sharp glass.

"Oh god!" I shudder. "That's horrible!"

I head to the window to free the bird, but Hugo puts out a hand to stop me. "Don't go near it! Those shards could cut you to pieces."

A protest is on my lips, but I stop. He's right, of course. I nod and turn away. "I can't watch. How did that happen?"

"Looks like it got stuck in the vines and smashed the window with its beak in a panic."

We both keep our eyes turned away from the gruesome sight, and the fluttering sounds diminish until only silence remains. But the image of the crow is seared into my mind.

The crow. All the blood. I struggled to free myself from the rotten floorboard, but each pull made the wood tear deeper into my skin, and a thick red river flowed onto the floor. The stabbing pain. My heart raced, and I fought waves of panic as the crow attacked, pecking at my face and drawing yet more blood. My eyes! Stay away from my eyes!

The memories cascade through my mind like it happened yesterday.

Hugo watches with tenderness as a tear streaks down my cheek. I wipe it away with a quick flick of my wrist.

"There's nothing we could have done to help it," he whispers.

"I know." Another tear escapes, and I puff out a sad laugh. "I have no idea why I'm tearing up. It's just a stupid bird."

But I do know. These childhood memories dredging up. This bird was trapped, bleeding to death. *I'm* trapped too. Forced to prove myself to my dad and jump through his circus hoops. Forced to always act happy on the outside while my doubts and fears eat me alive from the inside.

Forced to live in a body I hate. Forced to deal with bullies at school because I choose to express who I am. My whole life has been nothing but one obstacle after another.

And now this stupid house is back in my life, all mixed up with my feelings for Hugo. He's been nice today, but I'm simply the first available guy he's met. He'll ditch me once he finds out what a loser I am or finds another cuter, thinner guy. It's all too much, and this bird has put me over the edge.

"It's okay," Hugo says, his voice soft. "I mean, that was horrific. It's understandable that you're upset." He puts his hand on my shoulder in the gentlest way.

That act of kindness overwhelms me, and without thinking, I wrap my arms around him, bury my face in his shoulder, and let out a sob. Hugo stiffens in my grasp at first, but then he relaxes and returns my hug.

"Hey, it's okay," he says, rubbing my back. "Shh."

"I'm sorry," I choke out with my mouth buried in his shirt. "I don't know what's gotten into me."

"I don't mind," Hugo says. "But is everything okay? Is it more than the bird?"

"Yeah." With my hands still resting on his waist, I pull away but look down to avoid his gaze. "This house. My dad. School. It's all just a lot."

"You want to talk about it?"

"Not really."

Hugo lifts my chin and peers into my eyes. In his gaze is tenderness and understanding, but also something else—the slightest sparkle. My sadness melts away, and I'm overtaken by the urge to kiss him.

"Cameron?" Hugo whispers.

"Yes?"

The bird thrashes in a last gasp of life, snapping the glass shards holding it captive with a piercing crack. It flaps its shredded wings, falling to the ground in a bloody heap feet away. Hugo and I pull apart, horrified.

This is the moment Chloe dreamed about—Hugo and me hugging and crying. Did I do what I did because of that suggestion alone, stuck in my subconscious mind and waiting to bloom into a self-fulfilling prophecy? My heart sinks. I pushed Hugo into this awkward situation, and the bird saved him. He isn't interested in me. I'm fooling myself, like I was with Noah.

The doorbell rings, loud and jarring.

We both let out a sharp laugh—a release of tension, not because anything is funny.

"Who the heck could that be at this hour?" Hugo barks.

"I bet one of the gang forgot something. My phone is dead," I say. "We better go answer it."

Hugo stares at the floor. "Yeah. We better."

16
Life Goes On: Hugo

I race up the spiral staircase and down two flights of steps with Cameron right on my heels. The doorbell rings again.

"Coming!" I yell.

Cameron and I were seconds away from kissing, and that fucking bird ruined it. What was I thinking anyway, taking advantage of Cameron in his vulnerable state? Did he want to kiss me too, or was he simply swept up in emotions?

Not to mention this damn house. The calm that has descended over it is real, but how long will it last? Maybe it's over already, what with that bird's horrific death. Can I afford to get attached to Cameron given that we'll move away as soon as Pa finds out about any of this? I should know better. It always ends the same, so why even bother?

The doorbell rings a third time as we descend the last flight of stairs and head to the foyer.

"Dang it! We're coming!" I shout.

I swing the door open fast, startling the guy standing outside. He looks a lot like Cameron. A bit older, a bit taller, wearing a letterman jacket, but undeniably related. He could be a brother—he's got those same wonderful eyes.

"Cameron, there you are." The guy peeks past me into the house.

"Jack!" Cameron says in shock. "How did you find me?"

"We tried calling and texting a bunch of times, and you didn't answer. I texted Abby, and she told me where you were. Why didn't you text back? Mom and Dad are pissed."

"My phone died."

"Well, you better get back. They're calling Abby right now, and she's saying you lost track of time. They don't know I'm over here."

"Thanks."

"What are big brothers for?" Jack smiles. "You must be Hugo. I'm Jack." He puts out his hand toward me.

"Hey, Jack. Nice to meet you." I shake his hand.

"I better go," Cameron says to me with a gentle smile. "I'll see you later."

"Later."

Without another word, Cameron and his brother head across the street.

An unpleasant feeling swirls through me. It's hard to describe, but emptiness might be an appropriate word. Maybe it's seeing Cameron walk off, or maybe it's being all by myself again in this stupid house. Possibly both.

Despite my mood, I get the best sleep I've had since we moved in. The house is peaceful. Hopefully the bird thing was a fluke.

Speaking of the bird, I spend part of Sunday morning cleaning up that mess, removing all the shards of glass and disposing of the crow while wearing the same thick rubber gloves we used to remove the rats. Who knew crows had so much blood? And what does this house have against animals?

I retract the spiral staircase to the basement and lock up the nanny's room, not wanting to mention anything to Pa. Not yet. I'll wait until I'm certain the house is going to stay calm.

Pa gets home right before dinnertime, and we order more Chinese takeout.

"Anything exciting happen while I was away?" he asks.

"Not really. Pretty boring. Did homework," I reply. On the inside, I laugh. "Oh, and I met the guy who lives across the street. His name's Cameron."

"Is that the kid who cuts through our yard?" His gaze is sharp over his container of orange chicken.

"*Pa.*" I roll my eyes. "Now that I know him, it's not like a stranger is cutting through."

Pa winks and smiles. "Just messing with you. It's fine. You think he'll be a friend?"

"Yeah." I nod. "I think he will."

"That's good, mijo. You need more friends."

If Pa only knew what happened in this house yesterday. A spirit cleansing, a pizza party, an almost-kiss with a guy. I smile despite myself. "I'm working on it."

Later that night, I sit in front of my easel, touching up my painting, but my eyes drift to the glowing light of Cameron's bedroom. I reach for my phone to text him but change my mind and put it away. Not sure what I'd say—*Thanks for almost kissing me?*

For once, I can't wait for Monday. I even wake up before my damn phone alarm goes off. Of course, it starts blaring while I'm in the shower. Typical.

My first four periods go deathly slowly.

I head to the lunchroom, excited, nearly jogging, only to get held up waiting in line for what the school swears is a cheeseburger. I'm skeptical—more like two slices of limp bread surrounding some meat-like substance with an unnaturally orange cheese-like substance on top. With my tray full of questionable food, I head to where Cameron and his friends sit.

The closer I get, the more I second-guess everything. Maybe they were only being nice so they could have their spooky ghost hunt in Crimson

House. Maybe Cameron freaked out after our almost-kiss. Maybe it's better not to make friends and be a loner like usual. And yet my feet have a mind of their own. They ignore all the doubts swimming inside me, and I find myself walking right up to everyone. I better say something before I look stupid.

"Can I sit with you all?" I say to the group. Everyone looks up and greets me with enthusiasm and smiles, and I let out the breath I'm holding.

Cameron grins from ear to ear. "Saved you a spot." He pats the seat next to him, but then his smile drops. "I mean, if you want it."

"Of course I do," I say, and his smile returns. I plop down next to him, trying to conceal my joy and relief at being immediately accepted by everybody.

The group is lively after the weekend's events, still talking about the spirit cleansing and the pizza party. Cameron and I fill everyone in on the bird and the broken window. Chloe frowns but remains silent through most of lunch, which makes me uneasy, although I try not to dwell on it too much.

Neither Cameron nor I mention our almost-kiss. I guess that'll be our little secret for now. I smile at him, and he grins, his cheeks a pale shade of pink. This guy better never change.

"Hey, Hugo," Taylor says. "We're all going camping Saturday. The weather looks good, and it might be our last shot before next year. You wanna go?"

"Sounds fun," I say, but then I sigh. "But I've got this huge trig test next Monday. I need to study extra this weekend since I'm behind."

Cameron's eyes light up. "I'm great at trig. I can tutor you. You can come over to my house and study. I'm free tonight."

Wow. An excuse to see Cameron tonight sounds great, even if it means we'll have to study. Maybe we can do more than study.

"Thanks. That'd be awesome," I say. "I'll ask Pa about camping, but it should be fine. Where are we going?"

"Ever heard of Fort Warden?" Matty says with an evil grin.

"No," I say, taken aback. "Should I be worried?"

"Only if you don't like spooky abandoned military bunkers." Matty's grin gets bigger and more evil.

"I think I've had my fill of spooky for a while."

"Shush, Matty." Cameron stares daggers Matty's way, then turns to me. "It's not that creepy. You'll love it. They made all these gun battlements to protect Puget Sound forever ago. Now they're all abandoned and overgrown. It's so cool. I get a lot of ideas for my stories there. I bet it'd be awesome to paint."

"That sounds great." I smile. "Can't wait."

And I *can't* wait—for the tutoring, for the camping, and for the next time I'll be with Cameron in theater tech in a few hours. He's occupying more and more of my thoughts lately.

The next two classes drag on forever. Chemistry nearly makes my head explode, and literature is boring. I jog the entire way to theater tech, stopping well before the door so I'm not breathing too hard. Got to play it cool.

Inside the classroom, Cameron peeks up and smiles the moment he sees me. A rush of endorphins hits me, and I smile back.

"Hey," I say, a little breathy, still winded from my jog over.

"Hey," he says. "I like that we're talking in class now."

"Yeah, me too. Sorry—"

"Uh-uh." He cuts me off. "No more apologizing. I'm looking forward to studying with you tonight."

"So am I," I say. "It's the first time in my life that I'm looking forward to trig."

Cameron laughs, and I smile. He has such an adorable laugh. I want to say more funny things to him. I'll have to work on that.

After class, Cameron and I walk home together through the forest. I text Pa on the way and tell him I'm studying across the street. He says to take my time and study hard, and I promise him I will.

I'm struck with this unfamiliar sensation as we leave the trees behind and approach my house.

"Do you feel that?" I ask.

"What?" Cameron replies, a little startled.

"Nothing. I feel nothing. It's not oppressive like it's always been before. It's just...normal."

"Yeah." His apprehension melts away, and he smiles. "I *do* feel that. It's a nice change."

We continue past my place and across the street to Cameron's house.

"Dad! I'm home," Cameron yells as we go through the front door.

"Hey, Cam. How was school?" his dad calls from the other room.

"Good," Cameron calls back. "My friend Hugo from across the street is here. We're going to study in my room."

"Okay. Sounds good."

Cameron waits for a moment, like he expects his dad to say something else, but his dad is silent. I'm not sure what he's expecting, but he sighs and looks annoyed, so I don't bother him about it as we head upstairs.

We actually...study. It turns out Cameron is good at tutoring, and he explains the sines and cosines of complementary angles. In only a couple of hours, I'm well on my way to being caught up.

We're lying on the floor side by side, stomachs on the ground, propped up on our elbows, my trig textbook between us. Cameron knits his brow as he writes a formula on a sheet of paper, his tongue sticking half out of his mouth. Then his eyes light up as he finishes the formula. For about the tenth time today, I notice how totally adorable he is. Especially his cute butt as he kicks his legs back and forth behind him.

"You're so good at trig," I say.

He shrugs. "Just makes sense to me."

"That's because you're smart."

"You mean nerdy."

"No!" I say. "Smart is sexy."

"You think I'm sexy?" he asks, smiling, arching an eyebrow.

I *do* think he's sexy—like, very. He obviously meant it as a joke and expected me to be flustered or joke back, but I'm struck with this sudden moment of bravery.

"Yes," I say, with a soft smile and a hint of something more. "Yes, I do."

Cameron's face explodes into crimson, and he pins his eyes on his sheet of paper.

"Cameron," a woman calls out from beyond the closed bedroom door. "It's time for dinner. Does your friend want to stay? We're having spaghetti."

Cameron jumps up, flustered. "Coming, Mom. I'll ask Hugo."

Who knows what would have happened next if his mom hadn't interrupted, but now I'll never find out. Another mystery of the universe that won't ever be revealed, like whether we would have kissed the other night if not for that damn bird. The universe is trying to keep us apart. But I'll keep trying.

"You—um—want to stay for dinner?" Cameron asks, voice shaky.

I want to, but his mom interrupting my attempt at serious flirting has formed an awkward space between us, and Cameron is clearly uncomfortable. I stand up. "I should probably go."

"Please stay," he says with sad eyes, like a lost puppy picture posted on a telephone pole. How can I say no to that?

"Okay." I nod. "Let me text Pa."

His eyes light up, and he beams. I've never seen a smile so bright. "Thank you!"

After Pa gives his okay, Cameron leads me down to their dining nook right off the kitchen. His brother, Jack, is sitting at the table, and his mom and dad are next to him. The family resemblance is striking.

"Hugo, this is my mom and dad. And you know Jack from school."

Jack nods with a barely perceptible wink.

Cameron's mom offers her hand, which I shake. She has a firm grip and wears a hospital badge on a lanyard and blue scrubs. "Nice to meet you, Hugo."

"Pleasure to meet you, Mrs. Walsh. You're a doctor, huh?"

She laughs. "He didn't assume nurse. I like him already." She tugs on her blue smock. "Sorry about this. I'm afraid I have to head back to work soon. Duty calls."

Cameron's dad holds out his hand. "Hugo," he says curtly.

"Mr. Walsh," I say, echoing his tone as I grab his hand. His grip is tight, but I hold my own as his fingers clench mine like a vise.

"I hear you and your father are going to clean up that eyesore across the street," he says as he shakes my hand with all the care of a sledgehammer. My fingers start to turn purple.

"We'll try our best," I say, pulling my throbbing hand away. I've known Cameron's dad for less than thirty seconds, and he's already rubbing me the wrong way.

"Well, I hope it's enough. That place is bringing down the property value of the entire neighborhood," Mr. Walsh says. "Might be easier to tear it down."

Cameron's mom glares at his dad. "James, be nice."

"What? I'm saying I'm glad they're fixing it up."

She shakes her head.

We all fill up our plates with spaghetti. Cameron's dad and brother start a detailed discussion about a soccer match as they scarf down their food. I take my first bite, and it's delicious. Full of flavor and even a hint of spice.

"This is delicious," I say, glancing between Cameron's parents. "My compliments to the chef."

"He doesn't assume I'm a nurse *or* that I made dinner." Mrs. Walsh smiles. "A real progressive, aren't you?"

"I suppose." I shrug.

Mrs. Walsh's phone chirps. After a glance, her face goes serious in a second flat.

"Shoot. I've got to go." She gets up from the table and heads straight for the door. "It was so nice meeting you, Hugo. I hope to see you around more."

"Me too, Mrs. Walsh. Thanks again for the food."

She smiles and nods, then heads out the door without another word.

"Such is the life of the top heart surgeon on the Olympic Peninsula," Mr. Walsh says with an edge of sarcasm, then goes back to his spaghetti.

"That happen a lot?" I ask Cameron.

"Yep." He nods. "She's always running off. We're used to it."

"You play any sports, Hugo?" Mr. Walsh cuts in, his attention focused on me. I gulp.

"No, sir. My dad and I move around a lot. It's not very easy to get on teams when you move every six months."

"Too bad. Sports are the best way to impress girls," he says with a weird grin. "You have a girlfriend?"

I hate this shit. Cameron's face stiffens, his mouth forming a thin line. It's obvious he wants to say something but is holding back. The idea that Cameron deals with this every day makes me low-grade angry.

"Dad!" Jack says. "Don't be a jerk."

I hold back a laugh. Thanks for sticking up for us, Jack.

Cameron's dad glares at Jack. "What's wrong with what I said?"

"Literally everything," Jack shoots back. "Not everything's about sports, you shouldn't pry into his private life, and you shouldn't assume straight is the default."

"Oh." Mr. Walsh turns and stares at me, then stares at Cameron, then back at me. *"Ohhhh."*

Mr. Walsh's face pales a bit.

Cameron's face goes pink.

Jack continues, "I'm not saying anything about Hugo one way or the other. That's his business. You just shouldn't assume."

"Okay, well, I'm sorry if I offended anybody." Mr. Walsh puts his hands up. "I'm still figuring all this stuff out. I'm trying."

"That's all we ask, Dad." Jack pats his dad on the back.

"Well." Mr. Walsh clears his throat as the color returns to his face. "How 'bout those Mariners this year? Chance at the playoffs."

***

After dinner, Cameron walks me across the street. We stand on my porch.

"Sorry about my dad," Cameron says, looking down. "He can be a real idiot sometimes. But I do think he's trying to get better. He's trying to understand."

I want to tell him he should stick up for himself and not let his dad get away with that shit. Sometimes Cameron lets people walk all over him, and he doesn't deserve it. But I'm not in a position to tell Cameron what he should or shouldn't do with his dad since I'm a little behind in that department.

"It's okay," I say. "Your brother is awesome, at least."

"Yeah, Jack is great."

"And your mom is cool."

"When she's not busy." Cameron sighs. "We hardly see her."

The front door opens, and Pa pops out, eyes wide. "Oh, Hugo. It's you. I heard a noise at the door. Came to check it out."

"Hey, Pa. This is Cameron. He lives across the street, and he's helping me with trig."

Pa's face lights up, and he gives Cameron a big smile. "Hey, Cameron! Nice to meet you! Thanks so much for helping Hugo." He holds out his hand.

Cameron shakes Pa's hand. "No problem, Mr. Cruz. Nice to meet you."

"Us Cruz boys sometimes need help with math," Pa says. "Don't get me wrong, we're smart. Just easily distracted."

Pa looks between Cameron and me. He has this little smile I'm not sure I've ever seen. What is that all about?

"Well, I'm heading back in," Pa says. "See you in a bit, Hugo."

"Be done in a sec," I say as he shuts the door.

"He seems nice," Cameron says with a shy smile.

"Yeah. That was kinda strange."

"He—um—doesn't know, right?"

"No. I mean, I don't think so." Heat spreads across my face. *Could* Pa know I like guys? I've always imagined that he'd have a hard time with it.

"Well, I better let you go," Cameron says. "See you tomorrow."

"Bye," I say, unable to hold back my grin.

I can't take my eyes off him until he reaches his house. At his door, he peeks over his shoulder and waves in his adorable way. I wave back as he disappears into his house.

Cameron invites me over to study the next day. We study, but we also spend a lot of time talking about friends, parents, and hobbies. I talk about my artwork, and Cameron talks about his writing. He goes on for a while about one character in his story, and I ask him, "When are you going to let me read some of it?"

His cheeks flush. "Eventually, I guess. But not yet."

"How come?"

He shrugs. "It's personal."

I nod. "Yeah, I get it. Same with my paintings. No pressure, then." I'm willing to wait until he's comfortable. Sharing your art is hard. It makes you feel exposed.

On Wednesday, we study at my place with our papers and textbooks spread across the kitchen table. My bedroom has hardwood floors, and my desk is full of painting supplies, so the kitchen will have to do.

"If you asked me a couple of weeks ago if I'd ever study trig in this house, I'd have laughed at you," Cameron says with a smile.

"I was in the same boat when we first got here," I say. "I hated this place, and I still don't love it. But at least it's tolerable now."

Pa walks in and peeks at our work. "More trigonometry, huh? I'm so glad I'm not in high school anymore."

"Thanks, Pa," I say. "That makes me feel great."

He shrugs. "Everybody's got to go through it."

Pa hovers around the kitchen, distracting us and being annoying. At one point, he and Cameron strike up a conversation about fishing, of all things. Pa's tried taking me several times, but I suck, and it's boring as hell. But I guess Cameron loves it. Go figure.

Pa's eyes light up as he recounts fishing stories. "This one time, I hooked a forty-pound salmon. That was a sonofabitch to reel in."

"I bet," Cameron says. "Best I've ever caught was around thirty. We have great salmon fishing around here. My dad takes me every year."

"See if you can convince this one to go," Pa says, patting my back. "He hates it."

"Not going to happen!" I shout, but with a laugh.

Pa really likes Cameron, and he won't go away. I have to tell him to get the heck out of the kitchen and let us get some studying done. He mopes into the living room and turns on the TV. Sometimes Pa is like a kid.

Thursday rolls around, and we're back at Cameron's house. We've finished studying, sprawled out on his bedroom floor, with our textbooks and assignments everywhere. Cameron stands, his shirt riding up, and I glimpse his belly button and the tuft of hair heading down into his pants, and my stomach flutters. He sees me checking him out and blushes. He pulls down his shirt and sits on the edge of the bed, looking at me with his signature shy smile. I smile back.

Someone knocks on the door, and Cameron's dad bursts in without waiting for an answer. He glances between us. "Oh—um—oh."

Cameron's face turns bright pink.

"Uh—Hugo, your dad called," Mr. Walsh says. "He's been trying to get hold of you."

My phone has three missed texts. I must not have felt the vibrations.

"Thanks, Mr. Walsh," I say, waiting for him to walk away.

"It sounded important." He stares down at me, like he's not going to leave until I do.

"Okay." I hop up and straighten my shirt. The room is thick with awkwardness. I turn to Cameron. "I guess I better go. Thanks for your help, Cameron. I'll see you later."

Cameron waves. His dad bursting in has frazzled him. "Bye, Hugo. See you tomorrow at school."

"I'll see myself out," I say to Mr. Walsh, not wanting to spend a moment longer with him than I need to.

Mr. Walsh still has a shell-shocked expression.

Without waiting for an answer, I run down the stairs, let myself out, and head across the street. It turns out Pa only called to say he ordered us pizza for dinner. Why did Cameron's dad make such a huge deal about it?

Other than the awkward moment, it was a great day. My confidence in trig has skyrocketed, but even more importantly, Cameron and I know each other so much better now. And I like him. I like him a lot.

After dinner, I wander to the bathroom with Cameron on my mind. I saw him only an hour ago, so I should play it cool.

Nah.

Hugo: Thanks so much for the tutoring

Cameron: Np you're good at it!

Hugo: Eh I'm ok

Cameron: Nuh uh! You can't fake being good at math

Hugo: Can't wait for camping

Cameron: Same I really like hanging out

That makes me smile.

Hugo: Me too

The three dots appear and disappear a few times as I stare at my phone. Whatever Cameron's writing, it's taking a while. My smiling face stares back at me from the bathroom mirror. I can't remember the last time I was this happy. My phone chirps.

Cameron: I don't just like hanging out. I really like you

My breath hitches. Cameron really likes me. How is this shy and adorable guy braver than me when it comes to making moves? I thumb a reply that I really like him too.

But a rattling noise forces my eyes off the phone. The bathroom mirror shakes.

"What the heck?"

The window is still missing in the hidden room, and it's a windy night. There must be wind pushing in from outside—it's the only explanation that makes sense.

I put my hand up to steady it, and it stops. But a moment later, the rattling picks up again, the mirror jerking harder and harder under my hand. I steady it with both hands, but the shaking only gets more violent.

The force of the rattling cracks the mirror, so I pull back to keep from slicing my hands to shreds, powerless to do anything else. My eyes widen as the vibrations increase until a crack forms between the medicine cabinet and the wall.

At the last moment, I jump away and dive toward the door, covering my head.

There's an explosion of shattering glass behind me.

17
Adventure: Cameron

I lie in bed, staring at the glow from Hugo's window. He hasn't texted back. There's no sleep to be found as my mind races with what that could mean. I told Hugo I like him, and he left me on read. I bury my head in the pillow.

Why did Dad have to burst in at that exact moment? After that, Hugo was in such a hurry to leave. And who could blame him? Between me gushing all over him and my jerk of a dad, I wouldn't be surprised if Hugo wants nothing to do with me.

The way Dad looked between Hugo and me—the image won't leave my mind. That might have been the first time in a long while that Dad saw me for who I am, and the worst part is, I'm not sure he liked what he saw.

I'm breaking many texting protocols, but I can't take it anymore. I thumb out another message to Hugo.

> Cameron: Sorry bout my dad

No response. Nothing. No three dots, even. Minutes pass. I start and stop typing another message about ten times.

> Cameron: Everything okay?

Still nothing.

Hugo's light goes out, and my heart sinks.

I toss and turn for most of the night, but I nod off at some point. The harsh sound of my phone alarm jars me out of sleep.

Every minute of school feels like an hour as I wait for lunch, the first time I'll have a chance to see Hugo. My eyelids are heavy from lack of sleep, and my stomach is tied up in knots. I text my friends and ask if they've seen or heard from Hugo. Nope. What the heck happened? Did he fall off the planet?

Lunch finally rolls around, and I head to our usual spot. Abby and Taylor are already there chatting.

Abby looks up with a sad smile. "Hey, Cameron."

"No Hugo, huh?"

They both shake their heads.

"He wasn't in trig," Taylor says. "He must have missed school for some reason."

"He might be sick," Abby says, eyes hopeful.

"He was fine last night," I say.

As I sit down next to Abby, she puts her arm around me. "Sorry, Cameron. I'm sure there's a good explanation."

I do my best to smile at her, and she smiles back. Simply being around her lifts my spirits. That's what best friends are for, I guess.

Matty, Chloe, and Maya show up, and I tell everybody about the last few nights. Well, I might leave out the part where Hugo said I'm sexy. That's too embarrassing to tell the entire group, and I'm not sure he meant it. We were kind of joking. Kind of. I might tell Abby later when it's only the two of us.

"Well, dude, there's one thing I can say for sure," Matty says. "Hugo likes you. That's a fact. Give it some time. I'm sure it'll all work out."

Everybody nods in agreement—everybody, that is, except Chloe, who says nothing and stares out the window into the distance.

"Chloe?" I ask. "Everything okay?"

"Hmm?" Chloe's eyes focus. "Yeah. Everything's fine."

"You'd tell me if it wasn't, right?"

"Yeah." She nods, then smiles. "Of course."

The rest of the day goes by as slowly as the morning. Theater tech comes and goes with no sign of Hugo. The last bell of the day rings, and I walk out of class feeling pretty low.

As I'm leaving school, Abby runs up. "Hey, Cameron! We gonna do our movie night tonight?"

"Yeah, sure. But later. I'm headed to the library for a while." The library is where I go when I want to escape. It's my safe space.

Abby nods. "Okay. Text me if you need anything."

"Hey, Abby?"

"Yeah?"

"You're a good friend." I smile.

She smiles back and nudges me on the shoulder. "You're not half bad yourself, Cameron."

At the library, I find a quiet nook with comfy chairs and settle down with my laptop. I've been preoccupied for the last couple of weeks and have spent little time on my writing. It's one of the best ways to escape—losing myself in my fantasy world and characters. I let the real world melt away.

My story is about a boy who discovers he has magical powers. They're wonderful, but then he falls in love with another boy. He has to choose between losing his powers and losing the boy.

I'm so deep in my writing that I lose track of time, brought back to the real world only by the buzzing of my phone. It might be a message from Hugo. I almost drop the phone as I fumble for it. Nope, it's a text from Mom asking where I am and saying that dinner is almost ready. I pack up my laptop and head for the exit.

As I pass the main desk, Mr. Peterson waves.

"Hey, Cameron, there you are. Been looking for you."

"Hey, Mr. Peterson. What's up?"

"There's more I should tell you about 16 Sycamore Lane, if you want to hear it."

"That'd be great." I smile.

"Follow me."

We head down into the archives again.

"Remember how I mentioned the townspeople gathering around the house last time we talked?" Mr. Peterson says.

"Yeah. Trying to find out about the missing children, right?"

"That's right. There's more to it than I said last time. What happened is of…special interest to me." Mr. Peterson's expression is complex, with a hint of sadness. "It was the summer of 1958. Half the town formed a mob outside Emily's home, demanding answers. When she didn't come out, people started throwing rocks and breaking windows. Four men broke into the house. The crowd waited outside, chanting for them to drag her out and force her to face justice. After a while, the four men left the house empty-handed with blank expressions. None of them would talk about what they'd seen. They wandered down to a local bar, and all four of them drank until they passed out."

Mr. Peterson takes out four newspaper articles. "All four men were young and in good health. All four died in tragic accidents in the next couple of months." He sets the articles on the table one by one. "One died in a logging accident. One drowned. One was shot during a bank robbery. And one slipped and fell while he was hiking. Fell a hundred feet to his death."

Mr. Peterson pauses before he lays down the final article with the headline: HENRY PETERSON DIES IN TRAGIC HIKING ACCIDENT. His face draws into a deep frown.

"Henry *Peterson*?" I ask.

Mr. Peterson sighs. "One child who went missing was Fredrick Peterson—Henry Peterson's son. Henry Peterson was my grandfather. Fredrick would have been my uncle. Only thirteen years old when he went missing in 1958."

"I'm sorry," I whisper, feeling a lump in my throat.

Mr. Peterson's eyes are distant. "That's why I'm so interested in that house. Unanswered family questions. When I was about your age, I snuck inside."

"Really?"

"Yeah. I wanted to figure out its secrets, search for clues about my missing uncle. I didn't find any."

For a moment, something flashes in Mr. Peterson's eyes. I've seen that look on too many faces recently—fear of that house.

"Did something happen to you there?" I ask.

His eyes focus, and he returns from where he was. "Be careful, Cameron. I've warned you once, and I'll warn you again. That house is dangerous. You should walk away. Be glad you made it out with only that scar on your leg. That house can leave scars on people in more ways than one."

"It's kinda too late for that," I say.

"What do you mean?"

"My friend Hugo—the guy who came here with me last time? We've both seen things. We've found things. He lives in that house."

Mr. Peterson's face goes white as a sheet. "*Lives* there?"

"Yeah. He and his dad moved in a few weeks ago. They're renovating it."

"But that means..." Mr. Peterson trails off.

"What does it mean?"

"Your friend Hugo. What's his full name?"

"Hugo Cruz."

"I need to do some research." Mr. Peterson looks me in the eye. "Cameron, be safe. If at all possible, try not to spend time in that house. I'm going to give you my phone number. Call me if anything happens."

I enter his number into my phone and send him a hello text. "Got it."

"I have to go," he says, nervous and distracted. "I've got some things to look into."

"Okay," I say, at a loss for words. "Thanks?"

He walks off and leaves me in the archive room by myself. What an odd guy.

On my way home, I cut through Hugo's yard again. I peek into the foggy windows as I pass the house but see nothing—no Hugo. I stand beside his home for a solid minute, staring at the front door, wondering if I should knock. In the end, I talk myself out of it. If Hugo wants to talk to me, he'll get in touch. I have to let things run their course, so I cross the street with my head hung low.

Dinner goes by like it always does. Dad tells stupid dad jokes, Mom's work phone distracts her, and Jack heads off to a soccer match. Nobody mentions Hugo, and I don't bring him up. The last thing I want is to talk about him with my family tonight. Especially Dad.

After dinner, Abby comes over, and we watch movies. That bit of normalcy helps my mental state.

"I see his lights are on," Abby says, glancing at Hugo's bedroom. "No word from him, I assume?"

"Nope."

"Have you considered going over there and knocking?" she asks.

"I almost did, but I don't want to push him. I'll wait until tomorrow. He said yesterday that he still wants to go camping, so that will be a good excuse to get in touch."

"Sounds like a plan," Abby says.

Much later, after Abby heads home for the night, I find myself in bed, unable to sleep and staring at the light in Hugo's window again. An undercurrent of anger mixes with my sadness.

What the heck's up with him? He's right there but refuses to talk to me. My anger only gets stronger when his light turns out. How hard is it to text? What kind of friend leaves another friend hanging like that?

My mind is a hornet's nest of negative thoughts. It hasn't been this bad since my school bullies got out of control a few years ago, shoving me on the playground and calling me fat and the F-slur. I lie in bed for a long time, stewing in toxic emotions.

My eyelids are heavy and I'm on the edge of sleep when the slightest noise comes from the window. I sit up in bed. A pine cone hits right in the middle of the glass, and I'm struck with déjà vu. Could that be Hugo again? In a flash, I'm out of bed with my robe on, peering out my window.

Hugo stands in the yard, illuminated by soft porch light, concentrating as he aims the next pine cone. His face lights up when he sees me, which sends my heart into overdrive. I was sure he hated me and wanted nothing to do with me.

"Cameron!" he whisper-shouts.

"We've got to stop meeting like this," I call back. Despite my best efforts to be angry with him, my lips have a mind of their own and curl into a smile. "Where the heck have you been?"

"Come down here," he replies. "I'll explain everything. Wear something warm."

"Be right there."

I throw on jeans, a sweatshirt, and a jacket. In a moment of inspiration, I stuff a small blanket into my backpack, then sneak downstairs and out of the house.

Hugo smiles from ear to ear as I approach. I should be furious since he's ghosted me for more than twenty-four hours, but I'm ready to forgive him if he's got pretty much any excuse. Still, I can't go *that* easy on him.

"Have you tried texting me?" Hugo asks.

"Yes," I say with a twinge of hurt. "Of course."

"Sorry." Hugo glances down. "Pa grounded me. Took away my phone."

Relief.

Hugo is *grounded*. It instantly makes sense. He didn't freak out when I said I liked him or freak out about my dad. I go from depressed and angry to giddy in a matter of seconds—sometimes my brain is like a roller coaster.

"What happened?" I ask.

"It's a long story. Any place we can talk in private?"

"Yeah." I smile. This is what I was hoping for. "You up for an adventure?"

Hugo's eyes light up. "Intriguing. I know School Cameron, and I've gotten to know Tutor Cameron pretty well over the last week, but I haven't seen Adventure Cameron in action."

"Is that a yes?"

"That's a yes. Lead on, Adventure Cameron." He beams at me and gestures toward the street.

To Hugo's surprise, we cut across his lawn and head into the forest behind his house. The night is dark and moonless, so I turn on my phone flashlight to lead the way.

"Are you taking me to school?" Hugo asks, laughing.

"Wait and see. You'll like it, I promise."

Sitting under the stars is high on the list of things I want to do with Hugo, and I have the perfect place. I'm not wasting this opportunity.

Port Townsend High School is on the top of a hill overlooking the entire town and the surrounding area. On a clear day, you can see the Olympic Mountains to the west, Port Townsend Bay to the east, and all the way to Victoria, Canada, to the north. But tonight's feature will be the stars.

"You *are* leading me to school, aren't you?" Hugo asks.

"Haven't you ever been curious about that old boarded-up brick schoolhouse next to all the newer buildings?"

"Kinda." Hugo shrugs. "What about it?"

"It's the original schoolhouse, built forever ago. It just so happens to have the best view in the area, and I know how to get to the roof."

Hugo laughs. "I like Adventure Cameron."

We walk up to a large two-story brick building perched right at the top of the hill, standing apart from the rest of the school. Boards cover the windows, all decorated with brightly colored murals painted by students. For being well over a hundred years old, it's in good shape, but the grounds are overgrown with weeds, and ivy climbs the brick walls.

We walk along the cyclone fence surrounding the derelict building. A break in the chain links provides enough room to squeeze through. On the side of the building, a long metal ladder encircled by a cage, extends all the way to the roof. The bottom of the cage appears locked, but on closer inspection, the padlock is not engaged.

"I noticed the maintenance people never actually lock this," I say with a smile.

"You're full of surprises."

With the lock removed, we climb up the old metal ladder. The rungs are cold and unforgiving against our hands as we ascend. I've never been a big fan of heights, but the cage helps some. We reach the top, and my hands and shoulders burn from exertion.

"Wow!" Hugo says, scanning the horizon. "You can see everything."

Stars sparkle off the bay, and the landscape is a palette of purple, gray, and black as far as the eye can see. The Olympic Mountains form a dark silhouette against the night sky. The shimmering lights of the town dot the landscape with little specks of amber. A blast of salty air from the sea rushes past.

"Look up," I say, smiling and pointing skyward. The stars are spectacular. The moonless night really makes them pop.

"Amazing!" Hugo spins around, head tipped back. "I've never seen the Milky Way so bright!"

"I sometimes come here when I need to think."

"I can see why. It's so peaceful up here." He takes in our surroundings with a relaxed and content expression. The wind buffets his dark, wavy hair, his face aglow with starlight.

I pull the blanket out of my backpack and spread it out on the roof. This is just what I had in mind when I packed it. I sit down and pat the space beside me. "So, tell me what happened with your dad."

"Well, I guess I didn't do as good of a job securing the medicine cabinet as I should have. It fell off the wall," Hugo says as he sits down next to me.

"Oh crap! How did that happen?"

"Wind, maybe? The window is still missing in Emily's room, and it was a blustery night. It must have shaken the screws loose."

"Wind? Seriously?" I saw Hugo secure it myself, and it seemed pretty solid to me. A touch of anxiety swirls through me. Anything unusual related to the house has that effect.

"I don't know." Hugo looks down at his feet. "That's what I'm going with for now. I don't want to think about the alternative."

"Did your dad find the hidden rooms?"

"Yeah. Also, I guess the nanny's door scraped the floor when we opened it, so he would have found out anyway. He asked me point-blank, and I couldn't lie, so I gave him the key."

"You said he's superstitious, right?" I ask. "Did the rooms freak him out?"

"They didn't seem to bother him. He was more upset about me keeping them a secret. But there was something weird about the way he was acting. He got furious, and that almost never happens. Pa's usually so chill. But the strange thing was, I didn't feel like it was me he was angry at."

"What was he angry at, then?"

Hugo shrugs. "I'm not sure. The house? Sounds funny saying it. He might think we're in over our heads trying to fix it up."

"I can relate to being angry at that house."

"Anyway, he had me stay home from school today to help him clean up the mess in the bathroom and clean out the hidden rooms. He was obviously a little mad at me since he grounded me. That hasn't happened in years."

"Oh shoot, does that mean you can't go camping?" I ask. I so desperately want to go camping with Hugo. This better not mess up my plans—plans involving kissing him. Hopefully. Fingers crossed.

"No, I'm still going," Hugo says. "I think Pa's so excited that I finally have friends. He doesn't want to mess that up. It's funny—he really likes you. He's mentioned going fishing with you, like, three times. I'm only grounded until tomorrow. I get my phone back in the morning."

"Tomorrow? I hope you're not taking too much of a risk by sneaking out tonight."

Hugo laughs. "Nah, Pa sleeps like a log. And I really wanted to see you."

My breath hitches, and my stomach tilts. "You did?"

"Yeah." Hugo says. "I kinda left you hanging after you texted that you liked me."

"Yeah." I nod. "That messed with me."

"I'm so sorry about that," Hugo says, and I can tell he means it. "The mirror fell right after I read your message."

"It's okay," I say, a bit too fast. It was totally *not* okay for twenty-four hours while I was an emotional wreck, but at least it makes sense now.

"Here's the thing, Cameron." Hugo sighs. "Every time I make friends or meet a guy I like, I get the rug pulled out from under me when we move away in a few months. I hate it."

A sinking feeling forms in my gut, like Hugo's about to make some excuse about how complicated his life is. The guys I like always find some reason it won't work out. I frown, and the cold seeps in through my jacket, making me shiver. I wrap my arms around my stomach.

"But…" Hugo says, and he looks into my eyes. "After Pa found the hidden rooms and didn't immediately move us out—and given how much he's been talking about you—I have this bit of hope. Hope that I can have a normal life."

Hugo sets his hand on mine, and this jolt of electricity runs through me.

"And you know what else?" Hugo asks.

"What?"

"I *really* like you," he says, with this look in his eyes—a look no guy has ever directed at me. My whole body flutters like a swarm of butterflies surrounds me.

"You do?" I ask, breathing the words out and looking into those beautiful brown eyes.

"Yeah. And I don't want to miss this opportunity because I'm afraid." He pauses for a moment. "Cameron?"

"Yeah?"

"Can I—um—can I kiss you?"

"Okay—"

I barely utter the word before he leans over and puts his lips on mine. So soft. Tingles radiate through me, all the way to my fingers and toes.

His lips are gentle and warm, and the light exhale through his nose tickles my cheek. We separate, our lips making the subtlest sound, then share a glance for only a moment before we press our lips together again with urgency. Our mouths open, and he cups my cheek as the kiss gets deeper. The night is chilly, but I'm warm inside as my joy brims over with an intensity that sends my pulse into the stratosphere.

We part again and tilt our heads the other way as our kiss gets even more passionate. His tongue explores my lips, which sends a tingle through me that I didn't expect. It's electric. My tongue touches his, and the world around me disappears as we continue to kiss, lost in the moment—just Hugo and me.

After quite a few minutes, which are impossible to count, with my lips hot and raw, we pull apart and peer into each other's eyes.

"Wow," I whisper.

"Yeah," he replies, and we both laugh from the sheer joy.

Some people say their first kisses were sloppy and forgettable, full of bumped noses and clacking teeth. This isn't like that at all. It's perfect. And I'll never forget it.

We lie back on the blanket, holding hands and looking up into the night sky.

"The stars!" I say, waving my free hand up at the heavens and the radiating arms of the Milky Way above us.

I turn my head toward Hugo, and he turns toward me.

"They're amazing," he says. "Everything is a bit more amazing now."

We kiss again, soft and gentle.

And everything *is* amazing.

18
Fort Worden: Hugo

Cameron borrows his dad's car for camping. Fort Worden is just north of town, but it's too far to walk, and we have to haul all our camping gear there. We've stuffed the trunk with tents, sleeping bags, camping chairs, snacks, s'mores makings, and a cooler full of hot dogs, sodas, and fizzy waters—everything we need for the night.

Cameron's behind the wheel, and my lips curve into a smile as I look over at my…what, exactly? Friend? Kissing buddy? Boyfriend?

Was last night a dream? It's still hard to wrap my head around. Finding a guy I like who likes me back is so rare, and wow, do I like him. I *really* like him. And he's a great kisser. Cameron told me he was new to the whole kissing thing, but he could have fooled me. I guess he's a natural. Or he's practiced on pillows and watched a bunch of YouTube videos. I wouldn't know anything about that. Nope.

As we pull into Fort Worden State Park, we're greeted by large green lawns and old wooden buildings painted white that look like barracks from a hundred years ago. The ghosts of soldiers marching in unison are easy to imagine.

A smattering of white houses and other structures dot the landscape and the hill behind the barracks. Beyond the homes is a large hill and a dense forest. Dotted through the trees are ancient concrete structures—abandoned battlements and guard towers stained and rusted with age, their inhabitants long gone. At least the living ones.

"It may look like an old military base, but the whole thing has been a state park for the last fifty years," Cameron says. "People rent those houses for weekend getaways. We'll camp near the beach on the other side of the hill, near the old gun batteries."

"This place is so cool," I say. "And kinda spooky when you think about all the soldiers who used to live here."

"Wait until you see the abandoned gunnery tunnels on the hill," Cameron says with a big grin. "Then you'll think it's *really* spooky."

Cameron drives us along a road that ends at the waterfront, then turns left and passes several campsites right next to the beach. Most spots are vacant, which isn't surprising in late September. Even though the weather is nice, it's chilly for camping right on the water. Glad I packed some warm clothes. It's great snuggling weather. I peek over at Cameron and smile.

At the end of the road, Cameron pulls into a spot nestled against the forested bluff running along the water. The trees make it more secluded than the spots right on the beach. We park behind two other cars.

"Looks like most of the gang is here," Cameron says. "Oh, one thing I forgot—no booze or pot. Matty would get kicked off the football team if he was even near the stuff."

"No problem," I say. "I mean, I've snuck a beer from the fridge once or twice, but I'm not really into that stuff."

"Cool. Oh, one more thing," Cameron says, then peeks at me with a bashful smile. "Um. What do we say? About us."

I lean over and kiss him, and I don't care who sees us. Cameron blushes in the adorable way he always does. He better never change.

"Well," I say after we part, "I guess we tell them we're boyfriends."

"Really?" Cameron's eyes light up, and he smiles from ear to ear.

"If that's okay."

"Of course it is," he says. "Are you for real, Hugo, or am I just dreaming?"

"Sorry. You're just dreaming," I say with a laugh. "I'm a figment of your imagination."

"I like you, Hugo Cruz."

"Back at ya, Cameron Walsh."

We kiss once more, then exit the car. A cool ocean breeze and a blast of briny air hits me. Cameron shivers, and I put my arm around him to protect him as we hike up a small path to the campsite nestled in the woods. Several camping chairs sit around a fire pit. Matty and Taylor are setting up two large tents a little farther into the woods. Chloe and Maya are inflating air mattresses, and Abby is pacing around, supervising and organizing things on the picnic table, like the camp counselor she is.

Everyone watches as we approach, holding on to each other. Cameron pecks me on the lips to drive home the point.

"About damn time you two got together." Matty laughs. Everyone else lets out a cheer.

"You guys are adorable," Maya says, smiling wide.

Abby runs up to us. "Is it official?"

Cameron nods. "Mm-hmm."

"Yay!" Abby gives us both a bear hug while hopping up and down. "I'm so happy!"

"So are we," Cameron says. "Now stop gushing and let us unpack."

"Hey!" Abby snaps, but she's still beaming. "I'm allowed some gushing, okay?"

The gang helps us unload our gear from the car. It turns out the two tents are more than big enough for everybody. Matty, Cameron, and I will be in one tent with Maya, Chloe, Abby, and Taylor in the other.

I'm happy about how the tents worked out—it prevents an awkward conversation between Cameron and me. Don't get me wrong, I would love to share a tent with only him, but I'm not sure we're ready to go much beyond kissing. It takes the temptation off the table, or at least makes it more challenging.

With the site set up and the campfire started, we all sit around the fire pit, roasting hot dogs. A bag of kettle chips and some potato salad round out the dinner—a meal fit for a king, if that king were a camping teenager.

Once our stomachs are full and we "do the dishes" (throw the paper plates into the fire), Cameron turns to me with a smile. "Ready to check out the gunnery tunnels?"

"Let's go!"

Everybody else says they'll join us later, so for now it's only the two of us, and that suits me just fine. Since last night, the only thing I've been able to think about is getting more alone time with him.

Cameron takes my hand and guides me to a wooded trail behind our campsite that climbs through the woods, switching back several times. My lungs burn as we walk, but the payoff at the top is worth it.

We pause at a spot where the trees open up, providing a spectacular view of the beach and the water beyond. We can see for miles. Emerald islands of evergreen trees pop out of the dark blue waters of the Salish Sea. Fluffy clouds float in the bright blue sky like cotton candy. The view is breathtaking.

"Wow, so beautiful," I say in a whisper.

"C'mon. Wait until you see what's next."

Cameron takes my hand and guides me down a tree-lined path that opens onto a long row of concrete bunkers, steel ladders, railings, and stairs built right into the side of the concrete structures, stretching on as far as the eye can see. Overgrown trees and vegetation sprawl everywhere. Cracks and stains cover the cement, and years of wear have rusted every metal surface into organic patterns of orange and red, like a dystopian Escher painting.

"This is unreal," I say, my jaw dropping open.

"Isn't it? These are old gun battlements the soldiers used to protect Puget Sound from enemy ships. There are two other bases like this along the coast. They called it the Triangle of Fire."

"And we're just allowed to walk through all this?"

Cameron nods. "Yeah. Hard to believe, isn't it?"

"Yeah. Let's go check it out!"

We both run, following each other up half-flights of stairs, past rusted metal doors, and into dark, twisting tunnels. The temperature drops, covering me in goose bumps. The tunnels go on forever, turning into empty rooms, dead ends, and staircases leading up to old gun turrets. We have only our cell phone flashlights to guide us through the pitch black.

Cameron gets ahead of me, and I lose sight of him. I call out his name, the sound echoing off the barren walls. He calls back, laughing. I laugh too, and the echoes reach a deafening crescendo until we find each other again.

"I bet these are spooky at night," I say.

"Only one way to find out," Cameron says with an evil grin.

Occasionally, sunlight streaks into the darkness through a porthole or a door to the outside, turning everything into a stark silhouette. I take a ton of pictures with my phone, capturing unique geometric shapes, interesting shadows, and odd angles. Cameron was right. This is a treasure trove of artistic inspiration.

We leave the tunnels and walk along the road between two bunkers that form a concrete canyon. Soon the road descends into a short tunnel underneath a small hill. Halfway through, a doorway in the wall leads into darkness.

"In here," Cameron says, taking my hand.

We enter a small room, empty save for a metal ladder embedded in the concrete wall, heading upward. Faint sunlight shines at the top, at least twenty feet above us.

"That's a long way up," I say.

"Yeah, but it's cool."

"Adventure Cameron," I say with a smile. Cameron blushes and smiles back. Can this guy get any more adorable?

At the top, we find a small concrete room with a long window right at eye level, providing a panoramic view of the area.

"This was one of the main lookouts before the trees all grew up around here," Cameron says.

"Can you imagine being a soldier back then, just sitting here waiting and watching?" I ask.

"I wonder how many soldiers did *this* while they were waiting." Cameron presses up against me and joins our lips together. I've been wanting this all day, and having him make the first move turns me on in a heartbeat.

I kiss him back and nuzzle him up against the wall, running my hands down his chest. My fingers continue to explore, slipping between his shirt and jeans. The soft skin of his midsection is warm against my fingers. But the moment I touch him, Cameron tenses, and the mood changes in a flash.

"Sorry," I say. "Didn't mean to push. I should have asked."

Cameron is quiet and steps away, looking out the window. His arms wrap around his stomach, which he does whenever he's nervous. He's got some tummy fat, which I find cute, so I hope that's not what he's worried about.

We went from happy and carefree to sad and awkward in a second flat. Shit. I messed this up.

19

Written in Stone: Cameron

Why am I such a wimp? When Hugo reached under my shirt, my whole body tingled. It's what I wanted, but the second he touched my stomach, this surge of emotions welled up, and I had to pull away. It was pure instinct—I couldn't control it—and now there's this awkward energy in the air.

I honestly find it hard to believe that Hugo's even attracted to me. Any moment, he'll find out how gross I am and realize his mistake. Abby's told me a million times that I'm cute, that people should like me for who I am, and that I shouldn't force myself to be something I'm not to please them. That's all easy to say, but the idea of losing Hugo over it makes me want to scream and cry at the same time.

"Cameron?" Hugo says in a soft voice. "I really am sorry."

"No, *I'm* sorry. It's just—" It's impossible to talk about this with him, and the last thing I want is to draw more attention to it.

"I'm happy just kissing you," Hugo says. "We don't have to go past that."

The thing is, I *want* to go past that. But somehow, my broken brain won't let it happen. I breathe out long and slow. "Okay."

I wrap my arms around my stomach. That damn reflex. I'm not even aware I'm doing it until it's too late—Hugo has noticed.

"For what it's worth," he says, "I like you exactly as you are. I prefer it, actually."

He prefers my blubber to a nice flat stomach? How could he mean that?

But wow.

Hearing him say that forces a smile out of me.

"I won't push you if you need some time," Hugo says, "but I'm going to keep reminding you how sexy and cute you are."

"I guess if you say something enough, it becomes true," I say with a sad laugh.

"It's already true."

Hugo's eyes are soft and caring without a hint of deception. All those times Abby said the right guy would come around, the idea felt like a naïve dream. And yet here's this caring guy right in front of me who appears to like me as I am.

Still, my mind is a tornado of reasons why this thing between us is doomed to fail.

"All of this is new to me," I say. "You've had boyfriends."

"I mean, a few. But we never got past kissing. I'm as new to this as you are."

"Really?"

"Honest. Let's take things slow."

"Thanks," I say, unable to hold back my smile.

"Of course. Now, can I get back to kissing you?" Hugo asks.

I nearly tackle him and smash my lips against his.

"I guess that's a yes," he says, muffled by my mouth. We continue kissing until the only thing on my mind is how wonderful he is.

***

Hugo and I walk along the trail, heading back to the campsite. We turn to start our descent down the ridge when we spot a swarm of black specks swirling around in the sky in the other direction.

"Are those birds?" Hugo asks.

"Maybe. Let's go check it out."

As we get closer, the specks take shape, and the harsh caws make it clear that a flock (a murder?) of crows is circling a spot on the ground. We leave the shade of the forest and find ourselves near the barracks and other outbuildings. Past the buildings, the crows' target becomes clear. Row after row of white grave markers comes into view—a military cemetery—sending a chill through me.

"You've got to be kidding," Hugo says.

"Why does it have to be a cemetery?" I ask. "And what is it with crows?"

Hugo shakes his head.

Like most military cemeteries, the grave markers are spaced evenly, creating perfect little rows and columns that make crisscross patterns as we walk past them. The crows circle one particular spot along the back edge, near the forest. Back there is a much older part of the cemetery. The elements have stained the gravestones, and the etchings have faded.

I let out a gasp. A mangled chunk of flesh and fur lies in front of a headstone. It may be a rabbit or a possum, but it's too far gone to tell. Maggots have claimed the poor thing, and a putrid odor wafts from it. The crows circle above us.

"Oh shit," Hugo says.

"What?"

"Look at the gravestone."

Etched in faded lettering on the worn granite is a name I can't believe I'm seeing.

CHARLES THORNBURN
1842–1890

"Emily's dad? What the hell?" I say. "What are the odds of an animal dying right on this grave?"

"I don't want to think about it," Hugo says. "The last thing I want is more inexplicable coincidences."

"No shit. I'm going to take a photo of the grave and send it to Abby," I say. She's been getting more and more snippy if we don't share all ghost-related events, and I don't want to piss her off.

"Good call."

I take the picture, and we turn to head back to the campsite. The wind makes a faint whistling sound. High in the sky, a crow suddenly dives toward us.

Is it attacking?

In a flash, I'm back in the darkened hallway with the crow trying to peck my eyes out. I shield my face with my hands. And then there's that voice. *You left me. Now I have you.*

But soon it's clear the bird isn't diving but dropping like a stone, its body twisting and spinning lifelessly in the wind.

The crow lands hard directly on a headstone just a few plots away. Rivulets of blood streak down the front, highlighting the faded inscription in gory red.

LUKE BR____
1855–1903

"Luke?" I say. "Oh crap. That was the name of the nanny's lover."
Hugo nods. "I think we just left coincidence territory."

20
The Dream: Hugo

Back at the campsite, Cameron and I talk with Abby in hushed tones. We show her the pictures of the gravestones and tell her about the crow.

"I don't like any of it," Abby says. "But it's not worth ruining the camping trip for everybody. Let's keep it to ourselves for now."

"That sounds good to me," I say. The last thing I want to do is think about ghosts, my house, or any of it. I came camping to escape all that.

Abby inspects the picture of Luke's grave. "We might be able to look up the plot maps for the cemetery and figure out Luke's full name. I'll check into that."

The sun sets, and the temperature drops, so we all huddle around the fire, eating s'mores and telling jokes. Soon the memory of the crow fades as Matty and Taylor start a contest over who can tell the worst dad joke.

"Where do rainbows go when they break the law?" Matty asks.

"I don't know. Where?" Taylor says.

"Prism. But it's a light sentence, to give them time to reflect."

The entire group groans.

"That's way worse than my dad's worst joke," Cameron says.

"That sounds like a challenge." Matty grins.

"No way!" Cameron cries. "You wouldn't stand a chance against me. It would be unfair. I have to abstain."

No amount of taunting and begging will make Cameron relent. But he whispers to me that the real reason is that he hates dad jokes.

But then the dad jokes turn into dirty jokes, and Cameron is suddenly happy to join in.

"What do you call a masturbating cow?" he asks.

"What?" Matty says, using every bit of self-control to hold back a laugh.

"Beef stroganoff."

Everybody groans and laughs.

"Oh yeah?" Matty shoots back. "Well, did you know my cock was in the *Guinness Book of World Records*?"

"Was it?" Cameron asks.

"Yeah. But the librarian told me to take it out."

More groans.

We keep at it for way too long. The entire group is being silly, laughing so hard we're clutching our stomachs.

When the fire dies down and darkness creeps in, Matty springs up and yells, "Abandoned bunker hide-and-seek!"

We hike up the hill in the pitch black, our phone flashlights our only guides. I stay next to Cameron the whole way up. Something about being near him comforts me. I like knowing where he is and that he's safe. The occasional bump and touch are enough to set my mind at ease.

When we get to the top, moonlight drenches the bunkers. They were eerie in the daylight, but at night they are extra spooky, looking like old mausoleums. I half expect zombies and ghouls to stagger out of the dark tunnels.

We take turns being the seeker. When it's my turn, I find Cameron first, and it turns into a five-minute make-out session in a dark bunker. Come to think of it, he was barely hiding, so this might have been his plan all along, and I'm okay with that.

Soon hide-and-seek devolves into chaos, with each of us trying to scare everybody else. I scare the crap out of quite a few people, and people scare me back more times than I care to admit. Cameron has a particular talent for jumping out at just the right time.

After a solid hour, we've all had enough frights for the night. My legs are like noodles as we head back to the campsite. Matty, Cameron, and I pile into one tent, and everybody else takes the other. We let Matty have his own air mattress while Cameron and I share.

"How gracious of you two to give me my own," Matty says, his voice dripping with sarcasm.

"Just part of our good nature," Cameron says innocently, but nobody's fooled.

Cameron and I lie side by side in separate sleeping bags, so close yet so far away. I listen to my friends' soft breathing and the sounds of the night—the slight rustling in the underbrush of some nocturnal critter, surf splashing against the beach in the distance, and the hooting of an owl.

Soon Matty's breathing becomes deep and rhythmic with a light snore. The next sound is the unzipping of a sleeping bag and Cameron's gentle whisper.

"Hey, Hugo, you awake?"

"Yeah."

"You, um, wanna come over here?"

"Are you sure?"

"Yeah. I mean, just to snuggle."

"Heck yeah."

I unzip my sleeping bag and shimmy over to his side. Cameron turns away from me, and I nuzzle in as the big spoon, putting my arm around him. I kiss the back of his neck, and he squirms.

"Stop," he whispers between giggles. "You're going to make me wake up Matty."

We settle into a serious snuggle. We fit together just right.

***

In the early hours, before the sun comes up, I'm deep asleep with Cameron in my arms when a shriek tears through the silence, waking everybody. My pulse skyrockets as I shoot up out of my sleeping bag.

"What the heck is that?" Cameron cries, wide-eyed.

"I think it's coming from the other tent," I say.

Matty jumps up in a flash, throws on his shoes, and unzips our tent as the screaming continues. Cameron and I follow right behind him.

In the other tent, the screams have quieted, replaced by hushed voices.

"Everything okay?" Matty asks through the nylon.

"Yeah," Maya calls back. "Chloe had a bad dream."

"Anything we can do to help?" Cameron asks, his brow creased.

"It's okay—" Maya starts.

"Wait! Don't go away," Chloe blurts. "Come inside."

We all exchange surprised looks.

"Okay. We're coming in," Cameron says. He unzips the tent, and we squeeze inside.

Chloe sits up on an air mattress, Maya holding her as tears stream down her cheeks. Her face is haggard, as if she's had quite a shock. Taylor and Abby lie on the other air mattress, propped up on their elbows, looking startled and scared. We all crowd around Chloe.

"I had a nightmare, and I want to tell you all before I forget it. My dreams go away fast."

"Go ahead, Chloe," Maya says. "We're listening."

Chloe peers up at Cameron and me, her face white as a sheet. Being on the receiving end of a look like that is never fun, and dread creeps through my extremities.

"It's about the house," she says. "Are you sure you want to hear it?"

Cameron peeks my way, questioning, and I nod.

"Yeah," Cameron says, his voice small. "Let's hear it."

"I saw an old lady, like you all have described. She was standing in Emily's room. The medicine cabinet was back in the wall, and she was angry about it. She shoved it so hard it ripped out of the wall and flew across the room."

"That actually happened," I say, feeling the blood drain from my face. "But I thought we just did a bad job of fastening the cabinet and the wind forced it out."

"You didn't say it *flew across the room*," Cameron says, looking my way.

I shrug. "I thought it tipped over and smashed against the sink and—I dunno, ricocheted off it or something."

Abby scowls at both of us. "When are you two going to stop withholding stuff? I don't care if you think something's explainable. You should tell us. Every detail matters when it comes to that house."

Cameron and I both nod, heads lowered. "Sorry, Abby," Cameron says.

"Anything else?" Cameron asks Chloe.

Chloe nods. "The next dream was different. It was fuzzier. I don't like sharing those because I'm not as sure about them. That usually means I'm dreaming about the future, and I don't want to influence people's decisions."

"Chloe," Cameron says. "You don't have to share your dreams with us. It's your choice. If you think it's better not to, that's fine."

"But I can't keep this a secret. It's bad." Chloe's lower lip quivers. "My dream was bad."

Her words fill my stomach with lead. Cameron and I exchange a nervous glance and move closer together.

"It's a dream about you two and the house," she says.

"I think we need to know," I say, and Cameron nods.

"I was in a room I've never seen. You were there, Cameron. It was dark with no windows. A tomb or a crypt, maybe? I'm not sure." Chloe pauses for a moment. "It was filled with ash and bones. Human bones."

Matty yelps and everybody jumps.

"Jeez, Matty!" Taylor says. "Give us all heart attacks, why don't ya?"

"Sorry," Matty says. "I couldn't help it. This is freaking me out."

"Anything else?" Cameron asks, a shake in his voice.

She nods. "This was when I started screaming in the dream, and I guess in real life too. Cameron, you were trapped somehow and yelling for help. Hugo was trying to find you, but something was stopping him. I...I think it was her."

"The White Lady," I say. It isn't a question.

"Yeah." She nods as a tear runs down her cheek.

"Um..." Cameron trails off, unsure what to say. Everyone else is quiet. The silence is too much. "That's something," I say.

"I'm sorry for laying this on you two. I thought you should know. This dream wasn't as vivid as the other one. Sometimes you can't take them literally. They can be more like riddles or allegories."

"What now?" I ask, looking at Cameron.

"Not a lot we can do at this point," Cameron says. "We should sleep on it. See how things seem in the morning."

"That sounds like a good plan," I say, and everybody else murmurs in agreement.

"I think we need to talk to my aunt," Chloe says. "I need her help with this. It's too big for me."

"Pa still can't know about this," I say.

"We should meet with Margaret, though," Cameron says. "That can't hurt, right?"

I was hopeful that our ghost problems were over and we'd never have to involve Pa. This has resurfaced so fast. My friends must think I'm a broken record talking about how Pa can't find out, but now I have so much more to lose. Look at them, all so caring. Cameron peering at me with his soft eyes is making my heart melt. I can't risk losing all of this, now more than ever.

"That okay, Hugo?" Abby asks.

"Give me time to think," I say.

Abby doesn't seem happy with my answer.

"Okay, that's it, everybody," Maya says, clutching Chloe. "Everybody back to bed."

"Feel better, Chloe," Cameron says.

As soon as we leave the tent, Abby emerges. "Hey, you two. Got a second to chat?"

Cameron puts his hands in his pockets. "What's up, Abby?"

Abby's gaze bores into me. "That ghost cleansing we did was little more than a Band-Aid on an open wound. You know that, right?"

"I guess."

"Tell me right now that everything has been one hundred percent okay since the cleansing, and I'll let this drop."

My mind goes to all the strange crow behavior, and perhaps I've been kidding myself about how the mirror fell off, especially considering Chloe's dream. I secured it myself with hardened stainless-steel screws. I was in such a hurry to dismiss it as normal that it's possible I ignored what was right in front of me. I stare at my feet and say nothing.

"That's what I thought," Abby says. "We need to take this seriously."

Cameron watches me with a sad little frown.

"Okay, fine," I say, rubbing my hands down my face. "I guess talking to Chloe's aunt won't do any harm."

Abby's face brightens, and Cameron's frown goes away. "Thank you, Hugo. It's the right thing to do," she says.

"Yeah," I say, just louder than a whisper.

"And we'll do what we can to make sure your dad doesn't find out."

"Thanks."

Abby's eyes light up. "I hope sometime we can do a proper ghost hunt at your house with all my equipment. We never fully explored the basement room, and we still haven't figured out what's behind the iron door."

Don't press your luck is on the tip of my tongue, but I stop myself from saying it.

"Don't worry," she adds, apparently reading my face. "Only when your dad is away."

"Let's take things one step at a time," Cameron says.

Abby nods. "Okay."

"G'night, Abby."

On the way back to the tent, I'm lost in my thoughts. My rational mind collides with everything I've experienced over the last few weeks, and my rational mind doesn't like it. I've tried to explain away the things that keep happening, but hearing Chloe describe in detail things she knows nothing about is chilling and hard to ignore.

Cameron and I snuggle back into his sleeping bag. Soon Matty's snoring breaks the silence of the night.

Cameron whispers, "Are you doing okay? Hearing that kind of stuff from Chloe can be intense."

"I think so. She said it was a fuzzy dream, and those things don't always happen, right?"

Cameron is quiet. I almost think he has fallen asleep, but then he whispers, "I've never known Chloe to be wrong. But she's human and can make mistakes like the rest of us. Her fuzzy dreams aren't precise, and she has to interpret them. But she cares a lot about people and doesn't say things like this lightly. Her dreams are hard on her."

Cameron is so kind and understanding. The way he cares for his friends makes me like him that much more.

"You're a good person, Cameron. I'm so glad I met you," I say.

"Me too. You have no idea how much."

I turn around in the sleeping bag and kiss him. We kiss until we fall asleep in each other's arms. I'm shaken from everything, but having Cameron nearby makes me feel like it will be okay.

***

The next morning, we all abide by an unspoken pact not to discuss Chloe's dream. Other than an occasional hushed conversation, the mood is light as we break down the campsite, everybody talking about last night's dad joke competition and running around the bunkers.

On the drive home, Cameron and I trade smiles. It's almost enough to make me forget about Chloe's dreams and that damn crow.

Cameron reaches over and grabs my hand. "I had fun."

"Me too." I smile. "I'm going to do a painting based on one of my photos. That place was awesome."

"I can't wait to see it," Cameron says. He has this bright smile, and looking at him sends warmth spreading through me. I've never felt this way about somebody and want to share it with the world. I pause for a moment, choosing my next words with care. "I want to tell Pa. About us."

Cameron's smile is the biggest I've ever seen. He pulls the car to the side of the road and kisses me.

"You sure?" he asks with the sweetest puppy dog eyes that make me want to hug him.

"If I wasn't sure, that kiss pushed me over the edge." I laugh. "But seriously, yeah. I'm ready. It's been a long time coming."

"You want me there with you?"

"Nah. I need to do this on my own."

Cameron nods. "Okay. Let me know if you need anything."

"I will."

We drive the rest of the way home in happy silence, smiles on our faces.

Cameron drops me off, and my heart beats faster as I enter the house. Pa sits in the living room, watching a soccer match.

"Hey, Hugo!" Pa's face lights up. "Welcome back. How was camping?"

"Awesome. I had a great time. Fort Worden is amazing. You need to check it out."

"You take any pictures?"

"Yeah." I show him my phone and scroll through pictures of spooky concrete bunkers, views of the water, and my friends sitting by the campfire, their faces all aglow. I smile at a group shot of everybody making goofy faces. A picture of Cameron looking pensively into the fire makes my insides flutter.

"I'm glad you're making friends," Pa says, smiling. "You should have them over sometime. I really like Cameron. Maybe the two of us can convince you to go fishing."

"Good luck with that." I laugh. "But yeah, my friends are great."

A surge of adrenaline courses through my veins. This is the perfect time to tell Pa about Cameron. But what if it goes badly? I'm not sure I could deal with losing Pa's love and respect. It's all I can do to keep my hands from shaking, and my stomach is queasy.

"Everything okay, Hugo?" Pa asks. "You look like you're going to be sick."

I take a deep breath. "I'm okay." Or at least I will be if I can choke out the words burning a hole in my throat. Or maybe everything will be terrible, but at least it'll be out in the open. No more secrets.

"Hey, Pa?"

"Yeah?"

"Speaking of Cameron. I want to tell you something."

The tone of my voice gets his attention. He turns off the TV and looks right into my eyes. His expression is neutral with the slightest hint of a smile. "Go ahead."

"I like Cameron. A lot." I pause, my pulse pounding in my head. A touch of panic rises, threatening to overwhelm me. It has to be now or it'll never happen. "In fact, Cameron's my boyfriend."

I hold my breath.

Pa says nothing, his face still neutral. We sit there for what seems like forever, but it must be only about five seconds. *Say something, Pa.*

But all Pa does is lean over and wrap me in a hug.

"I love you, mijo," he says as we embrace. "And you could do a lot worse than Cameron. I'm happy for you, and I'm glad *you're* happy. You're happy, right?"

"Yeah. I'm happy." Relief floods over me in a cascade. Tears stream down my cheeks, and I let out a quick sob despite myself.

"Hey, shhhh," Pa says, patting my back. "No tears. This is a good thing."

I pull away and smile, wiping a tear from my cheek. Pa's eyes are glossy too.

"I'm not sad," I say. "Just relieved and glad I finally told you."

"I'm glad you told me too. You know you can tell me anything, right?"

I nod. "You don't seem too surprised."

Pa tilts his head. "I mean, I had my suspicions. You never brought up girls. And the way you and Cameron look at each other kinda gave me some hints."

I laugh. "I thought it might be—I don't know—harder? I mean, the whole Catholic thing."

"I'm not *that* Catholic." Pa laughs. "That was more your ma's thing. Plus, we always went to liberal churches. Didn't you ever notice the rainbow flags in the windows?"

"I guess I wasn't tuned in to that," I say. "We haven't gone to church since I was, like, twelve."

"I assume you've already told your hermana, huh?"

I nod. "Carla knows."

"Did your ma know?" Pa asks.

"Yeah. I told her about a month before—" I look down, unable to continue as my throat gets thick.

"I'm so glad," Pa says. "Glad she got to know the real you."

That does it. I'm flooded with this mix of happy and sad emotions and can't hold them back any longer. The tears pour out, and Pa hugs me again.

"I miss Mama so much," I say between sobs.

"Me too, mijo." Pa's crying now. "Me too."

We keep hugging and crying for a while. Then Pa pulls away, his hand on my shoulder.

"I know these last few years have been rough on you. We haven't cried enough."

"I guess we're making up for lost time," I say, choking out a laugh, and Pa laughs too.

"I'm sorry if I haven't always been there for you and Carla. But let's change that, okay? There's nothing we can't talk about."

I nod. "I love you, Papa."

"I love you too, Hugo. And I always will."

***

Pa heads out to go bowling with some friends he made at the carpenters' union meeting. He asks me if I want to join him, but I tell him bowling's not my thing. In reality, the only thought on my mind is inviting Cameron over.

I head toward my bedroom with a smile, wanting to straighten up a bit before I text him. But apparently I can't handle all this happiness, and my mind drifts back to Chloe's dream about the medicine cabinet. It's gnawing at the corner of my thoughts and won't go away.

Let it drop. Don't think about it, Hugo.

That lasts about thirty seconds.

Shit.

I head to the hall bathroom with a drill in my hand. Pa has already replaced the broken mirrors in the medicine cabinet, but I need some questions answered.

I unscrew the cabinet from the wall and set it down. Seeing the wooden framing surrounding the cabinet makes my head swim.

Three of the hardened stainless-steel screws I secured the cabinet with are shorn off, ripped right in two. Little nubs of metal are all that remain. The fourth screw is nowhere to be seen, but in its place is a nasty hole, gaping and full of splinters, like somebody yanked out a rotten tooth with a vise grip. The amount of force required is hard to imagine. There's no way the wind could have done that, short of a hurricane.

I inspect the dent in the wall across from the mirror. Pa and I haven't gotten around to fixing it yet. When the cabinet fell, I didn't see what happened since I instinctively covered my head and turned away as the glass crashed around me. I assumed the mirror had fallen off, bounced off the sink, and hit the wall.

But that explanation doesn't fit the evidence. The dent in the wall is *above* the sink, as if the medicine cabinet flew straight across the room with such force that it ricocheted off the wall, bounced back, and cracked the sink's porcelain.

I inspect the back of the cabinet, and ice flows through my veins. Two indentations in the steel are plain to see—the size and shape of palms. Something pushed the mirror from behind and blasted it out of the wall with the force of a cannon. The evidence is all here, but my mind wouldn't let me come to the obvious conclusion.

Chloe was right.

This goddamn house is still haunted.

21
Aunt Margaret: Cameron

My folks are gone when I get back from camping, so I go about my day, putting away the gear, showering, and trying not to obsess about Hugo and how things are going with his dad. I start and stop texting him about twenty times. The last thing he needs is me hounding him. I can wait. I have patience.

Never mind. I don't have patience.

I type out a message, but before I hit send, a text from him pops up. I thank the texting gods for making me not seem too clingy.

Hugo: It's done. Pa knows you're my bf

Cameron: [heart emoji] How'd it go?

Hugo: Perfect

Cameron: For real?

Hugo: Yeah. He was totally cool with it. I'm a little surprised to be honest

Cameron: That's awesome

Hugo: Dad digs you. Wants to go fishing

Cameron: Let's go!!!

Hugo: Ugh. No way! Know what else?

Cameron: What

Hugo: Pa went bowling. Gone for hours

Cameron: Be over in 5

Hugo: [face with sunglasses emoji]

When I cross the street to Hugo's house, he's waiting for me by the door, backpack in hand.

"We going somewhere?" I ask.

"Yeah. I hate that house."

"Something happen?"

Hugo lets out a long breath. "Chloe was right about the mirror."

"Crap." I rub my hand down my face. "I guess I can't say I'm surprised. Chloe's always right. What are we going to do?"

"I dunno. Talk to Chloe again, I guess. But you know what we're not going to do right now?"

"What?" I ask.

"Talk about this stupid house any more. Come on."

Hugo grabs me by the hand, and we head through the forest and back to the abandoned school building. On the roof, Hugo spreads a blanket he takes from his backpack and pulls out some chips and two sandwiches.

"Picnic." He waves his hand over the spread.

"I love a picnic!" I lean over and kiss him. Hugo's such a romantic.

"Oh, almost forgot." Hugo grabs a tiny bottle of champagne from the backpack. "This okay? Because if not, we don't have to drink it. Just wanted to celebrate our two-day anniversary."

I laugh. "It's fine. My parents don't love me drinking, but they're okay with it as long as I don't get drunk or go anywhere near a car."

"Cool." Hugo smiles as he pops the cork. "This will barely get us buzzed, anyway. About one glass each."

"Where'd you get it?"

"We've been carrying it around in a box for years. Pa doesn't drink much since Ma died. Not sure how fresh it is."

"Doesn't it get better with age...or something?"

Hugo shrugs.

We eat our sandwiches and chips and drink our champagne. It's gross, but I do get a bit of a buzz. It makes me a little giddier, if that's even possible. We talk about how things went with his dad and a little bit about his mom, which is sad, but I like that he's opening up. We talk about my parents and my brother. We talk about our friends and the school play. The one thing we don't talk about is Crimson House, and I'm okay with that.

We make out, marvel at the sunset, talk some more, make out some more, and then lie on the blanket and stare at the stars.

At lunch on Monday, the gang reminisces about camping. Everybody's smiling and having a good time, but Chloe is quiet.

During a lull in the conversation, she speaks up. "Have you two thought about what you want to do? Are you ready to talk to my aunt?"

Hugo blows out a long breath. "You were right about the mirror. I looked at the screws on the medicine cabinet. They were snapped in half. Something with a massive amount of strength shoved it out of the wall."

The whole gang stares at Hugo in shock.

He continues, "So if you were right about that, I guess we have to take your other dream seriously."

Having Hugo acknowledge it makes it real for me. I was clinging to the hope that maybe Chloe was wrong and the problem might go away if we ignored it, but Hugo is one of the most down-to-earth people I know.

Why does something bad happen every time Hugo and I are at our happiest? It's like that house has a personal vendetta against us. I wish Hugo had moved into any other house on our block. But wishing doesn't do much. We need to confront this head-on.

I look Chloe in the eye. "I guess we need to talk to your aunt."

The next few days go by without incident, and I push the ghost stuff to the back of my mind. I'm so eager to ignore it that it's easy. But on Thursday, as Hugo and I approach the lunch table filled with our friends, Chloe looks up expectantly.

"My aunt wants to meet with you two," she says as we sit across from her.

I take a moment to get back into that mental space. Hugo and I texted for hours yesterday, well into the night, until we agreed it was silly to keep texting and we both snuck out and went back to the roof of the schoolhouse. That's our spot, I guess. The stars were spectacular again, although to be honest, we didn't look at them much. Other things kept us busy that were more spectacular.

For now we're sticking to kissing and snuggling with the occasional "inadvertent" rub through our clothes—maybe a hand under the shirt, which still sets me on edge every time, but I'm getting better.

And maybe one time, my pinkie finger went under the elastic band of Hugo's underwear. But that's it! *I swear.* That's okay with me. We have plenty of time to do other stuff when we're ready. I like taking things slow, and Hugo agrees.

Chloe continues, "Aunt Margaret wants it to be on neutral territory."

Okay. Focus, Cameron. Aunt Margaret. I shove away all thoughts of kissing Hugo and concentrate. I look Chloe in the eye. "Okay. What does neutral territory mean?"

"It means she wants to meet at a place with no emotional significance to any of us," she says. "Not her shop, and obviously not Hugo's place. Your place is off-limits too, Cameron."

"They could meet at Inkwell Books," Taylor says. "I'm working a shift there after school, and I could reserve a table in the back. It's pretty private."

"That sounds perfect," Chloe says.

"What about the rest of us?" Abby asks. "Should we come too?"

"Let's start with just Hugo and Cameron," Chloe says. "The rest of us can hang out at Salty's, and we can meet up after."

Abby looks disappointed, but she nods. "Make sure you two remember to write down everything she says. I'm keeping track of all the ghost-related evidence."

I raise an eyebrow at Abby. "Let me guess—you've got everything up on your bulletin board with pictures and articles connected by pushpins and strings."

Abby scoffs. "No way! I'm way more high-tech than that." She grabs an iPad out of her backpack and launches an app called MindMap. In it are the details of everything that's happened, organized into little squares with lines between them, all on a timeline. She taps on several of the squares, and up pop pictures she's taken of people, places, news articles, and floor plans. I recognize some photos I took in the library archives and the recent ones from the cemetery.

"Wow!" Matty says, looking over her shoulder. "It's all so organized. Hey, what's this?" Matty taps on a square labeled *Hugo and Cameron*.

"Hey! Don't touch!" Abby yells, but it's too late. The square opens up, and in it are pictures of Hugo and me kissing, sitting by the fire, and giving each other lovey looks.

My cheeks heat, and even Hugo's face is rosy.

"Abby!" I cry. "You've got a *file* on Hugo and me?"

"You two are important in all of this," Abby says in a huff. "Right, Chloe?"

"I'm staying out of this one," Chloe says, looking down at her phone.

Everyone laughs except Abby, who manages a weak smile. It's clear she put hours of time and effort into this, and I'm wracked with guilt.

"Abby, this is amazing," I say, smiling at her. "Thanks for putting it together. We should go over everything you've collected. Let's do it tonight at Salty's after we've talked to Chloe's aunt."

Her smile becomes genuine. "Thanks, Cameron. I'm glad *you* appreciate my efforts."

***

Inkwell Books is a classic brick building on Water Street with an entire bank of windows providing ample natural light. The store is quiet, save for the occasional hushed voice and the hiss of steaming milk from an espresso cart in the front. Books fill countless rows stretching as far as the eye can see, and the scents of printed pages and freshly brewed coffee fill my nose.

Chloe, Taylor, Hugo, and I weave through the bookcases to a large room filled with comfy-looking chairs, occupied by a smattering of people reading and typing on laptops. This looks like a perfect place to work on my stories. I'll have to remember it for later.

Beyond the chairs are a few large wooden tables, one set in the far back corner, away from the rest. I recognize Chloe's aunt from when I met her in her shop a couple of weeks ago. That bright red hair would be visible a mile away in dense fog. She's wearing a green turtleneck sweater and black pants. She smiles and waves as we approach.

Taylor speaks to us in a low tone. "I'm going to start my shift. Good luck, all."

Chloe approaches the table and waves us over. Her aunt gets up, and they embrace.

"Hugo, this is Aunt Margaret."

"Hi," Hugo says.

"And you remember Cameron," Chloe says.

"Nice to see you again," I say. "Thanks for doing this."

"Don't thank me yet," Margaret says, laughing in that gravelly voice of hers. "Nice to meet you, Hugo, and hello again, Cameron." She nods to both of us, then turns to Chloe. "I think it's better if we do this on our own."

Chloe nods. "I'll see you two later at Salty's."

She heads out, leaving Hugo and me staring at Margaret. The whole thing is a little bizarre.

Margaret looks at us with a half smile and squinty eyes, like she has just figured something out. "You two want to get outta here? I love a stroll along the water. Plus, this place is too noisy."

The place is dead quiet. I shrug and give her a quizzical look. "Sure?"

Without another word, she heads for the door. Hugo and I exchange a glance, wondering what we've gotten ourselves into, then chase after her.

Outside, she heads down the sidewalk with long strides and gestures for us to follow. She's only walking, but we nearly have to jog to keep up. We weave around people walking along Water Street until we're on the far side of downtown, where the businesses dwindle and there are fewer tourists. We stroll down a long brick promenade running along the waterfront, and soon the only sounds we hear are the water lapping against the shore and the occasional caw of a seagull. The air is thick with the briny scent of the sea.

"There, that's better." Margaret finds a group of three Adirondack chairs facing Port Townsend Bay. Beside them rests a bronze statue of a family of seals—mama, papa, and baby. She glances at the seals with a laugh. "I don't imagine they will bother us. Please sit."

We settle into the chairs, and Margaret glances between us.

"Now. Let's talk." She waits for a moment, like she's expecting us to say something. I'm about to chime in when she speaks again. "So. You two and that house."

"Did Chloe tell you—"

"Ump!" She puts up a hand. "Chloe has told me almost nothing. For now, please forget what she's said, and for spirit's sake, don't tell me any of it. Let's focus on the facts and your own feelings." She pauses, hands laced, index fingers tented in front of her mouth. "Before we start, I have a question for both of you. I don't know your circumstances, but I want you to answer this seriously."

We nod. She nods back, pauses, looks between us, then continues. "There's a connection between you two and that house. It's not a good connection, and I don't say that lightly." She pauses again, looking grave and letting her words sink in. They're not lost on me, and Hugo's expression is deadly serious.

"The easiest way to sever that connection is to leave," she says, sweeping her hands wide. "Have nothing to do with that house. Leave it behind you and never return. Is that an option?"

Hugo and I trade glances, but we already know the answer. We both shake our heads.

She sighs. "I didn't think so. Had to try. With that out of the way, I want each of you to tell me your connection to that house. I want to understand it."

"Well, I live there," Hugo says. "My dad and I moved in a few weeks ago to fix the place up. We're house flippers."

"Hmm. And how did you and your father choose that particular house?"

Hugo crinkles his forehead. "What do you mean?"

"I mean, that house is quite infamous," she says, eyes piercing into Hugo. "Most people wouldn't consider it. I didn't even know it was up for sale."

"I don't really know. Pa handles all that. I asked, but he didn't give me a real answer."

Aunt Margaret nods. "Asking him again might be a good way to start. It might be important." She looks at me. "And you? What's your connection?"

"I've lived across from that place my whole life and have always hated it. When I was twelve, I was exploring it, and I—um—I had a bad experience." I don't like talking about that moment.

Hugo peeks over at me. "You never told me much about it."

"It was nothing, really. Kids went in there all the time. I got scared, my parents found out, and they grounded me."

Margaret looks at each of us for a moment, then speaks. "Those are both connections, to be sure. But there's something else. Something deeper."

"Well, we're boyfriends," Hugo says, a smile forming on his lips.

I melt into a puddle.

He continues, "Sometimes I feel like the house gets angry anytime I'm happy. And especially when we're both happy."

"Now, that *is* interesting. And not a surprise, based on the deep connection I feel. I'll have to think about that. Young love is a powerful thing." Margaret smiles. "I certainly sensed that between you two when you first walked up."

"That obvious, huh?" I ask, cheeks heating a bit.

"Perhaps not to everyone, but it was plain as day to me. And that sort of thing can act as an amplifier to existing connections. But there's still something missing. Something physical. More direct."

I'm at a loss for what other connections I have. "I don't know," I say. "Does that mean you can't help us?"

"No," she says. "It just makes it more complicated. It'll be easier to free the spirit if we can find the physical connection and remove it. Spirits hold on to physical connections to stay anchored. Remove the physical connection, and they'll have less to hang on to. It's as simple as that."

"And if we can't find the physical connection?" Hugo asks.

"It'll take more force to free the spirit. It can be done, but it'll be harder. More...violent."

Something about the way she says *violent* doesn't sit well with me. Her eyes, full of life a moment ago, seem to dull as if she's remembering something unpleasant. In a flash, it's gone, and the sparkle comes back.

"Well, that's neither here nor there," she says. "We will work with what we have. I want you two to do some homework for me. Think of every connection between you and that house. Write down every detail. Leave out nothing."

"Oh, you should talk to Abby," I say. "She's created this whole chart of stuff related to the house. The entire history, including how Hugo and I are connected. She calls it a mind meld."

Margaret laughs. "You mean a mind map?"

"Oh yeah, that's it." I laugh. "She's not a Vulcan. Well, kinda, but not really."

"I look forward to seeing it. Now, when can I visit the place?"

"Well, that's tricky." Hugo hesitates, picking at a hole in his jeans. "We have to wait until my dad is out of town."

Margaret looks surprised. "Your dad doesn't know about any of this?"

"No. And it has to stay that way," Hugo says, eyes wide. "If he finds out our house is haunted, we'll move out the very next day."

"Wouldn't that be a good thing?" Margaret says. "Remember what I said at the beginning? The easiest way to deal with this is to remove yourself from it."

"You don't understand. We don't have a ton of money. If we leave now, we're ruined."

Hugo peeks over at me with a frown. He and I would be ruined too if he had to move away. The words go unspoken, but we both know it.

"I'm sorry, Hugo. But I'm afraid I can't continue without your dad's permission. It's simply not possible. I shouldn't even be talking to you right now."

Hugo stares at his feet. "I understand. Thanks for trying to help."

"Hugo." Margaret's voice has an edge. "I want you to reconsider. Your father should know about this. He has a right to know."

"Let me think about it."

"Very well. I should go. It was a pleasure meeting you both." She gets up, gives us a nod, and takes a few steps, then turns around again. "Remember what I said. Think about the connections. And when you're ready, I'll be ready too. Be careful in that house." She spins on her heel and strides away.

Once she's out of earshot, I turn to Hugo. "Are you seriously considering talking to your dad about all this?"

Hugo has a pained look. "It'll never work. The moment Pa thinks there's any danger in that house, we'll be gone. He already blames himself for Ma's death. It's one reason he's so superstitious."

I pause, worried about treading on tough memories, but this is important. In a gentle voice, I ask, "What happened?"

Hugo looks off in the distance silently for a while. He breathes deeply. "Pa and Ma had a huge argument right before—" His Adam's apple bobs. "Ma had a great-aunt who passed away from Parkinson's. Aunt Geraldine. She was difficult to like and had alienated most of the family. Ma was the only one she had a connection to. Aunt Geraldine didn't have any immediate family, so when she died, she left her entire estate to Ma. Ma wanted to give all the money to a charity for Parkinson's research, but we were broke, and Pa wanted to keep it. They never resolved the argument. Pa thinks the accident was his fault because she was so upset. Thinks it was karma's way of getting back at him."

We sit in silence, looking out at the water lapping on the shore.

"The thing is, Pa is wrong," Hugo says. "Ma wasn't distracted. The truck came out of nowhere. There was nothing she could have done. But Pa won't hear of it. Thinks he's cursed. Now he's superstitious about everything."

I take Hugo's hand in mine, and his eyes soften.

"We'll figure this out," I say.

He nods, leans over, and lays his head on my shoulder. "I haven't thought about that in forever. It makes me so sad, but talking about it helps. Thanks for listening."

"What are boyfriends for?" I smile. Being there for Hugo during a tough time makes my heart swell. That I can be the person who brings him comfort fills me with awe. I caress his head as we stare out at the water. After a little while, he looks noticeably less upset.

"Well, let's at least tell the gang what Chloe's aunt told us," Hugo says.

I nod. "Maybe we can research the connections. Find something we haven't thought of." I glance down at the spiral notebook in my hand, which is totally blank—I didn't take a single note. "Crap! Abby's gonna kill me!"

Hugo helps me remember everything we discussed. I write about our connections to the house, how Margaret thinks it's something deeper, and how young love can amplify connections. Hugo reminds me about this one, and I blush while writing it. I remember that freeing the spirit might be violent, and I shudder to recall the way she said it.

At Salty's, we all squeeze into our regular booth in the back. Hugo and I recount our conversation with Margaret, including what she said at the end.

Chloe's crestfallen. "I'm sorry, Hugo. I didn't realize she'd insist on getting your dad's permission."

"I understand why she said it," Hugo says. "She just doesn't know Pa."

Abby updates the mind map with all the extra details we provide. She taps her lip. "Maybe there's some connection between you two and the history of the house."

"Oh, that reminds me," I say. "I talked to Mr. Peterson last Friday, and he told me a bunch more history." I recount the story about his uncle being one of the missing kids and his grandpa dying tragically a month after confronting Emily. Abby adds all those details, side-eyeing me for not telling her earlier. I remind her under my breath that I was more than a little distracted by Hugo ghosting me that day.

"Mr. Peterson was surprised you had moved in," I say to Hugo. "He said he was doing more research."

"Research about what?" Hugo asks, looking taken aback.

"No idea. I need to talk to him."

Abby's eyes light up. "Oh, and I'm trying to find out more about the nanny's lover, Luke. I submitted a request to Veterans Affairs for information about the grave, but they haven't gotten back to me yet."

"How do you even know how to find stuff like that?" I ask.

Abby shrugs. "Just good at it. Google is my friend."

"Abby, you're incredible," Taylor says with a big smile, and Abby's cheeks turn a light shade of pink. What's that all about? Abby doesn't blush about anything. I'll ask her later.

With nothing more to say about Crimson House or Margaret for the moment, we all forget our troubles for a while and descend into discussions about how awesome the weekend was, how the prep for *Oliver* is going (the props and scenery are coming together nicely, and

Hugo's backdrops are amazing), and how annoying our teachers and parents are. Overall, it's great to be a normal kid for a while. Scratch that—a normal kid with a boyfriend.

22

GHOST HUNT: HUGO

I hate being alone in this house. With nothing to do on Friday night, I wander from room to room, looking for something to occupy my time.

Pa took a roofing job from some people he knows down in Portland for extra cash. He left first thing this morning, and missing another school day was unacceptable, so I had to stay back. Typical Pa. I'm used to it, a true latchkey kid.

Cameron and his family are visiting his aunt in Seattle and won't be home until Sunday. I consider texting the gang, but I can't shake the feeling that they're really Cameron's friends and just being nice to me around Cameron. It's probably stupid, but it's my loner instincts kicking in. So, it's only me and this stupid house all weekend. Lucky me.

In the course of a few days, the weather has gone from sunny with highs in the seventies to rainy with highs in the fifties. Some trees in our yard are changing color, and the air has a bite to it. Fall is here, and it's freezing in the house. I head to the circular metal thermostat made in the early 1900s and tap the display. The dial reads just below sixty. No wonder I'm cold. Does the heat even work in this house?

Each room has old cast-iron radiators. I touch the intake pipe of one, and it's freezing cold. The water in the kitchen sink never gets warm either. The damn pilot light must have gone out on the ancient boiler. It's in the basement, of course—my least favorite place in the house.

I head down the old worn steps, taking each one with care. The wood groans and creaks under my feet. With all the rotten wood in this house, I wouldn't put it past these treads to collapse, so I hang on to the railing with a death grip.

When I hit solid concrete, it's at least ten degrees colder. My teeth chatter as I rub my arms, trying to warm up. The shorter days of fall combined with the gloomy weather makes the corners of the basement darker. Shadows are longer. The bare sixty-watt bulb in the ancient ceiling fixture fights to penetrate the darkness.

The massive boiler, which normally gives off a low rumble as it burns fuel, is quiet as a dead beast. I get down on all fours to check the pilot light through the little door on the side. It's out, of course. I click the trigger of the long utility lighter we keep nearby for just such occasions several times until the flame on the end sputters to life. As I reach in to light the pilot, a cold draft blows by, hugging the ground and blowing the flame out.

"Goddammit. I forgot about that draft," I say to the darkness. The darkness answers with another gust of cold air and the faintest whistling sound as it eddies around the basement floor.

The pilot light ignites on the second try, and the roar of burning fuel fills the room. At least the house will warm up now, but it'll take some time, especially if that draft blows the pilot light out again.

I hate the idea of spending a second longer in the basement, but I should check on that draft. Maybe I can put a cinder block in front of the hole I found the last time I was down here. But as I approach it, my heart speeds up. Where once there was a small crack, now a whole section of plaster has flaked away, revealing a brick wall with a single brick missing in the bottom row. The draft pushes out of the hole in gusts.

That's strange. Pa must have found the crack and wanted to figure out what was behind it. That's the only explanation that makes sense. Unless…

I press my cheek to the cold concrete floor to peer into the hole and the darkness beyond. No light penetrates—only inky blackness. The breeze makes me blink, creating the subtlest noise as it pushes through the hole. I swear I hear something. I keep dead still, straining my ears. The whistling sounds like a faint whisper.

Hugo.

God, that sounds like Cameron's voice.

Stop, Hugo. Just stop. Why are you creeping yourself out like that?

I've got to get to the bottom of this, so I shine my phone flashlight into the hole. Something reflects the light—an orb shining in the darkness.

The orb blinks.

It's an eye staring back at me. The shadow of eyelashes is unmistakable.

I yelp, tripping as I try to stand and landing hard on my butt with my feet inches from the hole. My heart pounds, trying to burst out of my chest.

As I kick my feet to scurry back, a hand reaches out of the hole and grabs my ankle. The grip is strong, the fingers cold, like icicles digging into my skin.

I scream—a real scream from the depths of my lungs.

The sound from the hole gets louder until it drowns out everything—the distinct sound of weeping.

I kick my legs hard until I'm free and fight to hold on to my phone as I race up the stairs, head swimming, vision darkening, trying to stay conscious. Bile rises in my throat as I reach the front door. I race outside, slam the door shut, and spit up my lunch in the front yard.

I glance back for only a moment. Rain cascades down the front of the house, and rivers of red flow from the siding. Fucking Crimson House.

I race across the street to Cameron's porch, getting soaked on the way. No one's home, but I'm about a hundred times better off shivering on their porch than anywhere near that wicked house.

What the hell am I going to do now? My heart pounds as despair sets in.

Texting Cameron will only make him worry, and he can't do much from a hundred miles away in Seattle. Pa is even farther.

I text the only person I can think of who might be able to help—Abby. She's been a little annoyed with me lately because I've been putting off talking to Pa about the ghost stuff, and I get a passive-aggressive vibe from her sometimes. But I guess it's tough when your best friend directs their attention away from you. She might just tell me to figure things out on my own, but there's nobody else to talk to.

Hugo: Hey, where you at?

Abby: With Chloe and Maya looking for PSLs downtown

Hugo: PSL? Is that a ghost thing like EVP

Abby: Lol no. Pumpkin spice latte. Maya really wants one

Okay, banter. I can do this. Like a normal person who didn't just get grabbed by a ghost.

Hugo: OMG [skull emoji]. I'm an idiot

Abby: What's up? Everything ok

I rarely text Abby. She sees right through me.

Hugo: Sorry to do this. I need to talk

No response for a moment, and then my phone buzzes with a Face-Time request. I sigh and accept it. Abby's on Water Street wearing a black knit cap with Maya and Chloe right behind her, in each other's arms, sharing an umbrella. I look like a wreck in my selfie video, but I have bigger worries.

"Hey, Hugo, what's going on?" she asks, brow creased.

I try not to sound like a mess, but I fail miserably. "Hey, Abby. I...um...shit." My voice cracks as I fight back rising emotions.

She's serious in a heartbeat. "Is that Cameron's porch?"

"Yeah."

"Don't move! I'll be there in five."

"Thanks," I say, and then the call ends.

The cold and wetness make me shiver as I huddle next to Cameron's front door. In a few minutes, Abby speeds down the road on her longboard, cutting through the rain. In one fluid motion, she hops off, kicks up her board, grabs it in the air, and runs to my side. She wraps me in a wet bear hug, but I don't mind. It's exactly what I need at this moment.

"The house?" she says, still hugging me.

"Yep."

"You wanna talk about it?"

"Yeah, but give me a minute."

"Let's get out of the rain." She releases me, then reaches up to the top of the front door frame and grabs a key. "Cameron's family won't mind."

Once inside, we head up to Cameron's room without a word. On the way, Abby grabs two towels from the linen closet, tossing one to me and keeping one for herself. We dry off in silence, Abby looking my way, words on the tip of her tongue. I beat her to it.

"It touched me."

Abby's eyes go wide. "Holy shit, really? The White Lady?"

"I dunno. It's possible. Something grabbed my leg through a hole in the basement wall."

Abby's jaw drops as I pull up my pant leg. Faint red marks wrap around my ankle where the fingers were. My heart beats faster as the gravity of the situation hits me. Most things that have happened in the house could be explained away as coincidences, freak accidents, or my imagination. But this was real. It left a mark.

"What happened?" Abby asks.

I tell her everything, leaving out no details—the draft, Cameron's voice, the eye in the hole, and the hand that reached out, like icicles on my skin. She sits listening, taking in everything, her face getting graver by the second.

"Hugo, this is serious. Getting physically touched—that's a whole new ballgame. We have to do something. You aren't safe."

I nod, my shoulders sagging from this weight descending upon me. It's too much. "I don't know what to do."

"Chloe and Maya are on their way over. Let's talk it over with them."

"Okay."

"In the meantime, I want to check something," Abby says, pulling out her phone.

She opens up the MindMap app, swipes through a few things on her screen, and brings up a photo—the floor plans of my house that Cameron and I got from the library. Thinking about Cameron makes a lump rise in my throat. I miss him so much.

Abby holds up her phone. "This is the floor plan for your basement. Can you show me where the hole is?"

I zoom in and scroll to the right spot. But instead of a wall, it shows a hallway with a large room beyond it. I point to the screen. "Right there. That's where the wall is. That must be what's on the other side of the iron door we found in the basement room."

"Somebody walled up the other side," Abby says. "Like 'The Cask of Amontillado.' That house couldn't be any creepier if it tried."

"Poe fan?" I ask, a slight laugh breaking through my gloom.

"Duh."

I crack a smile and feel a little better. "Guess that was a dumb question. You are kind of a horror freak." I bump my shoulder into hers. "Hey, thanks, Abby. You didn't have to do this. Any of this. But it means a lot to me."

"What are friends for?" She shrugs.

"I'm glad you're my friend," I say. "I haven't had many of those. And I know you're Cameron's *best* friend. And I know I've been taking up most of his attention lately."

Abby shakes her head. "Hey! Shush! You're the best thing ever to happen to Cameron. In a few weeks, you've given him more confidence than I have in the last few years."

My heart swells. "You're a good person, Abby."

"You too, Hugo."

Abby's phone buzzes in her hand. "Chloe and Maya are outside."

We gather in Cameron's dining nook. As I tell them the story, Chloe's pale face gets even paler, and Maya's forehead creases as she shoots looks at Chloe.

"Hugo, I'm so sorry," Chloe says. "I feel responsible for this since my aunt won't help you."

"You are in no way responsible," I say. "But is there any way you can tell your aunt what happened? Maybe she'll reconsider."

Chloe sighs. "I already know what she'll say. We talked after, and she was quite clear about her feelings. She wants to help, but there's no way she's getting involved without your dad's permission."

"Hugo, this is getting serious," Abby says. "It's time to bring your dad into this. People could get hurt."

Just thinking about losing Cameron and all my friends makes me sick to my stomach. I stare down at my feet and say nothing.

Abby puts her arm around me. "He might surprise you. Cameron said he was cool about you two dating. Maybe he'll understand this too."

"This is different. This is about my ma. It's raw for him, even now."

"Okay." Abby nods. "Well, the first thing we need to do is find you a place to stay. There's no way you can be alone in that house. I was looking at the patterns of the hauntings, and I noticed they get more intense when you or you and Cameron are alone in the house."

"I noticed that too," Chloe says. "And the spirit calming failed the first time because you two were holding hands and thinking lovey thoughts about each other. Am I wrong?"

I let out a short laugh. "You're not wrong. But what does that house have against Cameron and me?"

"I think it all goes back to your connections to the house," Chloe says. "Both my aunt and I sense a strong bond."

"Cameron mentioned that Mr. Peterson was surprised when he heard you'd moved into Crimson House," Abby says. "How did your dad end up choosing that house?"

"Margaret asked me the same question," I say. "I don't know. Last time I asked Pa, he didn't really answer."

"You need to ask him again. It could be important," Abby says. "How long is your dad gone for?"

"Who knows? At least until Sunday. Maybe longer."

Abby nods. "Well, we don't want you alone in that house. That much we know. My parents are gone the whole weekend on some hippie retreat. You can stay at my place."

"Abby, that would be so awesome," I say.

Suddenly her eyes light up. "I have another idea!"

"Uh-oh," Maya says. "Why do I think I'm not going to like this?"

Abby gets this manic look in her eyes. "With your dad gone, this is the perfect opportunity to do a real paranormal investigation. We haven't been able to do that yet. Not really. We can go right now."

"Yep," Maya says. "I knew I wouldn't like it."

I'm about to agree with Maya when Chloe cuts in. "I think it's a good idea."

Maya and I simultaneously say, "You do?"

We both gape at Chloe.

"Yeah." She nods. "I think we might be able to uncover what's causing all of this. My aunt said we need to find more connections."

Maya's gaze bores into Chloe, concern written all over her face. "You sure about this?"

"I am," Chloe says. "I'll try to help."

"Chloe," I say, "if this has anything to do with you feeling guilty about your aunt—"

"I *want* to help," she says, her voice more intense than I've ever heard it. "Please. Let me do this."

I nod. My ankle tingles in the spot where that thing grabbed me, but I bury my fear and look her in the eye. "Okay. Let's do it."

***

We walk across the street carrying boxes of ghost-hunting equipment that Abby keeps stashed in Cameron's closet. I pause by the front door to my house. Am I really going to do this after what happened earlier? Panic claws at my insides, threatening to spill out.

Abby looks my way, eyes soft. "Hey, we're in this together," she says. "We'll never leave your side."

I'm used to doing things by myself and don't like depending on others. Relying on people always gets me into more trouble than being on my own. But something about having everyone here smooths over those feelings. I guess these really are my friends. They've got my back, and they aren't going away, even when things get tough. My panic ebbs.

"Thanks." I smile as I open the door and walk into the house with Abby beside me.

My phone dings as I set down the box I'm carrying. It's Cameron checking in. I didn't want him to worry, so I've been holding off on texting, but I can't lie to him. I tell him what's up without all the gory details. He immediately calls me.

"Are you okay?" he asks, sounding frantic.

"Yeah, I'm good. Your bestie Abby's got my back."

"Yeah." He laughs, the worry draining from his voice. "She's pretty awesome, isn't she?"

"You've got yourself one heck of a best friend."

"I miss you," he says, and I can tell he means it.

"I miss you too." Right now, nothing would be better than having him by my side. A twinge of sadness hits me as we say our goodbyes.

Abby sets up her "base of operations," as she calls it, on the kitchen table, which we've carried into the living room so we can all be together. She removes countless electronic devices, explaining each one. She has IR cameras, motion sensors, digital voice recorders, and several other things that go over my head. A lot of it sounds like pseudoscience, but who am I to judge?

We spend the next hour setting up the equipment throughout the house, getting just the right angles based on Abby's exacting instructions. We put cameras in all the places we've seen activity: the hidden rooms, the upstairs bathroom, outside Pa's bedroom, the kitchen door, and near the hole in the basement wall. I'm not proud of it, but I let Chloe and Maya set up that last one.

With everything connected, Abby does a systems check. She's nothing if not thorough.

"Digital recorders, check," she says. "IR cameras, check. EMF meters, check. And I've got the ghost box right here. I think we're all set."

Chloe, Maya, and I gape at her.

"What?" she says as we continue to stare. "If you're going to do something, you should do it right."

"I'm glad you're on our side," Maya says.

The doorbell rings.

"Oh, Matty and Taylor found out what we're doing," Abby says, cringing at me. "Hope that's okay."

"Of course," I say, laughing. "Why fight the inevitable?"

Matty and Taylor have brought snacks—lots of them.

"We can't do an all-nighter ghost-hunting session without lots of sustenance," Matty says with his arms full of grocery bags. "Oh, crap! Twinkies! Taylor, we forgot the Twinkies!"

All-nighter? What have I signed myself up for?

We pile onto the couches while Abby inspects all the feeds. Taylor goes over to help, sitting beside her. They have the slightest smile on their face as Abby explains everything in nauseating detail, taking it all in.

"All the cameras, mics, and other devices feed into this app," she says as Taylor nods. "So, at any point, I'll know what's happening throughout the house."

"That's awesome." Taylor smiles at her. "How did you learn all this stuff?"

"Figured it out on my own." She shrugs. "And lots and lots of TV and YouTube."

I detect the slightest blush on Abby's cheeks. Interesting.

She flusters for only a moment, then focuses on the display again. "When we go lights out, the cameras will all automatically switch over to IR."

"Why is *lights out* even a thing?" Matty says, eating a Flamin' Hot Dorito. "I like lights. Don't you just record in the dark to creep people out more?"

Abby doesn't even glance up from the display. "The theory is that spirits have a harder time manifesting with UV radiation everywhere. Turning off lights also makes the EMF meters give fewer false positives." She pauses for a moment. "And yeah, doing it in the dark is creepier for my YouTube channel."

"I knew it!" Matty smiles like he won the argument.

Chloe pipes up, "I think it helps you be more attuned to your surroundings. When there are fewer stimuli, you notice things you can't detect with your normal five senses."

Matty fights the urge to make a smart-ass remark. Knowing him, it's something about *seeing dead people*, but Maya glares at him, and he backs down, munching on another Dorito.

"Well, either way, we don't have to turn off the lights yet," Abby says. "The equipment is ready. Do we have any volunteers to do the first investigation?"

"Oh, I'll do it!" Matty puts up his hand, waving it back and forth.

"I'll join him," Taylor says, smiling at Abby. Abby looks noticeably impressed. I bet that's why Taylor was eager to volunteer.

"I'll tag along too," Chloe says, getting up from the couch. "I'd like to scope out how the house feels."

"Perfect," Abby says, handing out three walkie-talkies. "These are better and faster than cell phones for group talk. The rest of us will stay back and monitor things from here. Taylor, you want to wear the selfie cam?"

"Sure." Taylor nods.

Abby outfits Taylor with a device that goes over their head with a flexible arm holding a tiny camera extending from it. She points the camera toward Taylor's face.

"There we go," Abby says as she adjusts it. "How does that feel?"

Taylor smiles and gives Abby a thumbs-up.

"Okay, let the investigation begin." Abby raises her hands above her head in a sweeping motion. She lives for this stuff.

Taylor, Matty, and Chloe head to the foyer and then up the staircase while the rest of us gather around Abby's command center, watching the feeds. They enter the second-floor bathroom. Taylor asks questions to the White Lady, Matty is waving an EMF meter around, and Chloe is standing still with her eyes closed, looking calm.

The doorbell rings.

"Are we expecting anybody else?" I ask Abby.

She shakes her head. "Not that I know of."

"That's strange." I head to the door. "Wonder who it is."

I open the door and see Cameron standing outside. I'm breathless and can't hide my wide smile.

"Hey." Cameron smiles back, his cheeks turning rosy.

"Hey!" My huge grin is uncontrollable, and relief floods through me in waves. "What are you doing here?"

I go in for a hug when I'm stopped in my tracks by what's over Cameron's shoulder in the front yard. All my joy turns into horror.

A ghostly white figure with a haggard face stands no more than twenty feet away.

23
Unexpected Events: Cameron

Hugo's expression transforms into one of dread, and fear hits me like a freight train. I spin around. A figure dressed in white is headed right toward us.

I let out a yelp and stumble backward, and my heel hits the uneven surface of the porch, sending me tumbling into Hugo. He tries to steady me, but it's useless, and the two of us crash to the ground in a tangle of limbs.

We both look back toward the figure, trying to scramble away, but the illusion is gone, and my fear turns into fury.

It's somebody in a Halloween mask, wrapped in a white sheet. A teenage guy stands behind the idiot in the mask, holding his phone up, convulsing with laughter and clutching his stomach. I'd recognize that mop of red hair and that ugly laugh anywhere. Bryce Hunter.

"Ha! We got 'em, Jimmy!" Bryce cackles. "Wait until you see the looks on their faces. This is going to be awesome on TikTok."

Jimmy removes the mask and laughs at us lying on the ground.

"You fuckers!" Hugo yells, jumping up. "I'm gonna kick your asses!"

I follow Hugo, but Bryce and Jimmy are already running away.

"Go, go, go, go!" Bryce yells as they head for a car parked down the street.

Hugo chases after them, but it's no use. He's only halfway to their car when the tires spin on the wet pavement and they pull away. One thing

I find so amazing about Hugo is the way he protects me, running into danger without a second thought.

When I catch up, his face is contorted, his teeth bared as his chest heaves up and down, his fists clenched.

"Those assholes are so dead!" He spits out the words.

"Don't even give them the satisfaction, Hugo." I put my arm around him and rub his back in small circles. "Did you see the way they ran away from you? Those two are cowards."

Abby calls from the front porch, holding up her phone. "You're right. They are cowards. And I got a video of them running away from you, looking terrified."

Hugo turns to Abby, a smile cracking through his anger. "You did?"

"Mm-hmm." Abby's mouth forms into an evil grin. "And wait until you see the close-up of their faces. Scared shitless."

That's my Abby. Always on top of everything. I honestly don't know what I'd do without her.

"Abby," I say. "When was the last time I told you how awesome you are?"

"Pretty recently, but I never mind hearing it again."

Once we're all back inside and feeling calmer, Hugo hugs me. I sigh as I melt into his warm embrace.

"How are you here?" he asks after we pull apart. "I thought you were gone all weekend."

"I was supposed to be, but after we talked on the phone, getting home was all I could think about. I...um...made up an excuse. My aunt let me borrow her extra car."

"What excuse?"

I peek over at Abby with a sheepish smile. "Abby? You're suddenly feeling sick, aren't you?"

Without missing a beat, Abby coughs into her hand. "Yeah, I've totally come down with something. You're the best, Cameron, cutting your trip to your aunt's house short for little ol' me."

"I mean, with your parents gone all weekend, somebody's gotta take care of you," I say, sounding serious.

"Totally. And the fact that they're at a hippie retreat with no cell phone service means they have no way to verify—I mean, to find out I'm sick and come home early to take care of me. You're a lifesaver, Cameron."

Maya, who's staring at an iPad, interrupts our little hug fest. "Everybody, I think you should check this out."

We all head over to Abby's ghost-hunting command center—her iPad shows a bunch of different video feeds and telemetry readouts. When did her setup get so huge? I knew she'd been collecting equipment for a while, but I didn't know how much.

"Look at the light," Maya says, pointing to the fixture in the upstairs hallway. It's swaying back and forth and flickering.

"What the heck?" Abby says, then reaches for her walkie-talkie. "Hey, ghost team. We're seeing something strange on the video feed. You seeing anything there? Over."

After a squeal and some static, Taylor's voice comes through the walkie-talkie. "Yeah, we see the lights flickering. Over."

They start to flicker in the living room as well. We all look up at the light fixture and frown. I grab Hugo's hand, and he squeezes back.

Through the walkie-talkie, Abby says, "Chloe, are you feeling anything unusual? Over."

No response.

"Chloe, are you there? Over."

Still nothing.

"Uh, Chloe was here a minute ago," Taylor says through the static. "But now I don't see her. Do you have a visual on her? Over."

Abby scans the video feeds, her normal ironclad calm showing the slightest crack. "I don't see her."

Maya grabs the walkie-talkie from Abby with a frantic expression. "Chloe's gone? When was the last time you saw her?"

"I'm not sure," Taylor says. "Matty and I were doing an EVP session. She was doing her own thing right here in the corner of the bathroom. It's probably been at least five minutes since we talked to her. Over."

Abby goes into full command mode, taking the walkie-talkie back. "Okay, we're splitting up into groups. Taylor, you and Matty search the second floor. Maya and I will search the main floor and the basement. Cameron, you and Hugo search the third floor and the attic." She hands me a walkie-talkie. "Let's stay in constant communication until we find her."

The lights go blindingly bright, and a bulb explodes in the kitchen, making everybody jump. They flicker again, then go out entirely. The whole house is pitch black, save for the glow of Abby's iPad. I yelp, but it's drowned out by shouts and screams from every direction.

You left me. Now I have you.

That voice. I haven't heard it since we calmed the spirit, but it's back, banging around in my mind again. The stressful situation mixed with my anxiety about this damn house, no doubt.

"Calm down, everybody!" Abby yells, and we all go quiet. "This changes nothing. The first thing we need to do is find Chloe."

Hugo cuts in. "Abby, let's switch. Cameron and I will take the basement. I know where the electrical panel is."

"Good plan," she says. "Okay, everybody knows their assignment. Let's go."

We all separate into groups, using our phone flashlights for guidance. Abby and Maya head upstairs while Hugo and I walk hand in hand to the kitchen. The shattered bulb crunches beneath our feet as we open the door to the basement. A cool breeze hits us, blowing up the staircase and carrying a strong scent of must. Hugo flips the light switch, but as expected, nothing happens.

He takes a deep breath, then descends the stairs with me in tow. The temperature drops, and the air gets danker with every step. Hugo's grip tightens around my hand so much that my fingers hurt, but I wouldn't trade it for anything. His grasp is the only thing holding me together at this point.

Leading with his phone flashlight, Hugo guides me around shelving and boxes until we arrive at the electrical panel. The bobbing of our flashlights makes the shadows dance, and a prickly sensation forms on the back of my neck.

"Luckily, Pa already replaced the old panel with a breaker box, or we'd be unscrewing fuses right now," Hugo says as he flips the main breaker. The lights go on, casting away the darkness. "Whew. Glad that worked."

Abby's voice crackles through the walkie-talkie, sounding more panicked than I've ever heard her. "Everybody, get to Emily's room right now!"

We share a quick glance, then run for the stairs. Abby is tough as nails, and it takes a lot to scare her. My mind races, thinking about the horrible things I've experienced in this house. I've let my guard down since we calmed the spirit, but now all the malevolence of the house has come back full force and then some. The air is thick with it. I stick as close to Hugo as I can.

Neither of us stops until we reach the third floor, then descend the spiral staircase into Emily's room. The entire gang hovers around Chloe, who's sitting on the ground cross-legged, Maya by her side, arm around her, whispering into her ear. Tears stream down Maya's face.

The scent of cookies fills the room. It's overpowering, and visions of the old lady on the porch flash through my mind. Chills ripple down my spine.

Chloe's eyes are open but rolled upward, only the whites visible. Her entire body is shaking like she's having a seizure. It wrenches my heart, seeing her like this. An old leather-bound book sits in front of her, open to a page with writing and symbols all across it.

"Should we call 911?" I ask.

"No!" Maya shouts. "They won't know what to do. It'll only make things worse."

"What do you mean?" I ask. "What's going on?"

"I recognize the book," Maya says as tears roll down her cheeks. "It belongs to Chloe's aunt. She started the cleansing ritual."

"What!" everybody shouts at once.

"I didn't think she'd do it," Maya cries. "She felt guilty about her aunt not helping. She had another dream. She made me promise me not to tell and said she'd tell you on her own. It was about your dad, Hugo."

"What about him?" Hugo's voice rises, and panic sparks in his eyes.

Maya cries harder, unable to speak.

Abby steps in. "Maya, can we call Chloe's aunt?"

"I don't have her number." Maya's voice is barely audible between her sobs.

Abby reaches into Chloe's pocket and takes out her phone. She holds the screen up to Chloe's face. I would have never thought to do that, especially under pressure. Abby is next-level smart.

"Dammit, face not recognized," Abby says, then tries again. After a few more tries, she shouts, "That did it!"

She taps the screen in a flurry and puts the phone on speaker as it begins to ring.

"Chloe, what have you done?!" Margaret shouts the moment the call connects. "I felt it the moment you started."

"This is Abby. Chloe is having some kind of seizure. She has your book. Maya thinks she started the cleansing ritual. We're in Hugo's house."

"Listen to me very carefully," Aunt Margaret says, her voice calm and deep and full of gravitas, snapping everyone to attention. "It's critical that you don't disturb Chloe. Make her comfortable, but don't wake her. That is of the utmost importance."

"Got it," Abby says. "What else can we do to help?"

"Take a picture of the book and send it to me. I want to see what page she's on. And send me a picture of Chloe too."

"Okay," Abby says, and she takes the photos. The camera's flash blinds me for a moment. Spots form in my vision, and I blink them away.

"Photos are on their way," Abby says.

"Okay, give me a moment," Margaret says. "In the meantime, have Cameron and Hugo made any more progress on finding their physical connections to the house?"

Abby looks at Hugo and me, and we both shake our heads. This is something I should have been concentrating on, but I've been so distracted by Hugo. My stomach sinks.

"I'm afraid not," Abby says.

"Okay. I'm about half an hour's drive from you. I'm getting in the car right now. Based on where she is in the ritual, there isn't much we can do at this point besides finding those connections. Beyond that, Chloe's on her own." Then, much quieter, Margaret says, "Stupid girl. Brave, wonderful, stupid girl."

"We'll do what we can," Abby says. "See you soon. We'll keep the line open." Abby hands the phone off to Taylor. "Can I put you in charge of this?"

Taylor nods. "Yep. What would we do without you, Abby?"

Abby leaves the question unanswered and heads toward Hugo and me. "We never fully explored downstairs. Maybe we can find something."

"Let's do it," I say as I head over to the sconce that opens the bottom stairs.

As I do, Hugo approaches Maya. "What did Chloe say about my pa?" he asks, voice shaky, struggling to clamp down on his rising emotions.

Maya peers up at Hugo with sad eyes, but her tears have stopped, her face full of steely resolve. "She dreamt your dad got hurt."

"Hurt?" Hugo blurts. "Hurt how?"

"She wouldn't tell me the details. She wanted to tell you herself and was going to do it tonight."

I put a gentle hand on Hugo's shoulder. He shrinks away from me, but then his shoulders relax and he lets me touch him.

"Hugo," I whisper. "Let's focus on trying to help Chloe. Then she can tell you herself."

Hugo nods with a frown. "Okay."

"Maya and I will stay with Chloe," Taylor says. "Good luck!"

Hugo, Abby, Matty, and I descend into the basement.

"Search everything," Abby says.

Matty takes the table, searching through the tools and clay jars. Abby inspects the patch of straw and the manacles. Hugo and I check out the large iron door.

The door doesn't budge no matter how much I yank the handle. "Locked."

"That looks like the keyhole of the nanny's room upstairs," Hugo says, taking the iron key from his pocket. "Let's try it."

He inserts the key just as Abby shouts, "No, wait! In case the key—"

The faint sound of metal hitting concrete rings out from beyond the door.

"—is on the other side," she finishes. "Drat. We could have put a paper bag under the door to catch the key."

"Shit. Sorry," Hugo says. He tries to turn his key, but it doesn't budge. "This one doesn't work."

I peer through the gap under the door, scanning with my phone flashlight. A faint glint of metal shines a little more than a foot away. "I see it. I bet we can fish it out with a wire hanger or something."

"Hey, guys, check this out," Matty says. He holds a silver locket. An open clay jar rests on the table beside him. "What do you make of this?"

"That looks familiar," I say. "Let me see it."

The heart-shaped locket has small vertical stripes all along it. I've seen it before. "Abby, pull up the photo of Emily and the nanny."

"On it." She opens her MindMap app on her phone, taps a few times, and then turns the screen toward us. "Here."

The photo of ten-year-old Emily smiling vacantly and posing with her nanny is up on the screen. Abby zooms in on Emily's neck.

"It's the same locket," Hugo says.

"Wait!" I shout. "This might be one of the physical connections holding her here!"

Abby nods, a smile spreading over her face. "Exactly."

She grabs the locket and runs for the staircase with the rest of us right behind her.

Back in Emily's room, things have not improved. Chloe's convulsions are worse, and drool dribbles out of her mouth. She's unconscious and powerless, a captive of the house. Maya wipes up Chloe's drool with her shirt, but more takes its place. The scent of burnt cookies hangs in the air.

Chloe utters several guttural sounds.

"What did she say?" Abby asks as we approach.

"Not sure," Maya says. "Sounded like gibberish."

But I recognize it. That cadence is unmistakable, each syllable etched into my brain.

You left me. Now I have you.

For all these years, I was sure it was something I'd made up, the delusions of a terrified mind. But now I know the truth: It came from the house. My head spins.

"We're running out of time!" Maya cries. "I don't think she can take much more."

Abby speaks into the phone Taylor is holding. "Margaret, are you still on the line?"

"Yes. I'm about halfway there."

"We found something of Emily's. A locket. She was wearing it in an old photo."

"Excellent! Destroy it. You'll need fire," Margaret says. "Smash it to pieces, then burn it. Any flame will do. And take it out of the house."

"On it!" Hugo says, taking the locket from Abby and heading up the spiral staircase. I follow right behind him.

Downstairs, Hugo takes a hammer from the jumble of tools in the dining room and empties the contents of a metal wastebasket onto the floor. The lights in the house flicker again.

"We better work fast," Hugo says. "Grab some matches from the kitchen. Drawer next to the sink."

I race for the matches as he throws the locket into the trash can and smashes it with the hammer. The sharp crack of metal and glass fracturing fills the room. He smashes it several times.

"Okay, let's take this outside," Hugo says.

He sets the trash can down on the lawn as I strike a match. A flame bursts out, then dances on the end of the matchstick.

"Let's hope this works," Hugo says. "She said any flame would do."

"Here goes nothing," I say, dropping the match.

The moment the flame hits the smashed locket, a column of fire bursts up from the trash can, blue and green flames twisting furiously like a tornado, unlike anything I've ever seen. I swear faces appear within the swirling maelstrom. The acrid odor of burning metal assaults my nose.

The locket burns longer than I expect, and an ear-piercing shriek erupts from the trash can—the noise of the metal expanding and contracting from the heat, no doubt. But it could be mistaken for screaming.

A final ball of blue flame shoots out, rising twenty feet in the air and trailing a mushroom cloud of smoke in its wake.

Silence.

The fire is gone, leaving only a thin column of twisting smoke behind.

We peer over the edge of the trash can. Nothing remains of the locket—no melted metal or shattered glass.

"Well, something happened," Hugo says.

"We've got to go check on Chloe," I cry. "I hope she's okay."

As we enter the house, I feel immediately that the oppressiveness is gone. No voice whispers in my ear. We run the entire way back to Emily's room. The lights are steady. The house is calm. The smell of burnt cookies is gone.

Maya is crying again, but they're tears of joy this time. Chloe's in her arms, conscious but haggard and worn thin, her eyes sunken.

Her voice is weak, but she cracks a smile. "It worked. Emily is gone."

24
THE AFTERMATH: HUGO

"Here, sweetheart, drink this. It'll make you feel better," Margaret says, handing a steaming-hot cup of tea to Chloe, who's wrapped in a blanket on the couch. She's still visibly wiped out but about a hundred times better than she was half an hour ago. Maya is still by her side, arms wrapped around her.

Margaret arrived at the house about five minutes after the end of the ritual. I guided her to Emily's room, and she ran right to her niece. Several quiet words passed between them as Margaret touched Chloe's cheeks and kissed her forehead. As Margaret spoke, Chloe nodded with downcast eyes.

We're all in the living room now, contemplating the night's events. Everyone knows what Chloe did was brave but foolish. Everyone is relieved Emily's spirit is free and grateful for what Chloe did. Everyone knows we were lucky to come out of this unscathed. Everyone knows these things, so we haven't said them out loud. Everyone, that is, except Maya, who lets Chloe know in no uncertain terms that if she ever tries anything this stupid again, then so help her god, she will kick Chloe's ass right into next week. Chloe smiles and kisses her.

Cameron's on the love seat by my side, our arms wrapped around each other. Waves of relief spill out of both of us; the house is calm, truly calm, for the first time.

"Is it really over?" Cameron asks.

I nod. "I think so."

Margaret stands up and looks around the room, taking long breaths. "This house is still filled with energy. Some houses are like that. It feels like calm energy, but I've never felt this house before, so I don't have any point of reference."

Chloe speaks between sips of tea. "Emily's spirit is gone. I'm sure of it. I felt it when she left. The locket might not have been the only thing she was holding on to, but when you destroyed it, the shock was enough to make her lose her grasp."

"Did she go smoothly?" Margaret asks Chloe. "Was it a clean break?"

Chloe shakes her head. "She didn't want to go. She's protective of the house. It felt..." Chloe trails off.

"Violent," Margaret finishes for her.

Chloe nods, looking down into her tea.

That word—*violent*. The way Margaret said it the other day sat wrong with me, and it's the last thing I want to hear now. A glance at Cameron tells me he's not glad to hear it either.

"A violent cleansing can leave a mark on a house," Margaret says with a deep sigh, then looks at Cameron and me. "Be vigilant. Let us know if there is any more activity. I do sense that you two still have physical connections to the house. I recommend that you try to get to the bottom of it."

Cameron and I both nod. Margaret's gaze bores into me. The intensity of her reproachful stare is extreme and makes me shrink back.

"Hugo," she says in a level tone, but the edge of her voice is razor-sharp. "It's time to tell your father about all this. You can't keep it hidden from him. It's impacting more than just you."

Deep down, I know telling him is the right thing to do. But for some reason, the thought of talking to Pa about this scares me even more than coming out to him did. I have so much to lose.

"Yeah," I say after a long pause. "But I want to tell him on my terms. I want to break it to him in the right way."

Margaret nods. "Of course. But don't wait long. I'll give you until the end of next weekend, and then I'll check in with you."

My stomach churns, but I nod anyway. "I'll get it done by then."

"Very good. Chloe, I think it's time to get you home. I'll figure out how to break this to your parents."

Chloe, Maya, and Margaret head for the door. On their way out, I intercept Chloe and wrap her in a hug.

"I'm so glad you're okay," I say. "I don't know how to thank you."

She smiles. "You just did."

"One more thing. Maya said you had a dream about my pop."

Chloe nods. "I dreamed he fell and got hurt."

"What?"

Chloe puts her hand on my shoulder. "It was Emily who pushed him. Now she's gone. It's part of why I did what I did."

I hug her again. "Thank you so much."

"Come on, Chloe," Margaret says, putting her arm around her niece and guiding her to the foyer.

We all wave goodbye as Chloe, Maya, and Margaret head out the door.

For the next hour, we work to get the house back to normal. In Emily's room, I crank up the spiral staircase. We have more questions to answer, but I'd rather save them for another day, and I don't want Pa discovering the basement room until I'm ready to tell him everything.

We put away all the ghost-hunting equipment, and I replace the bulbs that broke throughout the house while Cameron sweeps up the broken glass. Once we're done, we all meet in the living room.

Matty pats me on the back. "Hugo, you sure know how to throw a fantastic party. But it's late. I better go."

I thank Matty, and we all wave goodbye.

"Taylor's giving me a ride home," Abby says. "Can you two carry these boxes back to your house, Cameron?"

"We got it," Cameron says. "And thanks for everything, Abby. I'm not sure we would have survived without you."

We say goodbye to Abby and Taylor, and they head out. Taylor has their hand on Abby's shoulder. Interesting.

I turn to Cameron. "Is there something going on between those two? It seemed like Taylor was going out of their way to impress Abby tonight."

"It's possible." Cameron shrugs with a smile. "They've been friends forever. But I have noticed she's been acting strange around Taylor lately. Especially since camping."

"They'd make a cute couple."

"They would," Cameron says. "But not as cute as us."

He gives me the most bashful and adorable smile. My only option is to kiss him, so I do.

"Well," I say, looking into Cameron's eyes.

"Well," Cameron echoes. He pauses for a beat, and we continue staring. Then he says, "I need help carrying these boxes over to my place. And..."

There's a long pause.

"And?" I smile.

"And I don't like the idea of you spending the night here alone. And my family is gone. So..."

"Cameron Walsh, are you inviting me to spend the night with you?"

He smiles. "Hugo Cruz, that's exactly what I'm doing."

"And you're okay with that?" I ask.

"I don't think I've ever been so okay with anything in my entire life. Are *you* okay with it?"

I look him right in the eye, deadly serious. "Yes."

I smile and grab one box. "Race you back!"

The next two minutes consist of us running with boxes, bumping into each other, juggling keys to lock my door, racing across the street, juggling more keys to unlock Cameron's door, elbowing each other on our way up the stairs with lots of giggling, kicking off our shoes, and jumping onto Cameron's bed.

We tumble together onto the bedspread, kissing with our hands all over each other. Our kissing gets deeper as we roll around. I pause for a moment to take Cameron in. He looks back at me with these seductive eyes that make me lose my breath. This is not the bashful Cameron I met just weeks ago.

He slides his hands under my shirt and tickles my back, sending shivers down my spine. We've done this before over the last week, but after the time in the bunker, I'm glad he's making the first move. He brings his hand to my front, squeezes my pec, and then runs it down my chest, sending a wonderful tingle through me, and I let out a gasp.

"Heh, you like that?" he says with a devilish smile.

"I do."

He reaches down, lifts my shirt clean off, and stares at my naked chest, running his hand back and forth over my stomach.

I follow his lead and put my hand under his shirt. For a moment, Cameron tenses, but then he relaxes.

"You okay?" I ask.

"Yeah."

His warm skin against my fingers is soft as silk. I glide my hand up his back, then down his chest, goose bumps springing up on his skin. I lift off his shirt and soak him in. Wow, Cameron is sexy. He's got natural muscle on him, with strong shoulders and arms, which really gets me worked up. We both stop for a moment, lying side by side, just looking at each other's half-naked bodies. My heart glows—this adorable, vulnerable, wonderful guy is lying next to *me*. I'm so lucky that things worked out like they did. I smile and run my hands through his hair, and he smiles back with pink in his cheeks.

We join again, pressing together, kissing with rising intensity. Something about our bare skin touching fills me with burning desire, and now I'm completely turned on. It's pretty obvious Cameron is too.

To my surprise, Cameron unbuttons my pants. We've never gone *this* far before, and it makes my heart rate skyrocket. He kneels on the bed, then yanks my pants off in one quick motion, leaving me in my tighty-whities with a serious bulge pressing against them. His sudden bravery leaves me breathless.

I sit up, then playfully push him off his knees, sending him falling into the pillows. "Two can play that game," I say, unbuttoning his pants. I rip them off so fast that I drag his underwear half off, exposing a tuft of brown hair extending down from his belly button. Cameron gasps.

"Hey, not so fast!" he cries with a smile as he swats my hand away and hikes his underwear back up.

He jumps on top of me, kissing me passionately as we smash our bodies together. This will send me over the edge pretty fast if we're not careful.

Things start getting more intense, but then Cameron pulls away a moment later with a touch of apprehension. "Um. We haven't talked about—uh—safe sex...and stuff."

I brush away a lock of hair covering his eye. "There are plenty of things we can do that are perfectly safe," I say. "That's all I want to do tonight anyway."

Relief washes over Cameron's face. "Oh, thank god. I'm new to all this. I do *not* know how it's supposed to work."

"I'm new to this too. Let's figure it out together. We'll do what feels comfortable."

Cameron beams. "How are you so awesome?"

"Lots of practice." We both giggle.

"Okay." Cameron gets up on his knees and guides me up to mine so we're face-to-face. He grabs the top of my underwear with both hands. "On three?"

I guess we're doing this. My heart beats faster as I grab the top of his underwear. "On three."

We count down, then pull each other's underwear down to the knees. We pause for a moment, staring, each taking the other one in. Seeing a guy I like naked in front of me is something I've dreamt of for years, and I'm not disappointed in the least. Cameron is perfect.

We push together, kissing with nothing between us. It's magical. The beating of his heart, the light scent of his sweat, and the taste of his kiss make me feel more connected to him than I've ever been to another person.

I pull him closer, and we tumble onto the bed, rolling and kissing.

Cameron ends up on top and gets to his knees, looking down at me with this fire in his eyes that I've never seen.

"One sec," he says, reaching over to his nightstand. He opens the drawer and pulls out a tiny bottle of lube.

I puff out a laugh. "Where'd you get that?"

"Walgreens," he says, cheeks turning pink. "It was super embarrassing."

"Adventure Cameron," I say with a smile.

He opens the lube and empties about half the bottle on my lower regions, then jumps on top, rubbing us together. Holy crap. At this rate, I won't last long.

We continue until the world melts away, and I'm only aware of our bodies pressed together. This is far more than just a physical act. My feelings for him are so powerful that my heart nearly bursts from my chest. Cameron's warmth, his soft skin, and the sounds he makes, combined with the emotions flowing through me, wrap me in bliss. I go back to kissing him, muffling his cries as I mash our mouths together. It's too much, and I can't hold back—we go over the edge. For about ten beats of my heart, I'm lost in total ecstasy. He collapses on top of me, both of our chests heaving. As my pulse slows, we share soft kisses, touching and giggling, coming down from our euphoric high.

"Um, wow," Cameron says.

"Yeah."

He reaches over the bed and grabs a towel for us to clean up. Cameron thought of everything.

We lie side by side, basking in the afterglow. Cameron rests his head on my chest, running his hand up and down my stomach. "I'm so glad I met you."

"You have no idea," I say. "Before you, I wasn't sure I'd ever have a real boyfriend."

"What?" Cameron says, shock in his voice. "A hot guy like you? You could have your pick of guys."

"Well, I pick you." I kiss the top of his head.

"I'm still not sure why."

"Because you're kind, funny, and smart, and because I find you absolutely, irrefutably adorable and sexy as hell."

"Okay, it's starting to sink in."

"Hey, bullies suck. They didn't make you lose your confidence overnight. It took time. So, it'll take time to go in the other direction too. But I'll keep reminding you." I smile and kiss him on the forehead, then sigh. "I've had my own issues, having darker skin. It's so easy to hate yourself."

"Yeah, I've thought of that, seeing idiots and bullies at school. The little comments they make."

"Tell me about it," I say with a sad laugh. "Death by a thousand cuts."

"I deal with that with my dad. But I'm sure it's nothing compared to what you go through."

"It's not fun for anybody. But yeah, it ain't great."

Cameron sighs. "People suck." He puffs out a laugh. "And not in a good way."

I raise an eyebrow and look at Cameron with a wry smile. "What is this good sucking of which you speak?"

Cameron smiles wide, cheeks pink. "Ready for round two?"

***

The next morning is leisurely, and we linger in bed. After such a long day and an even longer night, we deserve it. Cameron is tucked under my arm, resting on my chest. Drool has dribbled out of his mouth and formed a pool on my left pec. Even his drool is adorable. This is my boyfriend. Joy brims out of me, forcing me to smile. I replay the words in my mind—*my boyfriend*.

"Hey, Cameron," I whisper, nudging him. "Time to wake up. It's almost eleven."

Cameron makes a noise that sounds roughly like *Saturday*, then rolls to the other side of the bed. Guess I'll let him rest. I slink out of bed and slip on my clothes without making a sound. I kiss him on the forehead and whisper, "I'll see ya soon. Sleep tight."

Cameron grunts, and I slip out the door.

On the way to my house, I check my messages. Chloe is doing great today, thank god, and things went fine with her parents. Abby says she's going to review all the ghost-hunting evidence we collected. That should be interesting. Pa says things are going well in Portland and he should be back by sometime on Sunday afternoon.

My stomach ties itself in knots as I read his text. How will he react to the fact that we have a prison cell in our basement and we exorcised a ghost? But Chloe's aunt gave me a week, so I've got time to figure out how to break it to him. I can put it off a bit longer.

For the next hour, I scour the house, double-checking everything. I find only a few stray shards of glass under the kitchen counter. Other than that, it's like nothing happened.

I take a shower and put on fresh clothes. A message flashes on my phone.

> Cameron: Where'd you go [sad face emoji]

> Hugo: Home to shower and change

> Cameron: Why didn't you wake me

> Hugo: I totally woke you. You grunted like a [zombie emoji]

> Cameron: Need [brain emoji]

> Hugo: You only like me for my delicious [brain emoji]

> Cameron: Nuh uh!!

> Hugo: What else?

> Cameron: Need [eggplant emoji]

> Hugo: Be right over [sunglasses emoji]

I head over to Cameron's house, rereading our text chain. Our humor meshes so well that I can't help but laugh.

With my nose in the phone, I barely see the car coming toward me. I jump back just in time to avoid being roadkill, letting out a yelp of surprise. Our houses are near the end of a dead-end street, so traffic is unusual.

A man yells out of the driver's side window of an old 1950s Chevy. "Watch it, kid!"

"Sorry!" I call back.

As the car passes, I glimpse someone in the back seat. It's only for a moment, but I swear it's an old woman with long gray hair and yellow crooked teeth, smiling at me. When she sees me looking, her smile gets wider. Unnaturally wide.

I gasp.

In a flash, the car zooms by. Through the rear window, the head is only a silhouette, and she doesn't look back.

Shit. That stupid haunting really got to me. How long will I be seeing the White Lady everywhere? It wouldn't surprise me to see her face on a piece of toast. I shake my head and head over to Cameron's.

25

You Can't Choose Them: Cameron

Hugo and I spend a lot of time together, savoring the time away from our parents and, more importantly, away from stupid Crimson House. We stay at my house for most of the weekend. My parents text me to ask how Abby is. I tell them she's doing better and it's just a stomach bug. A pang of guilt hits me for lying to them, but I couldn't very well say I had to leave my aunt's place early because my boyfriend had a ghost emergency, so I cut myself some slack.

Saturday is filled with hanging out with Hugo, talking, goofing off, and the occasional make-out session. I work on my urban fantasy while Hugo draws in his sketchbook. He wants to draw the characters in my story. I'm working up the courage to let him read enough to do that—any day now.

Saturday night is even more fun as we continue to explore ways to make each other happy. We're still keeping things totally safe. Nobody's sticking anything into anybody anytime soon. To be honest, the safe stuff is awesome.

But the best part is being close to Hugo. Being with him so intimately makes these feelings deep inside me bubble to the surface. Honestly, it's a little scary how much I like him. I've never felt this way about another person, and the idea of losing him makes me ache, so it's easy to understand why he's afraid to talk to his dad. If there was even a chance it could break us up, I'm not sure I could go through with it myself.

On Sunday, we straighten up both of our houses, erasing all evidence of our nighttime activities, both ghost-related and not. But reality sets in when Hugo's dad and my parents come home. It was fun while it lasted.

On Monday at school, I'm eager for lunch to come so I can check in with my friends. Although our group text blew up all weekend, I haven't shared anything about what Hugo and I did. It's too intimate to mention over text, even to my best friend.

Abby waves as I approach the lunch table. She has this funny expression, a smile forming on her face.

"What?" I say as my cheeks heat.

"Something's different about you." Her smile gets wider, and my face gets warmer.

"I don't know what you mean." My cheeks are on fire now, and I fight back a smile.

"Oh my god!" Abby shrieks, then whispers, "You and Hugo did it, didn't you?"

"Wellllll," I say. "We didn't *do it* do it."

"Did you or didn't you touch Hugo's penis?"

"Abby!"

"Cameron!" She folds her hands. "Spill it."

"Yes, okay? We did it. Kinda. I mean, we were, like, naked and—you know."

"Oh my god, Cameron!"

Taylor, Chloe, and Maya walk down the aisle toward our table.

"Don't say anything!" I whisper to Abby, and draw my index finger across my throat to show I'll kill her if she does. She mimes zipping her lips.

"Hey, gang," Chloe says in a singsong voice as everybody finds a seat. It's a relief to see her in such high spirits.

"Hey, Abby," Taylor says as they sit down right next to her, smiling.

"Hey, Taylor." Her voice hitches a bit, and she breaks eye contact. I've never seen Abby so flustered around Taylor before. Maybe Hugo was right. Maybe something is going on there.

I turn to Chloe. "You look about a billion times better than you did Friday night," I say.

"Thanks," Chloe says, smiling. "I feel about that much better too. Aunt Margaret's tea is like magic. Or maybe it *is* magic."

"Friday still seems like a dream," Taylor says.

"Or a nightmare," Matty cuts in as he sits down at the table. "Any more ghost-related news?"

"No," I say, "but I'd rather wait until Hugo gets here before we talk about any of that."

As if on cue, Hugo arrives. My pulse speeds up as he approaches. He gives me a big smile and a peck on the lips before sitting down next to me. Our thighs touch, and my mind goes right to the things we did this weekend. Matty glances back and forth between us, his eyes narrowing and his lips curving up.

"Did something happen between you two?" Matty's grin is ridiculous.

Hugo and I say nothing, but we can't hold back our smiles. Even Hugo is blushing now.

"Oh my god!" Matty gets up from his chair and jumps up and down. "That's awesome!"

People around the cafeteria glance our way as Matty continues to act like an idiot.

"Matty, stop!" I glare at him.

"Sorry!" Matty sits down, but he still has this absurd grin. "I'm just happy for you." He puts his chin on his interlaced fingers and dreamily stares up at the ceiling. "I'm jealous. I wish I had someone."

He sits there for a moment, and we all gape at the train wreck that is Matty. If you looked up *extra* in the dictionary, it would be a picture of him. Then he does a total 180. "So, ghost stuff! Anything new?"

Abby laughs at Matty's randomness. "It took all of Saturday to review the evidence. There's some interesting video from when the lights exploded. Also some moments we may not want to relive. Other than that, nothing extra ghostly."

"I spent the weekend recovering," Chloe says. "My aunt and I talked a lot. She's going to tutor me more directly. I guess I was lucky things worked out like they did."

"Chloe," I say, "we are forever indebted to you for what you did over the weekend, and you were so brave. But never do anything like that again! Please!"

Maya gives Chloe a knowing look, and Chloe stares down at the table. "Yeah," she says. "Sorry about that. I shouldn't have gone rogue like I did. I didn't want to scare anybody or have anybody talk me out of it, but I know what I did was dumb."

"It was brave," Hugo says. "And you don't have to apologize. Thank you, Chloe."

Everybody nods and agrees, giving Chloe hugs and pats on the back.

"Did you tell your dad about the hauntings yet?" Abby asks Hugo. "Or ask him more about why he picked that house?"

His mouth curves into a frown. "No, I haven't talked to him. I'm still figuring that out."

She doesn't probe further. Hugo's clearly not excited about the subject. I make a mental note to talk to him about it later.

"Hey, everybody. It's October now. You know what that means?" Taylor says, apparently detecting the awkwardness and trying to change the subject, always the peacemaker. "Anderson Farms is opening their Halloween fair and corn maze. Anybody want to go this weekend?"

Hugo lights up at the new topic. "That sounds awesome."

"I've suddenly got the worst craving for apple cider and kettle corn," Matty says.

"And I still haven't gotten my pumpkin spice latte," Maya says.

I smile. "Let's do it!"

When lunch ends, Abby catches up with me on the way to my next class. "Hey, Cameron, got a sec?"

"What's up?"

"Do you...uh..." Abby picks at a hole in her jeans. "Do you think Hugo's going to talk to his dad soon?"

"I hope so. He gets defensive when I bring it up, but he says he will. Why?"

"I was thinking about what Margaret said about the spirit cleansing being violent," Abby says. "Something about the way she said it put me on edge."

I nod. "Same."

"Have either of you noticed anything? Anything at all out of the ordinary?"

"No. Nothing."

"You'll let me know if anything changes, right?" she asks.

"Of course."

Abby's phone buzzes, and her eyes light up. "Holy shit. I got an email back from Veterans Affairs."

"You did?"

"Yeah." She scans the email for a moment. "Plot 14a belongs to Luke Brannagh. We finally have the last name of the nanny's lover."

"Wow! Abby, you're amazing!"

"Does that name mean anything to you?" she asks.

"It sounds familiar, but I can't think of why. Does it say anything else about him?"

Abby continues to scan the email. "He was born in Ireland in 1855 and immigrated here when he was eighteen. It doesn't say his cause of death, but he died in 1903 during military service. I guess that's why he ended up in the military cemetery."

"I'll ask Mr. Peterson if he can dig up any more history about him," I say. "He's good at that stuff."

On my way to class, I send a text to Mr. Peterson, telling him about the letter we found in Agnes's room, signed by Luke Brannagh. I leave out the details about the crow falling on his grave—that'll be easier to talk about in person. No need to freak him out about ghost stuff over text.

> **Mr. P:** That's fascinating, Cameron. It fills a huge hole in the house's history. I'd love to see that letter.

> **Cameron:** I'll have Abby send you a picture

> **Mr. P:** Excellent. I'll do some research and let you know what I find.

"Mr. P's on it." I smile at Abby.

***

With Hugo and me getting more serious, I decide it's time to tell my family about us. On Tuesday evening, when my whole family is present for dinner for a change, I invite Hugo over to eat with us. Jack and Dad are locked in a heated debate about how the U.S. soccer team will do in the World Cup trials. Mom is polite and asks Hugo questions between glances at her phone. Her work always butts into family time.

Finally, the conversation lulls, and it's time to make our announcement.

"Mom, Dad, Jack, I have something I want to say."

Everybody gets quiet and directs their undivided attention my way. Hugo squeezes my hand under the table. I had no idea I'd be this nervous.

It's not like I'm coming out or anything. There's no going back now, so I blurt it out. "Hugo's my boyfriend!"

Everybody sits there for a moment, saying nothing. So, for emphasis, I add, "As in the kissing kind."

Jack nearly chokes on the water he was drinking as he bursts into laughter. "Yeah, we know what a boyfriend is, Cameron. But that's awesome."

Mom smiles, wide and genuine. "I thought there might be something going on between the two of you. With how you look at each other, it's not a surprise. Hugo, I can't think of a nicer young man for Cameron to have as his first boyfriend."

"Mooommm," I groan. *First boyfriend.* Does she have to spell it out like that?

"Thanks, Mrs. Walsh," Hugo says, smiling.

Dad clears his throat. "You two will need to keep the door open from now on when you're up in your bedroom."

Finally. This is the first time he's acknowledged that I like guys. "Dad, that's the nicest thing you've ever said to me. Thank you."

"And we're going to have to talk about safe sex," Dad adds. "Where's that banana and condom?"

"Never mind!" I shout as I melt into my seat, mortified. "I take it all back. You're the worst dad ever!"

The rest of the dinner is extremely...normal. Hugo and I continue holding hands but move them to above the table. Mom asks Hugo questions about his artwork, and Jack takes every opportunity to tease Hugo and me. Dad continues to be Dad. He still has a ways to go in his "my son likes guys" journey, but overall, nothing too awkward or uncomfortable happens, banana-condom comment notwithstanding. In other words, my family has accepted us as boyfriends, and they're treating Hugo like a member of the family.

It feels great.

The next few days are among the happiest I've had in years. The entire school knows Hugo and I are boyfriends. I guess the kissing in the lunchroom and hand-holding in the hallway gave it away. Go figure.

I even catch Noah, my former crush, watching us walk hand in hand to theater tech. His face is neutral, but the slightest shift in his eyes betrays his feelings—he's jealous of the thing he once rejected. Evil satisfaction bats at my insides, but I swat it away. I don't want to be petty.

Even Bryce and Jimmy are quiet. After they posted the video of themselves pranking us, which only made them look like the assholes they are, Abby linked a video of them running in terror from Hugo, which got ten times the likes.

Hugo hangs out with me after school pretty much every day. With the door open, mind you. We like each other's company and have the same Monty Python–esque sense of humor. Or perhaps Key and Peele. We can go on and on, talking for hours about nothing, cracking each other up with goofy nonsense.

On Thursday, after Hugo goes home for dinner, my dad comes up to my room. "Hey, bud. Got a minute to talk?"

Nothing good ever comes after that phrase. A nervous pit forms in my stomach.

"Sure, Dad. What's up?"

"I've noticed Hugo hanging out here a lot."

"Yeah, we really like each other." Where in the heck is he going with this?

His eyebrow twitches. Something's bothering him.

"Yeah." He draws out the word. "Seems like a lot."

"He's my boyfriend," I say, feeling even more tense. "And we always keep the door open, like you asked."

He does the eyebrow twitch thing again. That was not the answer Dad wanted to hear, but that's exactly why I said it. There's a principle here.

Jack hovers behind Dad. He must have overheard the conversation from his room across the hall.

"I think you're spending too much time together," Dad says. "Maybe you should cool it a bit."

"*Cool it?*" I'm trying to keep myself under control, but my voice has an edge to it.

Dad nods. "Yeah. See less of each other. I'm worried about you getting distracted at school."

"I'm getting straight A's," I shoot back.

"That's not the point. I—"

"You never told me to see less of Abby even though she was over almost every day last year."

Jack cuts in, "He's got a point, Dad."

Dad's eyes light up like he's about to win the argument. "Yes, but as you like to point out, Abby's not your girlfriend."

"As I *like* to point out?" I say, just below a yell. I've officially lost it. All the times I've let things slide with my dad, all the comments he's made, all the negative body language—it has piled up like a towering garbage heap in my mind, and now it's toppling down in an uncontrollable cascade.

"I *hate* pointing it out! And I shouldn't have to, because I'm gay, Dad! I like guys. Always have. Always will. But that doesn't stop you from insisting I keep the door open when Abby's over. It's messed up!"

"Hey, bud..." Dad gestures downward with his hands. "Let's keep this civil—"

"Every time you do it, it makes me feel sick to my stomach. Do you have any idea what it's like to go through that in your own home?"

"Now you're being dramatic."

"I'm with Cameron, Dad," Jack says, coming to my rescue. "I dated Angie all last year. She was over here all the time, and you never said a word."

"Hey, no ganging up on me. I'm the adult here. And what I say goes."

Anger builds in me like wildfire, and I have to get away. "As soon as you start acting like an adult, I'll start listening." I shove past Dad into the hallway and head for the stairs.

"Cameron! We're not finished here. Don't walk away. You can't talk to me like that!"

Dad tries to follow me, but Jack puts his hand on his shoulder. "Dad, let him go."

I race down the stairs and blast out the door with my head spinning. This is how I always suspected my dad felt, but until now he's kept it hidden behind passive-aggressive comments. Today it has turned into *direct* aggression. I've always hoped having a boyfriend would help him accept me for who I am, but it looks like all it's done is reveal how he really feels.

I run to Hugo's house and head for the back door so my dad doesn't see me and try to follow. I knock on the door while texting Hugo that I need to see him.

The back door opens a moment later, and Hugo's dad comes out. "Hey, Cameron." He takes one look at me and frowns. "What's wrong?"

Hugo's dad being so caring to his son's boyfriend brings tears to my eyes.

"Come here, come here." Mr. Cruz opens his arms and hugs me. My tears flow faster as he rubs my back. "Hey, hey, everything's going to be okay. Shhhhh."

"Sorry, I just—" I choke out as I pull away.

"What's going on?"

I rub the tears off my cheeks. "Parent stuff."

"Oh man, that's the worst!" Mr. Cruz says, and I cough out a laugh.

"Tell me about it." I smile at him.

"Anything you want to talk about?" he asks.

"No. Honestly, being nice to me is the best thing you could have done to make me feel better."

Mr. Cruz smiles. "Anytime, niño."

Hugo comes into the kitchen and runs over to me. "Cameron! What's going on?"

"I'm okay," I say. "Dad and I got into an argument."

"Why don't you two head up to Hugo's room and talk about it? I'll just get in the way."

"Thanks, Pa."

"Thanks, Mr. Cruz."

"But no funny stuff up there!" He gives us a big smile as we head out of the kitchen.

"Chill out, Pa," Hugo says with a laugh.

The whole interaction between Hugo and his dad is so delightfully normal that it makes me smile. But the joy mixes with melancholy. Perhaps someday, *my* dad will act like a normal dad to his normal son—a normal son who happens to like guys.

***

As we walk upstairs, my head starts to clear. Being next to Hugo makes everything feel like it'll be okay. He smiles as we enter his room. The painting of the tree is much further along than it was the last time I was here.

"Wow, that looks great," I say. "Are you almost done with it?"

"Getting close. Still need to paint highlights."

"Oh! The swing. I just noticed that," I say. "Is that a kid in it?"

"Ghost kid." Hugo smiles, then sits on the bed and pats the spot beside him. "So, tell me what happened."

I tell him about the argument with my dad and how Jack defended me. Hugo listens quietly the whole time.

"I've never stood up to my dad like that," I say. "I mean, I'm plenty snarky to him, but we've never had a yelling match."

"That sucks," Hugo says. "I'm sorry he's acting like that."

"I wish he was more like your dad."

Hugo laughs. "I'm still in shock that Pa is so cool about everything."

My phone buzzes.

> Jack: Hey you okay

Cameron: Better than I was

> Jack: Dad was an ass

Cameron: Didn't mean to yell at him

> Jack: He had it coming. I talked to him

Cameron: Really?

> Jack: Yeah. He calmed down at least

Cameron: K

> Jack: Still doesn't get why he was wrong

Cameron: [eye roll emoji]

> Jack: You at Hugo's

Cameron: Yeah

> Jack: Stay there as long as you want. But it's cool to come back

> Cameron: K. I'll stay here for now. Back in a while

> Jack: K love you dweeb

> Cameron: Love you too freak. And thanks. A lot

I show the text chain to Hugo. We talk a bit more about my dad but then move on to other things, like Abby's possible crush on Taylor, the school play, and the corn maze we're going to this weekend. My troubles slip away for a while.

At one point, I go to the bathroom. I peer into the mirror as I wash up, running my hand through my mop of messy hair. My acne has cleared up. My cheeks don't seem too chubby. My hair looks cool. My smile is relaxed, not forced. For the first time in a long while, I don't find stuff to nitpick. I like the person looking back at me, which makes me smile wider.

I walk out of the bathroom and into the hallway, the smile still on my face.

Every single door in the hallway is open wide.

I swear they weren't like that when I went into the bathroom. Hugo's still sitting on his bed, staring at his phone.

For a moment, the tiniest bit of panic washes over me. My promise to tell Abby about anything strange weighs on my mind, and Margaret said to be vigilant and watch for more activity. Does this qualify? Things have been going so well, and I'd hate to ruin it by being a wimp and making a big deal out of nothing.

"Hey, Hugo?"

"What's up?" he says, hopping off the bed and heading my way.

"The doors. They're all open. Were they like that before?"

Hugo's eyes widen for a moment, then return to normal. "None of the doors are hung right in this house, and the latches are old. They're always doing that."

"You sure? Margaret asked us to watch for any strange activity."

"If I told Margret about every strange thing this house did, I'd be texting her four times an hour," Hugo says with a laugh, but his voice has a note of finality to it.

"But you're still going to talk to your dad about what happened, right?"

"Yes! I wish people would stop bugging me about it," Hugo barks, and heads back to his room.

Wow, Hugo's never snapped at me like that. At least not since the first day I met him, when he stormed out of the lunchroom. It leaves a knot in the pit of my stomach. Still, he's told me plenty of times why it's a tough subject for him and his dad. I guess he's right about the doors. It's easily explainable. *Stop freaking yourself out, Cameron.*

It's nothing.

26
ANDERSON FARM: HUGO

I didn't mean to raise my voice with Cameron, but anytime Pa comes up, I can't help myself. People need to leave me alone and let me deal with it my own way. I'm going to talk to him. Eventually. I'm working on figuring out how to do that.

Cameron hangs out for about an hour longer before he heads home. I walk him to the front door and tell him I hope everything goes well with his dad and to call or text later to tell me what's happening. He says he will and waves to me as he heads home.

Pa is hovering in the living room near the foyer. "Everything gonna be okay?"

"I hope so."

"Does it have anything to do with the boyfriend stuff?" Pa asks.

"Yeah. It's not fair."

"C'mere," Pa says, sitting on the sofa and gesturing me over.

Pa's soft expression is comforting. "Every parent has expectations for their kid. We dream about what you'll be like. It's silly, but we all do it. And when those dreams don't work out like we expect, it can take some time to adjust."

"How about you? You having a tough time?" As soon as the words leave my mouth, my chest constricts, not sure I want the answer.

"Nope," he says easily, his look sincere.

"How come?"

"I think Cameron's dad doesn't know that most of his dreams can still come true. He hasn't lost anything."

"You think so?" I ask.

"I know so," Pa says. "My best friend in high school, Pete Gibson? He came out to me when we were eighteen. I was shocked at first, like people often were back in the nineties. But I got past it once I realized he was still the same guy I'd always known. I just knew more of him, and we stayed best friends. He found his dream guy, got married, and had kids."

"Really? How come you've never mentioned him?"

"Lost touch with him years ago." He shrugs. "It happens. I should look him up again."

"You should."

"Anyway, that's why the whole boyfriend thing isn't a big deal for me. You can still do all the things I've imagined for you. Like get married and give me some nietos."

I laugh. "You might have to wait on both of those."

Pa laughs too. "Yeah, I expect to wait. And I'm not trying to pressure you. You can live your life in the way that makes you happy."

"Thanks, Pa." I smile at him. He's surprised me. Here I was, not realizing I could talk to him about this stuff all these years. It feels great. I only wish I had done it sooner.

Maybe I should tell him about the things that have happened in this house. This would be the perfect time. But even though Pa has been so cool about everything else, the stakes are too high. The idea of losing Cameron and all my friends makes me feel hollow inside. I've gotten so used to hiding things about myself that it has become an instinct. Still, Margaret expects me to do it, and she'll check on me soon. I should talk to him about it right now. Like, right this second. I'll start the conversation by talking about the mirror. I open my mouth and draw in a breath, ready to begin.

"Does it feel cold in here to you?" Pa asks, rubbing his hands on his arms.

I exhale. "Kinda. It's probably the boiler." I hop up and head to the radiator. The intake pipe is cold against my hand. "Yeah. That stupid pilot light. Happened last week."

Pa gets up. "I'll go check."

"It's okay," I say, cutting him off on the way to the kitchen. "I got it."

"Okay. Thanks, mijo." Pa sits back down on the couch and turns on the TV.

A weird mix of relief and regret swirls through my insides. I jumped so fast at the excuse to hold off on the ghost conversation. It's a special kind of torture, waging a battle in my head between the need to tell Pa about the hauntings and the fear of losing Cameron and all my friends. That could break me in a way I'm not sure I'd recover from.

I head down the steps to the basement, clutching the railing in a death grip as my knuckles go white. Ghosts or no ghosts, going into the basement still freaks me out each time.

The boiler's pilot light ignites after several tries with the lighter.

The draft is stronger than it was the last time I was down here. I should patch up the hole or at least put a cinder block in front of it to stop the gusts of air, like I planned to do last time this happened.

As I head toward the hole, my ankle tingles, and I wonder why the hell I thought I'd be okay down here by myself. A cold descends, making me shake, and it's not just the draft.

My eyes widen as I approach. Where before only one brick was missing, three are now gone, and the plaster is more cracked around the edges. My mind goes to terrible places, imagining the White Lady with her wicked smile, chipping away at the bricks.

I shake my head and laugh. Pa must have found the hole himself and has been trying to figure out what's behind the brick wall. That has to be it. It's the only logical explanation.

But I still run out of the basement as fast as my feet will carry me.

***

School can't go fast enough on Friday. I'm excited to hang out with Cameron and the gang at the corn maze tonight—anything to take my mind off that evil house.

I should tell everybody about the hole, but the simplest explanation is usually the right one. I don't want to seem like a coward, freaking out about every little thing.

On the way to theater tech, I cut across the school courtyard. I got stuck talking to my lit teacher about extra credit, so I'm running late, and the courtyard is empty of students.

The wind blows, howling as it makes its way through the buildings on either side, and the air has a serious bite to it. Everything gets darker as a storm cloud rolls in, blocking out the sun. A flash of something white behind a shrub at the courtyard's edge catches my eye.

I freeze.

Somebody is definitely behind the shrub. The shape of a person dressed in white is plain as day behind the greenery, but only the shape. No details. I think of the lady in the back of the car the other day. This is stupid. How long will I be cowering at everything I see out of the corner of my eye? I need to confront this head-on.

I jog over to the shrub and stop in my tracks. There's nobody there. What the heck? I walk around the hedge in a circle. The person is gone, and there's no sign of them anywhere. I circle back around again to where the person stood mere moments ago. Sitting on the ground is a crumbled-up chocolate chip cookie.

Ice flows through my veins. What the heck is wrong with me? Am I losing it?

I run the entire way to theater tech, not looking back, stopping only when I'm inside the door.

Everybody else is chatting and building props, and I head over to Chloe.

"Hey, Chloe," I say. "Looking forward to the corn maze tonight?"

"Kinda," she says. "Not exactly my thing. But Maya is excited."

"Well, that's super sweet of you to go for your girlfriend's sake," I say, then pause, choosing my next words carefully. "Hey, can I ask you a strange question?"

She laughs. "I'm getting used to those."

"I bet," I say, then take a deep breath. "Can a *person* be haunted?"

Her piercing emerald eyes bore into me. "That's a disturbingly specific question, Hugo. Why do you ask?"

"I dunno," I sigh. "I keep seeing things out of the corner of my eye. It's stupid. I know I'm just freaking myself out."

"After what we've gone through, freaking yourself out is understandable. I see things too. A flash of white somewhere I didn't expect. Then it's gone."

"Exactly!"

"Yeah, I think it's your mind still dealing with things," she says. "Finding patterns that aren't there."

"Thank god," I say, relief coursing through me. "That makes me feel so much better."

"No problem. Let me know if it gets worse. And to answer your question: Yes, a person can be haunted. A spirit can latch on to them and appear wherever that person goes. But it's rare. It means there's a serious bond between the spirit and a person. Only a terrible thing could cause such a bond. I wouldn't worry about it."

***

It's eight o'clock in the evening, and we all pile into two cars to head to Anderson Farms. It's Cameron and me in the front seat of Pa's SUV and Abby and Taylor in the back. Chloe and Maya hitch a ride in Matty's old 4Runner.

The farm is only a ten-minute drive from Port Townsend. I've spent most of my time in bigger cities, so it always surprises me that we can go from being in town to being in the middle of nowhere in the blink of an eye.

In the rearview mirror, I see that Abby and Taylor are sitting close to each other in the back seat, possibly holding hands, but I don't want my spying to be obvious. I send Cameron a glance saying, *Check them out*. He peeks back, all nonchalant, then smiles and nods. Looks like we were right about them.

Near the farm, a line of cars stretches down the road, waiting to park. I guess the nice weather has made people want to get their fall festivities on. Even from here, the lights of the farm cast a glow into the night sky, and the grounds are all done up in Halloween decorations. Kids' screams and spooky sound effects drift out to the road.

We park in a massive field with rows of cars lined up. Since it's evening, the clientele is less families looking for pumpkins and more teenagers looking for thrills. I recognize more than a few kids from our school.

I take Cameron's hand in mine and walk to the entrance. Large hay bales are stacked up high, covered with scarecrows, ghosts, and jack-o'-lanterns.

Roasted corn and apple cider aromas hit my nose as we head down the main thoroughfare lined with concessions, carnival games, and people dressed up as zombies, vampires, and werewolves, trying to scare the wits out of unsuspecting teenagers. The occasional scream floats over the murmur of voices when one of those monsters hits its mark.

Abby and Taylor are right behind us, holding hands and not trying to hide it. Cameron stops and looks at them.

"So, is this a thing?" he asks with a big smile.

"It is what it is," Taylor says nonchalantly, and Abby's face turns crimson.

"Well, for what it's worth, I think it's awesome," Cameron says.

Maya, Chloe, and Matty come up behind us, also noticing this new turn of events and giving each other knowing looks.

"I knew it," Maya says to Chloe in a loud whisper that everyone hears.

"Hey, everybody," Cameron says. "It is what it is. Right, Taylor?"

"Right," Taylor says with emphasis, smiling.

"I hate being the seventh wheel," Matty says, with a big flourish of his hands.

We stop at the concession stands first. Maya finally gets her pumpkin spice latte, Matty gets kettle corn, and Hugo and I grab some cinnamon churros, then queue up for our ride tickets. Of course, it takes Matty all of one minute to start chatting up a cute girl named Riley in line behind us. With tickets in hand, we head straight for the midway. A long row of carnival rides extends all the way to the edge of the corn maze, including a Tilt-A-Whirl, a fun house, and a ride-through haunted house.

Matty takes Riley by the hand and runs to the haunted house. Everybody groans. Is he serious? The ride is done up like an old Victorian mansion, of course, complete with ghosts, ghouls, and skeletons.

"C'mon, everybody," Matty yells, getting onto the ride with Riley.

Cameron and I send each other a look that says, *Why did we think any of this would be a good idea?* Don't we have enough real scares in our real lives without a fake haunted house?

"It's just a dumb ride," Cameron says.

"You're right." I take him by the hand and line up behind our friends.

We squeeze into a tiny vehicle, squished together, the entire length of our bodies touching. I put my arm around him, and Cameron tucks right in with a gentle smile. I kiss him on the cheek, and then the vehicle lurches forward, going through swinging doors and plunging us into darkness.

Cheap thrills, flashing lights, and clunky animatronics greet us at each turn as our car twists along the track. It's all pretty cheesy. A werewolf with his left paw falling off lurches toward us with the grace of a robot. A strobe flashes, and a poorly recorded werewolf roar plays from a tiny speaker. We trade glances and laugh. Well, at least it's not scary.

Midway through the ride, the car careens to the left, pushing Cameron deeper into me. Our eyes meet, and I kiss him gently. This ride isn't so bad after all.

We go by a large Victorian dining room with a long wooden table covered in fake rotten food and surrounded by skeletons and ghosts. Compared to the rest of the ride, it's not half bad.

One ghost in particular is quite realistic.

I blink.

It can't be.

I clamp my eyes shut, breathe deeply, and open them the tiniest bit. A crooked smile stretches across the all-too-familiar wrinkled face. Sitting at the head of the table is the White Lady. Her eyes lock on mine as her mouth grows unnaturally wide, flashing jagged, yellowed teeth.

Panic threatens to overtake me, rolling through my body in sickening waves. A quick glance at Cameron's cheerful face tells me he hasn't seen her.

The car veers right and pulls through another set of swinging doors, and the ride ends.

I'm stunned. Did that actually happen? Cameron glances my way, smiling, unaware of what I just saw, but then his smile melts away.

"Hugo? What's wrong?"

I can't speak. I jump up from the car and race down the steps of the ride. Our friends stand around in a circle, talking and laughing. There's no way I can go up to the group and pretend nothing happened. I need time to think, so I break into a jog, running by them.

"I feel sick!" I shout as I pass, then run straight toward the Porta-Potties near the entrance to the farm. I ignore the long line and run right up to one of the opening doors, shoving my way in. "Sorry! Emergency!"

I fight for air, only able to draw in hurried, shallow breaths. My pulse pounds in my neck, and surges of lightheadedness threaten my consciousness. I sit down hard on the toilet seat and run my hands through my hair, trying to make sense of what I saw.

It couldn't have been her.

We freed her spirit, and even before we did, she never appeared to us outside the house. Is it possible that she's not only still around but has somehow grown stronger? How? Do *I* have a serious bond with the White Lady?

There's a light knock on the door.

"Hugo?" Cameron's familiar soft voice calls out. "Is everything okay?"

"I—uh—" My voice cracks, and I clear my throat and try again. "I'm not feeling so great."

"Bad churro?"

I laugh despite myself. The charm of sweet Cameron makes me feel a bit better. At least well enough to function half normally.

"I'm not sure," I say. "Give me a minute or two."

"Okay. I'll be waiting outside. Take all the time you need."

My thoughts race. Is it possible I'm making all of this up, finding patterns like Chloe said? I'm not sure if I'm more or less excited by the idea of it being a hallucination. If it is, then at least that's an explanation that doesn't involve the supernatural. But if it's not in my mind...

As the shock dissipates, I form a plan. I have to tell Pa. After that, I'll talk to Margaret and ask for help. I've been putting it off long enough. But the thought of Pa moving us away plays like a broken record in my mind. If that's the sacrifice I need to make, then so be it. But it makes my heart ache.

Okay, I can do this.

I leave the Porta-Potty and find Cameron sitting patiently on a nearby hay bale, his face wracked with worry. I approach, and he hops up. "How are you feeling?"

"Been better," I say. "I think I need to go home."

"Yeah, I figured," Cameron says. "I already told the gang. I'll drive you home. Matty offered to take everyone else back."

"You should stay with your friends. I'll be okay."

"Hugo, there's no way I'm letting you drive home alone," Cameron says. "Besides, I'm not sure this whole thing was a good idea anyway. Let's go."

"Okay." Despite my protest, I'm relieved to have Cameron with me. I'm not sure I'll be safe on my own. That, and I want to be with him as much as possible. Our remaining time together may be short, depending on how things go with Pa.

Cameron insists on driving. He sits behind the wheel with his brow knitted in concentration in the most adorable way. My chest swells as I look at the guy beside me.

We head home in silence. I contemplate telling him what happened, but I don't want to worry him, especially since *I'm* not even totally sure what I saw. The more time passes, the more seeing the White Lady feels like a dream. So instead, I tell him part of the truth.

"I'm going to talk to Pa tonight."

Cameron nods with a frown. "Yeah. It's the right thing to do."

"I don't know how he'll react."

Cameron reaches over and grabs my hand. "Whatever happens, we'll face it together."

Together. That word rips at me. Together is the one thing we won't be if things go badly.

We pull up to my driveway, get out, and stand side by side.

"Do you want me to come in with you?" he asks.

I'm about to say yes or suggest we go to his place. But then I'm struck with a thought. If the White Lady is following me, it's not safe for him to be around me. I'm a danger to Cameron.

"No." I sigh. "I'm still feeling off. After I talk to Pa, I'm going to head straight to bed."

Cameron's sad eyes peer into mine. "You sure?"

"I'm sure."

"Is there something else going on?" Cameron's gaze pierces into me, and I have to look away.

"Sorry. I gotta go." I have to leave this instant. If I so much as look at him, he'll slip past my defenses. "Bye." I turn around and head for my door.

"Bye. I hope you feel better," Cameron says, sounding sad and small.

I don't look back. His expression would break my heart, so I run to the front door and slam it behind me, instantly regretting not kissing him goodbye. My heart aches.

The house is oppressive—cold as ever and thick with this negative energy I've never felt. Across the street, Cameron's house is warm and inviting. I watch him duck inside, and I'm pulled by the temptation to go over there and stay with him. But I can't put him in danger.

I head to the living room, determined to talk to Pa. But the TV is off, and only a single light is still on downstairs. On the second floor, the faint sound of Pa's snoring breaks the silence. I head into my room, lock the door behind me, undress, and lie in bed, trying to calm my racing mind.

Tomorrow I'll talk to Pa. I play out scenarios in my mind about how he might react. Almost all of them end with us leaving the house the second he finds out. We have relatives down in Oakland, which is where Pa would probably move us until we figured out what to do with the house. I lie awake, tossing and turning, wondering if this is the last time I'll sleep in this house and if this was my last night with Cameron.

A tear runs down my cheek, and I brush it away.

27

DISCOVERIES: CAMERON

I lie awake, looking at Hugo's room through my window. His light went off, so he really must have gone right to bed. Did he have time to talk to his dad?

What the heck was up with him tonight? One minute we were having fun on that stupid haunted house ride, and the next minute he totally transformed. He looked terrible, and I'm not sure a bad churro explains it. It certainly doesn't explain his sudden decision to tell his dad what's going on.

On the ride home, he wanted to say something. I'm sure of it. When we got to his house, he ran off without even a proper goodbye or a good night kiss, which messed with me more than anything else. I tap out a text to Hugo, asking him what's *actually* going on. But then I delete it. He must be asleep by now. I'll talk to him tomorrow.

The next morning, I wake up and go about my day, trying not to obsess about him, but I still check my phone every thirty seconds. Nothing. I type out another text asking how things are going, but again I delete it. He doesn't need me hounding him.

After breakfast, I'm sitting in my room, distracting myself by working on my story, when my phone buzzes in my pocket. I nearly drop it on the ground as I fumble to see who it is.

Mr. P: Hey Cameron. This is Mr. Peterson from Port Townsend Library.

Is a book overdue?

Oh. Maybe he has more house info or some information about the nanny's lover, Luke.

> **Cameron: Hey, what's up**

> **Mr. P: I found something out about the house.**

> **Cameron: Cool whaddya find**

> **Mr. P: It's easier to show you in person.**

That's strange. Then again, everything Mr. Peterson does is strange.

> **Cameron: K, be there in 10**

At the library, Mr. Peterson glances up from the front desk, looking excited.

"Cameron. Excellent. Come, come." He heads toward the back room and gestures for me to follow. From there, we go into a small, cluttered office. A desk rests against the wall with countless books and papers spread across it. Above it is a bulletin board filled with pictures, notes, and news clippings connected with pushpins and strings. Among the pinned items are pictures of Crimson House, Emily, and the nanny. It's like a scene from a detective mystery. This is what I thought Abby's research would look like, but she has her MindMap app.

"Whoa," I utter with my mouth hanging open.

"This?" Mr. Peterson says, pointing at the board. "This is nothing. You should see what I have in folders."

"You and Abby should compare notes."

Mr. Peterson nods. "Smart as a whip, that one."

"So, what did you want to show me?" I ask.

"Ah, yes." Mr. Peterson searches through a pile of folders on his desk. "Where did I put it? Oh, here we go." He opens a folder packed with papers. "When you told me your friend had moved into that house—"

"Hugo," I cut in.

Mr. Peterson nods. "Yes, your friend Hugo—"

"Boyfriend," I correct.

"Oh." His face scrunches up as he thinks for a moment. I might detect the slightest smile. "Well, that's a pretty bizarre coincidence."

"What do you mean, coincidence?"

"I'll explain," Mr. Peterson says. "I was surprised to hear that your boyfriend, Hugo, moved into that house. You see, it's been vacant for more than sixty years, other than one short stint. But even that was over fifty years ago."

Mr. Peterson takes a piece of paper from the folder—some sort of legal document. "When Emily died in 1959, her will specified that the house should go to her nanny, Ms. Finch. But the will was more than seventy years old, drafted by her father, and Ms. Finch was missing and presumed dead. Instead, the house went to Ms. Finch's closest relative: a great-great-grandniece, Maria Flores. Mrs. Flores and her family moved into the house in 1962. But they moved out after less than a month."

He takes out a newspaper article titled: FAMILY MOVES OUT OF THORNBURN RESIDENCE WEEKS AFTER MOVING IN.

"Where are you going with all this, Mr. P?"

"I'm getting to it." He takes out another paper. "After Mrs. Flores moved out, she put the house in a trust. The terms of the trust were private, but people speculated that it mandated that the house remain unoccupied. There were several generations of trustees before it came into the possession of Geraldine Flores. Geraldine passed away three years ago. She had no direct descendants, so it went to her grandniece Sofia Flores."

Mr. Peterson pauses and glances up from the document. "Her married name was Sofia Cruz. She was Hugo's mom."

"What!" I cry.

"She died—"

"Yeah, I know," I say. "Are you telling me Hugo and Emily's nanny are related?"

"Yes." Mr. Peterson nods. "By my calculation, Hugo is Ms. Finch's third cousin six times removed. It's distant, but they are related."

"Wow." My head swims. Hugo told me his mom and dad had argued about her inheritance before she died. Hugo's mom wanted to give it away, but his dad wanted to keep it. His mom died right after that. Does that mean Hugo's dad went against his mom's wishes and kept the house?

"I have to tell Hugo about this," I say.

"There's more I need to tell you, Cameron."

"I'm not sure I can handle any more," I say.

"You'll want to hear this." The seriousness of his tone snaps me back to attention. "Remember the letter you showed me from the nanny's lover, Luke Brannagh?"

"Of course."

"Brannagh is a common Irish name. It comes from the word for 'British' and means 'foreigner.' Many Irish immigrants with that name changed it to one that sounded less Irish, so they chose a word that meant the same thing but was derived from the word for 'Welsh.' Luke changed his last name to Walsh."

"Walsh?" The blood drains from my face.

"Luke is your four-times great-grandpa, Cameron. He built the house you live in."

My entire world tilts on its axis as I put the pieces together. That's our deep connection to the house. Hugo and I are descendants of Agnes and Luke, and now those descendants are boyfriends. Agnes Finch held Emily captive for forty-nine years, and Luke disappeared. That explains the extreme hostility Emily's spirit had toward Agnes's and Luke's descendants. Hostility toward Hugo and me.

It all makes sense: why the house always seemed to react to me more than other people, why the spirit activity was worse when Hugo and I were together, and why Chloe could so easily sense the connection between us and the house.

"I have to go," I say, heading toward the door.

"Cameron, I'm sorry if this impacts you and your boyfriend. I promise I won't say anything about the trust. But if I found out about it, it's likely other people will too at some point."

"Thanks, Mr. P."

I leave his office and head out of the library, texting Hugo on the way.

Cameron: Hey, got a sec to talk irl

Hugo doesn't respond. Nothing. Not even a read receipt. He's not looking at his phone. But I have to talk to someone about this right now or my head will explode.

Cameron: Hey, you heard from Hugo

Abby: Nope whats up

Cameron: You'll never believe what I just found out

Abby: What

Cameron: It's about me Hugo and the house. Let's talk irl

Abby: K. Come to my house. Something I want to show you

Something she wants to show me? That sounds ominous. But Abby doesn't live far, so I head right over.

Abby's waiting for me by the front door, tapping her foot. Her house is another old Victorian mansion with a big turret and a wraparound porch, but it's been restored to its former glory, right down to the pristine pastel gingerbread trim on the eaves.

"Hey, Cam. What's up?" she says.

"Let's go inside."

Abby guides me to her bedroom, where posters of famous skateboarders, snowboarders, and punk rock bands cover every square inch of the walls.

The door closes, and I can't hold it in any longer. "Hugo's related to Agnes Finch, Emily's nanny!"

Abby's jaw drops. "What?"

"And I'm related to Luke Brannagh."

Now her face explodes with shock. I tell her everything Mr. Peterson told me.

"That explains why Emily's spirit was so upset about you two being together."

I nod. "It was a slap in the face."

"And Hugo doesn't know about inheriting the house?" she asks.

"He's never mentioned anything about it to me. In fact, he said his dad put his life savings into it. Maybe his dad kept it a secret from him."

"Why would his dad keep something like that a secret?" Abby says.

"He said his dad and mom had a big argument about her inheritance before she died. I bet his dad feels guilty about it."

Abby nods. "Well, we better tell Hugo so he can talk to his dad about it."

"I wish he'd respond." The message I sent earlier still shows as unread.

"We'll have to go there and knock on his door, I guess," Abby says.

"Yeah." I stare down at my sneakers, my stomach tied up in knots. "I'm nervous it'll mean he'll have to move away. Part of me wants to ignore it."

"We at least have to let him know. Let him decide what to do with the information."

"Yeah, you're right." I nod. "So, what did you want to show me?"

"Oh yeah! I've been reviewing all the digital audio from the ghost hunt. I found this right before you texted. I want you to listen to something."

"Let's hear it."

Abby heads to her desk and waves me over. Displayed on her laptop is a program with a big grid of video and audio feeds with time stamps. She grabs a pair of fancy-looking headphones that cover the entire ear and hands them to me.

"Here, listen to this. It's from the basement. Tell me what you hear."

I adjust the headphones and give her a thumbs-up. She starts the recording. The low hum of static and the occasional boiler noise are the only sounds. Then something rises above the white noise. It's faint, but it almost sounds like talking—muted and indecipherable, but undeniably there. Then I detect another voice. It is similar but with a lower pitch. The voices have the cadence of a conversation.

"Sounds like two people talking, but I can't make the words out," I say. "Did it pick up one of our conversations?"

"No. Watch the videos." She rewinds the recordings. "Everything is synced. At that point, we were all up in Emily's room with Chloe. Nobody was talking."

"Abby, you found an EVP!"

"Just wait," Abby says.

She scrolls to a new part of the recording. After more quiet static, the voice speaks again. This time, it's talking faster and louder and sounds more distraught. But there's no second voice in this recording.

"That sounds like only one voice. And whoever it is sounds sad. Or pissed."

Abby nods. "That's what I thought. The first recording happened before Chloe freed Emily's spirit. The second one..." Abby pauses for dramatic effect.

"Abby, spit it out already!"

"The second one happened five minutes *after* Chloe finished freeing the spirit."

The hair on the back of my neck stands on end. "That means—"

"Either Chloe didn't really free the spirit, or—"

"There's more than one spirit," I say, sitting back in my chair.

"We better text Chloe," Abby says, going for her phone.

As she texts, I let the whole thing sink in. Hugo might not be as safe in that house as we thought if there is more than one spirit.

"Maybe it's the nanny?" I say. "And somehow her spirit is connected to Hugo since he's related to her?"

Abby nods. But there's something else. Something at the edge of my mind, gnawing at me. Something that's been bothering me since the night we freed Emily.

"Abby, can you pull up the picture of Emily and Agnes?"

"Sure." Abby clicks a few times with her mouse, and an image appears on the screen. In it, Emily is smiling vacantly, her nanny beside her. "What are you looking for?"

"Not sure yet. Can you zoom in on the locket?" I ask.

"Yep." She does.

"There's no doubt that's the locket we found. I recognize the markings, those little vertical lines across it." I tap my chin. "Bring up the other photo of Emily."

Abby clicks a few more times, and the other photo comes up. This one is Emily with a terrible scowl, now all by herself.

"Now zoom in on the locket in this one," I ask.

Abby does.

"Look!" I point to the photo. "It's subtle, but the patterns on the locket are different in the two photos."

"Wait a second," Abby says, as she pulls up the photos side by side. She aligns them, and my jaw hits the floor. The edge of the nanny's dress cuts off on the left side of the first photo. On the right side of the other one is a barely perceptible slice of the same dress. They line up perfectly.

It's one photo cut in two.

We both stare with our mouths gaping open. I have to grab on to the desk as my head swims, dread spreading through me like wildfire.

"Emily didn't have a split personality," Abby says.

I shake my head. "She had a twin."

28
The Return: Hugo

Among the many things that suck about being the son of a guy who fixes up houses for a living is Saturday, which should be a day of relaxing and being lazy, is instead the day Pa finishes all the projects he can't do by himself.

He came into my room early and told me to wake up. It was time to work on the crown molding, he said. I dragged myself out of bed, threw on clothes, scarfed down a bowl of cereal, and we got right to it.

A few hours have passed, and we're still going strong. I haven't had a moment to do anything else. A knot forms in my stomach as I consider how to tell Pa about the house.

The way I left Cameron yesterday is also gnawing at me, eating me up inside. I've got to level with him. I should have told him what I saw last night, but seeing the White Lady freaked me out, and I was more than a little worried that I was hallucinating, which wasn't a great feeling.

Almost like a taunt, my phone buzzes on the coffee table, where I set it down earlier and where it will stay until this job is done. Each buzz is a bit of torture—it's probably Cameron wanting to talk about last night.

Pa and I work in silence as I feed him the crown molding piece by piece. He has a look of concentration, and I feel a surge of pride as he works tirelessly, providing for his family. I'm struck with a moment of bravery. I have to tell him about the house, like, right now. If I let this moment pass, I might chicken out, and hiding the truth is putting a strain on everything.

"Hey, Pa?"

"Yeah?" he says, half distracted, driving nails into the molding.

"Have you seen the hole in the basement wall?" I ask, my pulse rising. "Near the boiler."

Now it's out there—there's no taking it back. Once he answers, I'll know for sure. If he didn't remove the bricks—if it was something else—I'll have no choice but to tell him about everything.

Before he answers, my phone buzzes on the table again.

"Hugo, can you do me a favor?" Pa says, straining to keep his hand steady as he holds the heavy nail gun above him.

"Sure?"

"Can you silence your phone before I shoot it with the nail gun?" he says with a laugh.

"Sorry. Are you sure you've got the molding?" I ask.

"Yeah, I can hold it steady for a bit."

I let go of the molding and run over to the table, glancing at the screen for only a second. There are messages from Cameron. My breath hitches, but Pa's arms are beginning to shake, so I don't have time to look at them. I switch my phone to silent mode and slip it into my pocket.

I look up at Pa, and ice flows through my veins at the sight before me.

Standing next to Pa's ladder is my absolute worst nightmare. The White Lady stares at me with a wicked smile, like she knows I was about to tell Pa. She has one hand on the ladder and another held up, palm facing me, commanding me to stay where I am.

"Hugo, hurry up! I can't hold this for much longer!"

I try to call out, but my voice is gone. All that comes out is a strained gasp. The moment I move, the White Lady emphasizes her gesture and shakes her head. Her sick smile gets unnaturally big, covering most of her face. Her teeth are yellow and rotting away.

"Hugo!" Pa yells, then glances down and sees the horror below him. "What the hell?!"

The White Lady shoves the ladder.

I yell as Pa tumbles toward the ground. I race forward, not caring about the White Lady. I have to help him.

"Pa!"

The White Lady comes toward me, blocking my path. I throw my hands out to shove her, but they sink right through like she's vapor. My fingers are cold as a corpse as they plunge into nothingness, sending me stumbling forward.

The White Lady drifts away like smoke. As she fades, Pa hits the ground hard, the snap of cracking bones sickeningly loud. It's a familiar sound from my past. *The truck striking the side of the car...Ma's body crumpling...no, no, no!*

The nail gun follows Pa, striking his head hard and then clattering to the floor. I race to his side, yelling "Pa!" over and over. His eyes are closed, and he's not moving or responding.

Pa! I can't lose you too! You're all I have left!

I put my ear to his mouth. He's breathing. He's alive!

I fumble with my phone.

"Nine-one-one. What's your emergency?"

"My pa," I cry. "He fell off a ladder. He hit his head, and he's not awake, but he's breathing."

"Can you verify your address as 16 Sycamore Lane, Port Townsend?"

"Yeah." My voice hitches, tears streaming down my face. "Come quick!"

"An ambulance is headed your way. Please stay on the line."

It takes only three minutes before I hear the wail of the sirens, but it's the longest three minutes of my life as Pa lies motionless on the ground with a nasty bruise forming where the nail gun hit him.

"Pa, please don't leave me!" I cry, kneeling beside him, hands on his chest. "Please! I need you, dammit! Don't leave me alone!"

In a blur, the paramedics come in and surround Pa. I barely register what happens as they guide me away, asking questions. They tend to him, brace his head, and then put him on a stretcher. It's all distant, like I'm watching from far away.

As they wheel him out the front door, one paramedic puts their arm around me and guides me out of the house. I'm on autopilot as I shut the front door and head toward the ambulance.

I reach for my phone but come up empty. Crap. I've left it behind, but that's the least of my worries right now. I get into the back, where Pa lies on the stretcher. One paramedic puts a mask over his face as another inserts an IV.

Someone says something that's probably meant to be comforting. I don't even hear the words, but I nod anyway, watching Pa's chest move up and down. The siren blares, and I brace against the lurch of the vehicle as the ambulance races away.

I glance back at the house and see the White Lady peering out the living room window, head tilted back, laughing at me.

29

Ashes to Ashes: Cameron

Abby and I race through the woods on our way to Hugo's house. I text him several times, but there's still no answer. Calls go to voicemail.

Abby texts Chloe to catch her up on the recent developments. The time for tiptoeing around this is over. We have to tell Hugo's dad what's happening and beg for Margaret's help before somebody gets hurt.

"When Chloe freed Emily, she said it felt violent," Abby pants as we run along the path. "I think Emily and her twin were intertwined. Chloe must have ripped them apart."

"We freed the friendly spirit and left the wounded evil one. Perfect!" I shake my head. "Why did the house feel okay at first after we freed Emily?"

"I'd guess the violent split injured the twin and she went to lick her wounds. But like a cornered wild animal, she's sure to lash out eventually."

I pick up my pace. "Let's hurry!"

We burst out of the forest and run straight to Hugo's front door. Parked in the driveway is the familiar blue SUV.

"Looks like Hugo's dad is home, at least," I say as we ring the doorbell and knock. I only wait a few seconds before I try the door. Unlocked.

"Hugo?" I yell through the open door, and it echoes off the barren walls.

A wave of sickness envelops me as I enter the foyer, sharper than I've ever felt—more wicked. Compared to this, the other feelings were muted and restrained. Now the full impact of the spirit's malevolence punches at me, sending me off balance.

Abby looks at me and nods with a sour face.

A blast of cold hits me, and I'm twelve again. The shadow circles me, the memory playing in my mind like a movie. The voice calls out louder than ever.

You left me. Now I have you.

Luke.

It was Luke who left her. Emily's twin must have cared for him, and then he disappeared from her life.

You left me. Now I have you.

Now she has *me*—Luke's descendant.

A chill runs through my entire body, rippling along my skin and outward to my extremities. We have to find Hugo fast and get the heck out of here.

"Hugo, are you here?" I call out. "Mr. Cruz?"

"Let's search the house," Abby says.

"Yeah. But let's stick together."

She nods.

Abby and I go from room to room but find the first floor empty. A ladder rests on the ground in the living room.

"Strange," Abby says. "Looks like they were in the middle of a project."

"Look, Hugo's phone." I pick it up from where it's resting on the ground next to the ladder. Notifications fill the lock screen. "He's gotta be here somewhere."

We make our way to the second floor.

"Hugo?" I call out. "Hugo! Where are you?"

The second floor is empty. No Hugo and no Mr. Cruz.

"Third floor," Abby says as she stares up the stairs at the shadowed third-floor landing.

The air is oppressive as we head up the steps. I continue to call Hugo's name, but we find no sign of anyone. The nanny's room, like all the others, is empty. We head to the edge of the spiral staircase.

I sigh. "That's next, I guess."

"Let's go."

Emily's room is empty, the lower staircase descending into the darkness. A blast of stale air shoots through the stairwell.

"I thought Hugo closed this," I say. "He might be down there."

"We better look," Abby says. "I want to check it out anyway. The basement room might have belonged to the twin, and this one was Emily's."

"Oh god, I didn't think of that," I say. "No wonder her twin was so messed up."

"Here goes nothing," Abby says, turning on her phone flashlight as we descend into the depths.

The room is exactly as we left it. The straw bed sits in the corner with the manacles resting beside it. The iron door dominates the far side of the room, closed and impenetrable. It is hard to fathom that perhaps the nanny imprisoned Emily's twin down here for years while Emily slept upstairs in her comfortable room. She must've built up a staggering amount of animosity.

The wood table covered with iron tools and clay jars rests against the wall. One jar is open. It must be the one Matty found the locket in. Abby inspects it.

"Um...Matty forgot to mention the ash in these jars."

"Ash?"

She tilts the jar to show me. "Yep."

"What's that on the side?" I ask, spotting little scratches and hash marks near the top of the jar.

Ash and dust cover everything, so it's hard to make out. Abby blows on the jar, and the markings become slightly more visible. She rubs the edge of her shirt against the marks to clean off the last of the ash.

"Oh, shit," she says. The markings are actually writing. Etched into the clay is a name and date.

EMILY—NOVEMBER 1939

Abby sets the jar down like burns and backs away. "Emily was supposedly buried in Laurel Grove Cemetery. In 1959."

"I guess her twin sister is buried there instead," I say.

I pick up the other jars one by one, each etched with a name and date from the 1940s and 1950s, until I find one that makes my chest ache.

FREDRICK—APRIL 1958

"These are the missing children," I say in a flat tone, stunned. "This is Mr. Peterson's uncle. He was only thirteen when he went missing."

We both stare at the jars in shock.

"This is a crime scene," Abby says.

"So, Emily actually died in 1939, not 1959," I say. "Her twin sister cremated her. Since nobody knew she was a twin, she took over Emily's life. Then kids went missing until 1959, when she died."

"She was a serial killer," Abby says grimly. "But her sister must have kept her in check. Until Emily died, that is."

I nod. "Emily kept her in check in this life and in the next one. And since we freed Emily's spirit, now her sister is the only one left in this house."

We stare at each other in stunned silence, horror trickling through me like thick molasses.

A faint voice calls out from beyond the iron door. "Cameron, help!"

"Hugo?" I shout. "That was Hugo. He's behind the door!"

"Hugo, is that you?" Abby yells as we run to the door.

"Help, Cameron. I'm stuck!" the voice cries out.

I bang on the door. "Hugo, how did you get in there?"

Abby lies down on the ground and points her phone flashlight under the iron door. "The key is still on the ground on the other side."

"Hugo, can you grab the key?" I shout.

"I'm stuck," the voice replies.

"I bet I can get it," Abby says from the ground. "Hand me one of those tools."

On the table, I find a long, narrow iron tool with a hook near the end that looks like a fire poker. "Here." I hand it to Abby.

She puts it under the door and fishes for the key.

"Please, Cameron, help!" the voice cries.

"We're coming, Hugo!" I yell back.

"Ugh!" Abby grunts. "I can't quite grab the key. Cameron, run and see if you can find a wire hanger. Might be easier."

"On it," I say, as I run up the spiral staircase.

I run down the steps to the second floor, head into Hugo's room, and root through his closet. Only plastic hangers. Crap. Next I go to Hugo's dad's room. Same thing.

I run downstairs. The coat closet is empty.

"Dammit!"

"Cameron, please! I need you." The faint voice comes from the kitchen.

I run in and see that the door to the basement is open. Without a second thought, I race down the stairs and head toward the boiler. I fight back the fear spreading over me, desperate to help Hugo.

I find the hole in the wall next to the boiler, but it's much bigger than Hugo described. It's nearly two feet wide and almost as tall. I bet I could squeeze through it.

"Cameron, I'm back here!" the voice calls, coming from the hole, sounding more frantic.

"Hugo, hang on! I'm coming through," I yell.

On my stomach, I peer into the hole—pitch black. My phone flashlight provides a guiding light as I shimmy in, but it barely penetrates the inky darkness. I fight back my rising fear, desperate to help Hugo.

It's a tight fit. The edges of the brick scrape against my back as I shove my way in. The voice of Bryce Hunter plays in my mind: *Hey, Tubby—you're stuck because you're so fat.* The voice feels foreign, like it's coming from outside my own consciousness.

"Fuck off, Bryce," I shout, and push forward.

The brick catches on my sweatshirt, and now I'm stuck. I can't move any farther. Panic builds inside me, and my head swims. I clamp my eyes shut and take slow breaths. When the panic ebbs, I reach back and pull the sweatshirt loose, then continue to squeeze and shove my way in.

I'm almost through when a massive spider crawls over my outstretched hand. I yelp as I shake it off, and it scurries away. If I make it out of this, I swear I'll never go in this house again.

With one final shove, I'm through the hole. I find myself in a short hallway opening into a larger room. The darkness is so thick it swallows the light from my flashlight.

I enter the room and explore the perimeter, keeping my hand on the wall to anchor me, avoiding the dark abyss in the middle.

"Hugo, are you here?" I call out.

"Cameron?" Abby's muted voice comes from farther into the room. "Is that you?"

"Abby!" I yell as I continue along the wall. My foot bumps into something on the ground, and a metallic clatter echoes through the room. I come to a small slit of light shining under the bottom of the iron door—it must be from Abby's flashlight on the other side.

"Abby, I got in here through a hole in the basement wall by the boiler."

"Did you find Hugo?" she asks.

"Not yet."

"Grab the key and let me in."

I shine my flashlight on the floor, but the key is nowhere to be found. "Oh crap. I might have just kicked it away."

"Okay, I'm coming," Abby says. "Don't do anything. I'll be there in a second."

The faint sounds of Abby's footsteps echo behind the door as she runs up the spiral staircase.

"Hugo, where are you?"

I shine the flashlight around the area, looking for the key and any signs of Hugo. The light reveals a sight that will be etched into my memory forever.

Against the wall are the long-decayed remains of a human, arms bound with shackles. I let out a yelp and fumble to keep from dropping my phone. The skin has shriveled, leaving the face frozen in a permanent ghastly grimace. Only a few wispy hairs remain on the scalp. A tattered black dress with frilly lace around the neck, frayed and rotted, covers the corpse.

"The nanny," I whisper.

I back away one cautious step at a time until my back hits something hard and cold. An iron furnace covered in rust dominates the room. It's massive—six feet deep, four feet wide, and tall enough to stand in. It looks like a huge kiln or something that belongs in a crematorium. My mind flashes back to Mr. Peterson saying this was set up to be a mortuary. There's a large closed iron door on the front with slots like prison bars.

"Cameron, help!" Hugo's voice cries out, loud and insistent. It's coming from *inside* the furnace.

"Hugo, are you in there?" I shine my flashlight through the grate on the door, but it's too dark to see.

"Please!" the voice yells, closer than ever.

I turn the handle on the furnace door, unlocking the mechanism that keeps it shut. I pull with all my might. The door groans, its iron hinges rusted. It sounds like a scream, the whole furnace protesting that its long slumber has been disturbed.

When the door is open enough to peer in, I shine my flashlight inside but still see nothing.

"Hugo, the door is open. Where are you?"

Bitter cold descends around me, my breaths coming out as fleeting misty clouds.

"Cameron, behind you!" Abby's voice cries out.

Icy hands press against my back, and a shove sends me tumbling into the furnace. I trip on the edge of the furnace doorway and fall into a pile of cinders. My hands blunt the fall, but I clamp my eyes and mouth shut tight to avoid being blinded and choked by the ash.

The furnace door groans behind me, punctuated by a massive boom like the door of a coffin closing. The click of the latch is the final nail driving in, sealing my fate.

Abby runs to the door and tugs on the handle with all her might. "It's stuck!"

I stand up and dust myself off as best I can, but the ash is in my eyes, and the charred taste of soot coats my tongue, making me cough.

"Hugo's not here. It was a trap!" I yell.

"Hang tight, Cameron. I'll see if I can find something to pry the door open with." Abby says, heading away from the door.

A slight warmth and the smell of fresh smoke come from behind me. I spin around. Spent wood and charred coals surround me, heaped in piles.

Deep within one of the piles, a faint orange glow gets brighter. I gasp as silhouettes of skulls and bone fragments take shape amongst the embers. Right before my eyes, a flickering flame springs to life.

You left me. Now I have you.

30

CONVERGENCE: HUGO

Blinking lights and the soft beeps of medical equipment surround me as I sit at my pa's side. He lies motionless in his hospital bed with the IV line snaking up his arm and an oxygen mask covering his mouth and nose.

Doctors and nurses come and go, taking vital signs and talking in hushed voices, but it's hard to hear them over the pulsing in my head. I watch them in a daze, my senses dulled.

A doctor walks up and stands beside me. "Hugo Cruz?"

I force myself to focus on her, but I manage only a nod.

"I'm Dr. Wilson, your father's doctor. I wanted to give you an update."

"Okay." The word comes out sounding hollow, like somebody else said it.

"Your father is stable. He has a concussion, two cracked ribs, a broken collarbone, and a broken arm."

I let out a sad laugh. "That all?"

"We have every reason to believe he'll fully recover. He's still young and strong. But with head trauma, we can never be certain. We'll have to wait until he wakes up to know the extent of his injuries."

If he wakes up, I think, but I keep my mouth shut and simply nod.

"We're going to take him to surgery now to set the broken arm."

"Okay" is all I manage.

"We'll keep you posted," the doctor says, and she puts a hand on my shoulder. "We'll do everything we can to make sure he pulls out of this."

"Thanks. Oh, my sister, Carla. She should know. I left my cell phone."

"We'll try to get in touch with her."

Several people wearing ER scrubs haul Pa away. I sit in the empty ICU stall, staring at the people rushing past, unable to focus. I bury my face in the palms of my hands and let my tears flow.

A sharp pain on my ankle snaps me back to reality, and my mind sharpens. The spot where something grabbed me through the hole in the basement burns like it's been scorched with a branding iron. I lift my pant leg and stare in shock as welts form in the shape of a handprint.

I reach down to touch it and recoil in pain.

Details of the last hour come back to me in a flash. A fog lifts from my brain, and I remember the White Lady shoving the ladder. How could I have forgotten that detail?

Oh no. *Cameron.*

He texted several times before Pa fell. What if he went to the house to find me? He might be in danger.

In a flash, I'm running down the hospital hallway, shouting to the nurse behind the desk that I'll be back as soon as I can. They call something back, but I'm already out the door.

Home is two miles away, so I keep running. My lungs burn as I try to maintain my pace, my feet hitting the pavement like hammers against an anvil, my legs screaming.

An old yellow Volvo drives up beside me, and the passenger side window rolls down. A man inside calls out, "Hugo Cruz, is that you?"

It must be somebody from the hospital trying to stop me. I keep running while calling out, "Who wants to know?"

"It's Mr. Peterson from the library. I was on my way to your house to speak with you and your father. Need a lift?"

I stop and run to the car, opening the passenger door before I even answer. "That would be awesome. I have to get home right away. Um, why did you want to speak with me?"

"I talked to Cameron earlier today and realized I should have included you. Has he spoken to you yet?"

"No," I say. I don't explain why; I'd rather not discuss what's going on with Pa.

"Well, the first thing I have to tell you may come as a shock. No easy way to break this to you, so I'll just come out and say it. You are related to Agnes Finch, the nanny of Emily Thornburn."

"*What?*" I gasp. "What are you talking about?"

"You're her third cousin six times removed. It's a distant relationship, but 16 Sycamore Lane has been passed down through your family. Your mother inherited it when her great-aunt Geraldine died."

Mr. Peterson continues to explain all the details, and my head swims. So, the house was part of the inheritance Ma wanted to give away. Why did Pa keep all this from me?

Then Mr. Peterson tells me about Cameron's connection to Agnes's lover, Luke. It's all so hard to believe. I sit there without saying a word, letting everything sink in.

"I found something else," he continues. "The birth certificate for Emily Thornburn. Mr. Thornburn had influence with the local judge, who ordered it sealed for one hundred years and stored it in the mayor's office. Luckily, I'm friends with the mayor, and it's been well over one hundred years."

"Okay, get to the point!"

"Sorry." Mr. Peterson cringes. "I can rattle on. What I found was not one birth certificate but two. Emily had a twin sister, Eunice. Mr. Thornburn kept it hidden all those years."

A twin. That means... It hits me like a punch to the gut. We must have freed Emily's spirit and left Eunice's in the house.

"Fuck!" I shout. "Mr. Peterson, please get me home fast!"

"What's wrong?"

"Cameron might be in danger. It's kinda hard to explain."

Mr. Peterson speeds up. "Try me. I'd believe almost anything about that house. I had my own...experience there when I was sixteen, looking for answers about my uncle's disappearance."

I catch Mr. Peterson up on what's been happening, at least as much as possible in the few minutes it takes to drive the rest of the way to my house. He nods and appears to believe every word. I guess he must've had quite an experience in that house. It seems to happen a lot.

We pull into the driveway behind an old sedan I don't recognize. As we open our doors, Chloe and Margaret get out.

"Hugo! There you are! Where have you been?" Chloe yells.

"My pa's in the hospital. He fell off a ladder."

Chloe's face darkens. "Oh my god, I'm so sorry, Hugo."

"Is that what you saw?" I ask. "In your dream?"

Chloe nods, looking down at the ground. "More or less. I didn't see specifics."

Margaret cuts in. "We can talk about that later. We have work to do."

"Abby thinks Emily had a twin sister," Chloe says as we approach the front door. "She might still be haunting the house."

"Her name is Eunice. Here's the proof," Mr. Peterson says, holding up the birth certificate.

"Hey Hugo." Mr. Walsh comes across the street. "I'm looking for Cameron. We're supposed to go visit his grandma, and he's not answering his texts."

My mind races as Cameron's dad approaches, not sure what to say. This has gotten complicated in a hurry. "Um..."

"James." Mr. Peterson gives Mr. Walsh a curt nod. "Been a while."

"Eric." Mr. Walsh replies with a curt nod of his own. An entire silent conversation passes between the two men in an instant. Mr. Peterson's expression is complex—regret mixed with sorrow, and something else.

Mr. Walsh's expression is stony, as usual. He stares back at me. "So, where's Cameron?"

Abby throws open the front door. "Hurry! Cameron's trapped!"

"Trapped? Where?" I shout.

"Come quick," Abby says.

"What do you mean, Cameron's trapped?" Mr. Walsh shouts. "What's going on?" Everybody ignores him and runs into the house.

The moment I cross the threshold, it's like I hit a sheet of ice, frozen and unforgiving. Chloe and Margaret double over as they enter the foyer, and Mr. Peterson and Mr. Walsh follow behind them, looking like they might be sick.

"This is far worse than I thought," Margaret says, trying to steady herself. "I've never encountered something this strong."

"This is much sharper and stronger than I've ever felt before," Chloe says.

"Where's my son? Will someone tell me what's going on?" Mr. Walsh shouts.

"Have you blocked it all out, James?" Mr. Peterson says. "Remember when we were sixteen and we broke in here?"

"I don't know what—" Something flashes in Mr. Walsh's eyes. "Oh god. How could I forget?"

"We don't have time for this!" Abby yells, and heads up the stairs.

As we run up to the third floor, Abby fills us in on all the details, including finding the skeleton they think is Agnes Finch and Cameron being trapped in the furnace. Shock, rage, and despair swirl in my head, but I press on.

I run down the spiral staircase two steps at a time with Mr. Peterson right behind me. "I can hardly believe what I'm seeing," he says as he takes in the hidden rooms.

We reach the basement, and I run through the open iron door and into the large room beyond. A faint orange glow and wisps of smoke emanate from the grate of a massive iron furnace dominating the room.

"Cameron, are you in there?" I yell.

"I'm here!" Cameron shouts, panicked. "Hugo, is that really you?"

"Yes, it's me! We'll get you out." The handle is freezing, and my fingers burn like I've touched dry ice. "Argh!"

"It's no use," Abby says, running up. "I've tried hitting it with a sledgehammer, and it won't budge."

"Cameron!" Mr. Walsh shouts as he comes up beside us. "Here, let me." He reaches for the door but shouts as he touches the handle, then backs off, clutching his hand.

"It's warded by Eunice," Margaret says, walking briskly into the room. "Our only option is to free her spirit, but she won't go easily."

"Spirit? What are you talking about?" Mr. Walsh shouts.

"It's getting warm in here!" Cameron yells from inside the furnace. "And the smoke is getting bad."

"Have you tried water?" I ask.

Abby nods. "The fire springs back to life worse than ever."

"We have little time," Margaret says. "We must do this now."

"I insist someone tell me—" Mr. Walsh starts.

"Shut up or leave!" Margaret's voice booms through the room, and she appears to grow larger right before our eyes. Mr. Walsh shuts his mouth and backs into the corner.

Margaret sets an old leather-bound book on the ground, sitting cross-legged in front of it.

"Chloe, you will be my external eyes and ears." Margaret taps the spot on the ground next to her. "Sit here and put your hand on my shoulder.

Whatever you do, don't let go." Then she looks around at the rest of us. "You all will need to protect us," she says.

"Of course," I say. "But protect you from what?"

"Eunice has learned to command the physical world. She will make every effort to stop us. Be vigilant."

We all trade glances, then nod to Margaret in solemn determination.

"Let us begin," she says.

Chloe puts her hand on Margaret's shoulder, and Margaret reads from the book. The words are foreign, but they sound lyrical, like soft music.

The ground vibrates. The entire house compresses around us and springs back like we're in the chest of a breathing beast. Sharp cracking noises come from the brick wall covering the entrance to the back room. The bricks cascade down with a deep rumble, forming a pile of rubble. A gust of wind blows through the room and swirls around us, carrying the scent of rot. Weak sunlight streams in through the newly revealed doorway.

The light exposes a horrific mummified corpse chained to the wall, held together by the slightest bit of leathery skin and dangling by its skeletal arms. Mr. Peterson shouts, and I put my hands over my mouth to keep from doing the same. Mr. Walsh stares in horror, speechless.

"The nanny," Abby says.

As the shaking continues, her remains crumble to the floor in a heap of bones and tattered clothing.

Margaret's eyes glaze over, and her face goes slack. Chloe seems like she's in a trance too, but she's still half alert and able to speak. "Eunice is very strong." The words sound modulated, like it's two voices in one. "And very angry."

"What can we do to help?" I say.

"She won't go easily," Chloe says in that same haunting voice. "Agnes Finch wronged her, and Luke Brannagh abandoned her in her time of need. Eunice is on her way, seeking vengeance. She's almost here."

Margaret's and Chloe's eyes clamp shut at the same time. The shaking stops. The soft sound of crying echoes through the room from no describable direction.

Then their eyes snap open, glazed over with blank stares. An unfamiliar voice comes from both of them, their mouths moving in perfect unison like marionettes on a string. "The descendants of Agnes Finch and Luke Brannagh must suffer."

Cameron cries out. "The fire's getting hotter!"

"No!" I cry, my panic spiking. "Eunice, we didn't do anything to you!"

"Your ancestors kept me trapped for forty-nine long years," Chloe and Margaret drone in unison. "Trapped like an animal. But I escaped and showed Agnes Finch what it meant to be trapped. She served fourteen of the forty-nine years she owed me before she perished. By my measure, you owe me much, Hugo Cruz. She took what was dear to me, so I will return the favor."

The house shakes again.

"The physical connections!" Abby yells. "Margaret said spirits can hold on to physical connections. Hugo, her body would be a very strong physical connection." She points at Agnes Finch's remains.

Burn the locket, Margaret said when Chloe was trying to free Emily's spirit.

Burn it.

"We have to burn her remains!" I shout. In a flash, I run through the pile of bricks and into the basement.

The sharp shattering of glass comes from all directions. Outside every basement window, black crows stare through shards of broken panes, letting out deafening caws. Fucking crows.

I ignore them and continue up the stairs, then dump a metal trash can filled with construction waste onto the floor. I grab matches from the kitchen and run back to the furnace room.

"Hurry!" Cameron pleads.

I set the trash can down, and Abby and Mr. Peterson gather the nanny's remains and place them inside. I strike a match and toss it into the can.

A churning inferno of lustrous, dancing blue-and-green flame bursts forth. The fire is unbearably hot and impossible to go near—a supernatural flame burning supernatural fuel.

Chloe and Margaret scream in unison, an unearthly sound that comes from the depths of another's soul.

The fire in the trash can erupts higher, licking the concrete ceiling, dancing like a demon trying to break free. Then it dies into a wisp of smoke, leaving a trail of scorch marks radiating outward on the ceiling.

Cameron cries out, "The fire in here is weaker, but it's still burning!"

I run over to the door and reach for the handle again. It's still ice-cold, but I'm able to touch it this time. The latch still won't budge.

"Cameron's still stuck," I say to Chloe, hoping someone in there hears me.

Chloe opens her eyes, but it's clear she's still connected to Margaret. "Eunice is weakened but continues to hold on," she says. "There's still something physical she's clinging to—a blood bond."

"Blood bond?" I say. "Is there another corpse hidden somewhere?"

"Wait!" Abby shouts. "Could she be talking about actual blood?"

Chloe and Margaret nod in unison. "Yes. Actual blood is the strongest bond."

"When I got stuck in the floor when I was twelve, there was blood everywhere!" Cameron yells. "But that was years ago."

"On the third floor?" I ask.

"Yeah," Cameron says. "It couldn't be there still, could it?"

"Um, I think it is. Under the floorboards."

Chloe and Margaret both yell. "Eunice knows! She's coming again! Beware!"

Their eyes snap shut again, and the house shakes worse than ever. The pile of rubble trembles, and individual bricks begin to move on their own. One flies through the air, striking Mr. Peterson in the head, and he crumples to the floor.

Abby holds the fire poker in front of her like a sword, and Mr. Walsh grabs the sledgehammer. A brick flies toward us, and Abby swats it out of the way with a loud grunt. Mr. Walsh deflects another brick, crushing it to dust.

"Go, Hugo!" Abby yells. "Burn the blood!"

Mr. Walsh nods. "We'll hold down the fort here!"

"On it!" I run out of the room, dodging flying bricks on my way to the basement stairs. I'm past the rubble, ten feet from the stairs, when a brick smashes into my back, knocking me over. The pain is blinding, radiating between my shoulder blades, and it takes my breath away. I grit my teeth, hop up, and start running again.

The cracks in the basement floor widen as the entire house shakes. I steady myself to keep from falling over as I run.

Wooden treads crack under my weight as I race up the basement stairs. Three stairs from the top, the whole staircase gives way beneath my feet. As it collapses, I leap toward the kitchen floor, catching the edge and hanging from my hands. My body dangles where the stairs used to be.

The house continues to shake, and I begin to slip.

I have to be strong. There's so much at stake.

I close my eyes and think of Pa and his kindness. I think of Cameron on the roof of the old school. I think of Ma and her smiling face, her voice soft like music: *I love you, Hugo.* A warmth spreads through me like a soft blanket against my skin. "I love you, Ma."

Cameron needs me.

I have to make it.

Drawing on my inner reserves, I find a strength I never knew I had and hoist myself up to the kitchen floor.

In the dining room, glass shatters all around me. I shield my eyes as I grab a cordless circular saw and an ax from our pile of tools, not knowing what it'll take to rip the floorboards up. I head to the stairs, leaping up three steps at a time.

At the landing, I turn to face the third story. Large cracks form in the plaster walls, and chunks fall on me like jagged snowflakes. Staircase treads buckle under my feet, and I dance around the broken places, avoiding falling by sheer will alone.

At the spot in the hallway where Pa replaced the floorboards, I fire up the circular saw, the metal blade whirring as it comes to life. I plunge the saw into the wood, cutting through it like a hot knife through butter. With the first pass done, I lift the saw, ready to start on the second, when a horrendous shrieking comes from the blade. The nut securing it to the saw spins off and flies away, clattering down the hallway. The blade wobbles, threatening to rip me to pieces, so I throw the saw across the hallway. The blade whirls off, flying toward my face. I duck just in time to keep the spinning teeth from tearing through my flesh. With a loud *thunk*, the blade embeds itself in the wall.

I grab the ax, and driven by fury and pure adrenaline, I bring the blade down into the floorboards with all my strength. Splinters fly everywhere, getting in my hair and scraping my face. I ignore them, only one goal in mind.

Soon, the red-brown stain on the subflooring shows through the splintered wood.

I take the matchbook out of my pocket.

One match left.

Typical.

I drag the match head over the strike strip, sending sparks flying up. The flame dances and bobs at the end of the matchstick.

It goes out.

"Fuck!"

Suddenly it roars back to life, a cascading flicker of yellow and orange. I drop the match into the hole. An explosion of the unnatural blue-green flame flies out with a force that pushes me off my feet, knocking me to the floor.

The house shakes more violently than ever, so powerfully I fear the whole structure might collapse.

In one last crescendo, the walls seem to expand around me as if the house is about to explode from some unseen internal force. Timbers groan and crack. Just as I'm sure the straining beams can take no more, the house snaps back.

The flames burst from the hole in a torrent, exploding outward in a wave of unbearable heat. They surround my body, then disappear in a cloud of wispy smoke. My hands and arms should be burnt to a crisp, but there's not a single blister or a red mark.

A monstrous scream echoes through the house with such intensity that I plug my ears to keep them from bursting. Then it stops.

Utter silence.

Only the gentle patter of dust settling disturbs the quiet.

I breathe for the first time in about thirty seconds.

Laughter breaks the silence. I fear it's coming from some unwanted spirit before I realize the laughter is mine.

I'm alive.

Cameron!

I race into the nanny's room, twist down two flights of stairs, and burst through the iron door. Everyone lies on the floor, bruised and battered, surrounded by bricks and chunks of rubble.

"We did it!" Chloe yells, pumping a fist in the air.

I turn to the furnace. The orange glow and smoke are gone. I'm afraid to look, but I'm driven by an unstoppable need to learn Cameron's fate. I turn the handle, which moves easily, swing open the door, and look into the total darkness.

"Cameron?" I call out, holding back dread.

Cameron runs out, covered in soot, and nearly tackles me to the floor as we embrace.

"I love you," he says.

"I love you too." I smile as waves of relief and joy flood through me.

He pulls me in tighter, squeezing my ribs. And we hug, and hug, and hug.

31

Tale of The White Lady: Cameron

Hugo and I clear away chunks of rubble and help everybody to their feet. Mr. Peterson groans, rubbing his head where the brick struck him, but he's okay. Besides a few scrapes and bruises and being shaken up, everyone is in good spirits, relieved the ordeal is over.

Dad comes over and wraps me in a hug. "I'm so glad you're okay. I love you, Cameron."

"I love you too, Dad."

Then Dad hugs Hugo. "Thank you for saving my son."

"Of course," Hugo says.

As everybody shakes the dust from their bodies and assesses their injuries, the gravity of what just happened unfolds in my mind. Being trapped in the furnace, the heat of the fire around me, choking on the smoke…I won't soon forget those things. But throughout it all, I had faith that my friends would see me through it, that Hugo would see me through it. And he did. I love him so much.

"Let's take some time to get cleaned up and recover from what just happened," Margaret says. "But before anybody leaves or contacts anyone from the outside, we need to talk. Let's reconvene in the living room."

Once we've tended to our wounds, we sit on the couches. Everyone still has wide eyes, shell-shocked from the day's events.

"Surprisingly, the condition of the house isn't that bad," Hugo says. "After the way it was shaking, I was sure it was ready to collapse. But there's only some cracked plaster, a few broken windows, and the ruined basement stairway."

"Spirits can alter your perceptions," Margaret says, "exaggerate what you see. Speaking of which, let's address the matter at hand. How do we want to talk about what happened?"

"We can't hide it," Abby says. "We discovered a crime scene down there."

"This is true," Margaret says. "There is no doubt we will have to get the authorities involved. The discovery of the missing children's remains will provide closure to the families of the victims."

Mr. Peterson nods with a deep frown, his expression grave.

"But I can tell you from experience that the world will not believe everything that happened here," Margaret says.

"What *did* happen here?" I cut in. "Can you explain it?"

"I think I can explain most of it," Margaret says. "Chloe and I expelled the spirit of Eunice Thornburn—with all your help, of course." She gives a gracious nod to everyone in the room. "And during the ordeal, we learned quite a bit. Releasing a spirit is an intimate process. You have to empathize with them. You literally see things from their perspective. In a way, it's like seeing your life flash before your eyes, but in this case, it was Eunice's life."

"You know what happened to her?" I ask.

"In a vague, dreamlike sense, yes. Combined with all the facts we've discovered, I think we can paint a decent picture. Because of complications at birth, Eunice had special needs. But she grew up in a world that was unkind to children who were different. So, her father hid her and told the world he had only one daughter. The nanny disliked Eunice. She'd make cookies for Emily and give none to Eunice. This more than anything became a symbol of Eunice's anger."

"I wondered why cookies were significant," Abby says. "That's one mystery solved."

Aunt Margret nods. "That brings us to Luke Brannagh, the nanny's lover. Luke felt sorry for Eunice and was the only person to treat her with kindness. Because of this, Eunice cared for him deeply. But then Mr. Thornburn—who had developed feelings for the nanny himself—discovered Agnes and Luke together. He flew into a rage, threatening to kill Luke with a gun. Eunice exploded with anger and wrestled the gun away from her father. In the struggle, Mr. Thornburn was shot."

"It wasn't suicide after all," Hugo says, frowning.

"That's right," Margret says. "From the letter you discovered, we know Luke was wracked by guilt about Mr. Thornburn's death and never returned. The nanny blamed Eunice for driving Luke away, so she locked Eunice in the basement. She treated her like a monster, and in doing so, she created a monster. She held Eunice captive for the next forty-nine years."

Abby's eyes light up. "That matches what we figured out based on the hash marks on the walls. And we found a jar of Emily's remains dated 1939. Did Eunice escape after Emily died?"

"Correct," Margaret says. "Emily was the one thing keeping Eunice stable and when she was gone, it didn't take long for Eunice to turn the tables on Agnes and lock her up."

Mr. Peterson cuts in. "The last known sighting of Agnes Finch was the winter of 1939. It wasn't long after that children started going missing."

"Locking up the nanny wasn't enough," Margaret says. "Eunice felt her childhood had been taken from her and took revenge by taking the town's children. It made sense to her warped mind. She lured them in with the same cookies the nanny had made for Emily." Margaret shivers. "It was hard to see those images. Something I'd rather not have seen."

Mr. Peterson sighs and rubs his eyes.

Margaret puts a gentle hand on his shoulder. "I'm so sorry."

He puts his hand on Margaret's. "Thank you. Thank you for everything. Uncle Fredrick died before I was born, but his disappearance impacted my family long after that. It tore my father apart, and it's been my life's goal to find out what happened to him. Now we know."

"I hope it will help to ease your family's pain," Margaret says.

Mr. Peterson nods.

"What about the nanny's spirit?" Abby asks. "Or the children's, for that matter? Did you free them too?"

"I didn't detect any other spirits," Margaret explains.

"Why do some stay and some go?"

"There aren't any hard-and-fast rules about what traps a spirit," Margaret says. "At least none that I understand. Often spirits have unfinished business. I suspect Eunice wanted revenge and Emily stayed to watch over Eunice."

"But why didn't you detect Eunice's spirit after Emily was gone?" Abby asks.

"That's an excellent question," Margaret says. "What we detected was a violent separation. Eunice's spirit was intertwined with Emily's. My best guess is that the force of Emily's spirit leaving weakened Eunice. But like a stretched spring being released, first it contracts before it springs back with immense force."

Margaret stares into the distance for a moment, and everyone's quiet. Then she turns and addresses the entire group, "Now, how do we explain to people what happened here? What's our story?"

"A localized tremor," Mr. Peterson says. "I'm sure that's a thing. Caused by groundwater overuse. I think I've read about things like that in the news."

"Not half bad," Margaret says with a smile and a nod.

"The tremor collapsed the wall in the basement," Hugo adds, "which led us to the iron door and all the jars."

"But what about Agnes Finch?" Abby says. "Her remains are gone now."

"I'm afraid hers is a story that will be lost to history," Margaret says. "Only her family will know." She looks at Hugo.

Hugo nods with tight lips. "I'm not proud of what she did to Eunice. But at least we've uncovered the truth."

A buzz comes from my pocket, but I soon discover it's not my phone. It's Hugo's, which I picked up earlier. The caller ID says Jefferson Hospital.

"Hugo." I hand the phone over to him. "A call from the hospital!"

"My pop!" Hugo grabs the phone, answers it, and listens. He nods and says a few quiet words as a smile spreads across his face.

"Pa's out of surgery, and he woke up. He's okay!"

***

Hugo and I drive his dad's SUV to the hospital while the rest of the group stays at the house. We run the entire way from the parking lot to the recovery room. Hugo's dad is sitting up, looking alert, his arm in a cast. Hugo runs up to the bed and gives him a gentle hug.

"Pa, you're awake!"

"'Course I am, mijo. I'd never leave you."

"I love you, Pa."

"I love you too," he says. "Oh, and look who else came to see me! The boyfriend! Hey, Cameron."

I smile. "Glad to see you looking so good after that nasty fall, Mr. Cruz."

"Ah, this is nothing." Mr. Cruz waves it off. "I've been through worse. I'll be back at it in no time."

Mr. Cruz looks from me to Hugo, and his face transforms into a frown. "Uh, Hugo...there's something I need to tell you." He hesitates. "It's unusual."

"Spill it, Pa. It's okay."

Mr. Cruz lowers his voice, but I'm blessed with good hearing, and I can still make it out.

"Our house is…" Mr. Cruz glances back and forth, seemingly worried that someone else might overhear him. "I think our house is haunted." He cringes, waiting for our response.

Hugo and I both let out a big laugh.

"Ya think?" Hugo says, trying to catch his breath.

"I'm serious." Mr. Cruz looks hurt. "You might think I hit my head too hard, but some crazy old ghost lady pushed me off that ladder."

"I know, Pa. We both know. I was about to tell you about her right before she did it."

"Oh god, you knew?" Mr. Cruz's eyes widen.

Hugo nods. "Yeah, we knew."

"I saw her once before, but I tried to ignore it. Thought I'd imagined it. Thought it was stress." Mr. Cruz shakes his head and frowns. "That house was our last resort, but it's too dangerous. We have no choice but to leave. I can't risk either of us getting hurt any worse. We'll have to move in with my cousin in Oakland until we can figure all of this out."

"Pa, we've got something to tell you."

Hugo tells his dad about everything that has happened in the house, including what Chloe and Margaret did today. Mr. Cruz listens intently, his expression softening from shock and concern to relief.

"I'm so sorry for putting you through that," Mr. Cruz says, eyes glossy. "If I had known what you were going through, I would have done something right away. Or at least made sure you didn't suffer alone."

"I wasn't alone," Hugo says, grabbing my hand, making my heart flutter. "And I'm sorry for not telling you sooner. I was afraid you'd make us move, and I didn't want to lose the friends I've made here. But I know I should have told you."

"Come here," Mr. Cruz says, ushering Hugo in for a hug.

They embrace, both of them crying. A tear rolls down my cheek as I watch.

"New policy," Mr. Cruz says. "No more secrets in our household."

Hugo nods, wiping his nose.

"Speaking of which, you heard about the will, huh?"

"Yeah," Hugo says.

"When your ma inherited that house, she didn't want to move in. I respected her wishes for as long as I could, but the bills stacked up after our last house, and I didn't have a choice."

"How come you didn't tell me?" Hugo asks.

"I felt guilty going against Ma's wishes, and I didn't want to dredge up old memories." Mr. Cruz sighs. "But now I know it was a mistake not to tell you. Like I said, from now on, no secrets."

"Agreed, Pa. No more secrets."

Soon the doctors return. Mr. Cruz needs rest, so we say our goodbyes and return to the house. Flashing blue-and-red lights greet us when we arrive. Crime scene tape cordons off the house, and several police officers are standing around, snapping pictures and asking questions to the rest of our group. Mom and Jack have joined Dad, who's talking with Mr. Peterson.

I whisper to Hugo, "I didn't know my dad and Mr. Peterson knew each other."

"Yeah, I overheard them talking about exploring the house when they were young."

That's a serious shock. Neither Dad nor Mr. Peterson has ever said anything to me about knowing each other. Did they have a falling-out?

But before that sinks in, Mom runs up and hugs me. "Cameron! I'm so glad you're okay."

Dad and Jack come in for hugs too. Dad whispers in my ear, "I love you, son. And I'm sorry I haven't been supportive. That ends today."

"Thanks, Dad."

Maybe he means it. Time will tell.

Dad gestures for Hugo to join us. "C'mon, Hugo."

Hugo joins our group hug, smiling.

We end the hug, and Dad takes Hugo by the shoulders. "What you did in that house was brave. It shows me how much Cameron means to you. And I'm sorry if I didn't make you feel welcome in our family. I was wrong. You're a great boyfriend to Cameron."

"Thanks, Mr. Walsh. That means a lot."

Dad pats Hugo firmly on the back. I had no idea my dad could admit he was wrong and apologize. I didn't think he had it in him.

"Guess even old dads can learn new tricks." Jack laughs. I love how he has this gift of saying out loud what I'm thinking. We bump fists when Dad isn't looking.

Mr. Peterson fields most of the cops' questions. He's friends with the mayor and knows the police chief, so things go smoothly, but they've got a lot to investigate.

After an hour of answering questions, we're allowed to leave. The sun is setting, and I turn to Hugo. "Hey, you wanna get outta here?"

Hugo beams. "I know just the place."

We run through the forest and don't stop until we reach the school. Hugo wins the race to the ladder, and I scamper up behind him. We reach the top, and I tackle him, both of us rolling on the roof, hugging and kissing.

Hugo peers deep into my eyes. "Did you mean what you said?"

"That I love you?"

"Yeah."

"I did. I love you, Hugo Cruz."

"I love *you*, Cameron Walsh."

We kiss some more and watch the sunset. The sky darkens, and we marvel at the spiraling arms of the Milky Way above us. The stars are amazing.

Everything is amazing.

Epilogue: Hugo

Twelve months later, many things have changed in my life. The cops closed ten missing children cases and finally solved a bunch of local mysteries. Eunice Thornburn and 16 Sycamore Lane got a lot of press. People love it when unsolved mysteries turn into solved mysteries, especially when those mysteries involve serial killers. All of us got a little famous—for about two weeks, anyway—and then the world moved on.

Mr. Peterson updated the history of the house with everything we'd learned. We never got to the bottom of what he and Cameron's dad saw in Crimson House back when they were sixteen. They're keeping their mouths shut, and I can relate to not wanting to relive bad memories.

Since Mr. Peterson is on the board of the local historical society, he convinced them to make the house a historical landmark. Even better, the board earmarked a million dollars to restore the house and turn it into a museum. Pa and I were thrilled and signed on to do most of the work, which meant we could afford to live in a house that didn't need renovating while we fixed up 16 Sycamore Lane.

The downside, of course, is that I don't live across the street from my boyfriend anymore. That's right—Cameron and I are still going strong. Last week we celebrated our one-year anniversary on the old school's roof with a tiny bottle of champagne.

On October 7th, exactly one year after we kicked the spirit of Eunice Thornburn out of 16 Sycamore Lane, the Thornburn Historical Museum opened to guests. Cameron and I both got jobs as tour guides, having fun leading people through the house and telling ghost stories. Of course, we can't tell the real stories. Those are only for our little group.

Cameron and I are taking a break after a long day of tours, hanging out in the kitchen, which is now a museum display with an old-fashioned stove and icebox that are fully restored but haven't worked in years. A little girl I recognize from our last tour walks up to us. She's no more than seven years old, with a cute dress and little curls.

"Hey, sweetie," I say, crouching to talk to her. "Are you lost?"

"I'm *not* lost," she insists in a precocious tone.

"Then what can we do for you?"

"I'm hungry," she pleads.

"I'm sorry, but we don't have any food in the museum," I say with a sad smile.

She frowns. "But I smell cookies."

Cameron and I stare at each other in shock.

We only look away for half a second, but when we turn back, the little girl is gone.

ACKNOWLEDGMENTS

This being my second book, some aspects of writing it were easier than the first book, but some were harder. The story itself came together quickly, but getting the characters right took more time. Overall, this book is more personal to me. I drew from my past for many of Hugo's and Cameron's personality traits. Digging into some of those old memories, Cameron's insecurities, in particular, required some serious self-reflection.

Thanks to my super-star beta readers, Andy, Nick, and Brian. Your willingness to slog through first drafts and answer all my detailed questions was invaluable.

Thanks to my friend Patti for creating the inspiration for Hugo and for providing insight into her own experiences as a queer Mexican American growing up living a nomadic life very much like Hugo.

As usual, my queer book club provided a great beta-reader think tank. In addition to Nick and Andy, thanks to Brian, Tyler, Eric, Beau, Peter, and Kiyon. Thanks to the Seattle Writers Group for helping to critique many of the early chapters.

Thanks to my editors, Maria Tureaud, Alison Cherry, Michele Cacano, and Misha Kydd, for helping make this book what it is and giving it the polish it needed.

Thanks to Marcela Bolívar for the stunning cover illustration and Valerie Gomez for the amazing cover design.

Thanks to my husband, Peter, for providing encouragement and always being willing to work through ideas.

Thanks to my sister, Jennifer, for beta-reading and being my biggest fan, and my mom and dad for always being there when I needed them.

Thanks to Oreo and Minou for keeping me company in my office, requiring lots of petting, and reminding me to take breaks from time to time.

Finally, thank you, the reader, for taking the time to experience all the highs and lows with Hugo and Cameron. Without your enthusiasm and support, my writing dreams would not be possible.

About the Author

Paul is a lifelong creative writer whose life is filled with queer joy. His passion is to spread that joy through storytelling, writing books where you might not typically see queer characters. He lives in the Pacific Northwest with his husband and two tuxedo kitties and might have a slight addiction to reading queer fiction. But it's not a problem. He could stop any time he wanted. Honestly.

Email paul@pmwinters.com

Facebook www.facebook.com/paulmichaelwinters

Instagram @pmwintersauthor

Website www.pmwinters.com

Together in a Broken World

Heartstopper meets ***The Last of Us*** **in this heart-wrenching post-apocalyptic romance adventure.**

Two boys fall in love in a deadly world, but it's the secrets they keep that might kill them.

Amazon

Apple Books

Barnes & Noble